# 384 days

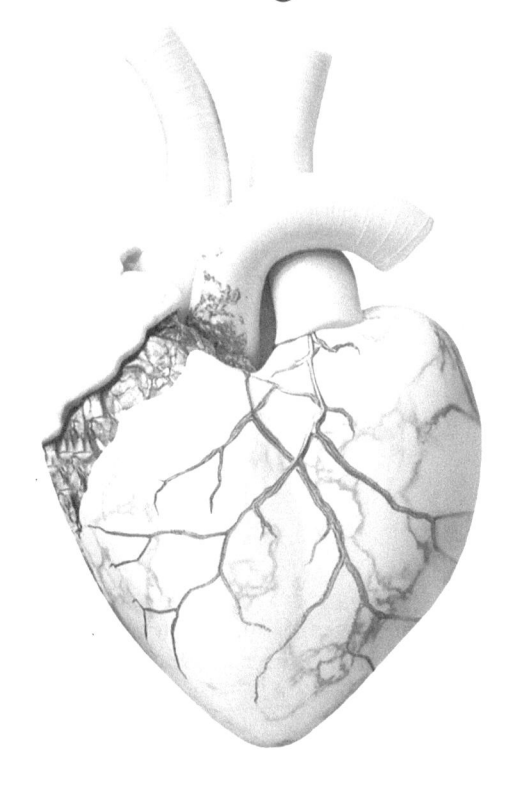

María J. Pahmer

# 384
# days

**First edition: March 2025**
@ María J. Pahmer

ISBN: 978-980-18-5978-9

All rights reserved. No part of this book may be reproduced, stored, rented, transmitted, or adapted in any form or by any means without the prior written consent of the author. All rights are reserved for Maria J. Pahmer.

**Content Warning:**

This book contains descriptions of emotional and physical abuse that may be disturbing to some readers. While the story is based on personal experience, much of the content has been adapted or modified for literary purposes.

It is important to note that this is a work of fiction and any resemblance to real events or people is purely coincidental. The purpose of the story is to explore the emotional impact of difficult situations, not to recreate them faithfully. The reader's discretion is adviced.

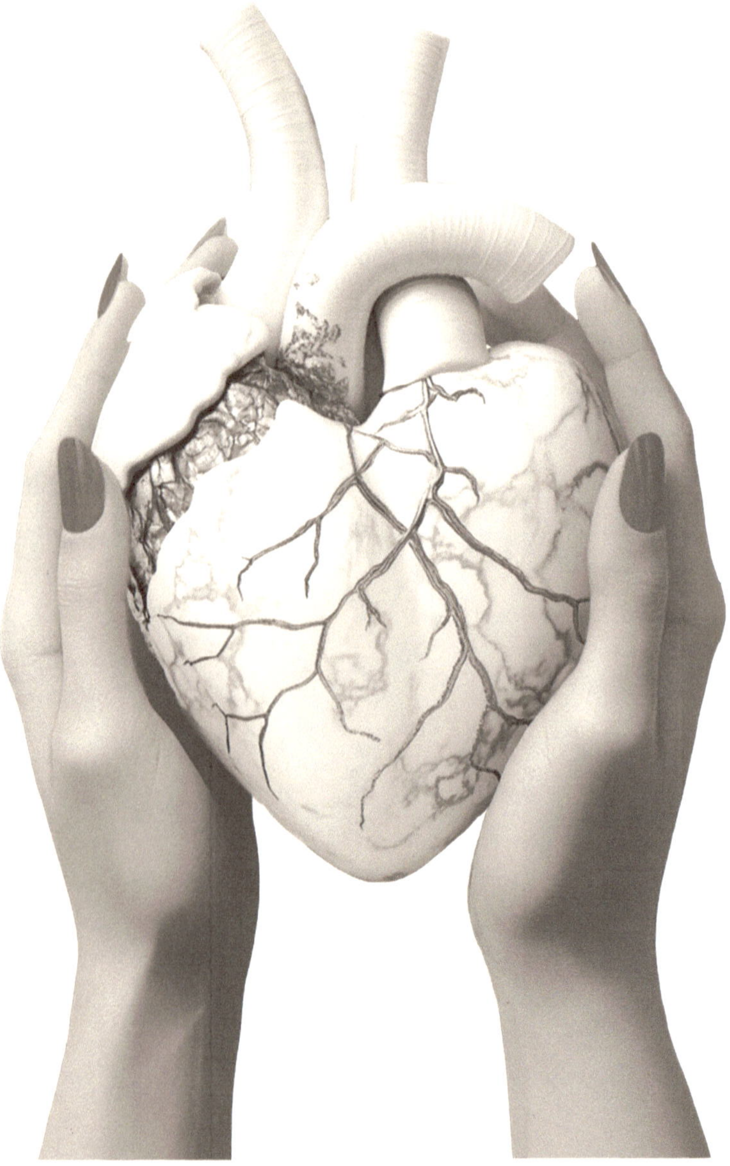

To all of the broken women that still dream with a
*happily ever after*

*Acknowledgements:*
To God,
For holding me in His arms like the apple of His eye.
To my Ohana,
For blowing the sails of my ship
and lending me warmth when the cold sets in.
To H's mom,
For having baked, with such exquisite precision,
such a delightful sweetie pie.

# Index

**CHAPTER I**
About dreams and realities ........................................... 15
    Prelude ............................................................... 17
    Old friends ......................................................... 20
    Madrid, here I come ........................................ 26
    Old Nightmares ................................................ 30

**CHAPTER II**
Everything is possible if you wish for it with all your heart 37
    The reunion ..................................................... 38
    In defense of the rumor ................................. 42
    Unforeseen apathy ......................................... 48
    H, the great ...................................................... 51
    The tramp ........................................................ 59
    Under the skin ................................................. 65
    Is this real? ....................................................... 70
    Mischief managed ........................................... 76
    Drool, lies and anxieties ................................. 86
    LibrAries ........................................................... 95
    Departures ....................................................... 100
    Oh! I'm leaving you, Madrid ......................... 103

**CHAPTER III**
Unreachable sunset in France .................................... 107
    Detectives & unexpected clues .................... 108
    Dancing through the night ........................... 114
    Tarot .................................................................. 120
    At 360 kilometers per hour ........................... 124

Juliet, please! .................................................... 131
Ghosts on the prowl ............................................ 138
Therapy, my dear friend ..................................... 143
And if they meet, what then? ............................... 147

## CHAPTER IV
Shadows of desire ....................................................... 150
   Between friends and alliances ............................ 152
   Repowered friendships ........................................ 156
   Spicy curiosities ................................................... 161
   Caution: falling in love ........................................ 163
   Face to face with the past .................................... 165
   The truth chamber ............................................... 177
   The call for change ............................................... 181
   Instigations ........................................................... 183
   Vices, discussions and comparisons ..................... 185
   On any given monday ......................................... 190
   911, H emergencies ............................................. 194
   Atitigo .................................................................. 199
   Swifties ................................................................. 205
   From Milan to Paris or Paris to Milan? ................ 211
   Pucca .................................................................... 217
   To the Netherlands and the Nether-worlds .......... 224
   Gossip grenades .................................................... 228

## CHAPTER V
At the edge of the twilight .......................................... 232
   The tower ............................................................. 234
   A menu of bitterness ............................................ 237
   432 Hz .................................................................. 243
   Endless loops ........................................................ 248
   Not your ordinary day ......................................... 249
   The wheel of fortune ............................................ 256

 Parallelepiped .................................................... 260
 Christmas............................................................266
 Now, it's Luismi's turn............................................ 270
 Unapologetic ....................................................... 276
 Morning tales ...................................................... 279

## CHAPTER VI
Forming the unseen ................................................. 284
 New year. New me ............................................... 286
 Theo's pacience ................................................... 291
 It's in the air ....................................................... 294
 Intimate ..............................................................298
 Scary! ................................................................ 302
 The unexpected ................................................... 305
 My cortisol is on its own ....................................... 310
 From a breeze to a hurricane ................................. 313

## CHAPTER VII
The never ending Paris ............................................. 318
 Blues in April ...................................................... 320
 All too well ......................................................... 324
 Peace treaty ........................................................ 328
 Maslow .............................................................. 332
 We have a wedding .............................................. 335
 Welcome to Budapest ........................................... 337
 Yes, I do ............................................................. 340
 Birthdays and empty spaces .................................. 345
 Doubt-full monday .............................................. 353
 Running away ..................................................... 356

## CHAPTER VIII
Kintsugi ................................................................. 358
 Wild and melancholic Madrid ............................... 360

Tantrums and concerns .................................................... 369
Ripples of Friendship ...................................................... 377
Too much red, too much «Reputation» ......................... 385
Like a Miss ....................................................................... 390
Handbags on the run ...................................................... 395
Seven of Swords .............................................................. 398
**About the Author** .......................................................... 400
**Playlist** ............................................................................. 402
**Resources** ....................................................................... 404

# CHAPTER I
## About dreams and realities

«If you can dream it, you can do it».

—Walt Disney

# Prelude

My name is Maria Valentina Santini Duque, and ever since I was old enough to think about love, beyond the love that we give to our friends and family, I declared myself as a **ROMANTIC**; yes, just like that, with all caps and in bold font.

I don't know if there's an instrument that can measure the level of fantasy and wishes that women usually have, but if there is, I'd break it: I am a romantic in the highest degree.

Since the time of having a boyfriend came to my life, in combination with my hobbies of movies and literature, I have spent hours and hours writing, manifesting and contextualizing what the right person for me should be like, I've made collages where I visually describe, as if it was a mental map, places, smells, sensations and, of course, I became obsessed with creating the «perfect man» and imagining him as a whole with all of his characteristics: physical, intellectual, emotional, moral and even socioeconomic. So, in a small diary, along with those mental maps, I also have a list of attributes of what that perfect man is like:

He's respectful, honest and kind.

He cares about me, honestly. He makes me feel warm, welcomed, at home, like a blanket; he makes me feel appreciated.

We are the perfect complement to each other.

We trust in each other.

We mutually support each other's dreams.

We are intellectually compatible.

He's the best listener and the adviser, always. He knows what to say, he gives me perspective.

We have the same values.

He's committed to his career and is successful with what he does.

He's patient.

He's an incredible cook.

We have the same sense of humor.

He's committed to himself, goes to therapy if he needs to, eats healthy, works out and doesn't have addictions like drugs, alcohol or cigarettes.

He has a great sense of style, he can dress casual attire or with a fancy suite, and he'll look great in both.

He cares about the wellbeing of his loved ones, he's a family first man, he treats his parents with respect, he thinks highly of his mother and sisters (if he has any).

He knows what he's worth and he reminds me about my own when it's necessary.

He's disciplined, ambitious, hardworking, tough and intelligent.

He shows me the most authentic version of himself, even the rawest or most vulnerable.

He finds me incredibly attractive; he knows what I'm worth and inspires me.

He rarely gets angry, and when he does, he handles it perfectly. If we have disagreements, he doesn't get irritated, we can talk about it.

He has perfect teeth and pretty hands.

He has financial freedom.

He always smells good and is super tidy and clean.

You might think that the list is long; but what woman in her right mind – and in her not-so-right mind- hasn't set some minimum number of wishes of how the «love of her life» should be? I know I'm not the only one. The truth is that, as time has gone by, my list hasn't reduced in size, on the contrary, my experiences have helped to enlarge it, even if it reduces the population of boys with the potential to be a part of my life.

I do have to state that, despite my best efforts, «the wish list» hasn't really worked as a stop to prevent disgusting beings from entering my inner circle, because you can't catch all of the characteristics that someone has with a single glance; how the other person is, is something that you discover slowly, or it reveals itself unexpectedly and in the blink of an eye, but when it's already too late. In that process, I have destroyed myself in ways that I can't even contextualize, I have died so many times in the hands of people that I haven't even loved, that I'm even embarrassed to admit it.

I learned astrology and some tarot, and I got into the habit of manifesting in writing my desires as a desperate act of faith, and I would be lying if I didn't admit that these practices saved my life... and yes, on countless occasions my life has ceased being a life, but like the Fenix, I have risen from my ashes. Each new stage brings fragments of previous ones with it, scattered along the road, reminding me, that transformation isn't simply wiping the slate clean, but a journey filled with lost memories that dance between shadows and light. That is how we live, die and are reborn, until our soul becomes eternal in the ephemeral nature of existence.

# Old friends

I toss and turn in my bed, trying to find a shred of energy, I've been trying to get up for about half an hour, but - I swear - the blankets are covered in lazy dust... When I finally manage, I crawl over to the loft stairs where my bed is and go down, dragging my feet over to the bathroom to take a shower, I open the tap and brush my teeth at the same time as I shower. It's not an ecological thing, although it helps, the reason being that my studio apartment in downtown Milan doesn't have a sink. The only water tap, besides the shower, is in the kitchen, and I think it's disgusting to brush my teeth where I do the dishes.

When I finished showering, I went to my bed-living-dining-room to get dressed. I get rid of the towel to look at myself in the mirror and recognize myself. I feel incredible. As Taylor says, "Long story short, I survived.

The last few years have been an emotional rollercoaster; when COVID came around, people had a terrible time and many even died. For me, however, the time in lockdown helped me rebuild myself after an abusive relationship that nearly killed me. This may seem like an exaggeration on my part, but the reality is that it was a hard time, a time I don't like to remember. That Maria Valentina Santini Duque, weighing only forty-five kilos and suffering from nervous alopecia, is long gone. Today I'm stronger than ever, I weigh fifty-five kilos, my hair is glamorous and shiny, and the gym has certainly helped.

I look spectacular, and for the first time I feel absolutely amazing in my own skin. "Hot mama," I flirt with myself before getting dressed.

In my small apartment, I have a single multipurpose table that I use not only for eating or as a centerpiece in the living room, but also for my laptop. That's where I start my work; I have to be really organized, today I have a videoconference meeting with the manager of a Spanish oil company, and I have to prepare 2 financial reports for a mayor in Mexico.

I work in the finance department of a sustainable energy company. It sounds great, and I make good money, but I'm not satisfied. Yes, I'm one of the many millions of people who work to make a living while planning their dream life.

I studied audiovisual production, the field I want to work in. When I lived in Maracaibo, I was a production assistant for an audiovisual magazine called Pasarela 360. Thanks to that job, I was called to be a production assistant for small events, such as theater plays in the county, and large nationwide events, such as concerts for bands like Caramelos de Cianuro. I even got to participate in the most important beauty pageant in my country: Miss Venezuela, when it was held in my hometown of Maracaibo.

All those days seem like a distant dream, a life I once had the chance to enjoy. Since I left my country, I have done an endless number of odd jobs, I feel like a different Barbie every year: I've been Waitress Barbie, Saleswoman Barbie, Technology Barbie, and now I'm Finance Barbie.

The horrible sound of a Microsoft team member's phone call pulls me out of my own thoughts; it's my boss, Anna. During our conversation, we organize the work day, and when we are done talking, I continue with my work arrangements.

That afternoon, while I'm fully focused on a meeting to explain to the Petro-España executive what's going on with their account and the disaster they're having with payments and new orders, I realize that I have four missed calls from Luis Miguel.

Luis Miguel Gil Montilla is one of my best childhood friends, I don't really remember how I met him, but between the ages of thirteen and eighteen we were inseparable. We drifted apart when we went to university: I focused too much on having artistic friends, and he on having friends who partied every weekend.

Despite the distance, Luis Miguel would show up from time to time, and when he did, we would talk every day until we got bored and everyone went back to their routines. This must be one of those times, because I think the last time we spoke I was living in Miami, and that was almost two years ago.

When I finished my meeting, I decided to give My Luismi, my cute nickname for him, a video call and when he picked up, he screamed:

-Mary Jane, honey! - That's his cute nickname for me; because I'm a redhead, he says I'm identical to Mary Jane from Spiderman, and in addition, to justify his decision, he reminds me that I used to work as a waitress.

-How are you, my Luismi? It's been so long, honey, tell me everything.

-Santi, honey. -Santi is short for my last name. It's what all my friends from Maracaibo call me-. I called you to tell you that I'm living in Madrid now, I have an apartment in Atocha, it's beautiful, okay? I want you to come over right away! As soon as possible, I want us to see each other, I miss you terribly. Besides, my mother asked me about you the other day, and I was with Andrés, my friend, and the three of us talked about you for a long time. Come here, come spend your vacation with me. When do you have time off? What do you do for a living, Mary Jane?

-Baby, I work in finance, but yeah, my boss just asked me last week when I'm going on vacation. Of course I'll go, I love the idea, let me find a ticket at a fair price, I'll call you later and *cuadramos* [1], right now I'm a little busy with some client meetings and all that, but give me this week, I'll organize everything right and, after that, you now, I'll buy the ticket.

-Great, baby, get to work and let me know, love you.

-I love you, bye. -I hang up.

Luis Miguel is like an absolutely unbearable little brother, but you can't just leave him on the side of the road, he comes and goes, and when he's in a loving mood, I make the most of it and fill him with love. Sometimes he just comes through to tell me about his drama, on those occasions I'm pretty firm with him and tell him off when he's focused on an existential crisis, I think it's one of the ways we have to express our love to each other, he acts like a victim, a drama king, and I tell him off.

Working at home doesn't mean that I don't have office hours, on the contrary, I keep them. I've finished the day's tasks with my boss and it's time for me to get out of work mode. I run to change into my gym clothes and hurry to the gym.

As I work out, I listen to Wisin y Yandel on my Airpods. Because of My Luismi, my muscles and my brain are taking different paths today. In my head I only have H, or as I like to call him, Hachito Sweetie Pie, Delicious Hachito, Hachito Papacito. My platonic love, my possible-impossible love, the love of my life, H, Hachito, I love you.

H is Heinrich Miguel Gil Montilla, Luis Miguel's older brother, my platonic teenage love.

I still remember the first time I saw him when I was thirteen years old. I knew that Luis Miguel had an older brother, but I hadn't met

---

[1] *Cuadramos* is used in Venezuela with the meaning of organize, square up (Editor's note)

him yet. It was a Saturday and Luis Miguel and I had planned to meet in the afternoon and play Wii, it was the first time that I actually went inside his house, before that I had only picked him up in front of the building with my parents to go to my house.

At that time, Mrs. Marisela -H, Luis Miguel and Graciela's mother- and my mother had already formed a kind of friendship, so Luis Miguel and I were allowed to spend a lot of time together; our excuse was that we met to do our homework, even though we didn't study in the same institution.

When Mrs. Marisela opened the door, I greeted her affectionately and she invited me in. It must have been around three o'clock in the afternoon, and Mr. Heinrich was drinking coffee and doing what looked like a crossword puzzle. He got up to say hello, and we formally introduced ourselves, since I had only exchanged a few words with him from the car.

Mr. Heinrich said something to me that I didn't understand, in a language I didn't know, and then Luis Miguel came into the living room and translated for me.

-He says hello in French, say "très bien, merci".

I repeated what Luis Miguel said as best I could, and Mr. Heinrich answered something else. I looked at Luismi to help me translate.

-He says this is your house, whenever you want to come by.

I blushed, and that's when My Luismi's brother entered the living room. The first thing I noticed was his unkempt, still wet, jet-black hair. The cologne immediately permeated the room. He was wearing a black t-shirt, jeans and white sneakers. My whole world stopped at that moment, "He's beautiful, I think I love him and that I'll wait for him all my life," were the words that echoed in my barely thirteen-year-old brain in front of this sixteen-year-old boy.

Bringing myself back to reality, I pause Wisin y Yandel and their

"Irresistible". Phone in hand, I go to Instagram and check out his profile, "what a spectacular man, I think to myself. He's too beautiful, he's become more masculine, but he's still beautiful, with that good-boy face, thin pink lips, a smile that lights up everyone's life, long eyelashes, not too long, not too short hair, he looks like one of those boys who plays golf with his father on Sunday afternoons".

There's a big difference between that moment when I was thirteen and now. Now he's a twenty-eight-year-old man and I'm a twenty-five-year-old woman, and anything can happen, if the universe allows, of course. I check on Instagram to see if he's following me, and he is, but I've never noticed if he looks at the stories I post or not. I don't think he's ever liked one of my posts, I would have had a heart attack if he had! It's been twelve years since that moment in their living room and I still look at him and think, if that man crashed my wedding, whoever the groom is, I would go with him and I would go with him in a heartbeat, no questions asked.

Every time I reconnect with Luis Miguel, it's like my eternal love for H is reawakened. This time, I think I've taken the time to thoroughly stalk him on Instagram, "Am I getting over him?" I wonder. I look at the last picture he was tagged in and my world stops again, "I don't think so - I answer myself. No. This boy is like a fine wine, he gets better with time.

# Madrid, here I come

I'm super excited, I already have a date for my trip and of course I have the ticket. I don't think there is a better place for a short summer vacation than Madrid. It's not just the place, it's also the people, it's like having a part of my family close by and being able to reconnect with, well, a step-family, but family nonetheless. I excitedly called Luis Miguel to give him the news he'd been waiting for. He gets right to the point:

-Hello, baby, tell me, did you buy the ticket?

-Baby, yes, I'll be there from the sixteenth to the twenty-second of July. Woohoo!

-Baby, I'm so excited! We're going to have so much fun, we're going to bring the house down!

-Stop it! -We both laugh, and then I ask the question I've always wanted to ask: Hey baby, what about H?, better known in my life as Hachito Sweetie Pie.

-Oh no, Santi. He has a girlfriend; they've been together for a while. He's working, as always, you know how he is, just working and with his girlfriend, we barely talked and I thought when I was here we would see each other or something, but no, he's MIA, I think I'll have to call him and go visit him in Paris or something like that.

-No! What do you mean he has a girlfriend? Every time I ask about him, he has a girlfriend, it's so annoying! When are God, the Universe, the Holy Spirit and the Virgin Mary going to put this man, single I might add, on my path so I can make him fall in love with me and have him forever?

Luis Miguel bursts out laughing and changes the subject.

———•·•→⦂←•·•———

My vacation in Madrid is coming closer and closer. I decide to go to the office instead of working at home for the last 2 weeks before my trip to make Anna happy, because even though she wants me to take my vacations and not add them up, she's a bit fussy.

Actually, more than fussy, she's one of those people who thinks that being in the office is a sign that someone is working. I find it illogical and hard to believe that in this day and age, especially here in Europe, people still cling to old, unnecessary habits: If you can get work done wherever you are, what's the point of occupying an office?

But well, fighting against your boss's nonsensical habits is like choosing to fight a losing battle, so I decide to go to my "workstation" for the last two weeks before my vacation.

When I get to the office, I notice that the screen, keyboard, and laptop charger are missing.

I open my laptop and contact the IT department to help me with this, and they tell me that they'll bring me the things I need in a few minutes. While I'm waiting, I grab my phone, open Instagram and record a story.

"I got to my workstation and things were missing, the IT department said they'll bring me my things soon, but why are they taking everything from me? What is this, Venezuela?"

I'm always creating content on my Instagram feed that relates to my own life story and aspirations, I think my antics on social media keep me alive and close to my artistic side.

Sometimes I feel like I'm living in a video game, I want so much to work with audiovisual productions again, but it's so hard here in Milan, even though I speak perfect Italian. The economy and the jobs have shrunk since COVID-19. I know how lucky I am to have part of my family here in the same city, to have a job - God bless! - to be healthy, to have a roof over my head and food on my plate, but there are days when I feel like I'm living in a world that isn't mine, acting like a robot, and I wonder what my life would be like if right now, at this very moment, I was doing what I love to do, what I'm passionate about, if instead of working with oil companies or government agencies or airlines, my clients were singers or actors, how can I put out this fire inside of me?

My iWatch vibrates and pulls me out of my thoughts, people start laughing at my stories and I have several interactions with my friends as the guys from the IT department set up my workspace and I get back to work.

Around three o'clock in the afternoon I take a cigarette break, I don't tend to smoke that much, but sometimes when I have a lot of work to do I feel like smoking. I leave the Azienda JEN&WA building and start chatting with Mattia, a colleague. While we are smoking, Gabriella from the sales department comes over and, since Mattia obviously likes her, he gives her all his attention. I felt a little uncomfortable standing there and concentrated on my phone to pretend not to notice. I'm checking the responses to my stories this morning and choke on my cigarette smoke. NO WAY!

Stop the world!

Heinrich had answered my stories. That's right, H, Hachito, Hachito Sweetie Pie.

"What?". I immediately took a screenshot and sent it to Luis Miguel.

My coworkers didn't even notice that I was almost choking on the smoke because they were too busy flirting with each other. "Idiots," I thought to myself.

I look at H's reply again and he had just sent a laughing emoji, but we've been following each other on Instagram for years and we've never interacted, more to the point, we've been Facebook friends since 2012 and we've never had any kind of interaction, not even a like on a picture or birthday wishes. NOTHING.

Universe, is this my time? Dear God, please open the way for me.

I stop fangirling and go back to my workstation.

# Nightmares

Late at night, when I'm in the gym with RBD and their "Tras de mí" blasting in my ears, I feel nostalgic, I remember my school days in Maracaibo and how different my time at the university was, and also this migrant phase. I don't know where I am now, but what I'm doing now is unblocking a lot of memories, changing a lot, getting rid of certain friendships and rekindling others. What I don't see a lot of is meeting new people, but we're still in the aftermath of COVID and that was a very hard time here in Italy, so it's all very complicated.

"I've been living here for two years and a year and a half of it was during a lockdown, it's like they stole this chapter of my life, máginate, several chapters have been stolen from me, it's crazy. I continue with my thoughts, and I get to the point where I realize that I have never really fallen in love, I have had three serious boyfriends, the longest for a year and a half, and I have lived through some dark times with all of them.

The first one was when I had just started studying at the university, "my first love", named Carlos Daniel. He was a dentist. He was a real prince charming for the first eight months of getting to know each other, but then it was like a switch went off in his head and a monster came out that I had never imagined could exist. I don't have any other way to describe it or compare it other than the It Ends With Us story by Colleen Hoover, it was exactly like that. I was the victim of physical and psychological violence from a narcist who painted the perfect con,

I knew he truly loved me, and in a way he still does, but even a murderer can love someone, and love isn't really all there is in this world.

I take the stabbing pain I feel in my heart and add an extra pair of five kilo weights on each side of the barbell, because if my heart hurts, my legs might as well hurt too.

My second boyfriend was an artist, Joel. For a while I thought I was really in love with him, but what was the problem? He was seventeen years my senior. I was twenty-three at the time and he was forty. I'm not sure you could really call that love. He was a journalist/writer/painter/photographer and all the other similar arts. When we lived together, I woke up every day to a love letter on my pillow, with breakfast ready and a movie set to a certain scene. This happened when he had to go to work and I didn't. When we woke up together, he would sing to me under his breath close to me, he was a music lover, his room had shelves full of old records and movie and show memorabilia like Star Wars and Friends. I still remember when he basically forced me to watch all the movies and chapters of Friends and I fell asleep during all of them. I don't know, I didn't really like them, I didn't hate them, the movies or the show, but for some reason I couldn't concentrate on them.

Joel wrote a column for an important magazine in Maracaibo, he was also the top editor for the most important newspaper in the country at that time. Whenever there was an important concert in Venezuela or Colombia or even Brazil, El Pitazo, a Spanish newspaper, would send him to cover the event. Joel had worked as a journalist at Guns N' Roses, Kiss, Juanes, Julieta Venegas, Camila and many other concerts. Not only that, he had also won a collection of different journalism awards in Venezuela.

For many different reasons - his hair, his pauses in his speech, even his body movements - he reminded me of Tom Hiddleston, only that

Joel had a darker skin color and wasn't quite as handsome, his greatest asset was his intellect. I still remember him and feel love for him, sometimes I even miss him, at least once a year I get in touch with him just to know how he's doing. Joel and I even got engaged. When that happened, my family, my family was up in arms: I was too young and he was much older. Obviously my mom wanted to die, I think the biggest fight I ever had with her was that we didn't speak for months, in fact I moved to Miami, and she didn't even say goodbye to me.

Joel and I broke up because he didn't want to leave the country. For him, in his forties, it was too hard to leave everything behind: his career and all his achievements were deeply rooted in the country.

Breaking up with him really hurt me. Because of the situation in the country, I had to go to Miami while I did the paperwork to get my Italian citizenship. The plan was for me to go back to Venezuela and get married so that he could get the citizenship and we could move to Italy together. But that didn't happen, while I was in my Miami our love ended.

I had to go through this separation alone, scared and living in modern slavery. I worked as a waiter in a Chinese restaurant, I spent twelve hours standing and only had ten minutes to eat my lunch. When I got home I cried my heart out, it was a very sad time for me, but the next one was the worst and it started with me moving to Milan and the third serious boyfriend.

When I moved to Italy, I still hadn't finished the official process and paperwork for my citizenship. I was in the country legally because my application was already an official legal process, but I didn't have a citizenship status that would allow me to have a work permit, and I needed to do something to afford living there for the time being. Fortunately, I have family here, so I moved in with my uncles, and later I moved into an apartment that belonged to a cousin who had moved to the city, and I shared that apartment with three other people. I didn't have to pay much rent there, so I could pay that with my savings, but I had to work somewhere to cover my other expenses, like food and personal hygiene products.

I got a job at a wholesale electronics store. It was a big store and they distributed and sold products in Italy as well as in Malta and other neighboring countries. The company had 3 big bosses: an American named Jackson, an Italian named Federico, and a Spaniard of some other origin, though I didn't know where from, whose name was Marco.

When I first joined the company, I noticed the guy in charge of import and export. His name was Ali and he was Zayn Malik's long lost brother - beautiful - and like Zayn, half British and half Pakistani. My job was to check and inspect products, I did quality control tests. Most of the time I worked in the containers that they used to ship the goods or in the warehouse, very rarely in the offices that had air conditioning. It was the middle of summer and every day it was almost 40°C; I was always sweating and about to faint. I lost weight like never before: besides the constant sauna-like conditions, I didn't eat anything, I was so exhausted all the time that I didn't feel hungry.

Ali had to supervise my work once a week, and I looked forward to these reviews to have an excuse to talk to him, knowing that time was an opportunity for intense flirting.

A few days passed before Ali asked me for my personal phone number, I gave it to him, and we spent hours texting each other. When we were at work, he acted nice, going to the trailer or the warehouse and buying me water and giving me easier tasks that didn't involve heavy lifting so I could have a break. During this time, I hadn't completely let go of Joel, in fact I still talked to him every day, but when Ali invited me to a Backstreet Boys concert, I texted him and asked him to stop contacting me.

Marco and Federico flirted with me from time to time and "rescued" me from Jackson's despotic rule. Honestly, the guy was crazy, he screamed at me that I was useless, but I used to work in art production, so I'm bulletproof, no amount of screaming or bad words can get the best of me.

On the day of the concert, I dressed up super pretty. I realized that the texts I was sending Ali weren't going through. He had texted me earlier to let me know the time and place at the venue where we would meet from the company phone, which made me think that his personal phone wasn't working, so I went to the concert waiting for further confirmation.

I arrived at the venue at the agreed time and smoked a cigarette while waiting, time passed and I smoked another one, time passed but I couldn't smoke a third one because it just felt too much. I texted and called him, but he didn't answer. I didn't understand what was stopping him. Even if his personal phone was broken - I assumed it was - he could have found me. I was getting worried, forty-five minutes had passed and the concert was about to start.

I decided to look for him inside the venue, next to the entrance we had to use. The concert started, the Backstreet Boys came out and started performing. The crowd was euphoric and I couldn't concentrate. As I stood in front of a beer and hot dog stand, I felt the place getting smaller and my heart started racing. People were yelling and the summer heat was starting to become suffocating.

I tried not to have a panic attack, but people kept screaming and clapping. I tried to find a place to focus my attention to see if I could calm down, maybe the concert video camera could help. It was pointed at the crowd when I heard Nick Carter say: "Hold on to your loved ones if you are here with them and dedicate this song to them. I focused on the crowd that was on the big screens, and I saw him. On one of the monitors, I could see Ali kissing a blonde girl. I was shocked. My ears started ringing and I had to get out of there.

The next day at work, Ali didn't show up and I was still in panic, feeling the fear beating in my chest, I was in the warehouse when I lost my breath, I fell to my knees and was on the floor fighting for air. Marco showed up, picked me up and when we were outside he asked me:

- What is going on?

Gasping for air and scared, I told him what had happened to Ali.

- Darling, you should be with a real man. He's just a little boy, an asshole. If you were with me, you wouldn't have to worry, he said.

And that's how an incredibly weird dynamic started at work: Jackson would yell at me every day, Marco would flirt with me more and more every day, Federico would occasionally show up to work and flirt with me, and Ali, in addition to blocking and unblocking me on WhatsApp depending on his mood, would often skip work, but when he did show up, he would sometimes ignore me, and sometimes he would bring me water and be nice to me again.

Slowly, flirting with Marco led to a relationship. It happened after he left me in charge of some goods because he had to go out of town. When he came back, he had bought me a purse as a gift and asked me very enthusiastically to give him a chance. And I gave it to him, just to get over Ali and forget about him. That was my first step into a world of nightmares.

What I lived with Marcos is something I'm not ready to share yet. It causes me so much pain that I feel incapable of bringing it out. Everything that happened with him and the context of that relationship was so infamous that in order to heal I decided to call him Voldemort. And no, I still can't talk about such a perverse thing...

Right now, the memories of that nightmare make me want to crawl under the covers and cry. I was pumping the iron hard at the gym. This new body that I have, with this energy and this unprecedented beauty that has awakened this feminine power in me, will never be touched by them again, nor by anyone at such a low level.

How did I survive what I went through? I don't know. When I was at my lowest point, I had only the certainty that Maria Valentina would rebuild herself and enjoy every second of her life. Now I think that the storm was a lesson, not a life sentence. This is my life now, and I'm going to live it to the fullest.

# CHAPTER II
## Everything is possible if you wish for it with all your heart

«For, you see, so many out-of-the-way things had happened lately, that Alice had begun to think that very few things indeed were really impossible».

—Lewis Carroll, *Alice in Wonderland*

# The reunion

Luis Miguel is a boy who is a little unstable, but he really wants to get ahead in this world. He majored in business administration in Venezuela and when the country's situation became unbearable, he decided to emigrate, but since he couldn't find what he wanted the way he wanted it to, he decided to study and become certified as a dental hygienist.

Physically, he is very handsome, like all of the Gil Montilla. His brown hair has a special glow to it now, on the video calls I realized he got some highlights in his hair that showcased his beautiful childish face. We both have the same age, twenty-five years old, but he looks like he's twenty and the rebellious, restless and immature nature of a thirteen-year-old teenager is what defines him. He's always joking about the two beauty marks that he has on his left cheek —one larger than the other—, saying they're the hook to win over his suitors.

When I walk outside of the airport in Madrid, I spotted Luismi in the crowd, with his thin lips showing off a warm smile that seeks affection, my heart melts when I see him, it's like looking at a little brother.

When I'm a few steps away from him, I run to hug him, and when he holds me in his arms I feel as if I'm about to break down and cry. «My baby boy, my beautiful baby boy, my colorful gay boy. I love you so much, my wrecking ball», I think to myself.

When we get to his apartment, I realize just how beautiful it is.

It's a single bedroom, two-bathroom apartment with a small balcony. The dining room table is all set, and Luis Miguel tells me that dinner is ready, that I only have to heat it up in the oven a little bit.

Once our dinner is warm, we sit down to enjoy that delicious meal. Dinner is baked salmon with vegetables and potatoes. He opens a bottle of champagne to celebrate and when the bottle pops, he says:

—Welcome to Madrid, Mary Jane!

I scream with excitement and Luismi starts to tell me juicy secrets about his life.

He tells me that he met Andrés via Instagram, that he's from Andalucia and that, despite being overly controlling, he stands up to him. And that thanks to Andrés he was able to move to Spain.

We had a spectacular evening, I really missed Luis Miguel and his crazy antics. I missed his little face, I missed this, the simplicity of just having a friend to talk to even about trivial things, I missed the human warmth of having a friend.

The next day, when I woke up, I have a lot of stomach pain, so much so that it's unbearable. Luis Miguel had to go and I was left alone with Lili, the Pomeranian that my friend adores.

I quickly take a painkiller and decide to call my parents to catch up with them. I'm lucky and I manage to get a hold of them, I let them know that I'm okay, that I have some stomach pain, but that everything is okay and that Luismi will be back soon. My parents tell me to send their regards to him and say Hello. It's six a.m. in Venezuela and over here it's almost noon. My dad is getting ready to go to work, while my mom is making breakfast. I let them know that I want to lay down for a bit and I hang up.

Once my dear Luismi comes back, we get into tourism and street mode.

Luismi takes me to the "Palacio Real" in Madrid, and I set up my very own photoshoot there.

I laughed so hard when he yelled:

—You go, Kendall Jenner! Give it to me!

Once the photoshoot is over, he tells me:

—We're going out partying tonight, and all of the celebrities from Maracaibo that live in Madrid are coming, are you ready?

—What do you mean by all of the celebrities? Who is that?

—Jennifer Hidalgo, Fernanda Portillo, Yuliana Pérez, Paola Ortigoza, Edgar Ramos, Ricardo Araque, that's all I know so far, but I'm sure the list is much longer.

I had forgotten about the sifrinería of saying first and last names.

—Damn! You forgot to say Mauricio Grimaldi that studied in Fátima school, the son of the owners of the De Candido supermarket. Come on!

—Mary Jane, please don't get started.

---

We got to the bar, and everyone stood up excitedly. They introduced me to the ones I didn't already know and we all sit down and got to talking. I ordered my cocktail by excellence, a Cosmopolitan, and the gossip talk that I already know by heart begins, but that for some strange reason I needed this. Everything focuses on the places where we have travelled to, restaurants, meals, things we have bought and forbidden romances that people gossip about on the streets.

I feel as if a part of me was asleep and was suddenly awake. Since I started my university studies, I became very philosophical, interested in different things in comparison to the people in the room. But after

---

[6] In Venezuela, *sifrinería* refers to the behaviors and mannerisms of individuals with high purchasing power, known as sifrinos or sifrinas. This includes their way of speaking, walking, and consuming. Rather than being derogatory, the term is used in a lighthearted and playful way. (Editor's note).

everything that happened to me, I have felt the need to build myself up from the simple things, and Luismi's phone call and invitation to come visit gave me that opportunity. Perhaps that's why I'm here, in Spain, a country with my native language, here, in this bar with these people that I've known for many ages. Even if the conversation topics feel shallow to me, I'm here with them, who have seen me fall and grow.

Even though I haven't always known everybody here, I somehow feel close to them. We share something more than an accent and a hometown; we also share the complexity and survival skills of immigrants. We share the hiraeth, we're bonded by the nostalgia of having to look at our loved ones through a screen, the disgrace of seeing our country fall apart.

But none of that matters today, today I only want to rejoice in the accent, the faces, that sounds of laughter that eco around in my heart. I don't want to think about the context of the gossip today, today I want to savor this Cosmo, and laugh with friends who saw me with acne and braces. I want to enjoy this small part of life that reminds us all where we come from.

---

[7] *Hiraeth* is a Welsh word that presents a longing for home. It refers to an emotion similar to nostalgia, but much more complex because it not only implies longing for a time or a person, but it also includes the sadness over something that no longer exists or can no longer be. (Editor's Note)

# In defense of the rumor

When the dawn breaks, I realize I don't have a hangover, even though Luis Miguel and I drank up the water for the plants, as we say in Venezuela. Luismi isn't home, I don't know where he is. I got up and went straight to the shower. Then, I check my phone and I have an unread message from Luismi:

> *Mary Jane, I had to leave in a hurry because Andres's puppy is sick and we are on our way to the vet's clinic. I didn't want to wake you up. I left your breakfast in the microwave, and the keys on the table next to the door. I'm going to text Jennifer and ask her to go out with you somewhere. Close the door when you go out. We probably won't go out tonight but I'll send you a Taxi so we can have dinner at Andres's house.*
> *Love you.*

Honestly, I don't have a schedule for these days in Madrid, but Jennifer is too nice and I'm excited about the idea of going out with her. I could also play dumb and text the guy that asked me out on a date tomorrow to see if he wants to do something. «Ugh! He's probably at work», I shake it off and stick to the idea of going out with Jennifer. She texted me and adds Fernanda to the conversation, the three of us are going to catch up in the afternoon, but first I'm going to go to my sanctuary, that is, the museum. The museum for me is like going to the

Temple of God, it inspires me a lot, and I decide to go to the Reina Sofia Museum.

I finish my breakfast quickly, grab my face mask and set my plans into motion.

Inside the museum, standing in front of the Picasso exhibition I can't help but to see myself like his women, especially when I look at Bust of a Woman, a painting that, according to the information, was stolen and passed through many hands. «Oh, to be a woman and getting passed through many hands without our consent», I say to myself. Besides, with Cubism I feel that we are all made up of pieces, rebuilt, «still trying to fit my pieces in».

When I leave the museum, I realize that I have a text from Fernanda:

*Mija[8], where are you? I'm with Jennifer, looking*
*for you. Let's have a picnic in the Retiro Park. .*
*I was enthralled with so much art and time*
*just flew by me.*

I send them my location and Jennifer says that they'll come get me in a couple of minutes.

Being at the museum made me forget about my plans and time, and here in Spain it's customary to have lunch at three o'clock, so we aren't that far off from Spanish lunch time, it's not even four o'clock yet.

The three of us get to El Retiro park, Jennifer has made some hamburgers and brought natural orange juice and a bottle of champagne. As we eat, we talk non-stop about the stories we have in common, including the details from the previous night. Fernanda goes too far with gossip and Jennifer looks for a reasonable balance between rumors and the truth. That was the topic of our table-talk.

---

[8] *Mija and mijo* are affectionate terms used to address someone in a familiar way. They are contractions of mi hija (my daughter) and mi hijo (my son), but they are commonly used regardless of any actual family relationship. (Author's note).

—I don't know why you have to hit the gossip so hard —Jennifer says—, you should let everyone tell their own story, you know, direct sources.

—Girls, don't hold me back, because you know I'm toxic —said Fernanda in her defense, as the three of us laugh—, if people weren't so toxic perhaps, I'd be more relaxed. Besides, it's not all bad, we also talked about other stuff, you know. And, Jennifer, «Direct sources?» —She said while air quoting—. If Madrid waited for direct sources about the romances between footballers and hostesses , we would never hear that Piqué was cheating on Shakira.

—Get out! For real? — I interrupt her with a heart attack from what she's saying.

—Of course, girl. But I'm using it as an example. If you don't know the details, it turns out that Piqué is always out at party, but he takes it to the limit when Shakira is out travelling. And people have seen him leaving the clubs with one and another. In any case, the point is that we have to expand on the gossip, and depending on how the parties involved defend themselves, they're confirmed or dismissed. And this gossip is an example, I know from a good source that it's true.

—Girl, kill me! Cheating on Shakira, now that's heavy—says Jennifer as she puts her hands on her head in disbelief—. If they do that to her, what's left for the rest of us. My God!

—Let's be honest, you know —says Fernanda—. A lot of stuff in the world are just gossip. From unconfirmed rumors even wars have broken out. My gossip doesn't have that much power, despite breaking up a marriage or two, because I can't find friends to spread them around —She says as she looks at me and Jennifer as if we're guilty of some crime—. So, I don't feel bad about my attitude and you're not going to convince me otherwise.

—Damn, mija, —I say—. You better not keep talking because we'll end up divorcing Messi and that would make me sad.

We all laugh.

—Now that's a saint. I've got gossip on that too. —said Fernanda. It's almost seven o'clock... We decided that we had had enough with debating about gossip and I text Luismi so he can send a taxi to pick me up. He says that the taxi will pick me up in a couple of minutes, and that they're ready for appetizers. The three of us say goodbye and we promise to continue our conversation, even if it's over the phone. Regardless of our opposing points of view about the topic of rumors, we really enjoyed our get-together.

---

I get to the apartment that Luismi told me to and Andres is the one who opens the door, I finally get to meet him.

—Andres? —I ask rhetorically and stretch my hand out.

—And you are, undoubtedly, Mary Jane — he pushes my hand away and gives me a friendly hug. He then raises his voice and says: —Luismi, your soul sister is finally here!

—Time to eat! —says Luis Miguel from the kitchen.

During the appetizer I notice that Andres is slightly older than Luis Miguel, he's a handsome, focused and well-grounded man, but you can see that he has a strong character from miles away. I immediately understand their relationship, even though Luis Miguel is a little bit immature, he's a boy with a golden heart and he loves to cook, host dinner parties and make people laugh, in other words, he's the partner that Andres needs to face his business world. My putative brother knows how to win people over, and in the world of business, that is a highly valued skill.

I seize the opportunity to have Andres tell me about Andalucía, its customs and traditions. Luis Miguel is a little bit jealous; he wants the conversation to be about him. I tell them about my day at the museum and with the girls, and I bring up the story of Shakira and Piqué.

—Girl, obviously, everybody in Madrid knows about that —says Luis Miguel—. Mija, if the walls at the clubs could talk, half of Madrid would be in jail and divorced, it's crazy!

—Ooh, that makes me nervous. I think Madrid is too wild for me. —I say a bit annoyed.

—Yes, Madrid is wild — Andres says—, but with good company you can find it to be charming. But with those friends, yes, it's wild.

—Well, it's not like I'm going to party with them —I said—. We just talked.

—Yeah Baby, that's why I only texted Jennifer, she's more your type —said Luis Miguel as he takes off to put some music on, he then pulls out some bottles of wine and shows them to me — Look, from Chile, just the way you like them!

The three of us talked and laughed. Suddenly, Andres gets up and says:

—I want you to listen to some music from my hometown, my native land —and he put on flamenco music.

Luis Miguel shouts out immediately:

—Oh! My soul sister also dances flamenco, Andres. —and then he talks to me—, humor me, Santi, dance a little bit, please.

—Well, I'm not an expert —I tell them, and I say to Andres—: I only took some flamenco classes when I was a teenager, I'll give it a shot, even though I don't have the right dress for it.

And I started dancing, as Andres and Luismi clapped their hands. I didn't feel embarrassed at all, on the contrary, we had created a moment of so much trust, it's as if we were family that got together after wishing it for too long.

When I feel tired, I signaled Luis Miguel that I wanted to go, and Andres tells us to stay the night.

—Thank you, Andres, but I need to take my make-up off, shower and the whole thing. I'm a bit of an old lady.

—Mary Jane, I'm going to keep calling you Mary Jane because Luismi was really on point with the nickname. Don't worry, I'll call you a taxi so you can go rest.

Luis Miguel has a mischievous smile, and says:

—I'll take a couple of bottles with me; in case we feel like partying when we get there.

And we did. We saw the bottom of the bottles that Luis Miguel brought with him while we talked about everything: the vulgar and the divine, with truth and with rumors.

# Unforseen apathy

The next morning, I wake up feeling surprisingly light, without a trace of discomfort, despite all the wine we drank the night before. I wouldn't call myself a regular drinker, but I have to admit—my alcohol tolerance has become impressive. There was a time when just one beer was enough to make my head spin.

I sit up in bed, and Lili immediately jumps onto my lap. I run my fingers through her fur, playing with her gently, careful not to make too much noise—Luis Miguel is still asleep beside me.

Suddenly, his phone rings. Half-asleep, he answers with a groggy mumble. Seizing the moment, I quickly grab my phone and hit record, capturing Lili's soft, rumbling growl.

A few seconds later, Luis Miguel hangs up, rubbing his eyes. "It was H," he mutters, his voice still thick with sleep.

I immediately stop recording the Pomeranian, because Luismi continues:

- He says that he bought a ticket to come here last night and that he's on his way to the airport, that he'll be here around noon.

- Why?

- He's heartbroken, he broke up with his girlfriend, he didn't say anything, that's why he was missing. They broke up six months ago. I didn't even know.

- Oh, okay.

- What do you mean "Oh, okey" -Luismi jumps up- but he's been your crush since you were a teenager and every time I call you, you ask me about him. This is your chance, he's coming single, baby.

For some reason, I'm not responding at all. My therapist would say that I'm afraid of being rejected, but I'm not going to talk about that with Luismi.

Bah, that's over, I tell him while making an I-don't-care gesture with my hand.

I get out of bed and take a shower to start the day. I have another museum to visit today, I know there won't be enough days here to visit them all, but I will try to make the most of this short time in Madrid and soak up the art.

In the Prado Museum I have the Naked Maja in front of me. It's a real spectacle. I've always said that if there's one place in the world that can drive my thoughts, it's a museum.

When I am finished with the exhibition, I stop by the gift shop and buy some souvenirs to take home for my little cousins. They're twins, and of course, like all the women in the family, they're called Maria, Maria Paz, and Maria Celeste. They live in Milan with my Aunt Maria Eugenia and Uncle Alessandro. I don't visit them often because I'm always busy, but I love them with all my heart. Yes, we're all Maria Santini. "That's so original," I say to myself.

On my way to the apartment, I remember that the capital H is arriving in Madrid today. I have no idea if he's already home, but I don't care. What I hadn't told Luismi is that the night before, when we went out with the "Maracaibo celebrities," I made eyes at a super hot guy named Pablo and we agreed to go out for dinner tonight.

"I'm a big, strong woman, I can't go around fangirling over a boy from my teenage years. It's not like he's Harry Styles. Enough about that. The new Maria Valentina can't go back to that silly moment with the typical crush on my best friend's older brother or running around looking for boys who look like her celebrity crush. First it was Joel who looked like Tom Hiddleston, then Ali who looked like Zayn Malik, ugh, no! I have to be a woman, now! I'm twenty-five years old, stop it. Otherwise, I'll risk bad things happening to me again, like with Voldemort,' I tell myself.

Around three o'clock, I ring the doorbell at Luis Miguel's apartment and to my surprise he is not the one opening the door.

# H, the great

H hides his jet-black hair beneath a Yankees baseball cap, with a few wavy, almost curly strands peeking out, adding to his effortless charm. His large, slightly slanted brown eyes are so expressive they seem to read my soul in an instant. When he smiles, his thin pink lips curve beautifully, revealing impeccably white teeth.

His sun-kissed skin glows, and his scent—intoxicating and unforgettable—etches itself into my memory like a cherished keepsake. He wears a simple black t-shirt that highlights his athletic frame, paired with classic Levi's and crisp Stan Smith Adidas, a look that is effortlessly timeless.

He is the perfect fucking combination of Charles Leclerc, Ian Somehalder and Alex Turner.

—Hi, Santi, please come in, how are you? —he says kindly.

When I come in, I greet him with a quick hug and he stands there waiting for the two kisses, in a very French way. I stare at him for one last millisecond.

«This man has my life in his hands», my brain speaks out while my heart pounds fast. I excuse myself by saying that I have to go to the bathroom and wash my hands. When I walk in, I look at myself in the mirror and think «He's beautiful, oh my God, what a beautiful man! My delicious Hachito Sweetie Pie».

When I get out of the bathroom, Luis Miguel and H have already opened a bottle of wine, they're waiting for me in the dining room to have lunch, but it could as well be dinner given the time, but it's the summer time and the days are much longer.

For lunch we're having pasta with shrimps made by Luismi, and the three of us start to enjoy that delicious meal.

H tells us a little bit about his job. The boy is a mini genius, a mini-Einstein, specifically in the field of robotics. He studied high-school in Maracaibo and then moved to Caracas to study computer engineering. When he finished his studies, he received a scholarship for the Paris Robotics University to study a masters. He graduated with honors, the first in his class, and he immediately started work in a Japanese computer and robotics company located in downtown Paris. Basically, H is like Hiro Hamada, the boy from Big Hero 6, and he works in a place like the one in the movie. It's unbelievable that both characters, besides having the letter H in their names, also look alike physically. He's hot, smart, speaks three languages fluently, I know where he comes from, and I know he's a good boy, brought up with strong core values and structure.

As I listen to H, I can't help thinking about Mrs. Marisela and Mr. Heinrich, with the two of them being so different and so alike. Mr. Heinrich comes back as being strict and very conservative, he liked things done in a perfect fashion.

I remember the moment when everybody found out that Luis Miguel was gay, we were fourteen years old. He stayed over in my house for a couple of days to wait for the tide to roll back. Mrs. Marisela had many conversations with my mom on that topic. I spied in on one of them and I remember hearing:

—Sandra, this situation is complicated for me, Luis Miguel is too young, how can he know what his sexuality is? He has to experience things first, perhaps he's confused.

—Look, Marisela —said my mom with her energetic Maracaibo accent

— you're either born gay or you're not. You have to love your son above all else. You probably already knew it, you're his mother, perhaps you hadn't given yourself time to digest it. Now, it's different with Heinrich, take it easy with him, he'll give in slowly. What you have to understand is that you don't stop loving a son because he's gay, the thing is that you think he's going to have a bad time because the world is very intolerant so you get mad at him, that's what's going on with your husband.

I jump out of my memories and look at Luis Miguel and H. They're entertained laughing at something and my heart just melts, the three of us were just little kids, and now we're adults and we're here, in Madrid, eating together. Life just takes unexpected turns!

The three of us dump ourselves on the couch and start telling stories. H starts to talk about the things that happened with his ex-girlfriend. The breakup boils down to communication problems, and not knowing how to manage a relationship after having being locked down, breathing the same air for months on end during the pandemic. As we're all there, I bring out the astrology skills I have honed and learned over time and I look for a website to check our birth charts and gossip.

—Well, my Luismi, it says here that you are stubborn and a tramp.

—Stars don't lie, girl —says Luis Miguel, and gives us a laughter attack.

—My turn now. What does astrology have to say about me? — H asks. When I have H's birth chart, I take a screenshot without him realizing it and save it on my phones loft bed for later so I can do synastry and composite charts. I just have to know if this Libra and this Aries have a future together.

—Well, let's see —I say as I take a quick glance at his birth chart —. You're Aries, so obviously impulsive, deceitful, fake and indifferent —I joke.

—Well, that's what people say, honestly. Everybody thinks I'm like that, but it's far from the truth. Yes, it's true that it's hard for me to put myself in somebody else's shoes, but it's that I don't understand the need to be excessively empathetic in every circumstance. I think that we have to look at things from other points of view too —he says.
—My dear friend, empathy and compassion are two different things. Not everyone has the capacity to be empathetic, but everyone can be compassionate, that is, you don't have to feel what the other feels to be compassionate and validate what they're going through. Compassion is enough —I point out, and H agrees with me.
—Well, my astrological friend, what do the stars say about you? — H asks.
—Well, honestly? —H nods with curiosity—. I'm a very dynamic person, and I get bored quickly. I'm also very aesthetic and pay a lot of attention to details. My mind goes too fast, and I think that the world moves too slow. I don't forgive and I don't forget. In the same way that you earn respect, I think that «second chances» are earned too. I think that covers the basics — I answer, almost without breathing, as if I knew and answered it by heart.
—Did you figure that out yourself or did the horoscope do that? — H asks.
—Not by myself, no way. I studied metaphysics during the lockdown, and psychology as well. So I think that I discovered myself in detail. Now, astrology only gave a better context to all that I had already discovered about myself, my therapist knows that I use astrology as a tool for self-discovery. And I always know that the stars pitch the field, but they don't force you to do anything. At the end of the day, you are the alchemist, you always have the power, nobody else does.
When I realize it, it's almost six o'clock and I have a date with Pablo at eight. If I want to look like a princess, I have to start to get ready now.

—Well boys, the conversation was good, but I'm going to take a bath and get real pretty.
—More pretty? Is that even possible? —H says.
I can't help but blush, but I seize the opportunity and throw it back to him:
—Yes. Well, you'll see, and have a heart attack.
We both share a flirty smile, and I run to the bathroom before I end up cancelling on Pablo because of H.
I put on the last splash of Setting Spray on my face, I put some perfume one and come out of the bathroom. In the living room, sitting there waiting like a figurine on a wedding cake is H. He also showered and changed, the combination of a navy-blue shirt with khaki pants makes him look casual and elegant.
—Well, we're both ready, where are we going? What restaurant do we have the reservation in? —asks H.
I freeze.
—No, but wait. What do you mean? I fixed myself up because I have a date.
—A date? With who?
—I'm sorry, but that's none of your business —I answered with an acid voice tone.
—Are they coming to pick you up or are they sending a taxi to pick you up? —he asks with intensity.
I realize that I had already assumed that I would get to the place myself. «Touché, H, touché».
—Well, I don't know. I hadn't thought about that detail.
—Well, figure it out and let me know, ask the name of the restaurant and if they made a reservation. You don't mind if we go eat at the same place, right? That way we can be your chaperones. —He gives me a naughty smile.

—Okay, let me call and ask.
When I'm going to step aside to make a call, H stops me and says:
—The call, here and on speaker. I'll tell you if the guy is worth your time.
I don't know why I'm being so submissive, but I do exactly as he says: I call Pablo and he answers after ringing a couple of times.
—Valentina, how are you? Don't tell me you're calling to cancel on me.
—Hi Pablo, no. Quite the opposite, I was calling you to ask if you're going to pick me up or if you're going to send a taxi for me. I also want to know where you made the reservation.
—Well, I was thinking of an Italian place that's close to my house, I didn't make a reservation, we can just go there and get a table. And let me see what to do, if I send a taxi for you, but if you take the subway, you can get here in twenty minutes.
—Oh, Pablo, can we change restaurants? The thing is I live in Italy, and I eat Italian food all the time. I'd like to eat something else.
—That's why I picked Italian, so you can tell me what to order and let me know if the food is done right and if I can recommend the restaurant later on to other people. —I did not understand. Did he assume that he could use me as a food critic? But the face that H made was a poem, he looked at me as if he was dying and signaled me to cancel it.
—Listen, Pablo, I think we should leave it at that. What do you say if we catch up some other time? I really don't feel like eating Italian or catching the subway right now.
—Well, it's your loss, goodbye. —He hangs up.
As soon as the call ends, H says to me:
—Let me break down what just happened. One: he did not have a reservation. A wise man is always prepared for the worst. If you got there and there wasn't a table available, what were you going to do?

Start walking around to see where you found a place? That sounds ridiculous. Second: He didn't plan on picking you up or sending a taxi over for you, and you're in high heels and dressed beautifully. What you're wearing and the occasion, definitely calls for him to pick you up.

As if what he said wasn't enough, H carries on with the list of grievances that he picked up on that short call:

—Third: he didn't think about what was probably better for you, but what was better for him, not only with the food, but with how easy it was to get to the place, he said that it was close to his house. If he didn't plan to pick you up, why didn't he choose a place that was close to you? He's thinking about what is easier for him, not for you. Fourth: When you said that you didn't want to go anymore, he answered as if he didn't care and did not look for a solution. As soon as you presented a small problem to him, he rather let the date be cancelled and not offer an alternative or solution. If the man can't give you a solution, he's not worth it.

I was speechless. He is absolutely right.

—Now, let's go and eat Japanese, feel like it?

—Yes, that's fine.

I don't have another option but to think «Wow, what a man! I have so much to learn in this world of boys and dating!».

———•··•→ ⚹ ←•··•———

    H managed to get a reservation for the three of us in a restaurant called Zuara, a Japanese restaurant with a Michelin star.

    When we arrive, they take us to our table. The service is so elegant and ceremonious that I feel as if we were the imperial family of Japan.

    The food is delicious, H took it to himself to order the food for all of us, he ordered a trout for me as a main course and I'm savoring each bite. The green tea is also spectacular, God, I love to eat. When we're done, we have a small debate over which mochi has the best taste and which dessert we should order.

Honestly, it feels so natural to be seated here with them, and especially so with H. There's not even a smidge of anxiety, a drop of fear, it feels as if I did this every day. Beneath this natural act I can feel gratitude about having him there, next to me, just existing. The reality is that I wouldn't know how to tell if what's happening is a potential romance.

I'm like a new person without experiences. There are chapters of my life that were stolen from me, in fact, I don't know how many, but for now I just want to enjoy him, look at him and admire him. I want to let myself get intoxicated in his perfume, I want my face to light up with his smile, I want to let him be, I want us to simply be, as we are in here: relaxed with our only concern being if the pistachio mochi is better than the chai tea, and besides, who even likes chai tea? Apparently, H does.

# The tramp

When we leave the restaurant, H asks if there's anything else we would like to do. I'm so comfortable with my sweetie pie that what I would like to do —talk to him until I ran out of words — didn't include three people, so Luis Miguel, who already had a few sakes up in his head, proposed to us:

—Let's buy something to drink and have a party in my apartment. We'll invite people over, of course. What do you say?

—That's fine by me — H replied.

—Yes. That's fine by me too.

Time goes by, and its already midnight. The house is full of people and I'm a little drunk.

People hang out between the terrace and the living room. They talk, smoke all kind of cigarettes, regular ones and the ones that make you laugh. There're bottles everywhere and Bad Bunny is doing his thing on the speakers with his «Dakiti»[5].

H has spent the night chasing me around, I have had to ask him to excuse so I could go to the bathroom. We talk about everything, from the new law that forbids wearing hijabs to why I think that men who have the moon at cancer are mamas' boys.

I think that neither of us expected the conversation to flow in such a natural way, and neither of us thought that we would share

---

[5] Dakiti - Bad Bunny

so many philosophical argumentations. I think that we both had the wrong impression about one another. I thought that he was a self-centered narcissist, and I'm sure that he thought that I was just mom and dad's little princess. But in reality, despite both of us being a little bit like what we thought of each other, we are also so much more, much deeper and complex. For me, acting like a spoiled little girl is like a defense mechanism, it always works for me, it protects me and takes care of me and it's the attitude I assume when I need to get out of a slump. Perhaps it's the same with him: being an asshole is a defense mechanism.

H and I continue with our conversation, and after a while I realize that I'm talking to the male version of myself, that, as I had deducted before, has a defense mechanism. We are both demanding, ambitious and perfectionists, we like things done our way because we can only trust in ourselves.

At that point I'm in battle with my feelings, he clearly likes me, I can tell by his body language —he's mirroring mine—, he makes me laugh, he blushes and acts surprised with the silly things I say to him. And when we both crack up laughing, we fall into a trance and end up staring at each other inside of our own personal bubble.

But the little voice inside my head starts to sabotage me and asks «Is this for real? Perhaps I'm just excited and I'm imagining it». The doubts make me a little anxious and I need to step out and smoke a cigarette. I need five minutes to think and put my ideas in place. H doesn't like it when I separate myself from him, and less if it's to smoke.

I step out of the building so I can smoke in peace without anybody around me, I think that I'm over stimulated from the number of people inside. I light up the Chesterfield and I start to roll around in my own thoughts.

«I'm sure that he likes me, I see longingness in his eyes, but a relationship with him could be very complicated for me. He lives in a different country from this and from where I live. Even though a long-distance relationship could work, having so much space in between would be troublesome for my emotions. I don't know how I would handle that, being H's girlfriend and having him so far away terrifies me. He's my dream come true since I was thirteen, and if I get into a relationship with him and it doesn't work out, it would tear me down. I would most likely spend my time crying, I would miss him too much. On the other hand, his ex-girlfriend lives over there, and they lived together and shared so many things, and that bonds people. If him and I aren't in the same place, not even close, how can we experience things? I think I'm terrified of everything, let's better not. Let's keep it as it is, Maria Valentina, and besides, in Italy men are at your feet it's just that with COVID, it has been impossible to socialize, give things time, and the summer is just getting started».

I head back to the apartment having made up my mind. When I look for H, I see him surrounded by a bunch of girls who are seconds away from throwing their panties at him and eating him up alive, he seems a little uncomfortable, but he doesn't completely hate it.

Seeing the commotion with H and his groupies , I sneak off to go to bed, because I'm starting to see double. When I try to open the door to Luis Miguel's room, it's locked. Then I remember that Luismi wanted to prevent people from going into his room because H's expensive and delicate work tools are in there, things like flash drives with confidential information.

I look for Luismi and ask him to open the room for me, that I need to look for something. I lie to him, because if I tell him that I want to go to bed he would kill me. He gives in, and once I'm inside the room, I lock myself in, throw the covers over me and try to fall asleep.

Suddenly, I hear the door opening and I don't even bother to open by eyes. From the perfume I already know that H entered the room.

He sits on the bed and gently strokes my hair.

—Are you asleep?

—Yes. Why don't you stay out there with your fans?

—Because I want to be here with you. Besides, you went to bed and didn't tell me. I was left without a party friend.

—Let's not make our lives complicated, go outside, don't keep your fans waiting.

— Is the distance from Milan to Paris so great?

—I don't know.

After I said that, he put his hand close to mine and gently tapped the back the back of my hand with his index and middle finger and says:

—1411 kilometers. Too many, right?

—Too many.

In between the rooms darkness I can feel his disenchantment, but his words confirmed to me that he likes me, that he would like for something to happen between us and that, like me, he's been thinking about the convenience of an us. Without another word he gets up and leaves, and I fell into a deep slumber.

I don't know how much time has passed, but when I get back into my own senses, I feel the urge to clean myself up, to brush my teeth and wash my face above all. When I step out of the room, there's nobody to be seen, everything's empty. The bathroom is right next to the bedroom, so I get there quickly.

I clean myself up without a hurry, I even take a long shower. I smell like cigarettes and party, I'm not sure who is going to sleep on the couch and who's going to sleep on the bed, but I prefer to be nice and clean in case I have to share the bed with someone special.

When I step out the bathroom, I realize that Luis Miguel is out on the terrace on what seems like a phone call. While I walk up to him and ask him if everything is okay, —because he has a frustrated look on his face— the doorbell rings. He hangs up and runs over to me to say:

—Go to the room for a bit, and please don't come out. Andres is here and he's in a bad mood, stay there and don't come out until I say so.

I comply with what he says and I go over to the bedroom quickly to give them space and let them solve their problems. When I open the door, H is on the bed with a tramp; one of the groupies that were harassing him earlier.

H has his body and faced completely against the wall. The tramp is very close to him with her skirt up, her bra unhooked and wearing H's black baseball cap. I'm boiling mad. Without a shadow of a doubt, I step out of the room immediately and close the door carefully. I regret having seen what I say, it's not something I would like to repeat, but Luismi nervously gets behind me, opens the door to the bedroom again and shoves me inside.

—Please, this will be quick. I'm begging you, it's life or death.

I reluctantly stay in the room; the tramp pretends to sleep and H is still motionless and breathing steadily. I deduce that he's also pretending to sleep. I lay on the empty side of the bed. I try to fall asleep, and after a while I feel that the tramp gets up from the bed and leaves the room. Almost immediately Luis Miguel steps into the room.

—Ugh, thank you, I fixed it. I'm going to sleep on the couch, you sleep here. Bye.

On autopilot, H moves his face from the wall, knocks over what seems to be a bag onto the floor and then I fix his pillow, take of his watch and open the covers so he can sleep more comfortably. «What was that, Maria Valentina? Why so submisive?», my brain drops on me. I shake that thought off and cover myself with the small piece of the quilt that's left for me. H immediately grabs my hand with a soft and delicate touch, slowly passing his fingers over my knuckles, and he repeats the two soft taps on the back of my hand with his index and middle finger, gently squeezing my hand as he says:

—Nothing happened with her — he says in a soft voice tone.

—You don't have to give me explanations.

—For some strange reason, I feel that I have to.

—You shouldn't.

—I know.

I free myself from his embrace and for the third time that night I force myself to fall asleep. The sun is almost rising.

# Under the skin

I wake up and H is completely pressed against me. The heat coming from his body has made me sweat. So much so that when I pull away from him, my pants are soaked with his sweat. He is still very sound asleep and my guts are rumbling with hunger.

I think that the sound coming from my stomach awakens H. He gently and lightly grabs my hand again, as if he wanted to say «I'm here». My heart melts, I look at his sweet face and as soon as he opens his eyes a little, I feel the urge to kiss him on his cheek and confess that I've had a crush on him for twelve years. But when I'm a millisecond away from doing it, my brain interrupts the romantic urge and shoves the mental image of the mardita tramp with his Yankees baseball cap on.

I feel a jab in my stomach. I gently release myself from his arms, I get out of bed, I grab some cloths from my suitcase and head straight to the bathroom to get dressed. My idea is to grab something for breakfast before I have a stroke.

As I leave the apartment, I see a coffee shop on the corner, I walk over, and when I get there, I order a large coffee with almond milk and a ham and cheese croissant. I look at my phone and see that I have a message. It's from some friends I met online a few years ago, they live in Madrid and they want to go shopping with me now that I'm

---

[13] *Mardita o mardito*: expression used in Maracaibo to say damned. This form of lambdacism is not as common in Maracaibo, as it is in the eastern part of Venezuela, so this expression is more of an extravagant used, opposed to a linguist custom or tradition. (Editor's note).

vacationing here in the city.

I accept the invitation with the idea of putting some space between me and H. «I have to focus, I think to myself, this man has the power to destroy everything that I have built, everything. If I'm not careful, I know he can crawl under my skin, and I'm not willing to give him that privilege so quickly, especially after that little scene with that tramp. He has to earn it.

When I get back to the apartment, I realize that the boys are still sleeping. Under the cover of silence I get into the bathroom for a long shower. One those showers where you exfoliate your skin, you shave… I need to drain out my thoughts, so I wash my hair again.

It's half past one and I'm ready to go out. Since it's still early to go out shopping with the girls, I decide to have a date with myself, I'll go to the Sala Canal de Isabel II, which is a museum-like venue that's on my way, and then I'll treat myself to some lunch.

I come out of the bathroom and H and Luis Miguel are having breakfast.

—Mary Jane, where were you this morning? — Luismi asks.

—I went to have breakfast.

—And now where are you going? — continues Luis Miguel with his interrogation.

—I'm going to catch up with some friends.

—Can we come with you? — H chimed in.

—No chance! Like they say here in Spain, it's a girl's thing.

—And tonight, are you coming with us? We're going to go out to a bar with the celebrities from Maracaibo. —Luismi tells me.

—Could be, depends on how it goes with my girlfriends. If we're done early, if I feel like it, etc., etc., etc.

—Anything you want to do is fine. Once you've finished with whatever you want to do, no matter the hour, send me your location and I'll send a taxi to pick you up. No matter the hour, no matter where you are, understood? —H insists.

—I can handle myself alone, and public transport in this city works very well —I answered, with my attempt to set some distance between us.

—That's right. But still, you could keep me updated. Could you at least share your real-time location? —H pushes. It's obvious that he seems concerned about me, and I'm decided to not give in.

—Again, in case you're deaf, I can handle myself alone. Okay?

—Okay —H said, and he immediately lets it go.

Jealousy is an emotion that I'm not familiar with. I don't know how to handle them. Honestly, I think that I had never really felt jealous, or at least not this type of jealousy. But the thing is, the situation with the tramp yesterday was out of proportion to me and it drove me crazy. I know that it's a contradiction to decide to not to get involved with H and having that tramp through me off board, but in my defense, I must say that emotions are worlds apart from reason. My head thinks one thing and my guts a very different thing. As much as I try, I don't have my emotions and my thoughts on the same page. «Shit! I know that I must not get involved with this boy, but I feel like I won't be able to control it».

---

I leave the house, and once I'm outside I look up on Google Maps the best route to get to where I want to go. After visiting the Sala Canal de Isabel II, where I saw an amazing photo exposition, I find a place to eat close to La Vaguada, which is where I'm going to be meeting up with my friends. I decided to go with Amazonia Chic and get going.

Once I'm in the restaurant, I order some steak with red wine, a Chilean cabernet sauvignon. Despite being in Europe, home of the best wines, my favorite is wine from Chile —a taste that Luis Miguel knows very well—. It's a drink that reminds me of times of abundance in my home, in Venezuela. For each special occasion, dad would buy Chilean wine, either El Gato Negro, El Rosario or, my favorite, Casillero del Diablo. For me, ordering one of these wines means rejoicing in its flavor and indulging in those family memories. Whenever I have the chance, I treat myself to my Chilean wine.

After satisfying myself with a delicious meal, I head over to La Vaguada Shopping Center.

When I find my friends, we go looking at the stores, one of them is a professional make-up artist, and so to hop on to that make-up train that she represents, I tell her that I want an all-new package with everything: foundation, blush, mascara, everything!

—Then let's go! If you want it all, you'll have it all! Let's go to Sephora and start hunting. I'm going to pick out the best, but with the best price as well so that you don't have to spend that much, okay?

I love the idea, because I don't want to leave my salary on it.

After half an hour, I already chose several things. When I look at my phone, I see that I have some messages from H on Instagram asking me what I'm doing, if I'm having a good time with my friends. It's a couple of messages and I really don't understand how I didn't see them. I think that I really disconnected for a couple of hours from the unexpected hurricane H. Maybe later, when I don't feel the anger that I've been dragging along since last night, I'll tell him what this girl's time out means for me.

When I was Carlos Daniel's girlfriend, the odontologist, he used to tell me that he loved me regardless if I had acne, if I wasn't wearing make-up or I didn't paint my nails. It was my first serious relationship and back then I thought that a man that loved like that was the right thing.

His words about how he found me beautiful no matter how I looked were so common and frequent that I slowly started to let go.

My friends used to tell me «I want to be loved like that, with messy hair and unkept». For some reason, those terms made me feel out of place, it was not until I started therapy that my therapist asked me in one of our sessions: «who are you», and I didn't know what to say.

One day I managed to answer him. I said, «I'm a woman who likes to take care of herself. I like to paint my nails, going to the hair salon, the smell of a hair dryer and nail polish makes me think more clearly. I feel happy when I have a new nail polish, a trendy new haircut, or a new color in my hair. I love being a woman and what that means for me».

And I still believe that. I love to wear make-up and, of course, if natives wore make-up to go hunting, as war paint, why can't I wear red lipstick as a way to state that I live a free life? It's okay if a woman prefers other symbols as a way to express themselves. There are girls that don't use make-up, they don't even shave, and that's the way they choose to manifest their freedom. I respect those decisions, but they're not mine.

The terms I apply to my femininity are my own, and I learned that there, I am the one that defines the word woman. I don't need the women around me to think the same way that I do, and I don't care if they judge me by the standards they have set for themselves. I understand that for a lot of women, taking care of themselves, using make-up or going to the hair salon is giving in to social pressure, but for me that means freedom.

Every time I have the chance to connect and bond with girls who think alike, that think that being a woman means dresses, perfumes or make-up, I seize the opportunity and enjoy my connection with them, in the same way that I can enjoy the bonds I have with other girls that differ from my point of view, because relationships don't revolve around the best lipstick or the latest lash curler in the market. That's my freedom. That's my way of being a *woman*.

# Is this real?

Once the make-up buying session is over, I see that it's still early. I give Luis Miguel a quick call to know where they are and he doesn't pick up, he only sends me his location via WhatsApp. They're in Picalagartos, a bar that, according to Google Maps, is on Gran Via. I check to see how far away I am, and it's thirty minutes from where I am. I only have to grab the subway.

When I get to the bar there's a small line of about three people. I take out my wallet to be prepared, I might have to pay an entrance fee or show my I.D.

—Good evening. Do you have a reservation?

—I have some friends inside waiting for me.

—Can I have your name, please?

—Yes, of course, Maria Santini.

—Mrs. Santini, please, right this way.

He leaves me for a second while he gets in touch through a 2-way radio, and then he brings me down a hallway to the staffs' elevator. I don't understand much of what's going on, I only do what I'm told. The guy presses the button on the elevator, but he doesn't come with me, and says:

—Once you get upstairs, one of your friends will be waiting for you to go to your table, they have been informed, okay?

—Okay, thank you very much.

I go up to floor number 9, the doors open and when I'm going to step out, I jump back scared, because H is leaning outside the elevator. «What the hell!?».

—Why didn't you answer my texts? And, why didn't you let me know you were coming? —he asks in a calmed authority tone.

—Mijo, you're not my dad.

He puts me back in the elevator with a swift but not harsh movement. He puts a key into the control system, the doors close and we are stuck in there alone without moving.

—Mijo. What the hell!? It's official, the visit has gone crazy.

—Can you please tell me, what's going on? —he asks in a calm tone, but with a smidge of concern in his voice.

—With what? I don't understand —I answered, truly confused. I don't know if he's asking why I didn't follow his instructions.

—Why are you holding back? Why are you fighting this?

—Fighting what? —I answer, in an attempt to ignore the fact that he's only a few centimeters away from me. I gulp, I know that he's talking about my efforts to avoid being near him.

H doesn't say anything else. He just grabs my hand and puts it on his chest. His heart is racing and he's breathing heavily.

I look into his eyes and I can't fight it any longer. I give up, I let it be. I let whatever is happening between us happen freely. I surrender to his eyes. I surrender to our hearts beating in unison. I let myself be, I let him be and I let us be. I surrender.

When H notices that my body has relaxed and that I'm not fighting it any longer, he pulls up very close to me. He gently and delicately grabs my face, I'm slightly taller than him, but my knees have agreed to bend down a little bit, because of the submission, I have just given in and we are at the same height.

We study each other's faces for a few seconds. H puts his forehead on mine without letting go of my face. I feel like I'm falling down a little bit more, and he pulls his whole body and presses it against mine. He puts his leg between mine so I don't fall down. Quickly and delicately, he puts some soft pressure on my thigh with his leg and, without letting go of my face, he brings it towards his own, breathing in my air and with our lips briefly touching.

After what felt like hours, he finally kissed me, slowly moving his tongue over my lips, and I can't take it any longer. After I put my hands on the back of his head, I grab his hair and bring him close to me, and we both fall into an intoxicating deep kiss. His hands are still holding my face and mine play with his hair, the hair that I had dreamed about for years… «Oh! My Hachito…».

H pauses for a second.

—What is this? —he asks, panting for air.

—I don't know —I answer, intoxicated with him.

We keep on holding each other with our foreheads resting on the other, while we slowly try to catch our breath. My mind throws at me the secret phrase I had hidden away for years, «We're home».

—I think we have to go—I say to try and get out of the heat.

—I think so too —he answers. Like me, he needs time to catch his breath, and then adds —: Can you stay close to me the rest of the night?

I nod my head in approval.

H takes the key out of the controls and hits a button; the elevator doors open and he walks out leading the way, but making sure that I'm close to him.

The table where our friends are is on a corner with a full view of the Gran Via, it seems like a movie scene. When we get to the table, nobody makes a fuss about the fact that me and H got there together. Everybody simply gets up to greet me enthusiastically. I kiss and hug everybody and when I look for a place to sit, H has already pulled out the chair next to him for me. When I sit down, the waiter comes by and asks me what I want to drink.

—A Cosmo, please.

The waiter gives me a list of the vodkas available for me to choose from, and honestly, despite having travelled around and knowing a thing or two, I don't know that much about alcohol, I'm really not that versed in all that. I only know about wines, especially if they're from Chile.

—Grey Goose will be fine, thank you —H answered for me.

I thank him with a little smile, and he acts stoically, just looking at me without saying a word. The waiter leaves.

An arm and a leg I have a hard time focusing on the conversation that the others have going on, when the only thing I want to do is kidnap H and talk to him about anything all night long.

I take a deep breath, settle myself in my seat, look straight ahead and make every brain cell that I have to pay attention to the topic of the conversation.

Once I'm paying attention to what they're talking about, I start to analyze the topic. They're talking about the privileges that we had back in Venezuela and how becoming migrants has forced us into living life from different perspectives and points of view.

When I started studying audiovisual productions, I decided to step aside from all of that circle that Luis Miguel called the «Maracaibo celebrities», the same group of people that are here tonight. I avoided them to run away from these conversations about privileges and the things they bought, but now I look at it from a different point of view. They all studied what they were supposed to study: law school, engineering, architecture, medicine and professions like that, the same as my cousins and my brother. I couldn't blame them; our families came from the same fields and their professional practice opened the door of success for this new generation.

During the university years, almost everyone gathered at this table in

Picalagartos was already struggling in some way, but it was still possible to make a living. Everybody had the illusion of growing professionally in the country, however, reality is a different story: we all became migrants and our professional careers are on hold.

The reality is that, despite having a certain degree of comfort and privilege, most of us came from hard working families, yes, business owners, but hard working nonetheless. Jennifer is a case in point, she worked the cashier at her father's bakery when we were teenagers, and like her we all worked on vacations or on weekends in our fathers and friends' businesses. We came from living a prosperous and hopeful life, but most of our parents did not. In fact, many of our grandparents were also immigrants.

My grandfather had escaped from the second world war. I can still remember when I was little, I would say things like «I'm hungry», and he would answer in a completely reasonable but authoritarian tone, line an army Captain and with a thick Italian accent: «You have an appetite, Tu non sai cos'è to be hungry». My grandfather died when Venezuela started to collapse, and when he died, the only thing he said about it was: «Venezuela is under construction, build it from the ground up, and build it as many times as necessary».

I'm sorry grandpa, but we all left, some because they didn't have another choice, and others, like my case, because my dream was to move since I can remember.

However, life has put me again in a Spanish country with the people that I grew up with, and after two years living abroad, I honestly don't have a stable argument regarding my thoughts on these people and their privileges. We all came from the same place, from the same social background, but why did I feel like such an alien? Why was it so hard for me to keep up with a conversation that I had had a thousand times before?

H grabs me and gently taps me twice with his two fingers on the back of my hand, his touch takes me out of my dissociated state.

—Your Cosmo is getting warm —he whispered in my ear.

I smile back at him and take a sip.

After an hour, I've already drank two Cosmo's. Edgar, who we have known ever since we lived in Maracaibo, and who is a part of the group of Friends that Luismi calls the «Maracaibo Celebrities», is jokingly acting along with me as if we were in a Mexican or Colombian soap opera.

# Mischief managed

Once I get to the apartment, I hop into the shower to wash off all of the dirt from the street. When I step out, H scares me again; he's standing by the door, wearing only a towel. You can tell that the boy hits the gym, he has a six-pack and big arms, «My god, what a delicious sweetie-pie» I pretend it's not happening, and I walk past him over to the room, it's almost midnight and I decide to read a book while H takes a shower. I try to focus on what I'm reading to not think about or set expectations about what is going to happen between us after that kiss in the elevator.

I'm reading the Crossfire trilogy by Sylvia Day. Even though I'm already twenty-five years old, I haven't been able to pull myself apart from these types of books, and to be honest, it's the first time I feel identified with an erotic literature book like this. Eva Tramel, the protagonist of the story, is a Latina woman with a strong character: she knows what she wants and how she wants it, she comes from a good family and there's not a lot of material things that Gideon Cross can offer to her that she can't get herself. Eva was also abused, like me, and Gideon was also abused, even though he has a hard time admitting it. To be together, they are both going to therapy. The whole story seems incredible to me. I wonder if H has a dark side, and, like Gideon, he has been abused and can't admit to it.

H walks into the room, and asks me what I'm doing.

—Reading a book.

—But you have your phone in your hand, are you reading it on your phone?

—Yes, it's a habit that I have, I only read on my phone.

—Why?

—Well, when I was a teenager physical books were too expensive, and I could read a book weekly, I was addicted. My parents couldn't buy all of them for me, and it was when BlackBerry's were "In", so I used to read previews on iBook's on an iPod, and if I liked the story and wanted to finish it, I paid for the book with my aunt Eugenia's credit card that was linked to my iCloud. If after I finished reading the story, my liking had turned into obsession, my parents would buy a physical copy for me. That practice became a habit. I think that I've never read a physical copy of a book for a first time, only re-read them.

Nowadays I don't read as much as I did when I was a teenager. I can read perhaps a couple of books a year, and I do it when I want to reconnect with myself. But reading has always been an essential part of my life, so much so that I couldn't decide whether to study audiovisual production or literature.

—Talk to me about the books you read as a teenager —says H while he lays down on the bed and gets under the covers with me.

—Well, I obviously read classics like Pride and Prejudice, The Great Gatsby, The Picture of Dorian Gray, The Tunnel by Sabato. I really loved Cortazar, I think he's one of my favorites, I also loved Poe. That, on the classical side, but the ones I felt more eager to read were fiction and teenage dramas.

—Like which? Let's see.

—Don't laugh. But I read Wattpad fanfictions. I bought the biggest ones, like Dark, or After, phew, I loved them, I also read the Divergent series, but my favorite one was always Hush Hush, my love for those books was so big that I read the Book of Enoch just because the mentioned it in the book.

—And out of all the ones you have read, which one is your favorite?

—Definitely Memoirs of a Geisha and The Book Thief, the movies based on them are spectacular too. And you? What about you?

—Mostly Edgar Allan Poe, philosophy, Plato, Aristoteles. But I also have to confess that I like Hemingway.

—«The world breaks everyone and afterward many are strong at the broken places» —I quote Hemingway with a blank stare.

H looks at me curiously. I clarify that it's a Hemingway quote and that phrases like that held me up in times of distress.

—What happened? —he asks me.

—I don't want to talk about that right now. Don't destroy the magic with that, my dear muggle.

—Come here —He brings me close to him, kisses my forehead and adds: I solemnly swear that my intentions are good.

My eyes begin to water and H interprets that it's time for whatever is going to happen. Softly and swiftly, he brings me close to him and we melt into a deep kiss. His mouth eats up mine and I push out all of the bad memories within me. I climb on top of him and we continue the attack on our mouths, needy but softly.

—You kiss so good.

—So do you —I answer.

I pull him back towards me by his hair, and our mouths look for each other to calm the thirst we have. H has his hands on my hips and squeezes them. He then moves on to my ass and I'm grateful to all the saints that I'm at my prime, this athletic body that I have now deserves to be touched by H, he deserves this, and I deserve his six-pack.

With a quick movement, we change positions: he's on top of me now. When I feel his hands on my stomach, I tense up and start to shake.

—Is everything okay? Do you want me to stop, did I do something wrong? Is there any spot you don't feel comfortable with me touching it?

The truth is that the last time that I had sex was a year and a half ago with Voldemort, but I felt comfortable and safe in H's hands.

—I'm just nervous, I'm sorry. And I'm on my period.

—Then we'll stop. If you're not thrilled to do something, we won't do it. It's essential for me that you feel comfortable, and that you enjoy it.

—But... —I haven't finished talking when he interrupts.

—Hush. No buts, you don't have to apologize for anything, nor do things that you don't feel happy doing. With me or with anyone. We can keep talking, do you want to do that?

—I want to do it, please, it's just that I'm on my period.

—I don't have a problem with that, with your period, if you haven't shaved, or any of that, if you want to do something, then we'll do it. And if you're uncomfortable with anything, we won't.

I grab his face and kiss him gently, his words calmed anything that might have been bothering me, and now I just want to eat him all up.

—Do you have a condom? I ask him with a shy smile that hides naughtiness and gives him the answer to his doubts.

—Yes, but I have to go get it.

He quickly kisses my forehead and gets up to look for the condom.

—Houston, we have a problem —he says when he gets back.

—Oh! What is it? You don't have a condom?

—No. Something worse.

—What?

He grabs my hand and puts it on his pajamas, right over his penis. I grab and touch it, and I realize that he doesn't have an erection.

—I'm sorry —and trying to find an answer, I said —: Is it because I was scared? Do you still think I'm uncomfortable with this?

—No, no, no. Hush, it's not that, shh, these conversations are necessary, we've only seen each other for a couple of days, and we're just starting to learn about each other.

—So, is it because of my period? Do you feel uncomfortable?

—No, it's not about that, I already told you that I don't have a problem with that. I think that the problem is that you intimidate me.

—What? Who, me?

—I know that you are aware of how beautiful you are, but do you really have an idea of the effect you have on men? —I don't say anything, the surprise leaves me silent and he keeps on —: You intimidate me, Maria Valentina.

His words and the fact that he's calling me by my full name makes me quiver.

—And you should know one thing, you'll intimidate any man that has his head in the right place. You're an imposing redhead, not only tall, pale, with strong distinctive features, you have a lot of self-confidence, you aren't afraid to say what's on your mind and you defend your arguments without invalidating the arguments of the other side. You're extraordinary, and any man should, no matter what, feel intimidated.

The truth is, he's right. I see myself that way, but I didn't know that people also saw those characteristics within me. In my teenage and university years, when I was in my country, I always had a hard time because of my «tough» character, I was always accused of having a bad temper, but a lot of things have changed.

When I became an immigrant, I learned to be humble. When I was in Miami working as a waitress, and later on when I just arrived in Italy, it wasn't easy. Where I was staying with my cousin, the landlady humiliated me, and at work I used to let Jackson scream at me and to be mistreated by Ali and Marco. Back then, I didn't see the line between being humble and being humiliated. But now I have overcome that, and the image that H has of me is, on the one hand, the imposing and confident teenager friend of his brother, and on the other hand, the nonchalant and restrained woman that I am. Now I have the precise dose of humbleness to recognize others' points of view, but I'm not in a place that makes me humiliate myself and accept truths that I don't share.

—Thank you. I guess.

—Shhh... Do you want us to watch a series or a movie? Do you want to keep on reading your book? Or, do you want to sleep?

—Let's listen to some music while we talk some more, okay?

He agrees, and when he grabs his phone to open Spotify, my stomach growls.

—Hungry?

I look at him through my eyelashes, and confirm his theory.

—I'll get some snacks; I think I saw some yoghurt.

—Hmmm... I'll come with you. —I don't want to lose track of him for one second.

When we step out, we try to tip-toe to the kitchen to not wake up Luismi, who's sleeping on the couch in the living room.

When we get to the kitchen, without turning the lights on, I open the fridge to see what we can eat. H gets behind me and has to stretch his head up to see over my shoulder. I see him and think it's the cutest thing.

—See, yoghurt. Or, do you want something salty? —he says.

—And you, are you hungry?

—Hungry for you, yes.

—What happened to feeling intimidated? Is that in the past now?

—Well, why don't you find out?

Without turning around, I press my buttocks against him and notice that he has an erection. Feeling him like that turns me on. I turn around and begin to kiss him. In a single movement, H moves me away from the refrigerator and leaves it open. He puts me on the kitchen counter, pulls up my pajama top and starts nibbling and sucking on my left nipple while gently pulling my hair. I moan with pleasure and arch my back. I let myself be taken away with the extraordinary excitement that I'm feeling. Along with my muffled moans, almost at the same time, the fridge alarm starts beeping because the door is open. Without taking his eyes off of me, H closes it.

—Do you want to do it here, or do you want me to take you to bed? —He grabs my hand and kisses it.

—I'd prefer the bed, I don't want to, eehmm... —I say, in doubt—. You know... to leave stains.

Without a word, he picks me up, and walks back to the room carefully without a sound.

Still in his arms, H closes the door behind us with one of his feet, and puts me on the bed delicately. Once I'm there, he takes off my pajama top and then my pants. I try to get involved in the process and take my panties off.

—Wait, let me —he says. He then delicately takes my panties off and looks at the sanitary pad—. You're in your last days —he says—. Nothing to worry about.

He carefully puts the clothes on the floor and takes of his t-shirt. He gets on top of me and grabs both my wrists upwards.

—Keep them there. Let me be in control. Just tell me to stop if you feel uncomfortable. Trust me.

I submissively keep my hands up, even though I'm dying to touch his jet-black hair.

H starts playing again with my nipples. He vigorously sucks and softly bites them, first on the left and then on the right. Instinctively, I lower my hands towards his head, inviting him to stay there a little bit longer, and he complies, and continues nibbling and sucking on my breasts. When I moan slightly in pain, he understands that my nipples are sore, and he goes down towards my stomach. He kisses his way down to my belly button, I start shaking again and I basically move him away with my hands, he stops, and I know that he's waiting for an answer.

—I'm fine —I reassure him.

His lips trace a path down my stomach, reaching the warm, sensitive curve beneath. I close my legs, a shiver running through me.

—Trust me —he says.

I let my legs relax. H closes up on my clitoris and blows on it, I'm so stimulated by it that I arch my back. Something as simple as the hot air from his mouth makes me feel like a jolt going down my spine. H comes closer; he feels around my clitoris with his thumb and massages it. I melt between his touch. He blocks the entry to my vagina with one hand and reaches to the clitoris with the other, pulling upwards to leave it completely bear and in reach. Then, he brings his mouth close and with his tongue he gently stars to lick and suck. I shiver and don't care about anything else, I just let go. H keeps on sucking, feeling bolder, I hear him moan, as I arch my back again. H keeps on tasting me and I can feel that he's extra fiery about it, as if he was charged with an uncontrollable onrush. I feel him pull away from me, so I bring his head closer so he'll keep doing it, he gives me a quick taste and says:

—I don't want you to come like this, I want you to come when I'm inside you.

In one second, he comes up with caresses and kisses to my mouth. He kisses my lips, and his tongue does circles inside my mouth right between my teeth and my lips. I'm surprised that his mouth doesn't taste like blood, it only smells like soap and tastes like him. As if he was reading my mind, H says:

—I told you to trust me.

I look at him keenly in the dark. This man is a subject expert, and

I'm a little girl, hungry to learn from him.

—I told you to leave your hands up, I also asked you to send me your location and to tell me when you were heading towards the bar. I'm not a controlling man, but if something happens to you, I want to know where you are and what you're doing —he says while grabbing the condom and starts to put it on— Do you understand what I'm saying?

—Yes —I say in a hoarse voice.

H puts the tip of his hard penis in the entrance of my vagina, as he grabs his hands and locks them with his, I can tell that we are both shaking, and he starts to penetrate me very slowly. We're both holding our breath, the penis slides inside without any problems, filling me up with him. When he is completely inside me, he puts his body on me and his forehead on mine and let's an «Mmm, you're so tight» slip out.

H starts to thrust me with steady movements, while I moan with each one. He covers my mouth because I'm apparently making a lot of noise. I take his hand away and bring him closer to me with a hug. I moan with his mouth next to mine, and in a few thrusts, I reach an orgasm. He starts to kiss me euphorically and then, he comes too.

His panting body rests on top of mine without putting a lot of weight on me, his head rests on my neck, he still hasn't pulled out of me.

—Be careful when you pull out, with the blood.

—Oh, yes.

He pulls himself up, takes off the condom, ties a not, puts it on the ground and lays on me again.

—H, my love, I need my panties with my little diaper —I say in the softest voice I can muster.

—One moment. —Without moving around too much, like when you look for the TV's remote control that fell on the floor, H grabs the panty and when he gives it to me says—: Do you need help?

—Yes, of course. —Laying down and very carefully I put my panties on, but I worry and say—: We probably made a mess, why don't we turn the lights on and have a look?

—Hush, I'll take care of all that tomorrow, let's go to sleep.

He hugs me, kisses my forehead and we stay silent. During the calm, I say to myself: «Don't think about where this is going to take you anymore, just enjoy it, Maria Valentina», and I mumble:

—Mischief managed.

I hear a faint laugh from H and we fall asleep.

# Drool, lies and anxieties

I open my eyes and feel a weight on my chest, it's H that is laying almost completely on top of me. «Good morning, Poliedro de Caracas», I think to myself. «Oh my! This is so wonderful, so beautiful, this is it, my delicious sweetie pie», I keep on going in my head. I stroke his hair and gently tap his nose.

—*Moin, Moin* —I say in German.

—*Morgen, Liebling* — Still sleepy, he replied

—*Du sprichst Deutsch?* —I ask, surprised.

—*Ja, ein bisschen* —he answers.

— Wait, I didn't know you could speak four languages! I know you speak Spanish, because it's our mother tongue; English, because we've all learned it since we were kids; French, of course, because you live in France and your dad speaks it too, you must have learned it at home, but German?

— You know Heinrich is a German name? -I nod- Well, for a while I felt it was my duty to learn German, because when I first moved to Paris, people would see my name and ask if I was German, but I'm the most Veneco person there is, as far as I know. So I decided to learn some German to be able to tell people that my grandmother on my mother's

---

[8] *Good morning*
[9] *Good morning, dear*
[10] *You speak German*
[11] *Yes, a little bit*

side was German, so they wouldn't ask me why I'm light-skinned when I'm Latino.

—I tell people that I'm Polish —laughing— for the same reason. I mean, I know that I'm Italo-Venezuelan, but it doesn't make sense for them that I'm so light, because Italians have tanned skin and I'm paper white, with red hair and people think that I'm Polish or Russian, so I stick with the lie. But I only say that to people who aren't important to me, to confuse them.

—And what other lies do you tell them? —he asks, as he caresses my knuckles.

— Well. I once said that since Maracaibo is a city of the oil industry, that the millionaires have faucets in their houses, and when they open them, oil comes out and goes straight to small ships that take it to the islands in the Caribbean, like Curaçao and Aruba, that this is part of their millionaire business.

— Wow, that is a good one! I like this lie, it's well constructed, I think I'll use it when they ask me stupid questions.

—Heyyyyy! Get your own lies, you idea thief.

We both laughed and when H gets off me, I realize that I'm completely soaked.

—I'm sorry, I sweat at night. Don't think that you peed the bed.

— How can a person wet a bed so much with just sweat? — I'm starting to shiver with cold — are you sure you didn't pee yourself, you dirty little pig?

— I sweat and you stain the bed. Neither of us showered after sex. — He makes a face like he doesn't mind, and then he opens the covers and shows me the blood stains all over the bed, he shows me his hands and they're stained with blood, too —. See? We slept between our fluids, and that's okay, now you're going to take a shower and I'm going to clean it all up, and that's it. — I make a worried face and he replies with an imitation of a Spanish accent—Hostias! It's only blood!

I feel curious with how he handles this period thing so naturally. I remember that Luismi once told me that H once had a three-year long relationship that had started in the university and ended before he got to Paris, then he had this other two-year romance that ended after the pandemic. Apparently, H has always been a long relationship kind of guy, I think it's part of his personality to fall in love and live together as a couple. So, I suppose, that gives him a broad and detailed perspective and knowledge on women.

I feel conflicted thinking about it, not because I'm jealous, no, it's just that it must be nice to live that experience. I've had many relationships, but nearly none of them escaped from being abusive, and the most I have been in one is for a year and a half. I keep on believing that I have stolen entire chapters of my life. I feel like a teenager that has no idea of what it is to love and feel loved, but one that has the illusion to live all that.

I got up silently when H asked me to so he could pick up the bed linens. I don't even ask him if he needs some help, I just let him do the work and I head over to the bathroom to take a shower.

When I get out, Luismi is gone; he left a note saying that he went to take Lili for a walk and that he will be back later, and H is in the kitchen making breakfast.

Suddenly I realize something that makes me desperately anguished, something that hits me like a bucket of cold water: my flight back is tonight at midnight. Tonight, I'm going back to Milan. I stop breathing. I walk back to the bathroom and lock myself inside again. I look at myself in the mirror. «Calm down, calm down, calm down. If it's going to be, if something else is going to happen, if he's the one for you, he'll find a way to be with you». I hear H knocking on the door.

—Hey, do you like to have a salty or sweet breakfast? Because I made eggs with toast, but if you don't like it, I can go and buy you a chocolate croissant or something else. And coffee, do you take it black or with milk?

—Plain coffee is fine, give me a minute. And eggs are fine too —I answered, holding my breath and controlling my voice so it won't shiver.

H said something else, but I didn't hear him; I'm panting and having a hard time breathing. My clothes feel like sandpaper on my skin, I take it off the best I can, trying not to fall over from lack of oxygen and dizziness. I get in the shower, open the tap and cold-water splashes on my skin. I give a muffled shout. I hate cold, I hate cold water. I start to cry. I wait for the water to warm up, and when it does, I get in, including my hair. I need two seconds to think. I need the water to wash away my anxiety. When I'm under the shower, I start to breathe slowly, I hug and cradle myself: «It's alright, baby. There's nothing to be afraid of, what's meant to be, will be, even if you get out of the way, it will always come back to you. You're safe, nobody can hurt you, I'll take care of you, you're okay». I start to caress my face, to hold myself tight as I keep on: «Everything is okay baby girl, we're safe, we're safe and protected». I hear the bathroom door open, and I know it's H. I don't bother, I just keep on doing what I'm doing, hugging and holding myself. H gets into the shower and hugs me; I feel like he's still wearing his pajamas. His hug is perfect, he just holds me and cradles me in, there's no rubbing against or squeezing.

—Shhh, nothing's going to harm you, I'm here. Somehow H knows that I suffer from anxiety and panic attacks, I have since I was a teenager. Perhaps my therapy sessions since back then have been an «open secret» between our families.

His pajamas quickly get wet, just like his hair, that starts to tickle my face, I'm still sobbing, and H just repeats the same words.

—Shhh, nothing's going to harm you, I'm here.

H lets go and brings his hands to my face, and he softly kisses my forehead. I start to get sleepy from the crying and anxiety session that I just had. As if he could read my thoughts, H says:

—You have to eat something before you take a nap, okay? Even a little bit, you have to put something in your stomach. You went to bed hungry last night.

—I ate something else —I said, half asleep.

—Let me wash up, and I'll fix you something to eat that's easy to digest, okay? And then we can take a nap.

I nod and H turns me around with him one hundred and eighty degrees and then pushes me back a little while he takes his pajamas off. I put my back against the wall and enjoy the show. Once he's naked, he grabs soap and starts to lather off all his body. The truth is that, for whatever reason, seeing him all lathered up in soap makes my anxious thoughts go disappear, I don't have the words to explain exactly the calm I got from this, but seeing him like that, care-free, taking a bath, with his head full of shampoo, the steamy shower and the smell of all these products, calms me down and makes me feel at peace.

Perhaps from the peace and quiet that this scene gave me, a memory becomes unblocked in my head.

I was fifteen years old and I was studying in a school close to Gil family's house. I was having a pretty bad time. It was a very hot day in Maracaibo, it was about forty degrees centigrade, despite being inside a room with air conditioning —the machine simply wasn't powerful enough— and I was also on my period and had a lot of pain in my belly. The teacher sees me as I'm about to pass out from the pain and she tells me that they're going to call my mom for her to come pick me up. When they got in touch with her, my mom let them know that she wasn't home and that she couldn't leave the place she was at, and they asked them to send me home in a taxi over to Luis Miguel's house, that she was going to call Mrs. Marisela Gil to tell her what was going on and have her wait for me at her house.

In about twenty minutes I was already getting out of the taxi in front of the house of the Gil Mantilla family. Mrs. Marisela worriedly opened the door. When she saw how pale I was she said, «Go take a nap in H's room, he's not here right now. I didn't fix Luismi's room for you because it was too messy and dirty, you know how he is, and Graciela locks her room when she's out. Besides, I already turned the air conditioning on, lay down over there, honey, I'll bring you a pain killer and something to eat».

After eating something and taking a painkiller, the stomach pain from hell started to give way, but I was still feeling a little numb.

I remember a lot of details from that moment: his smell on his sheets (navy blue with a black duvet), a guitar in the corner of the room, a collection of baseball caps on the wall, the half open closet where I could see all of his soccer team jerseys and t-shirts. There, with that scene, perhaps because of the pain killer's effect, I fell asleep deep.

I don't know how long I slept, but I heard something inside the room. I was too tired to pay attention to it, I was still feeling numb, but when the room flooded with the smell of shower gel and I felt a presence in the room, I slowly got up and sat on the bed. H was there wearing only a towel, with his hair dripping wet. He was looking for clothes in the drawers. When he realized I was there, the only thing he said was, «keep on sleeping, I'm already about to go, relax». I kept looking at him while he kept searching around. When he was done, clothes in hand, he left the room. «It's the love of my life», I thought. I insist, I was only fifteen years old.

My memories get interrupted by H's question, who's giving himself a final rinse-off.

—Anything you feel like sharing?

—Remember when I fell asleep in your room? When we were teenagers?

—Wow! Yes. I didn't let anybody inside my room back then, but I wasn't bothered at all by the fact that you were sleeping in my bed. And I never told you that, but you left a drool stain on one of my pillows. Still, I slept with them until they were old enough to get changed. —I looked at him in shock—. See? I'm used to sleeping on your fluids. I've got experience with that.

—Oh, sometimes I drool when I sleep, I answered, slightly embarrassed—. I don't know what to think about the fluids part.

—Nothing, you drooler —he says in a Spanish accent and then kisses me on my forehead.

H gets out of the shower, grabs a towel for him and then puts one on me.

—Go lay down, I'll bring you something to eat in a couple of minutes. No caffeine. Caffeine, nicotine and anxiety aren't good friends.

I agree, and with all the patience in the world, he helps me out of the shower.

I go towards the bedroom. H has already put on some fresh sheets, it's blue, but it still doesn't have a duvet and the pillows don't have a case. I lay down however I can on the bed, still in towel, and I wait for H to bring breakfast.

H walks into the room and leaves a food tray on the nightstand. The breakfast is a firm yogurt, and some fresh fruit. I start eating while he opens the closet, takes out the pillowcases and a black duvet, like the one in my memories. That many coincidences make me feel like I'm in a sort of dream where I'm not sure if what's happening is real or not, I'm not sure if I'm fifteen or twenty-five.

When the bed is ready and I've finished eating, H takes the dirty dishes to the sink. When he comes back, he gets in bed and gives me a kiss on each eye. I feel some pain, I know that they're swollen from my morning crying session, I feel melancholy hitting me again and I'm about to break down in tears.

—We'll figure it out —H says confidently, while he gently taps on the back of my hand with his fingers, and gently squeezes it after.

—And what if we escape? —I add, pouting.

—That's a good idea. Did you bring your work laptop? We can go somewhere and get organized.

I said no, still with tears in my eyes.

—Shhh, let's take a quick nap.

Cradled in his arms, feeling his breathing in his chest, I fell fast asleep.

A frenzy of kisses all over my face wakes me up. With a soft, almost whispering voice, H says:

—Let's go have lunch with Luis Miguel and his boyfriend Andres. —I pretend that I'm whimpering to tell him that I'd rather stay, but he insists—: Come on. —I keep whimpering and hugging the pillow. He strokes my hair and adds—: As tempting as giving in to the whimpering and staying here in bed with you is, Andres and Luis Miguel are on the other side of the wall, dressed up and waiting for us.

I get up jumping.

—Luis Miguel can't know what's happening between us —I said, terrified.

—Why?

—Because all of Maracaibo, Madrid, Milan, Miami and every city that starts with an M would hear about it, and me or you know where this is heading —I say, totally serious.

—As brothers, we have a loyalty code. If he says something I'll kill him. If that's what you want, of course. I don't care who hears about it —he says subtly, while he tucks a curl behind my ear.

—Please, let's pretend that nothing is happening between us. I'll trust that Luis Miguel won't tell anybody. I need to set my ideas straight —I answered.

—Understood —he said carelessly.

# LibrAries

Andres, Luis Miguel, Heinrich and I walked down the street looking for a place to have lunch. We left Andres's car in a parking lot close to Gran Via, to walk around a little and soak up the sunny day.

We're in a small street with almost no room left for cars. I stop for a second to buy some water, and when I step out of the shop, H's gaze finds me. He's just standing there, dumbstruck, looking at me, in the middle of the street. He gives me a half-smile; it seems like his expressive brown eyes shouted that I'm the most extraordinary woman in the world. I share the same look, smile and expression with him. For a few seconds we lock ourselves in a bubble where only the two of us exist. My heart starts racing, and there and then I confirm what my heart has been telling me since he opened the door a few days ago, «I love him with all the U's and I's». Undeniably, irrefutably, undoubtedly, indisputably, and, of course, irrationally.

A car's horn brings us both back from our own thoughts. H runs towards me and crosses the small street. When we're close, he grabs the water bottle from my hand to open it for me, without taking his eyes off of me.

—MJ —he says, and I look at him, confused—. You're Mary Jane to Luis Miguel. But for me you're MJ—and he adds—: Tom is my favorite Spiderman.

—Mine is Andrew —I said, pouting.

—Andrew is fine, but I prefer Tom.

I smile as we both cross the street, walking close by.

When we get to the restaurant, they say that we'll have a table in about twenty minutes and that we can wait at the bar. Luismi, Andres and H go inside, and I excuse myself so I can go back to a bookstore that I saw, just crossing the street.

There are a couple things that inspire me and make me find my center, and bookstores are one, as well as museums and concerts. They fill and heal a part of me, the same happens with the gym and, sometimes, swimming.

I'm going home today, after lunch I'll swing by Luismi's apartment to pick my things up and then I'll go to the airport.

In the library, I see bookmarks with zodiac sign phrases. I look for mine; the message on it says: «You can count on Libra to help you find a new magical sense to life». «Perfect —I think to myself— I'll take it and give it to H; I think that we both want to take our lives in a new direction and this is just the beginning.

H texts me to let me know that they're already seated. By then, I've already finished paying when a book catches my eye. The thing that gets my attention is the cover, I take my phone out and snap a picture, without looking at anything else; I walk out of there quickly towards the restaurant.

At the restaurant, the waiter brings drinks for all of us.

—Oh my god, stop! —I complain—. Madrid has me drinking alcohol every day, I think I haven't been able to step out of a hangover since I got here. Pleeeease, no more alcohol —I beg them.

—This is the last one, Santi. It's okay. Besides, we're here to eat, so everything will be fine — H answered.

He called me Santi, playing along while pretending that nothing was happening between us.

I'm not too convinced, but I take the drink, sometimes we also have to please others.

Andres starts asking me questions about my work, what I studied at the university, and my goals for the future.

—Well, I studied audiovisual production, and in Venezuela I worked as a producer at a fashion magazine, mostly, but I also helped produce events like Miss Venezuela, or concerts. Right now, I'm working in the finances department of a company, and my goal for the future is to work again with media, events, or something like that. I really miss my job. I feel happy and safe where I am, but, but I'm definitely not passionate about what I'm doing. I want to exude passion like I used to. I need that a lot, I miss it.

—Wow! —said Andres—. You know exactly what you want, that's not very common, I think that most people spend most of their lives trying to find themselves. It seems like you've already found yourself.

—I hadn't seen it like that. But perhaps you're right —I say to Andres.

—Following what Andres said, a lot of people, myself included, don't know what our passion is, and we spend and dedicate a big part of our lives trying to find ourselves. I find it refreshing that you're on a different path —H says.

—I think that it's also a curse sometimes. I'm a slave of my own passions because I simply can't just find myself in other places. It's like I don't have another option. I make it, or I'll die, as cathartic as it might sound.

—You'll make it. Don't worry —H says.

—You sound so sure that I believe you —I said back.

—I just know it. Just hearing you is enough to be sure —he answers without hesitating.

—Thanks, your confidence restores my own.

We have a monopoly on the conversation, we lock ourselves up in our own world until Andres interrupts us:

—And what's up with you two?

—He's dying to be my boyfriend. But I'm too pretty to be with him —I answer in a cocky tone.

—Exactly what she said —H backs me up.

Andres starts laughing and asks us

—But you slept together last night, right?

—I heard things —Luismi adds.

Everybody laughs at the table.

—He wishes, but not even in his dreams — I answered, and the topic dies with that.

The conversation carries on about our plans for the summer, and when Andres and Luismi are distracted, I make a quick move and take out the bookmark and put in H's pocket. I feel that his fingers gently tap the back of my hand twice and then give me a gentle squeeze. I manage not to cry, despite feeling that my eyes are itching, I'm thinking that I'm going to leave and I don't know when I'll see him again.

When we leave the restaurant, Luis Miguel and Andres decide to leave us. They had been arguing about silly things earlier and I honestly don't know if they leave us alone because they're in on it or because those two get too intense.

H and I look at each other, confused, and he says:

—Let's make the most of being alone and go to the botanical gardens, it's a beautiful walk.

—My time's limited —I said.

—Yes, you're right. I think I wanted to forget about that. Well, let's take the metro back, perhaps we'll get there faster by taxi. It'll be a short walk, I promise.

I agree and as we went down the stairs in a hurry, because the train was arriving, Heinrich stopped to help a woman who was in difficult circumstances —which I figured out by the way she looked— she had a stroller and a baby. «Can I help you?», he said, and without waiting for an answer, he helped her with the stroller.

My heart melted from the sweet sight. Heinrich didn't care who she was, or the poor conditions that the woman seemed to have, he only saw a person in need and he didn't hesitate to help. «H that stands for hero», I said to myself.

# Departures

Once we got back to Luis Miguel's house, I'm getting ready to organize my things in the bedroom and start packing while Andres, Luismi and H stayed in the living room talking. I gather my courage as I start packing. I say to myself that it's just a summer time love, and that until he doesn't fully put the words in the right place, that there's something more than just a fling between us, I'm not going to admit it.

I go to the bathroom to get my things. When I come out with my hands full of things, I drop a package of sanitary pads, but H is hanging outside the bathroom and he catches them mid-air.

—Thank you, Edward Cullen.

He just smiles, and grabs a couple of things from my arms to lighten the load. We both walk into the room. I drop everything on the bed and he copies me.

—How do you feel? How's your mood?

—I don't want to go.

—I don't want you to go.

—At least tell me that you'll come visit me on my birthday, in October.

—I'll try, of course.

H steps out of the room. I finish packing my things and I look at the clock. It's time to go.

When I leave the room, I put my suitcase and bag by the door.

—Well, the one you cried about is leaving —I said to everyone in a joking tone.

The three of them start laughing.

Luis Miguel is the first one to hug me.

—Take care, my house will always be yours. Your safe haven when you need it —he says.

—Santi, it was a pleasure getting to know you, get it and do it all. Take care and know that we'll always be here for you -says Andres when it's his turn to say goodbye.

—I'm going with her to get a taxi downstairs —says H.

We both head to the door. I grab the bag and H grabs the suitcase.

Once out on the street, H calls a taxi and says that we only have to wait five minutes.

—So? —he asks.

—I loved spending time with you and what else would I like more than to have you in my life, but the truth is that the distance makes me anxious. You have lived many things that I haven't and I'm afraid that the distance is a deterrent for this to flow the way that it should. I like you, a lot. I always have. But I don't think that I can wait for you.

—I feel the same, but I would like for us to be friends. Let's give that a chance. Don't you think?

—Yes, of course. I'd love that. We'll be in touch and we can see each other whenever you want.

—I'll do whatever is within my reach and abilities to make that happen. Okay?

—I want you to know that I've waited twelve years for this moment. I know it's saying too much, but I really like you a lot for the last twelve years.

I was careful enough to not say that I loved him, I wasn't really sure I wanted to start a full-blown romance, the distance and my own insecurities play a strong role in a possible relationship. Besides, if one of our mouths was to say «I love you» at some point, it had to be his.

The taxi arrives, and before H can say anything, I kiss him on the lips and I get in the car with my bag, while he still has the suitcase in his hands. The driver gets out, receives the suitcase and puts it in the trunk. When the driver gets back behind the wheel, I wave goodbye, and he smiles back sadly.

# Oh! I'm leaving you, Madrid

When I'm waiting in line to board the plane, I try to pick myself up and put some humor into the goodbye. I open Spotify and play Shakira's «Ay, te dejo Madrid» [12]. I'm humming the song in my head, when my phone vibrates. I don't have to look at it to know that it's from H.

*Already on the plane?*

*What are you, a wizard?*

*No. I get along well with time and I know how to measure it.*

*Oh okay. Well, but I am a witch.*

*And what does the witch predict?*

*That we're going to have a hard time letting go of each other.*

*Perhaps.*

When I'm finally in my seat, I text H one last time.

*I'm about to take off. Have a nice summer. Just like I wouldn't stop for you, don't hold back for me. Okay?*

*Okay.*

The plane starts to take off. I close my eyes to leave Madrid and H behind. I have to be strong and let him go now. I know I'll have a hard time, but the longer I keep him with me, the more I'll hang on. H is a wonderful human being, but something tells me that neither of us is ready for the other. I'm terrified. It's barely summer and we're

---

[12] Ay te dejo Madrid - Shakira

just getting back to normal. I can't be boxed in with a long-distance relationship, we both have to be free and have adventures of our own. If he wants to be with me, he's going to have to come get me.

The landing wakes me up. That's when I know that I'm back to reality.

I get a notification from H.

*I saw that you've landed. Please let me know when you get home.*

I get off the plane, and the moment that my feet touch the ground in Milan I say: «I'm in my comfort zone, I can think better here, but I know that me and H are not over yet».

When I get home, I send H a quick text to let him know that I'm in my apartment and then I hop in the shower.

With my pajamas on, it's nearly 4 a.m. I glance at my phone on the loft bed before quickly drifting into a deep sleep.

The next day, the first thing I do is check my phone. H sent me a message along with a photo:

*Nice comb, I could steal the t-shirt too.*

I laughed instantly, I hadn't realized that I left clothes over at My Luismi's house. The t-shirt is an oversized Spiderman one that I took with me precisely because Luismi calls me Mary Jane. And now H called me MJ. I find all the small connections super sweet.

> *You can send me the t-shirt. You can keep the comb, but honestly, I doubt the comb will give you a beautiful set of hair like mine.*

*MJ, I'm keeping the t-shirt because I might end up using it, I'm sorry, I'm stealing it. Now, the comb, does it have magical powers? Or does the witch, like you called yourself, have a spell to have a beautiful set of hair?*

> *Biotin & minoxidil. Give me back my t-shirt, you thief.*
> *But I don't think that your hair needs anything; I love the*

*way you have it.*

*It looks better on me.*

He sent me a photo wearing my t-shirt and I just melted over him. Before I can answer anything, I get another message and I focus on that.

*Biotin & minoxidil? What presentation?*

*Biotin pills, a minimum of fifteen milligrams, and*

*Minoxidil lotion after you wash your hair.*

*Thanks, it looks like you know all about care products. I might call you later so you can help me with some sunblock that won't leave my face like deep fried chicken.*

*Hahaha, yeah, I know about these things.*

*I like women who take care of themselves. Because I'm a bit jeva* [13] *and also take care of myself. I take better care of myself than most women, hahaha.*

*Hahaha, you don't have to be a woman to take care of yourself, I also like boys who take care of themselves. And by the way, enjoy your Spiderman t-shirt, it looks good on you, you're right.*

*Thank you, MJ.*

---

[13] A term used in Venezuela to a refer to a girlfriend, in some cases, or a woman, in other cases, like this one. (Editor's note)

# CHAPTER III
## Unreachable sunset in France

«Walking in a straight line, one cannot get very far».

—Antoine de Saint-Exupéry, *The Little Prince*

# Detectives and unexpected clues

It has been a week since I returned to Milan, and H and I have been talking every day. He tells me that he takes Lili for a walk every day and then goes to a nearby café to have carrot cake. It's my favorite cake and, as it turns out, it's his too. Although H is still staying at Luismi's apartment, he's not on holiday, so we've both been busy with work. But I think it's sweet that we're making time to get to know each other better; our WhatsApp messages go back and forth all the time.

> *Any plans for the weekend?*

*Yes. I'm going to Valencia with some friends, and you?*

> *Well, not much, honestly. Perhaps I'll go to a town nearby with my family to spend the weekend, especially because I haven't seen the twins in a long time.*

*Any reason why you don't see your family often?*

> *I don't know, I get overwhelmed easily. But tell me, what are your plans in Valencia?*

*Well, my friends have a birthday over there and they invited me.*

> *Party crasher*

*Obviously, but it's a real adventure. I haven't found a hotel to stay in.*

> *What? How are you going to travel like that?*

*Honestly, if I'm alone I can be pretty adventurous.*

> *It's not for adventure, it's for your safety. You're not planning on camping by the beach, are you?*

*Well, honestly, I thought about it. Are you concerned about my safety?*

*Obviously. All of you concerns me.*

(I say this too fast, so fast that not even I can believe what came out of my mouth. Well, from my fingertips in this case)

*That's cuchi[23]*

*Mhm.*

*Hey, you don't have to worry. I know how to take care of myself and nothing's going to happen.*

*Okay.*

I leave the conversation at that and I focus on finishing my days' work.

When I'm done, I close my laptop and run to get ready to meet some of my friends at a bar.

The bar is in an alleyway of bars and restaurants in the city. When I walk in, Soffia, Margot, Emiliana and Corina wait for me at a table by the door.

—Hi beautiful, are you okay?

—Hi girlfriends!

I greet all of them with a kiss on each cheek. It feels good to get together with friends every once in a while.

Emiliana set the meeting up because she suspects that her boyfriend is cheating on her and she wants us to help in FBI mode. All our conversation takes place in Italian, my friends don't speak Spanish.

—Okay, raga, we're all here, now I can tell you. This is the thing —Emiliana started— I went to visit my family in Perugia and I had to stay because my mother got sick and nobody was available to stay and

---

[23] In Venezuela, the word cuchi means sweet and nice at the same time. (Editor's note)

take care of my little brothers, so I had to stay over for like a month, remember?

—Yes— we said in unison.

—C'é, you also remember that we fought because, raga, we have been engaged for three years. So I ask him about the ceremony and he says that he doesn't have the money to. I'm sorry, but I'm not asking him to get married over the top, or for a wedding in Paris, I want to get married in Perugia in front of the mountains and drink wine from my parents' vineyard. I want something small and intimate. The thing is that since I got back, I feel that he's acting strange. And I don't know girls, but I suspect that he's cheating on me, something strange is going on and I just need to talk to somebody because I'm starting to collapse.

—Well, Emiliana —says Corina—, first off, you have every reason to feel conflicted about the wedding because you have been together for eight years, and, regardless of the wedding that you want to have, you have every right to demand it. You were with him for five years when he asked you to marry him; he got on his knees and proposed. He's the one that got on his knees, he's the one that proposed it, you didn't even expect it. I mean, it was his call. And now that you also decided to make it happen, he puts you on pause? What an asshole!

We all nod and agree.

—Now, on the other hand, what reasons do you have to believe that the problem is that he's cheating with somebody else, or that he likes somebody else? —I ask.

—Well, Netflix had a different account logged in when I got home, the account of a female friend of his. She supposedly came over with her boyfriend and the three of them were drinking in my house. But something tells me that's not entirely true. I also found some blond hairs in our bed, and, Hey! I'm a brunette. It was the same excuse: the girl was too drunk and they let her sleep it off a little and they kept drinking downstairs. The thing is that I haven't seen either of them post stories on Instagram together for quite a while now. I think

Giuliano is cheating on me with her.

—There's only one thing we can do —Margot intervenes—. There's a lady in Via Brera that reads the Tarot cards. Let's all go and get a reading.

—I agree —says Emiliana.

—Well, I've had her do me a reading and she's incredible. But she only does it on weekends, and today is Friday, so let's forget about that and we'll figure it out tomorrow —stated Margot.

—Okay, perfect —I say.

I excuse myself to go to the bathroom and when I get there, I realize my cheeks are all red and that my hair is a bit messy. Not to brag, but I look super sexy. I grab my phone, and take a good picture and send it to the great H.

He answers my message immediately.

*Nice photo. Are you drinking?*

*Yep, does it show?*

*Enough.*

*And you? What are you doing?*

*I'm already in Valencia, getting ready to go out and party.*

*Have fun.*

*You too. Take care.*

When I get back, my friends have another round of drinks on the table and you can feel in the air that we're all getting into a liquored-up party mood.

—Okay Valentina. Let it all out. Who's got your eyes all lit up? In the stories you posted from your trip to Madrid there was a gorgeous black-haired boy. Tell me, who is he and is he single, and if he's already yours? I want to know it all —says Corina.

—Girls, I don't even know how to put it into words. I'm really still processing it. —I tell them.

—But what are you processing? The black-haired boy or Madrid? —Corina asked.

—Both.

—Tell us and we'll help you process it —Soffia answered.

—Okay, it's like this. I caught up with my teenage crush and it was like an explosion of love, amazement, fears and anxiety. I like him a lot, and I'm aware that he likes me too. The problem? The distance and that he just broke up with his girlfriend of two years —I tell them.

—Girl, what's meant for you will always find the way to get to you. Perhaps this isn't the right time, but that doesn't mean it won't be in the future. We're old enough to not have those excuses. Do you know how hard and complicated it is to have someone you really like? I mean, someone you really want to share the routines and the complexities of life with. You'll find people in life that make you want to share the complexities and other people to share the routine with. I truly believe that if you find someone to share both aspects of life with, you'll have a great potential relationship that, I think, has to be lived, has to be executed and contextualized. It doesn't matter if it ends, breaks or destroys later on —says Corina.

—Don't you think that all that you're saying is too deep for the little context that Valentina gave you? You also have to consider that they just saw each other on a trip. I mean, what happened? What am I not aware of? —Soffia questioned.

—Yes. Well, we had sex, but we also shared a nice connection and pretty deep conversations.

—You can have a nice connection with anyone, it's not that hard. You turn everything into a romance novel and go to the extreme. Be a little more grounded and logical —says Soffia.

— Ah! But what's wrong if Valentina wants to have her hopes

up for a summer time love? If the girl has been through all of the shit in the world. We can ask the Tarot about your black-haired beau too —Margot says.

I laugh at Margot's comments, and I start to reflect upon the way we are, on how our differences nurture each other and bring us closer. Corina feeds the mystical part in me, she's the hippie friend, a vegan that wants to live from what grows out of the ground in a mountain. Margot is the one that's been in a long-distance relationship with a boyfriend in Mexico for years, she truly believes in love, she's a hopeless romantic. Soffia is a bit more logical and acid, she's been single for years because she doesn't stand anyone, but, she's never alone, she always has somebody around to spend the weekends with. And Emiliana, who we thought was the most stable one, is now having these problems with her boyfriend that I suppose are a part of life. I don't hate Giuliano, but it's not like i like him. He's indifferent to me.

The conversation on the «black-haired beau» ends, and then Corina grabs my hand and says almost like a secret.

—I've got a good feeling. Don't let go of the people that make you feel extraordinary and live your illusion to the fullest, you deserve everything that you dream of, princess. Put your heart and soul into it. Maybe he's your prince charming.

Margot chimes in:

— As long as it helps you grow, take it as a good thing.

The girls' words make my eyes water. H has made me feel so many things with very few actions and in such a short time that I don't know if I'm desperate to fall in love again, I don't know if this is how you feel when you fall in love with the right person or if it's all in my head and I'm going crazy. A part of me wants to run into his arms and another part wants to run in the other direction.

# Dancing through the night

As expected, me and my friends left the bar towards a place that had music and noise so we could move our body with the rhythm. After a while we're all liquored-up in a disco that's a bit nasty, but it was the only one playing reggaeton in that zone.

Rauw Alejandro is playing on the speakers with his «Cúrame»[15]. As me and my friends dance, the place is tiny, the floor is sticky and the number of different smells in the air make me nauseous.

I tell Cori that I'll be right back, I'm going to get some water. I order water at the bar and go out for a cigarette.

Once outside, I take the cigarettes out, and grab the lighter with one in my hand, I drop it and somebody passes over and steps on it making it pop. I'm sad for the loss, but I picked it up, because it's a lighter with the figure of an alien that I took by accident from Madrid, from Luismi's house. It was my summer time souvenir, and it'll keep on having that memory attached, even if it's broken. I grab it, broken as it is, and put it in my pocket.

When I get up a pair of green eyes catch me off guard. The gentleman, lighter in hand, strikes fire and lights my cigarette.

—*Pronta, signorina* —he says in Italian.

—*Grazie* —I answer in the same language.

---

[15] Cúrame - Rauw Alejandro
[16] Ready, Miss.

We look into each other's eyes for a few seconds, and I can tell, by the red in his eyes, that he's had a few drinks too many. That doesn't stop me from scanning him, «OMG! He's so handsome!»

—My name is Alex.

—Tina. —That's the name I use in Milan when I'm out and run into impersonal situations.

—Well, Tina, it's been a pleasure, I have to go. Have a good night.

—Bye! —I answered, acting indifferent.

When I get back inside the disco, the summer time hit song is playing, «Sal y perrea» by Sech, and I forget about everything and start dancing.

—Not even if I catch the bouquet I'll get married! —I scream in the disco while I walk towards my friends.

When I get there, I see that the group has grown, it has more people, I get introduced to everyone, I shake hands and one of them moves in to give me two kisses on my cheeks. He's tall, dark haired and super handsome.

—Tina, do you dance?

—What do you think?

His name is Theo, he starts dancing with me and then I realize that he's singing along with the songs.

—Hey! Do you speak Spanish? —I asked him, surprised.

—No, I just know the lyrics. I like Latin music and I'm always listening to reggaeton.

I just laugh and keep dancing with him.

Theo is an amazing dancer, and he doesn't doubt to grab me by the waist and take control of the dance.

The song ends and that awkward moment of silence between songs comes along. He takes that silence to ask me if I want a drink.

—Cosmopolitan, please.

—Okay, I'll be back in a second.

I quickly check my phone to see if H has texted me. He said he would go out partying, but he hasn't said anything since.

Nothing. I feel a little heart broken.

I check Instagram and I see that he posted something. I check to see and it's a repost of somebody else's story where they are toasting. Next to H's hand there's a female hand, and it's very close to his, and when they come in for the toast their hands touch. I feel nauseous instantly.

«There's nothing between us, nothing between us. He's just ended his relationship, and he wants to tramp around. So, if he's whoring around, we'll both tramp around. Because I believe in true gender equality. And if he's got options, I've got even more».

When Theo comes back, I look at him with «Take me to your place» eyes; as expected, he understands and gives me my drink and pulls closer to me. He grabs me by the waist and says to my ear:

—Wherever you want to go, or whatever you want to do today, tomorrow or whenever, just let me know.

—I'll think about —I answer, and I give him an innocent but manipulative smile, as I start to move my body so he understands that I want to dance.

Our bodies move to the rhythm of the music, and suddenly, he grabs the back of my head and puts his lips close to my mouth. We both melt into a passionate kiss. With each flashing light in the club, H shows up in my mind. I stop kissing Theo, I look at him and feel nauseated. I breathe in, and basically force myself to kiss him again, but even the smell of him starts to annoy me, and it's not like he smells bad. I try to find the reason why I'm rejecting this boy and my mind gives it to me.

«These aren't H's thin lips, it's not H's tongue, H's smell, H's touch, it's not H's hair», and I pull away from him again, faking a smile. I try to keep dancing, and when my heartbeat relaxes and my body doesn't feel so nauseous from Theo's smell and touch, I move in on his mouth again and I try, with all my strength, to enjoy the kiss.

Theo sees what's happening with me, he can tell that I'm fighting something. He whispers into my ear and says:

—I like women that simply enjoy the moment. Put your thoughts together gorgeous, and call me. If you want, we can just dance tonight, okay? For pretty girls like you there is always time and space, and above all, patience.

«Wow! I don't know if it's a post-covid thing, but, What? Why didn't I meet men like this before?», I think while I nod affirmatively, hanging my head in shyness and shame.

We keep dancing and I'm under attack by the same thoughts. «He's not H, he's not H».

I excuse myself and go to the bathroom, luckily, I don't have to wait that long. I get in, close and lock the door. I lay against the walls of the stall; I try to find oxygen and then I think, «why the hell am I looking for air in the bathroom when I could have gone outside». I can't find an answer and I grab my phone to look at the time, it's 3:33 a.m. and I can barely see the screen. I'm drunk. Before logic and reason could do anything about it, I see myself dialing H's number, and after a few seconds, he picks up.

—Hello?

—I made out with someone and I almost threw up because it wasn't you —I blurted, without even thinking about it. A deadly silence set in.

—I met somebody that I liked, I wanted to, you know. But I couldn't —he answered shortly after my wild confession.

—Why? —I ask, with genuine curiosity, and with the certainty that it was the girl that touched his hand in that boomerang I saw.

—Because... I don't know, there's you, I wouldn't know how to explain.

—You don't have to explain anything. The same thing just happened to me.

—Mmm...

—What are we going to do?

—Mmm... Where are you?

—In the bathroom, locked in like an idiot. And you?

—Show me.

—Okay.

I turn the phone's camera on and send him a picture doing a peace sign, very millennial and squinting, so it doesn't show how drunk I actually am.

—Mmmm —I hear him say as he exhales heavily.

—Do you like what you see? —I ask, acting naughty.

—Yes, of course. But I don't need to state the obvious.

—And what's the obvious, Heinrich?

—That you're gorgeous.

—And I look even more gorgeous with this outfit on the floor of your bedroom. —I hear him breath heavily again.

—Describe it —he asks me, shyly. What he doesn't know is that I'm an expert in describing enough to make him come.

—Well, I'm wearing a shirt that doesn't leave much to your imagination and a short skirt. Underneath that, I'm wearing a flowery thong that is probably wet right now, because, you'll see, I really like your voice.

—And how do we get this small shirt, short skirt and wet thong to the floor of my bedroom?

—First you have to come and get me in the club that I'm in, come and steal me away from the arms of another man that doesn't even come close to you, and then we'll go in a taxi to your place. On the ride over we're only holding hands, and when we get there, we take the stairs, because it's Paris. —I hear him laugh—. We get to the apartment and you go grab a glass of water and I start to take my clothes off as I come in, leaving a trail behind me. You see that and come eat me all up. I have the pleasure of sitting on your face and watching as my fluids drip from your mouth.

—More —he says, gasping for air.

—More? More? More, H Miguel? What more can I give you? If you have me at your mercy.

—That's not true. That's impossible.

—Do you think I would be locked in a bathroom reciting porn for any other man?

—It's not that, it's just that I need more to believe it.

—Give me an opportunity and I'll give you more.

—Take it. Come to Paris.

—To live there or to visit?

—To live here.

«This sounds like a dream come true»

—Let me find a job and I'll go.

—You don't need a job; you'll be with me.

—H, that's all nice, but I would like to do something, at least, to pay for my things. You know, at least to pay for my own gym and make-up.

—Whatever you want and decide to do, you'll do it great. My house has room for you in my bed, whenever you want.

My eyes start to water up.

—Okay, let's talk when we're both sober. —I say to him before he can hear me cry.

—Okay.

—Bye.

—Bye.

# Tarot

I wake up with such a headache that, I swear, that a vein is going to burst in my brain. As best as I can, I clumsily go down the stairs for some water and an aspirin. When I'm about to take the pill, I remember that I'm on an empty stomach and my body is simply going to reject it. So, I make myself a ham and cheese sandwich despite the pain, heaviness and having my battery dead; then I take the pill. Ten minutes later I feel more clarity and step in the shower. I once heard that cold water can help with a hangover, but I hate cold water, so I try to make it as less cold as my *ubriacco corpo* [18] can handle it. I stand underneath the shower and shake, «I hope this sacrifice will help myreboot», I say to myself.

After I leave the self-inflicted torture, I try to make a recap of what happened the night before. The boy with the lighter, who passed my scanners, Theo with his kisses and understanding, and the phone call with my sweetie pie H that I love so much. Wow! There are so many things that can happen in one night.

Of course, I clearly remember what H told me about moving to Paris. The truth is that I don't own anything but my clothes. Of course, I could grab my three *peroles* [19] and just go. I know that H is a responsible

---

[18] *Drunk body.*
[19] In Venezuelan slang, perol or peroles can refer to any object, such as a book, a car, or a bedsheet. While the RAE defines it as a way to avoid specifying an object, it is often used in a dismissive or minimizing way, reducing the perceived importance or quantity of the item(s), as seen in the author's usage.

person that would take care of me, but could he really assume that responsibility? I think I need some outside help, and I take a mental note: «I have to set an appointment with Mariana, my psychologist».

---

Later, Margot, Corina and I are going to Via Brera looking for the Tarot reader so she can read our cards. Sofi doesn't believe in this and Emiliana was afraid to come, so it's the three of us.

On the way there I started to think about Emiliana's fear. We had even agreed to this, precisely because of Emiliana's suspicions that Giuliano was being unfaithful. «It's obvious, of course, I say to myself. She's very scared of confirming the infidelity. If the Tarot card reader shows her skills to her, if the woman confirms that she's not a con-artist with a crystal ball and tells her he's unfaithful, she's going to have to make a decision: ignore the reading and deal with the infidelity or she kicks him out of her house and the relationship is over. And honestly, she doesn't want to be on that crossroad. I think that she's one of those people that prefers to wait for the inevitable, instead of taking a decision from within. It's just that, in matters of the heart, standing for final decisions, needs a lot of courage, don't I know it!»

When we arrive, Margot goes in first, then Corina and I'm in last.

As soon as I sit down in front of the lady, she says:

—What brings you here today?

—I think that I'm in love with my teenage crush.

—What happened?

—Well, I saw him this summer and I swear that I felt it all rush in. I don't know, but he lives in Paris and I live here.

—Okay. Let's see.

After that short interaction, the tarot reader starts to shuffle the cards. After a few seconds, she splits the deck in three parts that she places on the table as she asks me to choose one of them. I picked the third deck, the last one she put down, the one that's to my right. I chose the third one from an idea that anyone could call superstitious: last night, when I called H, it was 3:33, and the area code for France, where H lives, is +33.

The Tarot read starts to lift the cards from the deck and starts the reading:

He comes to me as the King of Coins, but also as the hermit. That speaks to me of a person that is very dedicated to his work and material earnings. With the Hermit it speaks to me of a person that hides away to solve his emotional issues. You might be dealing with a person that constantly disappears, but always shows up again. It's a person that needs loneliness to recharge, it's the type of person that also hides in his work and deals in an earthly way with the emotional world. The cards show a painful break up for that king, but it has nothing to do with you. There's something here about an ex-partner that can be very manipulative and play with this boy's feelings, even after that breakup. But I don't see new beginnings; that is, this girl will manipulate this boy's reality until he realizes that he can break with that pattern. You have nothing to do with that.

—The king of coins is also a king that moves slowly —the reader continues, while I just pay attention to everything that she's saying —. I see that this boy has a lot of love to offer. It's just that he can't do it right now. The cards don't show me how this story ends, but I can tell you that it's a long story, it's a story in which the both of you are going to be expanded. You can put a lot of expectations on him, because in some way this boy is the human manifestation of everything you have wished for romantically in this life. It's like the guides are telling me that you see him as if they found him in your thoughts, that he's the man of your life, your holy grail. —At that point, I'm drowning in tears—. Girl, listen to me very well, this one here —she points to a card— this one is you, the queen of wands and if the queen of wands wants to see rain, she will make it rain.

# At 360 kilometers per hour

My aunt Eugenia has told me that they're going to spend the weekend in Verona and she invited me to spend those days with them, so after the Tarot session, I get moving to meet with my family. It's almost three o'clock in the afternoon, I still haven't eaten anything, but in the hurry, I decide to eat on the train. Given the urgency, I'm going to buy the ticket for the Frecciarossa, the fastest train; It's only forty-five minutes from here to the town.

When I'm at the counter buying the ticket, I get a text from my cousin Estefania. It seems odd to me, since I moved out to live on my own, she distanced herself from me a lot. I crossed her distance off on the fact that I was a black cloud, and nobody wants someone next to them complaining all the time. Back then, I had the black plague with me, how was I not going to be a black cloud?

*Are you going?*

*Where to?*

*To Verona. With Aunt Eugenia.*

*Yes, I'm buying the ticket, why?*

*I'm on the train. I'll be there in twenty. Just checking.*

*Okay.*

I also find it strange that my aunt Eugenia didn't mention her coming too. «I'm not going to pay attention to it, as long as she's not bringing her friend, I don't have a problem» I think. But one thing is what you order your brain and another what it does, in that sense, it's like the heart.

I don't know if it's the double hangover I have today —Yes, it's double: one from the drinks and the other from the Tarot reader this morning, I'm still drunk from the words and the liquor–, so what I do is think about the girl that I don't want to see in Verona.

The train pulls away and all I do is remember Estefania's friend and how much that girl tormented me. My memories travel at the same speed of the train and bring a bitterness that I have to get over because I'm going to my family's house, and I want to be the happy Maria Valentina that wants to make others happy.

When I had just gotten to Milan, I didn't want to stay long at my uncles' house because I felt I was intruding in the family space. My cousin proposed that I move in with her; at that time, Estefania shared rent expenses with three others and I could sleep on the pull-out couch that they had for visitors.

I thought it was a great idea. «We all have more or less the same age and the location is centric», I said to myself and we did just that. I moved in with them to sleep on the pull-out couch while I tried to find a job and stability, and perhaps rent my own space, that was my intent.

In the apartment there was a room for Leonardo and Grabiele, both of whom were studying for master's degrees at the Universitá degli Studi di Milano, both of whom were from my country and both of whom had families with good economic resources to cover their expenses. They were almost never here, they only came to sleep and there wasn't a close relationship with them, almost like strangers, we almost never spent time together. In the other room was Estefania and her friend, and they had a similar situation to mine, Estefania was from Venezuela and the other was also Venezuelan but had lived in Chile for several years, but unlike me, they had been in Italy for some time, their migration situation had been regularized, and they had comfortable and stable jobs.

The reason why they shared an apartment was because each one was saving for different things and it was convenient for them to have two others pitching in with rent money.

During my stay there, which seems like an eternity now, Estefania's friend behaved and treated me without a hint of mercy. After the second day with them, I still hadn't found a job and she didn't hesitate to tell me, when Estefania wasn't around, of course: «Look for a job at a restaurant or a coffee shop, or at least clean toilets, that's something you can do». I knew what my situation was and I wasn't afraid to work doing anything, but I felt that her words were meant to humiliate me, she did it every time she could.

Once I came home early from work and was alone in the living room when she walked in without greeting me, went straight to the kitchen, and suddenly started yelling at me because there were dirty dishes in the sink. "I didn't leave them there," I said firmly, because it was true, but she ignored me and said contemptuously, "I don't have children to clean up after. You're not in a castle, princess, this is the real world." It made me cry with anger at the time, because it was the typical situation where I always ended up being the one who got caught up in other people's expectations, as if the people around me thought I lived in a perfect world. Two days later, I got a job at the warehouse, and I realized that Jackson's yelling was nothing compared to the way my cousin's friend treated me. She criticized everything I did. Even the way I folded and put away the blankets to make the sofa bed look nice and tidy, or when I tried to read a word in Italian that was difficult for me, she would react passively aggressive: «That's not how you pronounce the GL in Italian». But the worst thing happened when I was going through the black plague. When I told her and Estefania what had happened to me. Estefania cried with me, but Daniela —yes, that's the name I don't want to pronounce— laughed at me and said: «Don't act like a prude, you had a one-night-stand and that's it, the thing is you woke up, regretted it and now you're being dramatic about it». Estefania gave her a dirty look then, despite the fact that she admires her endlessly.

During the black plague era, I cried a lot, and I tried to do it quietly to not bother her, but one day she made a huge fuss and told me that I wasn't letting her sleep with all the crying. From Estefania's own suggestion, I had to move back with my aunt Eugenia one weekend so she could «take a break from me».

«Honestly, I say to myself, I don't understand why Estefania is friends with such a wicked woman, or why she admires her so much. Who knows what Daniela has told Estefania that made her distance herself from me».

I'm lost in those memories and suddenly a boy comes and greets me by my name.

—I can't believe it! Leonardo! —I say excitedly.

He surely thought that my excitement was because of him, but I was honestly just astonished with the coincidences. I was mortified with memories of Daniela and one of the boys that lived there suddenly appeared.

He ordered some coffees, I had completely forgotten to eat something, and we got to talking. It was normal for us to talk about the very few moments in which we had seen each other at Estefania and Daniela's apartment, and I, despite being angry with her, was talking nicely about her.

—I'm so glad Estefania and Daniela rented the place to you and Grabiele, otherwise we wouldn't have met, you would have walked straight to the dining car —I say, laughing— What have you been up to? —He looked at me funny, like I was saying something inappropriate.

—You're wrong, Valentina, the situation isn't like what you think or have been told. When Daniela moved here from her country she stayed at my parents' house, they knew her family, they gave her a place to stay, they helped her get her citizenship and found her the wonderful job that she has.

—I honestly don't know much about her and her story —I told him.

The truth is that she didn't talk about herself. I don't know if it's because we never managed to click, but the thing is that she keeps to herself, as if she was afraid to share with others. As if they would judge her the same way she judged others.

—Well, just so you know. Once she was economically stable, she rented the apartment and said goodbye to my parents, but not on good terms. I thought that I should also move out from my parents' house and I subleased the room. My parents didn't oppose it, they had the money to pay for my things, and they even thought it was a good idea, «That way you can help her out», they said.

—I thought you got here after Estefania.

—No, that's not the case. Not one month had passed since I moved into the apartment when she told me to find someone in the university to share the room with me, and that she would do the same. That way, supposedly, each one was going to pay less. I found Gabrielle and she bought Estefania over, but she didn't keep her word. She charged Gabrielle the same she charged me, and when I was going to pay her less, she told me to not be selfish, to pay the whole price, that she needed the money more than me, and that Estefania wasn't paying because she was an immigrant and she couldn't afford it.

"Estefania has always paid, as far as I know — I said. I didn't want to give him any more arguments to hate Daniela, but I considered it was my ethical duty to stand up for my cousin.

—Well, I don't know about that, I'm just telling you about my experience. The thing is that I felt moved by Daniela's situation, she was in a strange country, she needed the economic security and a long list of etcetera of being an immigrant, and from what she told me, she was also helping somebody else out, so I felt obligated and agreed to stay there, even when she told me and Gabriele to avoid spending time in the apartment during the day and that whatever was in her fridge belonged to her.

I was stunned, apparently Daniela is horrible to everyone, except Estefania, I guess. She treated him the same way she treated me, but I didn't say anything to Leonardo and he carried on.

—Like I said, I put up with the situation because I'm compassionate, but it got to a point where I couldn't take it anymore. When you moved out, she told me and Grabiele… —He stops for a moment and asks me—: Did you pay rent?

—Yes —I answered— since I got there, I paid Daniela with my savings. But I didn't give her an advance.

—Mmm, that's why —he says to himself, I don't understand what he means, but I don't interrupt him—. After you left the apartment she informed us, not that she asked us, she just informed us that she was going to change the beds for bunkbeds because she was going to use our room to rent it to two more people. At that point, I told her to count me out and find somebody else, that the room wasn't big enough for four people, and Gabrielle said to not count with him either. The point is that we no longer live there. Gabrielle, two other friends and I decided to rent an apartment, and share all of the expenses, not like a sublease, which by the way is probably illegal.

—I don't know what to say about all that you're telling me, honestly, I didn't know anything about that, I always believed you had got there afterwards —that's all I say to him, trying to circle back to my doubts, but he continued to tell his story as if he needed to tell what happened to him.

—I told my parents about it, because I was honestly upset with her attitude, I couldn't understand her. If she's doing well economically, why is she more worried about money than being friends with the people around her to the point of denying food. When I told my parents they didn't want to go into details about their breakup with her, they just advised me to stay clear and to understand that certain people can't break away from their past. —He gestures with his mouth to state that he doesn't know what his parents were talking about.

—Like I said, I didn't know anything, I don't know her story.

I want to make it clear that I'm not a part of it, but I'm not going to share with him what I went through with Daniela nor fuel the fire of the resentment he may still have against her. I feel somewhat sorry for her, something must have happened to her to make her act so ambitiously and bitter, the shortcomings and fears that shape her.

Now I realize that those are her two demons, her shortcomings and fears, and that the things she did to me wasn't because I had provoked them, I don't have the exclusive on her hate. That is her essence, she's like that with everyone. When I understand that, I sigh in relief.

When we arrive, we say goodbye like a good friend; I think we had never spoken as much as today. We make a promise that we're going to meet again, even though we both know that's not going to happen, we're just following up with the usual formalities. If we ever meet again, it's going to be an act of destiny, like this encounter at 360 kilometers per hour.

# Juliet, please!

The trip to Verona felt longer than it actually is, perhaps the conversation with Leonardo and the memories of Daniela made time slow down. When I get to Verona, I call my uncle to ask him where they are, he says that they are in Piazza delle Erbe, drinking some beers, so I head over there.

When I'm about to get to the table, I see her. I see Estefania's «friend»; a woman that I can only describe as Cruella De Vil's long-lost daughter. Despite the realization I had on the train, I thought, «Why! Why did this son of bitch have to come and ruin my weekend?». Of course, I don't say it out loud, Maria Paz is already running towards my arms.

—*Cuzzie* —she yells.

The twins are like all twins in this world, their personalities don't look alike. One of them is super sweet and nice, the other one is acid and bitter. And, since they're becoming teenagers, one likes to cry and the other likes to slam doors; one says you're not paying attention to her, the other says to leave her alone cause you're too intense. They're both Cancer, in fact, they're Stellium in Cancer, but Maria Paz has a moon in Leo and Maria Celeste has a moon in Cancer. The girls were born with a ten-minute difference and in those ten minutes the moon changed. And you can tell. When a personal planet is in Leo, it's as if it devoured them. It's as if it said, I'm in charge. In my opinion, Leo is an energy almost as strong as Scorpio.

I hug the little princess Paz, and I fill her face with kisses and cuddles.

When I get to the table, I proceed to say hello to Maria Celeste, the one that has the more acid personality. Like I did with Maria Paz, I kiss her face and give her a hug with lots of love, she lets me and smiles, and says:

—*I missed you, cuzzie.*

They both call me *cuzzie* because they couldn't say cousin when they were little, I mimicked them and we kept on calling ourselves like that. I think it's super sweet.

I proceed to say hello to my aunt Eugenia, who, despite being forty years old, looks like she's thirty. She doesn't wear makeup; she doesn't dye her hair and is a beautiful woman. She is Libra with Pisces rising, but she has a moon in Virgo. That is, she is a woman with an unbreakable patience, but she likes things done the right way. Otherwise, her personality will act up. And she's a *hippie* Libra, in my opinion, there are two types of Libras, the *hippie* and the snob, I'm more on the snob side.

I say hello to my uncle Alessandro, he's also a Libra and *hippie*, but with Aquarius rising and a moon on Gemini. He doesn't have earth on his chart, and with that much wind, he's forgetful and doubtful. He hugs me quickly.

Finally, I say hello to my cousin Estefania and her friend. Estefania is Stellium in Scorpio on the twelfth house and Gemini rising. I'd better keep my explanations to myself. I can only say that she fights with her biggest enemy every day: her own mind and paranoia. Perhaps I'm part of that paranoia and that's why she doesn't want to be near me. When I hug her, I feel pain in my heart, I miss her. But she doesn't want to be my friend. In Daniela's case, I have never been interested in knowing her astrology chart. My disdain for her made that. But I do know that she is a Gemini. I hate to use stereotypes and judge zodiac signs because I have met Gemini women that I love, but this is a bad walking-talking stereotype.

Once I sit down, I ask for some water, I still have *ratón*[20] and I'm a little hungry. I grab some prosciutto from the table, and we start to catch up with each other. As expected, I sit in between the twins, and Maria Paz has her legs on top of mine so I can cuddle her the way she likes.

After an hour and a half of catching up, we decided to walk around the Giardino dei Giusti, a beautiful garden filled with renaissance sculptures. I can't think of a better place to live than Italy, it's the country with the highest percentage of artwork in the world. Every place, corner, street screams out with opera and classical music. Or at least that's how I feel it.

On Sunday I wake up with a kiss on my forehead. I open my sleepy eyes, and right in my face I have Maria Paz. With her morning dragon breath, she says:

—*Boungiorno, cuzzie.*

—*Boungiorno,* little dragon.

—Mom says we have to go to church, so we have to get up now.

—Okay, okay, I'm coming.

We're staying in an apartment that belongs to a friend of my aunt Eugenia, who borrows her house in exchange for taking care of her cats when she's out of town. The place has two bedrooms and a living room with two pull-out couches.

The twins slept with me in the living room, on the couches. While Estefania slept in one of the rooms with her friend Daniela. Also, I think that she is somehow uncomfortable around the twins, I think she finds

---

[20] *Ratón* is an expression used in Venezuela for a hangover, to feel bad because you drank too much alcohol the night before (Editor's note)

them to be too noisy.

On the contrary, I adore them, but I sometimes need my space, and when I feel blue, I don't like to be around them. My friends tell me things like: «If your sad, all you have to do is spend time with your family» and «You're so lucky to have them close by», but I don't really understand them, when I'm sad, not only do I need to be alone, I also think that my uncles and the twins deserve a happy Maria Valentina; I don't think it's fair for our loved ones to be burdened by our sadness.

I checked my phone and I have unread messages from H. Along with the texts, he sent a picture of himself alone on a street at four in the morning.

> *I left the key to the apartment I'm staying in, inside the apartment. The owner's a nice old lady.*
> *I couldn't find a place to stay, but a friend told me that his grandmother had an extra room and that she could use a «decent houseguest», and since I only needed a room, because I'm not going to spend a lot of days in Valencia, I'm staying here.*
> *I'm waiting for the old lady to wake up and open the door for me. Luckily, she wakes up at five, so I won't have to wait long.*
>
> *Hey, that's scary. Well, at least you're not in a tent somewhere. Did you manage to get in? Did she open the door? Have you eaten something?*

I've noticed that my aunt doesn't like Estefania's friend that much either; but she doesn't show it, she just ignores her most of the time. When the priest announces that the mass is over in the Basilica di San Zeno, my aunt pulls me and Estefania aside.

—According to Shakespeare, this is where Romeo and Juliet got married.

And now we're going to ask Juliet to help you two find a nice boyfriend. —she says, with excitement in her voice.

My aunt Eugenia had married the only boyfriend she ever had. My uncle Alessandro has been her boyfriend since they started going to university. Like any good Libra, my aunt is a hopeless romantic.

We walk from the church to Juliet's house. I knew all northern and central Italy, that is, from Rome upwards, because I had already come over on a couple of different occasions, when I was a teenager, on vacations with my parents and my brother, to visit my uncles, but I don't really remember having visited Juliet's house.

Once we got to Juliet's house, I saw people in line to take a picture with a sculpture, as they grabbed her breast. As if my aunt Eugenia could read my mind, she says:

—According to tradition, touching Juliet's right breast brings you good fortune in your love life. Single women come and ask Juliet to find them a Romeo. That's why I brought you, my sobris , to ask for a nice boyfriend to love you.

My aunt's gesture makes me feel sweet inside. However, Romeo and Juliet were a super tragic story, it was a love that only lasted a few days: Juliet faked her death, Romeo committed suicide because he thought Juliet was dead, and then she ended her own life as well. And I'm not even mentioning that it was a forbidden love because their families hated each other. So, honestly, I don't find their story romantic. I find it sad that they didn't get to live out their love. «It's too dramatic, too much, even for me, and I'm an artist».

When it's our turn in line, I don't grab Juliet's breast, I find it a bit too much. Why should I touch her private parts? I understand that

...........................

[21] Abbreviation used to call your nieces and nephews. (Editor's note)

it's a statue, but still, I think that the woman deserves some respect, especially with how tragic her story was. Therefore, I decided to look at her and talk about my thoughts and feelings.

«Juliet, I'm sorry, I'm sorry you didn't get to live your love with Romeo. I know who I want my boyfriend to be, I want H, but I want to be able to live out my love with him, so this is what I'm going to ask of you, I ask you to let me live my love story with my prince Charming».

I realize that Estefania and her friend don't take a photo, or come close to Juliet's statue.

—What's the matter? You don't want to find a man? —I ask them.

—I don't need no man, I'm fine like this, single —says Daniela.

—Me neither —says Estefania, with an arrogant tone as well.

—That's so unromantic of you, Estefania —I looked at my cousin and ignored her friend—: Well, I ask her for the both of us. Hey Juliet, a good man for each of us, a handsome one, that loves us nicely, and with money so they can support us too —I jokingly add.

—Never —says Estefania immediately, reproaching what I said—. I don't need no man to pay and provide for me.

—Hey, it's just a joke. And there's nothing wrong with wanting somebody that has financial stability.

—For you. But I like to work and pay for my own things —she adds, with an acid remark.

«Ugh, what a bad vibe. Honestly, Some time ago she would have laughed with me, and she would have played along with my joke. I've worked since I was sixteen years old, and I don't expect to ever stop working, but I want somebody who has stability, and I don't think there's anything wrong with that», I say to myself, because if I say out loud to Estefania, and with her friend here, she could explode like Hiroshima.

It makes me sad that I can't even joke around with her.

My aunt Eugenia sees that, and intercedes and asks for the both of us, like me, ignoring Daniela.

—A good boyfriend for each one of my nieces, to love them like they deserve. Please, Juliet.

# Ghosts on the prowl

When we leave Juliet's house, we head out to a coffee shop nearby for a bite to eat before we head back. When we're about to sit down, Daniela comes up to me from behind and whispers in my ear:

—Pleased now? Juliet is going to provide you with a boyfriend like Marco, you couldn't be more delusional.

The atmosphere and her words immediately brought to mind the day Voldemort took me to a cafe and told me he was going to introduce me to some friends. When we arrived at the table, located at the back of the place, there were four men. He introduced them to me and left, supposedly, to place the order.

Those four 'friends' were undressing me with their eyes and kept asking bawdy and inappropriate questions. They were even blunt when they asked me point blank if I didn't know of any friends who wanted to be with them, because, you know, all Latinas were immigrants in need of money, «All Latinas are hot, or at least that's what I've heard», was one of the disgusting expressions they said to me.

They said everything as if it was a joke, but with the intention of provoking and stereotyping me according to their crude and disgusting beliefs. Latinas are hard working women, and there are tramps of all nationalities, no woman becomes a tramp because she wants to, but that's something that no man ever understands. I felt very uncomfortable and looked for Marco with my gaze. I couldn't find him and started to get nervous. I'm not shy, but I felt like I was facing a wolf pack that was going to tear me apart. There were no signs of Marco to be seen so I decided to leave after telling them: «I'm sorry, I don't think you can afford any of my tramp Latin American friends. They charge a lot and you don't have deep pockets»

Nowadays, I think that he was selling me or testing me out, «Was he trying to test how faithful I could be? Or was he doing business with some pimps? How could he do that to me?». Suddenly, the air disappears, I can't breathe and I start to have a panic attack.

My aunt realizes that something is wrong with me because I'm so pale and she asks me:

—Are you feeling okay, Maria Valentina?

I turn around to look at them. They're all seated. Daniela and my cousin are laughing with malice, I'm sure she told her what she had said to me «bitch». I can't stand it and tell my aunt that I'm going to the bathroom for a moment. I need to be able to breathe and confess to someone what's happening to me. I can't do it here; it would be too uncomfortable for everyone. I'm not going to ruin the moment; I'm not going to give that bitch the satisfaction.

Once I'm in the bathroom, I text Hachito.

*I feel so bad. I can't breathe.*

He doesn't text back. He calls me right away.

—What's the matter, MJ?

—I can assure you, I thought that woman couldn't hurt me anymore —I answered, and I couldn't help crying.

—What woman? What happened? Please, tell me.

So I tell him what Daniela did to me on this trip, and part of what she and my cousin had done to me before; I didn't tell him anything about my memories of Voldemort, that's something I still can't talk about. I also explain what I found out about her when I was coming over on the train and how, from that, I believed that she was a monster

I thought I had moved on, and that she would no longer hurt me.

H interrupts me, in a very delicate way, in some parts of my story to understand what I'm telling him; of course, avoiding the whole Voldemort story has made what I want to say become a waterfall of somewhat incongruous information. By talking to him, I start to calm down.

To calm me down he says:

—Okay, give me info on these women, their names and social media accounts. Let me stalk them just a moment and I'll call you back.

I think that, by omitting the black plague, H is focusing on Daniela and my cousin. I do what he asks and I send him the data by WhatsApp, I even attach a photo of that day they were both in.

I remained in the bathroom, waiting for his call. I have a cigarette in my hand. I'm not going to smoke, it's not allowed, but having the cigarette between my fingers relaxes me a little. I think that my nicotine dependence has to do with my state of anxiety.

Less than two minutes pass before and my phone rings with H's call.

—I know why they mistreat you, MJ— he tells me with utter confidence.

I'm looking forward to it. I have also stalked them, looking for answers to their behavior and I haven't gotten anything. «What could H have discovered that I haven't discovered?», I ask myself, and let him carry on.

"They're two ugly women— he tells me—. They're ugly inside and out. In terms of beauty, you're light years ahead of them, and, from what I could see on their media accounts, I can tell you that both are too mundane, they have nothing in their brains. It's obvious, MJ, that what they feel for you is pure and simple envy.

—But... —I try to find something to refute with, but nothing comes to mind and he continues:

- No buts, Maria Valentina. They envy you and they can't deal with their own envy, with their rage. Think of it this way: out of envy, there are criminals, large and small. The envy of the big ones sometimes ends in the bankruptcy of companies, and small criminals, what do they do? They rob and even murder to take control of what others have, because they envy, they want what their victim has and they don't.

»Let's see, let's see... — H keeps on, as if looking for other examples for his analysis - Do you know why they killed Canserbero? Not just out of envy but because of his ideals, because of his perspective regarding politics and Venezuela. His potential was a threat to the other rappers and to the government.

—Oh —l answered— It's true!

—Do you see it now?

H pauses, but I'm dumbstruck by his analysis. It immediately reminds me of the moment in Madrid when he masterfully broke down the problems of my date with Pablo. H interprets my silence and continues.

—Of course, they have a thousand reasons to feel intimidated by everything you represent. I know you hate to think badly of women in general. But believe me when I tell you that there are ruthless women, you are one of those women who makes other women nervous. They beg to have what you have, and what you have naturally.

—Hey, but I don't understand. What do they want from me? They are better off than me financially, they can afford clothing brands that I can't even save up for, in fact, I know that my cousin has just been approved for a house loan. I don't know, I have a life that I feel proud of because it cost me to get it, but, on the other hand, I feel frustrated because I can't do the things that I like and so... I don't know...

—Understand this, MJ. They don't envy your material possessions, they envy you as a whole, they envy you for who you are, because you have dreams and desires and the energy to make them come true. They fear, quite rightly, seeing you succeed in what you want to do and they try to prevent it by overshadowing your life. They are women who envy you now, not only for who you are today, but for what you will become in the future. That's a burden for them and they need to fuck with you, even if it's the little moments. Breathe easy and think that they are far, far beneath you, about three hundred floors underground.

The image he uses to illustrate his comment, makes me start laughing, between nervous and relieved to have someone like H by my side, he knows that I'm already relaxed and finishes off by telling me:

—Don't waste your energy looking for the reasons behind bad actions, focus on yourself, they are mentally disturbed.

I do not know what superpower H has to relieve each of my concerns. My hero

# Therapy, my dear friend

Despite the situation with Daniela, I spent a beautiful weekend with the twins. My cousin and Daniela wanted to make my visit bitter, but it backfired[22] because, after their attempt, the call with H put them in their right place, it comforted me and, above all, he became a little more attached to my heart.

My doubts before the trip were because of the reunion with the twins, sometimes I find it difficult to connect with them for some reason that I honestly don't know. There are still things that make me nervous, one of them is seeing the twins or my Aunt Eugenia, sometimes I feel out of place. It's like there's something inside me that's broken, that can't properly feel family warmth, but on these two days I felt really good.

I remember that I've got to call the office to make an appointment with my psychologist, Mariana.

I've been going to therapy since I was sixteen, it hasn't been that often, but I've always tried to seek help from professionals, especially when I'm going through emotional swings, those ups and downs of feelings that we call roller coasters.

When I was a teenager, I had fits of anger and I would break everything that came my way, I didn't know where that anger was

---

[22] The saying «It backfired» is used in Venezuela and other Caribbean countries to mean that some action turns out the opposite of how it was planned

coming from. And I still don't know.

The reality is that it's been hard to find a therapist who can help me, who can give me the tools to get to know myself better and overcome the barriers that are holding me back.

At university, I went to a therapist after having been with Carlos Daniel. I needed some help with the issue of physical violence. On the other hand, there was also the whole country's situation. We were taken out of class because of protests in the streets, the roads were closed and chaos was everywhere.

At that time my brain was chemically unbalanced. And my mom, poor mom! She didn't know what to do with me. She started giving me some pills that she had for her nerves, I'm not sure what she was giving me, but I started suffering from paranoia with the whole Venezuela issue and the protests. I had constant nightmares about the GNB, they would break into my home, vandalize my house, while I would hide under the bed or in the closet, only to be found by them and beaten. It was a tough time, I experienced an emotional disappointment, a situation where I felt I was somebody's personal object and then I became paranoid about being a state object, victim of the system and the Venezuelan dictatorship.

At that point I don't know if the medication aggravated or reduced the nightmares and paranoia, there are still parts of those memories that are cloudy in my head. Then came another broken relationship, and the unavoidable departure from the country, with all the desires, hopes, and frustrations that came along with it.

And in Italy it was Voldemort, and after him I found Mariana. I started from scratch with her, and it has been a complete adventure,

---

[23] Acronym for Bolivarian National Guard, before Chavez's term only National Guard, one of the five components of the National Armed Forces. (Editor's Note)

for her as well as for me, I think. We started from the basics, from childhood, and we did tests and drawings to get an idea of where I was standing at a psychological level.

Talking to her makes me feel safe, and the tools she has given me so far have really worked well for me.

Mariana hates diagnoses, she says it's putting me in a box. She told me at some point that we should go over the situations that happened during the "Black Plague" and all the abuse I experienced. So far, I haven't felt like talking about it, not even with Mariana, to whom I only briefly mentioned it. I keep putting it off.

I get off the phone with my psychologist's secretary and I have an appointment in a few days.

# And if they meet, what then?

H texted me and said that the day after tomorrow he will go back to his apartment in Paris. I know, from the conversation we had at Luismi's house the first day he arrived in Madrid, that he's the one who rented the apartment that *the she*, that is his ex, that she's the one who left.

Despite knowing that they no longer live together, imagining that they will be in the same city begins to gnaw at my brain, «What will happen if they meet? It's very common for couples to get back after an argument. Of course! That depends on the fight and those involved, I tell myself, I would never go back with Voldemort, but my sweetie pie Hachito is not a Voldemort and perhaps that relationship didn't have such a traumatic end either».

I don't understand this sudden jealousy for someone I should consider to be a ghost. I know that H has his casual encounters, I'm not a fool to think that he goes to parties with his friends and does not get any attractive women to spend a night with, but those encounters —if they happen— do not intimidate me, I know what they are.

However, the fact that he's in the same city where the person he shared his life with for two years still lives, brings me back to what the Tarot reader said: «There is something here about an ex of his who can become very manipulative and play with this boy's feelings». Yes, the ex can manipulate H's feelings even after the breakup. «If the ex-girlfriend sneaks back into H's life, our path to being together can get very complicated, and if you measure affection by the time shared together, then shit! With that cunt, I'm fucked, it's there two years against my few days, even if they've been intense».

I really don't know what would happen if H meets with his ex. It's a relationship that had stability, and the breakup, from what H said in Madrid, was the pandemics fault. Sharing the same space and seeing each other's faces every second of every minute for several months is enough to make anyone become bored, it was a litmus test and they got burned.

I decide to leave these absurd thoughts behind and reply to H.

> *That's so chimbo[24] Your vacation is over.*
> 
> *Yes, but I enjoyed those few days I took to clear up my mind.*
> 
> *Does that mean you'll be fully focused on your work? But I will always have time to talk to you, even to check my destiny in the decks or my astral chart, as we did the first day I arrived in Madrid, hahaha.*
> 
> *Oh, okay, and since you're still my friend, do you think we can have any calls to get astrological consultations? Hahaha.*

I write «my friend», on purpose, to see if he dares to answer me «we are more than friends», but no, he doesn't take the hint.

> *Of course, MJ, I like anything I can get to do with you, even having you read the deck to me or consult my stars. Anything that comes from you is something that I enjoy, but don't tell anyone about the deck. Can you imagine Luis Miguel telling the «Maracaibo celebrities» that I «get consulted» over*

---

[24] In Venezuela, when *chimbo* refers to a situation, such as in the context, it means that's too bad. Referring to an object, it means that it is of poor quality or that it's a hoax. (Editors Note)

> *the internet? Hahahaha.*
>> *Don't worry, that will only be between us. Oh, my new friend, I feel like a kid with a new toy, hahaha.*
> *I like being your new toy too, hahaha.*
>> *Thank you, toy friend. Should I put my name on your foot now? Like in Toy Story?*
> *Hahaha, I prefer it on my chest with red lipstick please.*

I love H's sense of humor. This is something that I don't have on the wish list of requirements, and I'll have to add it.

# CHAPTER IV
## Shdows of desire

«I've spent a great many moments since then imagining him. He was like a song I'd heard once in fragments but had been singing in my mind ever since».

—Arthur Golden, *Memories of a geisha*

# Between friends and alliances

A couple of days have passed and communication with H has been daily, to the point that I can't get off the phone. The last thing he told me was that he wants to talk to me once he gets to his apartment in Paris. He must be flying over right now, so I'm glued to the phone waiting for when he lands.

The level of anxiety I feel is not normal. He didn't say what topic or what he wanted to talk to me about, so I'm completely blank. «Could it be that he doesn't want to talk to me anymore? Did I bore him already? Did he fall in love with someone? Is he planning to get back with the ex?». Although from what we have talked about the issue of the ex does not seem to be in his sights, and that is the worst of my anxieties.

After a couple of hours of waiting, H's video call comes in.

—Hello —I answer.

—Hello.

—How was it?

—Good, I'm getting home. —I see him open the door of his apartment, walk in, put his things in the living room and then sit on the couch—. How are you? —he asks.

—Good, I was looking forward to your call. Do you no longer want to be my friend? —I ask him pouting. He laughs.

—No, not at all. The truth is that, look, I just got together with a friend, and after several conversations, well, we have a good amount of money to start a business, but we don't know what to do. I wanted to know if you would put your brain on the table, and obviously you'll have your percentage.

—ME? A BUSINESS? But, what kind of business? —I asked him, more than surprised.

—I don't know, you look like you know about that. You have a lot of ideas, come on, sell us one of your ideas.

I think for a moment about what he just said.

—Well, my dream is to have my own audiovisual production company, to have a studio where films, short films & photo shoots are made. With all the tools, obviously, and not only having the physical place, but also the human team. I would like someone to take care of all the financial parts and I would be the creative director; that is, when the client needs it, we help them organize and produce their ideas.

—Wow! That sounds great, but it does require several things. One, a market study to find the best location, if it's in Milan, here in Paris, Madrid or wherever. Two, it needs a lot of capital to buy the best cameras and stuff. It sounds like a life project, like something we can put on the list for later. Let's try to think of something more tangible, something we can do right now, that can help us create what you just told me, because it sounds amazing.

I'm stunned.

—But I'm dont understand anything. Why are you bringing me into a work project with your business partner-friend? And, why would you help me create my audiovisual production company?

—Because people like you, passionate about what they do, deserve to achieve things, they deserve to reach their dreams. You're worth it, you deserve it.

I don't know what to say. I really am wordless.

—I don't know H, I don't know what to tell you, honestly. I don't know how to help you, and a thing like that has never crossed my mind. I wouldn't know how to help you with something more tangible.

—Don't worry, we have all the time in the world. Besides, I like to keep my friends for a long period of time.

—It's okay — it's the only thing I can pronounce, but then I find the courage to tell him things that I reflect upon sometimes.

—H, can I tell you something?

—Of course.

—I tell you about my ambitions and my dreams because I think that one should do what we want, what we want most. It's true that life temporarily puts us in trades to survive, but we must see them that way: as temporary. Even if one gives it your all and ethically complies with a job, your dreams should be the permanent thing, what has always been your desires and your plans.

»My family taught me that we manage, but we don't settle, so if we have to do other trades that are ethically correct, then we do them with honor, but always working at the same time for the things we want. I believe that by doing what you want, the rest just comes to you. Now that you have this opportunity, think about what you want most and do what you have to do to get it.

—You're right, MJ. The thing is that your dreams are very clear to you, I'm still looking for mine. Honestly, I think that my thing is to make money and that's it. There is nothing that I am passionate about the way your audiovisual company idea does with you. Maybe that's why it comes to my mind that you put the idea. If money wasn't a problem, what would you do? What project would you carry out? I am very logical and practical, I'll tell you in two seconds if the idea is viable or not, but unlike you, I don't have that uncontrollable creation of ideas.

It reminded me of when Alice, after returning from wonderland, told her father's partners that she wanted to open a business in China, the truth is that it was crazy, but a tangible madness. H was putting the map on the table, and was just asking me, where do you want to go?

On the other hand, this conversation has once again questioned my entire past in terms of personal relationships. This is so crazy! Really. Voldemort always talked about starting companies and every time I told him an idea, he would say that it was stupid, that I was a fool and that I did not have the right vision for business. He insulted me so many times for the ideas I came up with, that on one occasion I told him, «I'm an artist, not an entrepreneur».

Unlike Voldemort, H took it with ice[25], he validated my dream and even with few words said that he would put the wings on my project when there was an opportunity. «You chose right, a part of my brain tells me. He's the right guy»

Never would the thirteen-year-old Maria Valentina have thought that, at almost twice her age, she would be talking to Heinrich Miguel Gil Montilla every day, that she would kiss him, that he would ask her to join him in a partnership and that, above all, he would be my friend.

Just thinking about it fills my heart with a gratitude that I have never felt before. I ask God to let me keep this man. To let me have H, H for hero.

---

[25] In Venezuela, the phrase *take it with ice* or *he took it with ice* is used to express surprise when someone assumes a relaxed attitude in the face of a fact that could be disturbing. (Editor's Note).

# Repowered friendships

When I was in Madrid, I connected a lot with Jennifer and Fernanda. I've known them both since I was a teenager. They were the kind of people that you know exist and with whom, maybe you crossed a couple of words once, but there was never a big bond.

However, in Madrid, when we saw each other, we had a good connection, so when they post insta stories together, I call or write them and we have that gossip session in a heavy Maracucho idiom that we just need sometimes.

The relationship I have with them now makes me think that we all need to create bonds and affections, either by supporting ourselves in our past or looking to the future. Being an immigrant implies, on the one hand, continuing to feed the root where we come from, and on the other, knowing that the tree will flourish thousands of kilometers from where it is planted. The affection I have for them is as if I could bring the root closer to the flowers, as if the tree was whole.

The way I connect with them is completely different from how I connect with my friends from Milan. Emiliana has an Italian father, but was born and raised in Croatia, she came over a couple of years ago. Soffia is Italian, but from the south, from Naples. Corina is half French, half Italian, and Margot is half Italian and half Hungarian. We all share an Italian origin that unites us, but we also have another place in our hearts. That makes us coincide and unite in a different kind of friendship than the one I have with Fernanda and Jennifer. With my friends here I don't talk about our home countries, there are no basic conversations about how I see Venezuela or memories of what we were when we were in our corresponding countries, the conversations with them are more along the lines of «How would you do it?».

With Jennifer and Fernanda, and in general with the others from the "Maracaibo Celebrities", the links are based on the need to recognize ourselves in our past, to remember our languague, to reconnect around common words and phrases due to the fact that we had all grown up in the same city, and that's something that I need sometimes.

So, I'm Hannah Montana, and I'm happy, I feel satisfied. I am very grateful for the bonds that I am slowly building, the friends in the city where I live, the friends from the city where I was born who were close and of course my Hachito. It feels wonderful, everything is starting to take on a nice tone, I keep thinking that if things start to go well it also means that, soon, perhaps, with God's favor, I will be able to get a creative job where I can feel more comfortable, more like a «fish in the water».

I write in the group chat with the five of us: Jennifer, Fernanda, Luis Miguel, Edgar and me, and as expected only the girls answer, so we make a video call.

Jennifer is at Fernanda's house and they are cooking something.

—Hello, *amiguis*, hello [26] - I say singing like the posh/snobby girls of *Somos tú y yo* [27].

—Hello, *amigui*, how are you? —Fernanda answers.

—Girls, all good, here we are spending this beautiful Saturday afternoon. It has been too hot and the truth is that if I catch the sun I burn —I tell them.

---

[26] *Hello, Amiguis, Hello* is a song from the Venezuelan TV series Somos tu y yo (2007-09).
[27] Venezuelan youth series available on streaming platforms.

—Obviously, Baby, in this weather you don't feel like going out —says Jennifer.

—And girl, you don't have to go around spending money. In saving mode, then —I say and then ask—: What are you cooking?

—We're making *patacones* [28] —Fernanda replies.

—Nooo, I'm dying! My mouth is watering, send me one, hahaha.

Conversations like this happen all the time between me and my friends. And although we usually chat in a group, Fernanda insistently tries to chat with me alone. She has also known H for a long time, and since "the world is a handkerchief" [29] She studied with H's ex in high school.

I've always tried to keep whatever I have with H privately, but both Fernanda and Jennifer know that H and I talk as more than just friends talk.

Fernanda, who is more than sure that I have something with H, has tried to talk badly to me about his ex, to make her look like a manipulative woman with a «Wasn't me» face [30]. She even takes screenshots of insta stories that she posts and sends them to me. Every day she has something new to tell me about H's ex and I feel like I'm invading the privacy of someone I don't know. I find it weird, bizarre and somewhat disturbing. It's like my friend wants to form a hate alliance against the ex, and I can't hate someone I don't know, much less a woman, no matter who it is... although, well, there have been exceptions.

...............................

[28] *Patacones* are fried green plantain, similar to a toston but much thicker, used as an hors d'oeuvre or side dish; they are frequently consumed in Maracaibo.
[29] *The world is a handkerchief* is an expression widely used in Venezuela to indicate that the world is small and that in remote places you can randomly meet people that you have some connection with.
[30] *Having a wasn't me face or a wasn't me cute face* is a colloquial phrase used in Venezuela to mean that someone is a hypocrite, false, who pretends to have virtues that they don't have. (Editor's Note).

I can't have Fernanda pouring gasoline on this anxious fire that is my relationship with H, even less so now that he's in Paris, in the same city as the blessed ex.

Honestly, I've never been in a situation like this before. In my previous romantic relationships, I never had to deal with any exes, much less with comments and gossip. Faced with this new context, I have tried to keep my distance and discretion; I try to conduct myself in an impartial way. I couldn't hate her, she was a girl, just like me, with mistakes and successes, I didn't know her personally, so I couldn't make any value judgments nor validate Fernanda's opinions.

I swear, with my hand on the Vogue, that I have done everything in my power to stay on the edge, to ignore, to not to have an opinion. I didn't want to violate anyone's privacy, but my friend is very intense with this topic and her gossipy attitude sometimes makes me feel like a child in front of a candy store, so when she called me, after H returned to Paris, I let her talk freely.

In less than an hour, I already had all the information about the ex from Fernanda's own mouth. I found out about her ex-boyfriends, ex-husbands and ex-friends-with-benefits, she told me about her parents and what they do, who her siblings are and a lot of irrelevant information about her. I also found out, and understood the reasons why my friend hated her so much.

It turns out that Fernanda, in some strange way, is tied H's ex life, not only because they studied together, but because from stories and tales and small-town gossip: years ago she broke up with the boyfriend she had when she was still in Maracaibo, because she heard that H's now ex was going out with her then-boyfriend. The exact type of situations I always stayed clear from when I lived there.

Once Fernanda's meticulous exposition was finished, I felt exactly the same as before, I didn't hate or despise the ex; she was a girl just like me, with mistakes and virtues. Although my friend didn't give me details about what had happened with H or why they had broken up, I told her:

—Honestly, Fernanda, you chose the wrong profession, you should be an investigative journalist— and then with as much tact as I could I told her: Girl, now I understand why you hate her, but you can't make me feel the same way. It's not the same situation and, honestly, I don't care. I'm not interested in what H's ex does or doesn't do; if there is a «pro H», and by that, I mean someone who pretends to be in his future, you tell me, but about this one, which is in the past, I don't want to know anything, and so should you. What good does it do to feed on past moments? As long as you have them with you, you will not be able to see the big picture or build expectations for your future.

# Spicy curiosities

After chatting with Fernanda and finding out all the details about the ex, I felt obligated, to myself, to find out more about her and I gave the matter the last push forward. For the first time, I actually checked her Instagram profile. In ten minutes, I already had her exact date of birth and, with the help of the pendulum, the exact time.

There are times when curiosity is an invasive fever that behaves like an itch all over your body and you can only get it off by satiating it. I have to know the astrological relationship between these two beings.

I look up her birth chart, and my analysis begins. I wasn't really looking for something specific, I just wanted to have a look.

The girl is a Gemini with a moon in Sagittarius and shares Venus in Pisces with H. It's only natural that H would fall in love with her, and her with him. She speaks his specific love language. It's a strong connection, as far as I can judge astrologically. It is an unspoken love language and they both love in exactly the same way. The only problem that I can see in her is that Sun squared to Uranus that usually makes a person a little disruptive.

From what I can see, she expresses her wounds in a way in which H could feel affected. I immediately remembered the Tarot reader. She knows how to put her wounds into words and actions in such a way that H can fall to his knees. That's a power that we women love, but it can also bring out a very manipulative part of us.

By analyzing that, it just gave me a twinge of pain in my heart. I tried to reflect on my own pain and understood that I felt sorry for H, and perhaps also for her.

I was sure that neither one had started that relationship thinking about ending it at some point. I do not know what led them to finish it, beyond what H said in Madrid, who dismissed the matter saying that it was about communication problems and the oppression caused by the pandemic lock-down. Whatever happened meant that it was time for them to take different paths, and that's hard to swallow. I felt sorry for both of them and for their Venus in Pisces.

Once again, my brain gets to work without authorization from me. «They are meant to be, they'll get back together at any moment. Maybe if they cross paths by accident, they'll get back together», I think and my anxiety attack is approaching, so I stop. «Stop it, Maria Valentina!».

I have satisfied my curiosity and I didn't like the results that much, but that does not mean that I am going to abandon my resolutions. The relationship between H and his ex is over and I am now the person he calls every day, the person with whom he shares everything and with whom he would even like to have a partnership with. Whatever has happened before or how deep their relationship may have been, it's in the past.

I am aware that this mediocre and meaningless research feeds in me an egomaniacal and small part that is that need-to-know things should not be any of my business. In my country they would say that I love *Looking for a fifth paw on a cat* [31], looking for what I haven't lost. I also know that these types of actions validate my insecurities, but I can't put into words what those insecurities actually are.

---

[31] *Looking for a fifth paw on a cat* is an expression that is used to indicate that someone insists, without important reasons, on doing things that can cause harm. (Editor's Note)

# Caution: falling in love

I'm waiting for my turn in the anteroom of the office. The context makes me think about the different occasions I've been here. Every time I've needed a place to break down, when I've felt like I can't get out of my crises without help, I've come here. This has been the place where they can sew up my wounds. Although I have not exposed my biggest ulcers with Mariana, she has taken the invisible thread of her wisdom and helped me to see the horizon. I ask myself: «What's bringing me here today is a wound or is it the need to clean up my past thoughts, or both»...

—Miss Santini —the receptionist interrupts my thoughts —Miss, Santini! —she repeats it louder to bring me back.

When I enter the office, Mariana greets me and asks me to take a seat.

—Tell me, Valentina, what has happened in your life? How was the trip to Madrid?

—I tell Mariana everything that happened and how I have been talking to H daily for weeks.

—Valentina, let's organize your thoughts a little. I get that there's a part of you that wants to run away, and another part that's excited about having something romantic with H. However, let's be honest, even if H told you that he wants you to go to Paris, that was an expression linked to the moment. And then you tell me that he confirmed that request in the call you had about a partnership, but he also told you in that call, according to your own words, «I like to keep my friends for a long period of time».

»Now, after covid-19 I have noticed that my extroverted patients are experiencing strong and fast feelings and introverted patients are having a hard time in undertaking everyday activities. From what you have told me, H seems to be a more introverted person than an extrovert, and you are more of an extrovert than an introvert. You both need a friend, a companion. But be careful, figure out what you want to do by yourself and then talk about it with him.

—I want to be his girlfriend —I immediately said to my therapist—. I think I'm about to fall in love with him.

—Okay, if that's your decision, then talk it over with him, H seems to be an easy guy to approach. Also, remember that you have a past that has hurt you, and something similar may be happening to him, because, as you told me, he is just getting out of a relationship. It is necessary for you to understand that there are no miraculous scissors that cut traumatic experiences in one single blow. You should both take things easy, calmly and, above all, with a lot of honesty. —Mariana makes a brief pause and then asks me—. Are you ready to talk a little bit about the past?

«To talk a little bit about the past», the past is the wound, the big one, the one that is hard to undress. It is the injury covered with guilt and shame, the one that doesn't let you sleep, the one that holds on in your life and the one for which you would like to have memory loss pills. But I know that when I start to talk about it, I will start, really, to get over it and I need to do that.

—Okay— I replied.

# Face to face with the past

For some reason, admitting to myself in front of my therapist that I want to have something stable with H gives me the strength I need to talk about my traumatic experience with Voldemort. A story that I have not wanted to share with anyone until now, that still breaks my balance, it is as if by verbalizing it I lived the moment, but the reality is that if I want to have H in my life, I have to have healed the past. This is part of what Mariana tells me and I share that thought: I need to calm the turbulent waters that still live inside me.

—Tell me in detail what happened with Voldemort. —I'm glad that Mariana respects the villain's nickname and does not call him by his name.

—The nameless one —I say—. Well, the story can get long, Mariana, but I'll try to tell it from the beginning. I had just arrived in Milan and I moved from my aunt's house to an apartment shared with my cousin, a friend of hers, who was renting to me, and two other students; I slept on the pull-out couch. Although I wasn't working yet, I paid the rent on time with my savings, despite that, the girl who rented to me was bothering me, humiliating me to go look for a job, as if she was annoyed by my presence.

»Well, the thing is that I finally got a job in infamous conditions, with overwhelming heat, and there I met Ali who treated me very well. I started to have feelings for Ali, but he was unstable, and I soon realized that he didn't feel for me the way I felt for him. To forget about Ali, I agreed to go out with Voldemort.

While I was dating him, I got sick, I suffered from panic attacks every day, the medications the psychiatrist prescribed me caused side effects and I was, like a guinea pig, trying different contraceptives; they all made me feel bad. I got to a point where I didn't even have the ability to go grocery shopping, choosing a simple cereal overwhelmed me.

»I got sick and skipped work and everything got complicated. Every day the relationship with the person who rented the room to me was getting worse. She behaved wonderfully when Marco visited me or when my cousin was there, but in their absence, she insulted me. Because of my mental and health conditions, the government granted me financial aid, which, although it was not enough, was useful, and Marco said that he was going to help me with the other things I needed.

Marco asked me to focus on more productive matters. He told me to look for an apartment closer to the company so he could take care of me, that he was going to take care of the rent, and then, if I felt like it, we could go and live together...

»At that time, many details related to Marco overwhelmed and confused me. Everything was confusing and cloudy in my head, I couldn't notice certain things, like, that I only saw Marco when he left work and came to pick me up to take me to a hotel, we spent a few hours there and we parted ways and went home. We never even spent a night together, although he couldn't stay where I lived, we could have stayed all night in the hotel, but that never happened; nor did I ask myself why we weren't going to his apartment. I didn't know where he lived, he paid everything in cash, he never told me about his family, and once I asked him about the origin of his last name, Kar, he didn't answer and got weird, as if he was angry.

"Anyway, in between my confusion, I realize that I haven't gotten my period. I blamed it on the number of changes in my contraceptive method. I had gone from pills to injections; however, I bought myself a pregnancy test and took it. The test was positive. When I saw the result, I was so excited, I was excited with a very beautiful feeling in my heart. "I'm going to be a mom", was all I could think. This made me so excited that I ran out to call Marco to give him the good news. He and I had already talked about becoming parents one day. I called him once, twice, three times, and he didn't pick up. I texted him saying it was an emergency. He replied saying that he was busy. I insisted on calling him and his response was a message saying, "Not now. You are being so annoying".

»So I decided to wait for him to call me, and when he did, I informed him that he had to come over because I had something very important to tell him. His answer was, "Valentina, I can't right now. I'm already at my house because you kept getting in the way, and calling and texting and I was busy. Tomorrow, if I feel like it, I'll stop by. Since you don't go to work, and all you do is sleep all day, you can spend all your time bothering me, Besides, when I met you, you were skinny, the way I like, now, you're even putting on weight" I had no choice but to tell him, on that same call that I looked chubby because I was pregnant. "Ugh! You're so manipulative. I'll be right back, I'm on my way", was what he answered, and then hung up the phone

I interrupt the story with Mariana because I'm starting to lose my breath.

—Valentina, I understand that this is hard to talk about. You are brave, I am here to listen to you —she adds, to encourage me.

After a couple of deep breaths, I continue.

—Well, at the time I just thought I was scared, but now I can see everything. No, I wasn't fat. I weighed forty-five kilos and I'm one meter and seventy-five centimeters tall. I was in the bones; you could see my rib bones. I was almost just a talking head. I think he said that because it's one of the most common insecurities women have, but if I was already feeling bad, imagine with that body dysmorphia on top.

»I remember that when he got to my house he brought me all kinds of pregnancy tests, and made me take them in front of him, when he saw all the positives test results, he said to me: "You don't know anything about life, you're a stupid and dumb little child, you should have an abortion because you're on medications on top of it all, it's already too much with all the annoyance that you are to now bring another irritation into my life. Find a way to have an abortion as soon as possible to get rid of this problem, otherwise I won't see you again. Here, that's a hundred euros. Find out what you've got to do, now! I'm not going to put up with your nonsense, or your crying".

»My heart dropped to the floor. It never even crossed my mind to have an abortion. My brain just wasn't ready to hear such a thing. I was broken, but at that moment I let myself be carried away by his words, my illusions went overboard.

»In the midst of that chaos, I turned twenty-four years old, I remember that Marco only stopped by the apartment to give me a rose when he found out that was the day I was going to get the abortion.

—Can you give me details of how the abortion took place —Mariana pressed on.

—I had the abortion at home, usually, during the day time, there was no one else there, my cousin and the girl who rented to me got back from work in the afternoon, and the other two guys got home at night just to sleep.

»I had to look for an association on my own that could give me some support, because I was afraid to go to the hospital and have to do it there, I thought I already had too much help from the government, I was... I don't know, afraid of what the nurses might think or say, I'm still an immigrant. With the money that Voldemort gave me, I bought the pills online and performed the abortion at home, during the day. It was very traumatic. I still remember the physical and emotional pain I was in. My cousin Estefania didn't know, when she got home in the afternoon, I told her that it was just a strong belly pain, Marco had already left; after seeing me bleeding, she said she would go buy dinner and didn't come back anymore. I called him several times, for several days and he never wanted to pick up.

—He was just there to make sure —says Mariana with a pinch of anger. I nodded with tears in my eyes.

—A few weeks later it was Christmas and the New Year —I carried on—. I could barely go and spend some time with my family. I had agoraphobia; I couldn't get up. My cousin Estefania would come and give me the food in my mouth, since all I could do was cry. She would fix my sofa bed, forcing me to take long showers, not just to clean myself up. She didn't ask me anything, she just helped me as if she knew that I needed that silence. I've never fallen so low.

I stay quiet for a while, it's hard to keep talking. Mariana understands the situation.

—And after that, was that relationship over? —she asks, guiding my thoughts.

—No —I reply—. But other things happened. —My voice is breaking.

—Do you think you can keep on or do you want us to stop? —Mariana asks me, and I decide to overcome it and continue with the confession.

—The first week of January I made plans to meet with a friend who was visiting in the city to go grab a beer. I forced myself to go out after four weeks locked in the apartment, I was already ending my relationship with Voldemort, I had to separate myself from the pain. After the first beer, part of my memory fades away. I have memory lapses about that moment. I remember being in his hotel room, holding on to my underwear and saying «NO», I remember when he tore my panties, I remember crying and feeling so disgusted.

»The day after this happened Marco showed up unexpectedly. I told him what had happened the night before, I was looking for his support given the fact that I had been drugged and raped, but what he did was question me for what happened.

»His response to the event still gives me as much disgust as the rape itself. Without an ounce of mercy, he said to me: "You were a tramp. That's what you are. What was raped was your soul, and you did that yourself. I step out of your life for one minute and look at what you're doing. I have no choice but to get back with you out of pity, to help you out, but I hope you know that another man wouldn't do this. We men like clean women, not tramps like you. You don't deserve a man like me, but I'm going to have mercy on you, because I still think there's something in you that might be worth it. But you can't go back to being a tramp like you were, or manipulating me with pregnancies, or calling me non-stop when you have those silly little girl attacks. Understood?". I remained silent after his words, I felt that I was depraved and that he was giving me a second chance.

—He gaslighted you —Mariana pointed out, after my interruption. It's a type of psychological abuse in which someone is made to question their own reality. It consists of denying reality, taking for granted something that never happened or presenting false information in order to make the victim doubt their memory and perception.

—At that moment, the only thing I felt was guilty, I believed I was one hundred percent responsible for what happened. Guilty of everything, even of getting pregnant — I carried on.

—Valentina, for a pregnancy to happen, you need two. It's not your fault.

I try not to think about the guilt so that I can continue with the story.

—I stayed with him, and by February I had already moved by myself to an apartment located one block away from the company where Marco worked. He always came by before and after work, stayed for half an hour or, when I was lucky, for an hour.

»On Valentine's Day we went to a hotel to celebrate. That was my gift, spending the day together watching movies. When he arrived, he opened a bottle of wine. I remember that I was the only one who drank it because he felt like drinking cognac. After two glasses of wine, it happened again. The blackouts. Memories come to me in pieces, and they're not so sharp. Me in the bathtub motionless while Marco was combing my hair, me tied up on the bed, me with his penis in my mouth, me vomiting, crying, clutching the pillow, me screaming in pain, bleeding, collapsing, me saying, for the thousandth time NO…

— The human brain can only process two sudden changes in a short time window, of around three to six months. You had a lot of changes in a year and a half, Valentina, you were very strong, stronger than average — Mariana gives me support so I can continue.

—Yes. It's crazy to think that all of that happened in the short span of a year and a half. Emigrating to Miami, emigrating to Milan, meeting Ali, breaking up with Joel, two rapes, an abortion; living with my aunt, then in a shared apartment and then alone. How did my body hold on through that storm? How did I not die? How did I not end up in a mental hospital?

»After moving to the apartment near his work, I thought that my life had already changed, that I was in a stable relationship, that the previous episodes were unimportant compared to the fact that we were together. Nothing could be further away from the truth. He was nice to me at first, but then he started calling me nicknames, derogatory nicknames. When I asked him out on dates, he always told me he was busy. It seemed suspicious to me, to be honest. There was a time when he told me that there were things that he hadn't told me, but he didn't bother to tell me and I didn't make a big deal out of it. I should have pressed on to find out.

Mariana makes a strange face and I finish spitting out everything that's missing.

— I was "the other one", I didn't find out until after I ended it. I found out about it thanks to a girl who worked at that company, whom I crossed ways by chance later on. What she told me was that he was married and had a child. I spent with him the few hours he visited me in the apartment he rented for me, for his «lover», which, basically, places me in the category of «husband-snatcher veneca[32]» even if I didn't know anything about it. That's why we didn't go out on dates as much, and when we went out to lunch, he always put me on the back tables and took me to weird restaurants. I don't understand, Mariana, I don't understand how I didn't suspect it before. The relationship with him gave me a lot of anxiety, but I couldn't focus on the elements that caused that state. My anguish was such that, one day, alone in the apartment, I looked at myself in the mirror and I had bald spots on my head: I was suffering from alopecia. On top of that, I weighed so little, you could see my ribs.

»And well, to finish with the story. A month after the rape I called him to tell him I had to pay the rent. He came by that afternoon, after work, and brought me the money but it was incomplete. When I asked him why, he told me that he was discounting my restaurant visits, that I couldn't expect that he was going to support me. That was when I

---

[32] *Veneco o veneca* is a pejorative expression used outside of Venezuela against Venezuelan immigrants. Its use began in Colombia, but has spread to other countries. (Editor's Note)

said to him, "This is as far as we'll go". And when I said goodbye, he just commented as if he was talking to a hysterical person: "Well, you'll get over it" and left. After that I called my parents, I told them what was happening without a lot of details, and they sent me money and took care of me until I got my current job — I finished the story, taking a breath of air.

— You told me at some point that you had taken pills that the psychiatrist prescribed you and that you were on contraceptives. Can you tell me exactly what pills you were taking? —Mariana asks me in a soft voice.

—Clonazepam.

—And what birth control?

—Well, I went through all the ones out there, pills, patches, injections, they all had side effects on me.

—When did you stop the contraceptives and when did you stop with clonazepam? Give me the chronological order of the story with Voldemort and the pills.

—Well, when the thing with Ali happened, when I was very attracted to him and he sometimes treated me nice and sometimes ignored me, that situation gave me a lot of anguish and they prescribed me clonazepam. When I decided to end it with Ali and started with Voldemort, I was only taking oral contraceptives. I had days when I forgot to take my birth control. In general, I was forgetting a lot of things. I also remember that I lost my sense of time and space for brief moments, you know? Like with Alzheimer's, I didn't know where I was or where I was going. Then when I got pregnant, when I took the test and I knew I would have a child, I stopped taking everything all at once. A few weeks later I had an abortion and, well, the abortion was with pills.

—Did you take any of the medications again after the abortion?

—Yes, birth control when I got back with Voldemort because I was terrified of getting pregnant again.

—When did the rapes happen? —Mariana asks, with the purpose of creating a timeline between the events and the medications.

—The one by my «friend» —I say doing air-quotes— a month after the abortion. And with Voldemort, a month after the first time; on February 14 to be precise.

—When did you get back with Voldemort? —Mariana is taking notes on her computer.

—One day after the night of the rape.

—When did you quit for good?

—A month after February 14th, when I had to pay the rent for March.

—Valentina, I think you compromised your body's hormones, without realizing it, especially with the contraceptives. Contraceptives alter hormone function and the interactions between them, which can lead to the loss of the ability we call "common sense", that's why you didn't ask yourself questions, that's why you didn't suspect, either that he was married or the seriousness of the rest of the things you're telling me. Besides, you stopped taking clonazepam all at once, and that has side effects too. It wasn't your fault. It's never been your fault. And you weren't stupid. No. You were chemically unbalanced. We have done tests and exams, and I have been seeing you long enough to consider that you have a high IQ, that you are able to identify a predator. What happened was his fault, you're the victim. You had the role of victim for too long because of the drugs that prevented you from having mental clarity, but it was in no way your fault. You can take that burden off your shoulders, and, my friend, you are not alone. You are a strong woman. Now, use your intellect to make a decision with H, whether it's just being his friend or telling him about your wishes. Don't be afraid. Believe in yourself.

---

As I leave the consultation, I feel an immense need to call H. Not to tell him that I want to be his girlfriend, but to tell him what happened. I want to take advantage of this impulse to confess to him where I'm coming from. I think he should know first about the baggage I carry, before I throw a romantic confession at him.

I get home, light a cigarette and decide to call H. Before doing that, I send him a message:

*Hi, can we talk?*

My phone rings right away. It's him.

—What happened? You don't want to be my friend anymore?

I laugh right away.

—I mean, yes, but no.

—Hey, let's switch to a video call so I can see you —he says.

I comply with his request, and when his beautiful little face appears on the screen, I blush.

—Now, look at you, with your nicely combed and perfect hair —he says to me.

—Well, in my defense, I have to tell you that I just got back from a consultation with my therapist.

—How did it go? —he asks while he's making a protein shake. He's disheveled and sweaty. He looks beautiful. I gather he just got home from the gym.

—Well, there are things I want to tell you, but they are heavy.

—You can tell me. I am always willing to listen to you. Tell me.

—It's just that I like formalities, and since what I have to tell you is hard, I would like us to talk about it one day when you have the time and all your attention is on me. I know you're getting home from the gym; I know you have things to do, and obviously I do too. What I want to tell you should be done in person, not through the phone, but given the circumstances...

—1411 kilometers, I know — he interrupts me.

—Exactly. That's why I was telling you. I would like us to have a serious meeting, also on a video call, when you can, when we are both free and we can chat. What do you think?

—Yes, of course, if that's what you want, it's not a problem for me. How about tonight?

—Yeah, that's fine. I can do it tonight. 7:00 p.m.?

—Yes, ma'am, seven o'clock is perfect. Now, I'm going to be intrigued all afternoon, hahaha.

I laugh too, and we say goodbye.

# The truth chamber

I'm back from the gym, I took a long shower and I'm in my bed dressed to go to bed and with the laptop on my legs. I know that the decision I have made to tell H everything is the right one. He's the one who initiates the video call we agreed to have earlier today.

—Hi, MJ. Here I am, ready for our date, without any interruptions and still very intrigued. —Like me, H is in bed with his laptop.

The blue sheets he uses bring back beautiful memories, not like the ones I have to share with him. «Life is full of contradictions», I think to myself, and I find the courage to tell him one of the most bitter chapters in the story of my life.

—H, I told you today that I went to see my therapist. Her name is Mariana.

—Yes, you told me that what you were going to tell me was heavy. I remember each one of your words.

—Well, I went to the consultation and there, I managed to unlock an episode from my past that I feel disgusted and ashamed about. I lived with that for over a year and a half; I hadn't even been able to tell my therapist. —I remain silent for a moment.

—Again, MJ, I'm here for you, for whatever, for whatever you need.

—Okay, if you are willing to listen, well I am willing to talk, it's important that you know what happened to me because I am a nervous person. Life fucks us all, no one leaves this world being a virgin, but there are some fucks that hurt. Sometimes we can make them not affect us, or, as is my case, we manage to ignore and hide them. What I'm trying to do is face them, but sometimes it seems that the same nightmare is waiting for the right moment to appear and fuck up your life, and I want you to know about me and my things, because I want you to be in my life, and I want you to know about my fears.

—Calm down, MJ. I can hear you. —He answered me with such certainty that I no longer had doubts about uncovering the past.

—Okay. —I grab some air and start telling him all about the «Black Plague» and the villain «Voldemort».

H listens carefully to me, and only opens his eyes from time to time with a sense of surprise, but most of the time he frowns without saying a word. He takes great care to not interrupt me. His silence makes me feel comfortable, so comfortable that I even give him other details that I had not told my psychologist, like that a few months ago I had found out, from a former employee of the company, that Ali, Voldemort and Jackson had bet money on whether we would get back together after the abortion. Federico found it to be despicable, but he never took any real action in the matter.

By the time I'm finished with my whole confession, H stares at me and adds:

—What a bastard, that son of a bitch. What a despicable being, I don't understand what the motherfucking hell is going on in people's minds *de pana* [33]. It makes me so angry that a woman that is so beautiful inside and out like you has lived something like that. As a man, I know there are women who go through this, but when it's someone you care about, it hits hard on the ego. —He takes a breath of air and in a calmer voice adds—: I'm sorry MJ, I'm really sorry. And I apologize to you as a man.

---

[33] In Venezuela the word pana means «friend», but the expression de pana means «really». That is the meaning in this context. (Editor's Note)

Tears come out, but they are not sad tears for what I just told him, I feel that's behind me, I'm excited because of H, because of his solidarity, his support and backing. «Human beings are so different. There are thousands of galaxies between this man and the one who offended me when I told him about being raped» is what I think. H brings me back to the moment.

—MJ, like you said, life fucks with us all, and it's fucking awful that life did that to you! Those assholes who passed through your life did not manage to tear down your essence. The whole thing has been a nightmare, shit! Now you've got to keep going; learn from that and improve as a human being

«H for Hero».

After such a confession, I decide that it's not the time to tell him that I love him just yet. Despite his receptivity and support, I think it was too intense. I think the both of us have had enough for today. I also want him to process the information I just gave him.

—H —I add— there are still many things that happened to me that I have not told you about, from other past relationships, but I will tell you little by little, okay?

—I'm willing to listen to it all, MJ. You could tell me all the bad things they did to you and you could tell me the bad things that perhaps you have done; that would never change my opinion, that you are an extraordinary woman.

Tears are coming out of my eyes. I love him. I swear I love him with all the U's and I's: Undeniably, irrefutably, undoubtedly, indisputably, and now with an r, rationally.

It's already the next day and I realize that telling H about my past made me sleep better. I know what I'm going to say sounds crazy, but I felt him with me last night, hugging me, like a good ghost that keeps me company.

# The call for change

H has told me that he wants to move, because after the break-up, there are only memories left there. Which inspired me to do the same; the apartment where I live is the same one from the black plague, so I could use a change.

I log on to the PC looking for apartment listings. And, the truth is, I don't know if the owners of my apartment gives me a special price or something, because everything I see far exceeds my budget. So, I simply convince myself that when the opportunity for a better apartment comes around, I'll take it.

For now, the only thing that is in my control is to change the things inside my apartment, to give it a fresh look. When I just moved here, the place was barely furnished: it had a bed, a sofa, a microwave, but there were no accessories, no dishes, no cutlery, no sheets or towels, and I only had my suitcase with my clothes.

I didn't have any money at that time either, because I was living on government aid, so I wrote to my government tutor to ask if he could help me with some things. He recommended a refugee Facebook group to me, where they were donating household items. There I met a very friendly Italian lady who invited me to her house and gave me a set of cutlery and dishes, as well as some towels and sheets, and my Aunt Eugenia gave me a blanket and a duvet for the winter.

Although the memory is still a little bittersweet, I'm not one of those who drown thinking about where they come from and where they are standing; I do not belong to the group of people who come to question themselves saying "I come from a private university, and my parents are business owners, and here I am, picking up towels at a strange lady's house I met in a refugee group." No, that's not my narrative. My parents taught me well that hard times exist, and you have to get through them. I just did what I had been taught, I didn't need to get sad with arguments about loss.

I know there are worse things, in fact, there are Venezuelans who have been hit much harder. By God, there are still families walking to other countries through inhospitable and risky areas to get out of the hole that Venezuela has become. When I had to receive help in the shape of plates, cutlery, sheets and towels, I felt privileged, but right now, I can buy new ones. It sounds silly, but «I can buy towels and sheets» in my reality, are big words that now fit in my mouth.

CHAPTER IV | Shadows of desire

# Instigations

The day at work has been slow, so I decided to paint my nails. Every time I do it, I ask H for a color; I've already made a habit of asking him. I take out my box of nail polish and send him a picture.

*It's time. Choose a color. Porfis* [34].
*Wine color. That color suits you.*
*You always choose red colors. How boring.*
*Well, I had to choose red, because lately you've been going for soft and neutral colors, which look good on you too, but I prefer reds, and especially when you have nails like that, a little longer.*

It feels sweet having H choose my nail polish, and having him say things like, it looks good on you, or that they're a little longer now.

When I crossed paths with him in Madrid, I remember that he told me that he didn't find it very attractive for a woman to dress up "too much", but I think his definition of too much had more to do with exaggeratedly long nails, with crystals, 2016 style makeup and platform heels. We both agree that some women look good and feel comfortable in those styles, but it's just not the style that I, Maria Santini, wear, and it's not H's style of preference regarding women. He even told me

---

[34] *Porfis, is a way used in Venezuela to shorten the expression Please. (Editor's Note)*

at some point that his exes never wore makeup or painted their nails, that it seemed unnecessary for a woman to do so. «They get carried away by your opinion, but that's not my case» I thought back then, but I didn't tell him.

He was very intimidated when we had that conversation. Back then he said to me, «Please, if I say something that isn't right, correct me. I don't want to step on a ground that doesn't belong to me as a man, but the reality is, that I have my preference for how I like a woman with whom I am romantically involved to look like. In my ignorance on the topic, I like a natural look better, but maybe tomorrow I'll meet someone and I'll like them with those eyelash and nail things, I don't close myself in because I don't think it's wrong, it's just that so far, I haven't liked anyone who is into that».

I remember that in that conversation I was provoking him, asking him about the weight of his romantic partners and about body hair. His answer was «I am a man who takes care of his diet and goes to the gym. I want a woman who does the same, but that doesn't mean she has to be skinny, there are many beautiful girls in my gym that aren't precisely skinny, but they're always there. I want someone who is active and eats well. They don't have to look a certain way. Regarding body hair, well, what do you want me to say? Venezuelan women got me used to no body hair, but if I like the girl, I'll take it as it comes. It's not like I'm not going to eat her out because she has hair, or I'm going to slow down because she has her period». I laughed at the memory.

I'm always provoking H with awkward questions just to check what he's thinking. And he, with his answers secures and saves his place in my life, the reality is that he is a man with the right type of mindset for me.

# Vices, discussions and comparisons

H and I are always debating on our points of view. Sometimes the arguments are provoked by me and other times by him, I think that's the way we have found to stay close and get to know each other. Today we discussed some of our beliefs. H is an agnostic, with all the letters, and I am a universalist, therefore, H's view on the subject is completely different from mine. We don't need to believe in the same thing, just respect each other and what we think, so it's fun to debate with H on this topic, or any other.

The truth is that sometimes, while debating, we get a little heated and the situation turns into quarrel mode; we are so fixated on our ideas that the other's point of view seems crazy to us. However, we always turn the table and return to our intimate way of communicating; if I say something like, «Shut up», he replies, «Come and shut me up». And H can say things to me in the middle of an argument, like «I like arguing with you». Needless to say, there is a very marked Arian energy. H is Aries, and I am ascending in Aries. These quarrels, that never end up with being angry, are a way of showing affection and fondness.

At some point during our talks, H asked me what I was doing, and I honestly confessed to him that I was smoking. I can't say he got upset, he never did, really, but he did talk to me in a paternalistic tone advising me to not keep doing it. I had to explain to him how my whole process had been with that vice, which was somehow also linked to the eating problems I had been through.

I used to smoke a pack of cigarettes in two days, given that Voldemort and all my exes also smoked; when I was with them, I smoked a lot. Once I was single and during covid, I organized myself and prescribed myself a routine that helped control that vice and didn't make me feel disgusted by myself or by the cigarette.

I usually only smoke three cigarettes during the day: one, at eleven in the morning; then another, at three in the afternoon; and the last one, before going to bed. I've gotten my body so used to that exact dose of nicotine that when I've only smoked two cigarettes a day I can't sleep, and if I smoke four, I feel bad and it makes me anxious.

After listening to my explanations about the cigarette habit, H congratulated me, told me that he admired me for the way I was taking on the challenge of quitting a harmful habit. H can really take any story to make me feel good about myself.

Unlike the exes from my past, H *doesn't smoke, doesn't drink, and he doesn't dance cheek to cheek* [35]. Well, he does, but only when he goes to summer festivals. It's not something that is part of his routine; in fact, H has as a no alcohol in his house rule.

In the same conversation about smoking, H invited me to start eating vegan. He said that he was doing his best not to consume animal-based foods, and that gave rise to another discussion, not because I disagreed, but because I had to explain my whole story with food to him. I even told him that I had to talk to a nutritionist and my psychologist about it, because my relationship with food has not been the best or the prettiest.

---

[35] The phrase is used in Venezuela to describe or criticize the attitude of someone when he is not a regular party goer. (Editor's Note)

When I was a kid, I only ate pasta and nuggets. My poor mom was desperate, as I didn't get the necessary nutrients and because of my bad eating habits I was always sick. During that stage, I was in the hospital at Christmas, birthdays and other holidays. This is also the reason why I developed late, at the age of fifteen, and now I have endometriosis. The truth is that I started taking control of what I eat and trying to adapt it to my body and my needs, in serious way and on my own, less than a year ago, and then I had considered being a vegan, because sometimes felt guilty, but my psychologist at the time told me: «Maria Valentina, eat! Whatever you want to eat, but eat! And then one step at a time we're going to organize your ethics regarding food, for now just give your body food».

The truth is that before I could spend up to twenty-four hours without feeling hungry or eating, and I didn't even realize it. I was so thin that a size zero from Zara was too big for me. And it seemed incredible to me how that idiot Voldemort had the nerve to call me «fat».

My problem with food didn't come from a fear of looking a certain way, my eating disorder was one of restriction, I just didn't like to eat. There were foods that by their texture, taste, smell or color gave me nausea. I also had episodes where in the middle of a meal, which I considered delicious, I got sick and had to run to the bathroom and vomit. But this doesn't happen anymore. Now I am more aware of what I do like and what I don't, I am more in touch with my body and I know myself better; I know that the combination of white rice with avocado in a single bite inside my mouth feels funny and pleasant. I know that I love roast chicken with mashed potatoes and that salmon with asparagus is something I would always like to eat, even when I'm not hungry, therefore, if I don't want to eat, I just make me some salmon, which is great progress because I didn't eat anything from the sea before.

For me, every bite, and every meal is like telling my body «I love you and I take care of you because you are important». After having lived through that eating disorder, it is obvious that, for now, it was not in my plans to be a vegan.

But, regardless of the fact that being a vegan was not part of my options, H's words moved me, I was pleased that H was looking for and challenging his own ethics at a time when he has to purge himself of so many things. And I say challenge because H's favorite food is a hamburger.

When I had this discussion about veganism with H, I remember saying to him: «I feel guilty and it doesn't feel good to eat animals, it's not ethical by any means, but on the other hand, taking into account my past story with food and the fact that I come from Venezuela, where I saw people rummaging through garbage on every corner to be able to eat, I also feel guilty, wouldn't it be disrespectful to my history and my country? Shouldn't I be grateful for what I have on the table and that's it?», to which H, as accurate as always, told me: «We all have a routine based on our needs, your greatest need right now is to give your body the nutrients it deserves, don't blame yourself for problems bigger than you at the moment, it's not time for that, remember that life is like a plane in an emergency, you put on the mask first, so you come first and then you can think about others. I have always had a good relationship with food, that's why I can give myself the opportunity to make changes in my routine, as your psychologist said, eat what you like as you like, but eat taking into account your nutritional needs».

These discussions with H are a way to get to know each other, to know our points in common around any topic, to respect each other in our differences, to feel close, but, fundamentally, H opens a window and an opportunity to be myself, he knows me, restores me and makes me feel good. When I talk to H I know that anything is possible because there are people as beautiful as him in the world.

# On any given monday

On Sunday nights you should dream of warning signs, with bright lights that remind you «tomorrow is Monday, it's a work day», but it never happens and Monday always comes without expecting it, so getting out of bed has been an ordeal. Really, on the first day of the week the sheets have more lazy dust than anyone other.

I had a protein shake and then I came straight to work because, as always, I'm running late. Bah! I packed myself a sandwich in case I get hungry in a while.

When I got to my workplace, I decided to check the meetings and emails for the day. I usually even put lunch time on my calendar so that the time doesn't run out thinking about pregnant birdies . Unlike H, my relationship with time is lousy and I don't know how to measure it well. A minute can feel like an hour and an hour can feel like a minute and it doesn't matter what the situation is, it just happens.

I see that I have a meeting with Antonio, the tax guy from Mexico. Apparently, a company has problems with its paperwork and we have been charging them wrong on many invoices. Therefore, we have to get involved in checking invoice by invoice, the process is called invoice reconciliation.

The meeting is at two o'clock in the afternoon here, which would be the first hour of the work day in Mexico. It's half past nine in the morning, so it gives me a chance to check my email inbox.

I answer a quick text to H on the topic we are talking about right now, about how I think the belief of God goes hand in hand with being in love.

---

[36] An expression used colloquially in Venezuela that means to be distracted, to waste time thinking about unsolvable or irrational issues. (Editor's Note)

*People believe in God more when they are in love, perhaps because they see everything through rose-colored glasses.*

I put my phone on sleep mode, and put it inside the drawer to make sure I won't be checking if H answered, because it distracts me a lot.

When I'm almost done cleaning my inbox, I get a message from Mattia through the chat at work; he asks me if I brought lunch. And then I realized that I was in the zone for almost two hours. Wow! What a great Monday! I managed to reduce my attention deficit. What music am I listening to? Ah! Yeah, it's One Direction. I always manage to do responsible adult work when I have my little British babies in my headphones.

I answer Mattia that I didn't bring anything and he recommends that I go down to the cafeteria to buy something before noon, that way I won't stand in line and we can eat together. I do as he tells me and grab my cigarettes to make the most out of it.

When I'm having lunch with Mattia in the office dining room, I get a notification from Google photos and, distracted, I go in to check what's going on. It's a memory line and among the memories there is a photo with Voldemort. I quickly log out of the app and try not to give too much attention to the matter because I don't want to ruin my meal. I need to be more responsible and not use the phone when I eat.

—Are you paying attention to what I'm saying? —Mattia asks me.

—Oh, dude, yeah, I'm sorry, I got distracted, Gaby agreed to go out with you and then canceled on you.

—Yes, but you didn't hear why she canceled on me.

—Let's see... - I say with curiosity.

— She told me that her day had gotten complicated, and then I saw that Michele posted an Instagram story with her.

—Stop being stupid and calm down. She was helping Michele to choose the engagement ring for his husband.

—Michele is gay?

—SUPER-GAY! The thing is that he doesn't want anyone to know, he is aware that with his looks he attracts many women and he likes the attention, one day he said to me: «I can't make it public, can you imagine all these disappointed women, no, I can't deal with all that sadness». —Mattia looks at me with a surprised look on his face—. Besides, I think he has an open relationship with his boyfriend because I've seen him here in clubs making out with girls. In fact, do you know my group of friends? —Mattia nods slightly. Well, once we met at a nightclub and Michele took my friend Soffia.

—But why didn't Gabriella ask to postpone it after canceling with me? I mean, if she was really interested in me, then she could say: I can't today, but I can tomorrow.

—Baby, she said so herself, she was full up, and complicated. If you really like her, then be patient and ask her out again, and make the date unforgettable. Try to think about her, about what she would like, now is not the time to think about whether she likes you or not, you are a guy who likes a girl, conquer her - I say in a soft voice so that he understands.

—It's true. I'll do that.

Italians are very intense and romantic, but Mattia came factory defective. It feels good to be able to help him.

In my short experience with men, I have stated that there are different groups, the Mr. Bingley's, who are shy, but full of love to give; the Mr. Wickham's, charming but narcissistic and/or with a victim complex, those who sell you a charade; the Mr. Collins, weird, just weird, I don't think they're bad, but they are not my type, and, of course, the Mr. Darcy's, confident, proud and defiant, it's not that they think they are better than the rest, they simply are. In this classification, the only ones I would warn the girls about are the Mr. Wickham's, those are the most common ones you'll find. There are also some that have a little bit of one and a little bit of another.

Mattia is from the Bingley group, he has a lot of love to give, but he is kind of clumsy in doing it and thinks things too much. He is the kind who builds ideas from a momentary rejection, he is the kind who thinks that if the girl says "I'm busy" it means that she doesn't want anything to do with him, his shyness doesn't allow him to ask and clear up his doubts, he takes the rejection for granted, even gets ahead of it or makes it up; he is a Bingley who is afraid of his Jane.

## 911, H Emergencies

My Monday continues, and once Mattia and I get back to work, I go to the bathroom to brush my teeth. Since it's still forty-five minutes until my meeting, I decide to check my phone again to see what Voldemort crap still exists in my digital life. I knew that I had deleted everything from my iCloud, but I didn't know that there was still evidence in Google Photos. I filter by year, 2019-2020, the time of the black plague. And I start checking.

«Ugh! It's all here. I have to delete it».

There are even screenshots, I go in to check that first and I say to myself, «I want to see what we were talking about, the truth is that I still don't understand what I saw in him, I guess at least we had good conversations». I find a 'poem' that he once recited to me:

«You are a beautiful rose that has so many layers that it blooms pleasantly and is the symbol of love and beauty. Even when you're dry, you're a rose. So, I promise today right now, to love you on your best and worst day. In the worst moments, even if the world reflects you, you will always see me behind you showing all my support, I will always be by your side». I decided to take a line from the 'poem' and Google it because I am sure that peanut head is not capable of writing poetry, besides that poetry seems from the 1600s, «Oh, yes, I'm a rose. Bastard!».

As expected, I got the poem on a website with the title poems about roses. I start to feel nauseous. I found another screenshot from a fight we had where he blocked me and disappeared for three days, typical of a narcissist. I also came across the list of gifts he asked me to make, which I then ended up buying out of pride because he didn't give me anything. And of course, I didn't have the money, but I had to show him that if I wanted something, I got it by my own means.

Then, I found some photos of a skin reaction I had, where I swelled up and had facial cellulite. Now I think that all that came from the level of stress I was subjected to.

I keep looking and I find the worst: videos of us having sex. Videos that I didn't want to make, but he begged and manipulated me until he got it. In fact, now I remember, he threatened to leave me because it wasn't normal for a girlfriend not to want to make a video with her boyfriend. I quickly turn down the volume of the phone to zero and lock myself in one of the compartments to see it, one doesn't know when someone else may come into the bathroom.

««Ugh! So disgusting». You can clearly tell I'm uncomfortable. It looks like I'm watching a rape video. He is visibly just masturbating with my body, and I am just there, there is no pleasure on my face, I am his flesh and blood sex doll, cheaper than a tramp, because at least they charge.

I delete everything I find, suddenly I find a conversation where he was telling me something comforting: «Hey, baby, I know you're not feeling well today, but if you need anything tell me, if I can help you, just let me know, I'm here for you, baby, I'm your boyfriend and I'll do anything for you». My disgust drastically changes to comfort. «What is this? Why do I feel this way?». I remind myself that he is a villain, that everything is a farce. I also delete that conversation and go back to my desk.

---

I'm on the video meeting with Antonio, the guy from Mexico, checking one invoice at a time. I've had a hard time concentrating, but I'm getting there, when we are forty minutes into the review, Antonio tells me:

—Hey, Valentina, I'm going to get up and pour myself a cup of coffee really quick, so if you hear some noise, it's me in the kitchen, okay?

—Yeah, no problem.

Sure enough, I hear noises, something falls, and he lets out a sigh, like a complaint.

The noise of the cup falling and Antonio's sigh makes me go into a hallucination where I can't move. My heart rate rises, I start to feel a headache, the oxygen in the room runs out and my tears start to flow, but I can't move.

The sigh. «Where have I heard that exact same sound?».

My brain remembers the sound and shows me a vivid image, the root of the trauma, in the middle of my paralysis.

Voldemort once called me to talk about «something important». We were arguing because he knew that I liked Ali, and he wanted me to explain, in great detail, about my relationship with him. When I'm explaining to him for the millionth time that Ali was just ignoring me, that nothing really happened, I started to hear panting, I asked him what the noise was, and he replied that he was lifting weights at home to relieve stress.

When my brain brings me to the present, still motionless, I say to myself: «That noise was not from exercises, he was masturbating while talking to me, because I was his private sex doll». When I reconstruct the moment in my head and become aware of what had really happened, the pain of knowing that I was somebody's object invaded me, that call was a violent act towards me that will never be recognized as such. «He used me. He used my voice to turn himself on. He's f***ing worse than the name I gave him».

Antonio's voice pulls me out of my paralysis, and I only manage to say.

—I'm sorry, I have to go. It's an emergency.

I hung up. I grab my things however I can and tell my boss that I have to leave.

—Valentina, you're pale, are you okay?

—I just want to leave. Please —I beg her between sobs.

—Yes, go ahead. Take the day.

When I leave the building, I call a taxi and light a cigarette while I wait. Getting into the taxi, still unable to breathe, I message H.

*Are you there? It's an emergency.*
*I'm in a meeting. Tell me, I can start reading.*
*I'm having a panic attack.*
*Just a minute.*

It's the last thing he types, his call comes in right away.
- MJ, what's up?
Between sobs I give him the details of what just happened.
—I'm sorry, baby. That's so fucked up.
I just cry.
—I don't know what else to tell you. I don't know what to advise you —H says—. I wish I was there with you to hug and comfort you.
The truth is that just with the sound of his voice, I find peace and calm. Knowing that he would never do a thing like that to me puts the air back in my lungs.
—You don't have to do anything, listening to me is enough.
—For what it's worth, I was in a meeting with the CEO of a Japanese company, a very important meeting, but it seemed to me that it was more important to listen to you, MJ. I'm here for you.
H, my good love.
—You know what? —I tell him—. I also found some old conversations, and it was strange because I felt like I was loved, like I had been important at some point for him.
—No, not that, Maria Valentina —he tells me in a serious and rough tone, it's the first time I've heard him like that. No aggressor, listen to me well, no aggressor deserves your empathy. He manipulated you, abused you, lied to you, played with you as he pleased. I'm asking you, please, to delete any positive feelings you have about him or whatever. That man hurt you, humiliated you and deserves absolutely nothing nice from you.
The rough tone of his voice didn't scare me, on the contrary, it alerted me and made me feel like I was in a boxing ring with Voldemort, I was winning, and H was my coach telling me where to hit him to finish him with a knock out and win that fight.

—Let's see. Don't harm yourself like that. If I'm honest, I do that sometimes. Suddenly, I find an album or something with a picture of my ex. MJ, it was two years, obviously, I have a lot of photographs and memories. And I understand, I know that you time travel just by seeing a photo and the memory becomes too clear. But it's not real, the fact that you time travel in that way is a mutilation. Please, put those thoughts far away, put the feeling away, it's not real. The only real thing is what is happening right now. Don't make a memory come true.

As always, he's right. I shouldn't hurt myself.

# Atitigo

I miss my family; I've hardly been able to talk to my mom lately. Venezuela is not getting any better and the problems with electricity and the internet have made it difficult for us to communicate. Today I need to listen to her voice a lot and tell her that I'm missing everyone here, that the friends I can communicate with aren't enough for me to feel the warmth of my home. I try to talk to her and send her a quick message to see if I can call her.

> *Hi, what'cha doing? What'cha doing that you don't love me? Do you have any other daughters? do you call them?*

LI'm writing to her like a spoiled child throwing a tantrum.
My mom's call comes in right away.
- Moommy!, my blessing? [37]. How are you?
—God bless you, my baby girl. Mi amor, we don't have electricity.
—We'll talk another day, then. —The tears come right away. I've been emotional lately, I don't like it when I don't talk to my mommy, my mom is one of my best friends in the world.
—No, mi amor, I'll tell your dad to add recharge money to my phone

---

[37] It is customary in Venezuela to ask to be blessed by parents, uncles, grandparents and godparents, it is the first greeting that is given. The answer is always "God bless you" and then the conversation continues as usual. (Editor's Note)

later. When there is power there is no internet, and when there is no power the phone works. Let's talk now, we haven't talked in a while.
My mommy and I are catching up. She tells me that she has joined the gym and that a friend of my brother's is her personal trainer.
My brother lives in North Carolina, together with his lifelong girlfriend, his high school sweetheart, Adriana.
—Oh, Mommy, that's great! And what do you know about Luciano? I haven't talked to him either.
—Mi amor, he's fine, he's working. He just got a big project for a Walmart that they're building and well he is pulling it off almost by himself.
My brother is doing very well in the United States, he has a position as project manager in a construction company. He has political asylum; I was in charge of gathering the evidence for him and his girlfriend for their asylum.
My brother had been a front of the line *guarimbero* [38], and Adriana was a professional making *miguelitos* [39]. But me, as a good Libra, was terrified of conflict. Those confrontation scenarios made me too nervous; if there was anyone useless in that war, it was me, so my contribution was with my mom: we made food for the *guarimberos*, that was our small contribution. We were all involved in those protests; my dad would build the boys shields from industrial oil metal drums that he would cut in half, and I, with my spiritual aura, would put a Viking symbol of protection on them with spray paint. My mom's part, in addition to bringing them meals, was to meet with the other moms of the neighborhood to pray the rosary every day for the peace of Venezuela.

---

[38] In Venezuela, street protests against the government have been called guarimbas , which consist of taking the roads and making barricades to hinder traffic and prevent the free movement of government forces. The government's repression of these protests has left people dead, injured, imprisoned and persecuted.
[39] Miguelitos are crossed nails that, when organizing the guarimbas, get thrown onto the road to deflate tires. (Editor's Note)

I don't know if it was the prayers or the Viking runes, but in my neighborhood, we didn't lose a single boy. We were lucky, my brother only had a few pellet marks, nothing serious or too major.

It was a war where many young people got caught and were submitted to physical and psychological torture, and got disappeared and imprisoned. Many mothers lost their children.

I remember once that in a neighborhood meeting the head of the guarimberos said in front of everyone, «I prefer that my blood be spilled on the streets of my country, then to live in a dictatorship that keeps us silent, kneeling and going hungry».

After the government repression, the entire group of guarimberos from my neighborhood had to go into exile, and, of course, most of them, including my brother, cannot set foot in Venezuela again as long as the corrupt government continues to be in place.

Venezuela is a long and painful chapter in the book of my life, and unfortunately, it's a story that still doesn't have a happy ending. But in my heart, I'm sure that will change one day.

I have a vivid image in my dreams of being in front of the Caribbean Sea, in a free Venezuela, giving my children their bath at the beach. In my mind, my future, who will be my children, will meet my past, they will discover themselves in the accent, in eating fried fish and tostones with their hands. I hope they'll find themselves there, where I have always been: in the blue of the sea, in the Andes mountains, in the sand of the dunes, in the rain of the Gran Sabana and riding horseback in the plains.

—My child, what's wrong with you? I'm talking and you seem distracted. My eyes are watery like a lagoon.

—Mommy, I just miss you. —My voice is breaking.

—Oh, my honey, me too. I promise I'll come visit soon, let me organize things with your dad —she says, like an oak tree. My mom is incredibly strong. I am too, but right now, talking to her, I feel like I'm a thirteen-year-old girl.

—Honey, tell me what's going on. I know something else is going on.

—Mommy, I'm in love with someone.

—With who, my honey?

—Mom, do you remember H?

—Luis Miguel's brother? Of course, you didn't stop talking about him when you were little. I remember, he was such a cute little boy!

—Well, Mommy, when I was in Madrid we met by chance and now I love him so much - I tell her in between sobs.

—Mi amor, but tell me, what's wrong? Why are you crying for loving someone? Doesn't he reciprocate?

—Mommy, it's just complicated. He lives in Paris, I live here, and he's six months into breaking up with his girlfriend of two years, and I've been really affected after Voldemort. I'm too sensitive, I feel like I love him to death, but let's be honest, it's complicated.

My mom didn't even know what had happened to Voldemort, that was a pain from which I wanted to protect her, both her, my dad and my brother.

—Honey, listen to me. Don't start crying because of that, my pretty girl. You are such an amazing woman, so beautiful, that, if he doesn't move heaven and earth to be with you, then someone else will.

Thinking about putting someone else on my horizon other than H, seems to me the most illogical thing in the world.

—But I want him —I say, in a tantrum tone of voice.

—Maria Valentina, I'm going to pray to the Blessed Sacrament for you, so that you have clarity — she says to me in a serious and dry tone.

I didn't need the church, I needed H.

—That's not necessary, Mommy. I'm just telling you.

—Well, okay, my girl.

We were silent for a few seconds and then my mom tells me:

—And what if I casually talk to Marisela? She plays bolas criollas where I play too. We're not as close anymore as when you and Luis Miguel were little, I hardly ever see her and when we say hi to each other it's a brief hello, but what if I track her down so that we meet «by chance», face to face, and then, you know, I buy her a coffee and we can talk, and I'll casually drop something like, you and H are…, to see what she has to say. They say that you have to conquer the mother-in-law first, so we can start by sweetening up Marisela. Right?

I burst into laughter.

-Mooom! You're so crazy!

—Well, but don't you want the boy?

—Mom, but that's just crazy.

—Oh, not that much, Marisela and I were very close friends.

My mom is the type of mom that, if I did something wrong, she would take the blame and fix the problem in two seconds.

—Thank you, Mommy, for all your ideas. But let's see what happens, I'll keep you posted.

—Okay, my girl, I love you, atitigo forever.

Atitigo means I want to be with you or at least that's what my mom used to tell me when I was a kid. It is one of the thousands of words in the special vocabulary of my house and I adore that. I love that the language can be so broad as to speak with everyone who speaks Spanish, and at the same time there can be the special words that we have in the privacy of our home, the words that we said as a child, or special names we gave to something, it's like, without an agreement, we build a unique code, the family code.

—Goodbye, Mommy, atitigo forever too. I love you.

# Swifties

I asked H, again, to choose my nail polish color. Asking for his opinion on these little things has become our habit. I enjoy it and I'm sure he does too. After choosing and painting my nails, I sent him a video modeling my hands, and in the background, you can hear «When I Look at you»

*Wow! Beautiful! I like them  .*
*You're listening to Miley Cyrus... Why don't you sing to me?*
*Aahhh, I can't sing!*
*Okay, but give it a try. I want to hear you sing.*
*Why?*
*Because I just want to hear you sing.*

I've never sung to anyone. But, for some reason, H asking me to do it makes me want to do it. So, I pluck up my courage and clear my throat.

«I'm not going to sing a cappella for my sweetie pie. Nooo, never». I play the song in the background quite loud and then I send him a voice note singing to him:

*Everybody needs inspiration*
*Everybody needs a song*
*A beautiful melody*
*When the night's so long*
*'Cause there is no guarantee*
*That this life is easy*
*Yeah, when my world is falling apart*
*When there's no light to break up the dark*

> *That's when I, I*
> *I look at you*

H answers almost immediately..

> *Hey, not bad at all, I knew you could sing and*
> *you could do it well*

I was in a choir when I was little, but I never thought I could still do it. Honestly, H awakens the unthinkable in me. «Me? Sing? What? », so I answered:

> *Thank you*

I attach a picture of my completely red face from how embarrassed I feel.

> *You're all red. Don't be embarrassed, even if*
> *you did it wrong, I would tell you politely.*
> *Mmm thanks again, I guess.*

H stops answering my texts and gives me a video call. I answer, and by then Miley Cyrus song is over and Taylor Swift is playing on YouTube.

—Mhm, you're already going for Taylor Swift.

—Oh, yes!, I like Sister Taylor. But I've hardly paid attention to this album, I'm a girl from Reputation.

—What's this one called?

—Lover, it's from 2019. If I'm not mistaken it was the album she wrote for her current boyfriend, I think his name is Joe.

—No idea. I have listened to Taylor and she is cool, I liked her country music and the «You belong with me» one was cool.

H never disappoints me. I remember the time he told me that he had seen Twilight like seven hundred times. I find it touching that he isn't afraid to show what he likes. He doesn't have fragile masculinity, he's a man who really doesn't care what people think, he's in his own world, his own vibe, doing his own stuff and is very self-confident. Typical of an Aries.

—Well, in this album there's a song with Brendon Urie, and, aaah, I love Brendon, he was a celebrity crush of mine, when he got married, I cried and everything. He made a song for his wife called "Sarah Smiles" , and, I died, the song is so beautiful.

—Play the song, I want to hear it.

—Which one? Sarah Smiles or the one with Taylor Swift?

—Both of them.

—Okay. Let's start with Sarah Smiles.

I play it on YouTube and as soon as the harmonica starts on the song I'm already smiling. When the lyrics start, H tells me.

—Sing a little too, I'll look for the lyrics here on the laptop.

—Okay —I say shyly, and I start singing

> *I was fine, just a guy living on my own*
> *Waiting for the sky to fall*
> *Then you called and changed it all, doll*
> *Velvet lips and the eyes to pull me in*
> *We both know you'd already win*
> *Mm, your original sin*
> *You fooled me once with your eyes now, honey*
> *You fooled me twice with your lies, and I say.*

Veo que H también empieza a tararear suavemente con la letra.

> *Sarah smiles like Sarah doesn't care*
> *She lives in her world, so unaware*
> *Does she know that my destiny lies with her?*
> *Sarah*
> *Oh Sarah*
> *Are you saving me?*

At the end of the song, I say:

—I love that song so much! I'll really like any song with a soft circus tone like that, and, matter of chance, Brendon and Taylor's song is like that too. —I look for the song and I say—: Can you look for it too? I feel that song is so powerful and so lyrically beautiful, but I don't know, I don't like the melody so much. You listen to it and tell me what you think.

—Okay. Let me look for the lyrics.

I wait a few seconds.

—I've got the lyrics here, Hit play on the song.

I blush and press play on the original video, which starts with an intro of them fighting in French. H listens carefully and laughs at the fight. I, obviously, don't understand a thing, but I'm content in just admiring H.

Before Brendon starts to sing, H gets up and leaves, with the video call still open.

—Is everything all right? —I ask, while I pause the video.

When I see him, he's coming back with a guitar. I look at him, with curiosity.

—Is there an acoustic version of the song? Because I already know what you mean.

—Bah, no idea – I answered, a little confused.

—Let me get the chords and we'll sing it together.

I'm floored. «Sing? With H? What! What!?».

—Okay, I found it. Look for the lyrics where the names appear, so we know when to enter and when the two of us sing and so on. What do you think, MJ?

—Okay, yeah.

Like a little girl who has just been given candy, I look for the lyrics. Once I have it, I let him know, and H tells me:

—I'm going to make the chords slow, so that you can sing nice and slow, so you don't have to worry about tone and all that, and you can sing comfortably. Okay?

With a wide admiring look, I shake my head to say yes.

H starts to slide his hands on the guitar strings, and I admire the dream I'm in for a few seconds. He's wearing a white t-shirt, his jet hair is unkempt and I can swear that his hands on the guitar make me feel happy, he seems to me like the most attractive man on the planet and the scene just adds value to all the fantasies that I've had in my head for so long.

The song is «Me!» and it's my turn to come in and sing so I get started:

*I promise that you'll never find another like me*
*I know that I'm a handful, baby, uuuhh*
*I know I never think before I jump*
*And you're the kind of guy the ladies want*
*And there's a lot of cool chicks out there*
*I know that I went psycho on the phone*
*I never leave well enough alone*
*And trouble's gonna follow where I go*
*(And there's a lot of cool chicks out there)*

I keep singing until it's H's turn to sing, and my ears are paying full attention.

*I know I tend to make it about me*
*I know you never get just what you see*
*But I will never bore you, baby*
*And there's a lot of lame guys out there*
*And when we had that fight out in the rain*
*You ran after me and called my name*
*I never wanna see you walk away*
*And there's a lot of lame guys out there*

I'm almost out of breath, he's an amazing singer, at some point I heard him humming a song in Madrid and it sounded good, but this is more serious. I am amazed at how well he does it.

H beckons me to join him in the choir.

>*Me-e-e, ooh-ooh-ooh-ooh*
>*and I won't stop, baby*
>*I'm the only one of me*
>*Baby, that's the fun of me*
>*Eeh-eeh-eeh, ooh-ooh-ooh-ooh*
>*You're the only one of you*
>*Baby, that's the fun of you*
>*And I promise that nobody's gonna love you like me*

When I finish, I just started laughing.

—I didn't know that you laughed as well when you finished singing?

—What do you mean by «as well»? —I asked, curiously.

—I don't know if you know, but when you have an orgasm, you laugh.

I'm left speechless.

—It's cute. I like that you laugh. Whatever the reason, even if you laugh at me, it would be fine. Don't leave the world without how beautiful your laughter sounds, or how beautiful your eyes look when you talk about the things that you're passionate about.

I have a knot in my stomach. «Am I dreaming? When did God decide to bless me like this?» I can't avoid having my eyes water up.

# From Milan to Paris or Paris to Milan?

I got paid, and before spending the money on dumb stuff, I decided to go to Ikea to buy new things for my house and give it a new look. Usually, Ikea stores are located on the outskirts of the city, and the company where I work is only two stops away from one. I decide to walk there right after finishing my shift and then return in a taxi with the *corotero*[44].

Once at Ikea, I'm picking out the sheets and I can't help but wonder what kind of sheets dear little Hachito would like. I would like to turn my space into something that would also be comfortable for him. I hold on to the illusion that he will visit me soon and that he will be able to feel as he makes me feel: at home.

Although I'm tempted to take a set of blue sheets with me, because they remind me of H, I don't. This is my space, and even if I want to share it with him, it's still mine. So, I opt for a light pink color and a cloud bed cover.

When I get home, I'm so tired that I decide to order McDonald's, the truth is that there is no Italian on the face of the earth who likes McDonald's, and that's fine, but they didn't live in a country where instead of French fries you got deep fried cassava. So McDonald's is also a privilege, through delivery service. So, as usual, I tell H. Specifically, I

---

[44] Any object that you don't want to mention, in Venezuela, is a coroto, and when it's an exxagerated amount, it's corotero. (Editor's Note)

write down each one of my moves.

> *Phew, I'm home now. I ended up buying sheets, towels, curtains. I'm starving and I ordered McDonald's delivery. Obviously, I just got paid and they gave me a bonus, but if you see me eating rice with lentils by the end of the month you already know why, hahaha*

> *Hahaha, let's see what you bought. Rice with lentils is a delicacy from the gods.*

I take pictures of everything and send them

> *Okay, you're making your house look beautiful, who's that for?*

> *For my husband.*

Which husband

> *You, Baby, who else? You are my husband.*

*Hahahahaha. And let's see, what pet name do you have for your husband?*

> *My papi bello, my sweetie pie, my hachito papacito, er jevito of mine.*

*Hahahahahaha my papi bello, I like it. Change my contact's name to that one.*

I do as he tells me; I take a screenshot and send it to him.

> *Hahahaha.*

...............................

[45] The expression er jevito is a colloquial one. The er refers to the article el that got the l swapped for an r to imitate the diction used in the eastern part of Venezuela. Jevito is a diminutive for jevo. Jevo or Jeva is used to refer to a boyfriend or girlfriend. (Editor's Note)

> *Hey, we're talking about everything like the crazy here, did you find an apartment to move into? The subject is worth an update, it's been several weeks.*

You have to ask H specific questions about what you want to know about him, he may avoid them, or he may answer straight to the point as well. It's as if you can only ask him yes or no questions. Which is the opposite of me, by inertia I even ask him if I should take an apple juice or a peach, I think I've really created a communicational dependence with him. I know that he also has a dependence on me, but he is definitely not as talkative. He always reads what I say, and gets busy, if I write something like «hey, answer me». When I turn to this strategy, he says that he is busy, but that he already read everything and gives me his absolute attention. It's as if Hachitos brain was modified so that when I was talking, his only focus was me, and if I needed something right away, I was the only thing that existed in the world. To receive this unlimited attention from my lifelong crush, and after being with a man who disappeared for days and didn't care about me, it felt like I was the queen of the world. But I cared about H more than my bones could handle, so I was trying to balance the communication streak and ask him a million things about his day.

> *The truth is I'm having a hard time finding one that I really like.*
> *Why?*
> *Because it's Paris! Over here you go and see an apartment and ten more people are going at the same time as you, and when you get to see it, it has the toilet in the hallway of the building and the shower in*

*the kitchen. I need a place where I really feel comfortable.*

*Oh, I understand. I hope you can find a place quickly. Hey, talking about everything and anything again, I remembered that we have a conversation on hold.*

*About what? Should I call you?*

*Yes, let me grab my food and if you want you can keep me company while I eat.*

*Sure, just let me know*

With my privileged Big Mac on the table, I call H.

—Bon Appetit.

—Thank you.

—Do you want to talk while you eat? Or do you want us to talk about something else and then move on to the pending conversation?

— Let's go and *darle plomo* to the conversation, cause the one who has to talk the most is you.

—*Plomo al hampa*[46], then. —He makes a gun with his hands.

I laugh. H and I are united by a country, a language and history in common, besides understanding each other in our idiomatic singularities, we have the same sense of humor.

—Do you remember, sometime ago, you and I were talking, and we were a little drunk, and you, probably because of the drinks, told me to go live in Paris?

---

[46] The expression *plomo al hampa* was used recurrently by a television journalist who became mayor in Caracas, Venezuela, to promote the fight against crime. It popularized and made part of common language in the country with the meaning of giving continuity to a situation: dale plomo. (Editor's Note)

—Yes, I do remember.

—Well, I want to do it. I want to move there.

H sighs in worry way.

—Maria Valentina, if I'm honest, now that I'm looking for an apartment, I've been feeling a little bit overwhelmed. Honestly, life here is not easy. Parisians are very rude, and it's not easy to make friends. Creating a life here is difficult, it's not that I don't want to, it's that I don't want you to make a drastic change in your life for me, and then if things go wrong, you'll find yourself in a city where all you have is me, and after what you've gone through, that worries me. Voldemort took you away from friends, family, work, and made him your only thing in the world, so he could hurt and manipulate you at his whim. Obviously, I'm not him, and I would never do even one percent of the damage he did to you. But what if, in bad luck, your brain takes it like that? I want you to do things for yourself. I'm not ready to take that responsibility, and you're not ready for that change either. Of course, I would love to have you here, but I want you to be happy, and this country can eat you alive. You're in Italy, where things are more colorful, people are nicer, you mention it to me all the time, even the greengrocer in the mornings says good morning to you, and when you tell me that, it makes me feel pretty jealous, I feel comforted because you have that human warmth close to you. Nobody does that here. It is a very lonely and cold country.

I felt it was a rejection until he mentioned that Italy had colors and that Paris was lonely and cold. «H is starting to feel lonely». I want to run over and hug him, to think that H has a pinch of sadness is like having the arteries in my heart ripped out one by one, in full colors.

—And what if you come over here? —I ask impatiently.

—To Milan?

—Yes. What immigration status do you have right now?

—I'm applying for French citizenship.

—How many months are we talking about?

—Like six months.

—Would you dare?

— I would go anywhere if I could keep my job and my salary.

—Well, when you have the nationality, we will talk about it again. Is that okay with you?

—Yes, of course. But I don't want you to take it for granted. I want you to do your things for you, I don't want you to wait for me, I'll give you the same advice you gave me before leaving in Madrid.

—Yes, that's what I'm doing.

I lied. I just bought extra blue towels in case he comes; my life revolves around him right now. I find it impossible to think that anything could go wrong, after everything I've been through H *is my happily ever after*. And I'm going to wait as long as it takes

# Pucca

I'm looking around in my closet for something suitable for a summer meeting with my co-workers. Although my economy improved with this job and I can support myself and give myself an occasional treat, I haven't bought clothes to go out. I have some, yes, but not enough. And today, almost at the end of the month, my coworkers had the idea to go to a bar-terrace.

I see a long sleeve red dress and I put it on. «Ugh! Terrible!» It's long-sleeved and it's summer time, but it's the only dress I have that's moderately light and suitable for going out with co-workers. The others show too much skin, I'm sure no one is interested, but dress etiquette is very important to me.

I'm running super late, there's nothing I can do but wear this dress.

Once at the terrace, I order a tinto de verano and I sit at the long table where not only my colleagues from the same area are at, but some colleagues from other areas like billing or sales.

Mattia has sat down next to the sales group and I see him talking to Gabriella. Good for him, let's see if he can finally win her over.

I have my boss, Anna, next to me and we are talking about the things we would do if we didn't have this job. My boss says that she would love to have a cafe in a village, work it herself and make cakes.

—Oh, Anna. Honestly, I see you're so focused in the office, so professional, that I thought you were living your dream job —I say.

—No, Valentina. Let's be honest. We all have this 9-5, office, corporate job, to create the life of our dreams. I doubt anyone's dream is the job we have.

—Well, that's not entirely true— says a guy from billings. I do dream of being the manager of the entire European headquarters of our company.

—Totally valid— Anna replies—. You're right, it was a generalization. What about you, Valentina? What is your dream?

—Well, mine is to have my own production company. I studied audiovisual production, so I would like to be the owner of a place where we not only have the human capital, but also all the toys, cameras, microphones... and offer all services. For example, if a singer wants to make his music video, he can go to my company to find the human and technical team and if he needs to, well, the idea for the video. I know it sounds big, and I don't necessarily have to be the owner, but at least be the creative director and to direct those projects. Being the owner of the company is the top, the biggest dream of all. However, working in an important company in the audiovisual area is the path I should be following, just as I did in my home country.

—Wow! That sounds amazing. I know the general producer of the Disney headquarters here in Italy, we studied together at school. So, if you see an open position that interests you, let me know, I could talk to her and make a reference — says Anna.

- Wow! That's magnificent! But that would mean quitting the job. And everything you've taught me, honestly, everything I know about finances and Excel is because you taught me. You have put in a lot of effort and energy to make the whole process perfect.

—That's right, but I can get a replacement in two days. My job as your boss is also to help you in your professional career. You are an excellent employee and there is nothing above your position that I can offer you, except a five or ten percent annual increase. The reality is that we know that the position you hold is something temporary, and if I can control how that's going to happen, it would be good for me. Besides, in recommending you to any friend, I know that you will do your job well, and that's a win-win for everybody.

—What do you mean win-win? What would be in it for you?

-Well, from the performance you've had with me, I know that you work responsibly and with passion, and that you will continue to do it wherever you are; and I know that by recommending you I would do a great favor to anyone who needs you, and that's a favor I can also use later on, that's why, for me, it's an act where three people can win: you, who would work in the area you dream of; I, who would feel very good about doing you that favor; and whoever hires you, because they get a jewel.

I want to erase every bad thought I ever had about Anna and her demands. I understand it now. She had created me to her liking for the company, she had managed to get me to reduce the total debt of the Latin American portfolio to forty percent. In theory, what was still pending were small things; the strongest and most hard work was already done. If she wanted to replace me, it wouldn't matter, the portfolio was clean and easy to handle. When I leave that job, she could hire someone for a lower price. It was true, it was a win, win for everyone, even for the company.

I have ended the unexpected thread of the conversation with a thank you to my boss for understanding that my path is elsewhere, and for wanting to be part of it. Women who support women, what a beautiful color life can have in the most expected and unexpected way possible. It's true what they say that help comes from the one you least expect.

In the bar where we're at, there's a game room and a mini bowling alley. Our teammates have decided to play and I have joined too.

I'm already a little drunk, so the topic of the off-season dress has been forgotten in my brain.

It's my turn at the bowling alley. When I try to throw, the ball falls backwards, and with it, I fall on my ass. All my colleagues start laughing, of course, I laugh too, while I try to cover myself so that I'm not showing anything I don't want to show.

Somebody helps me up and says:

—I think tintos de verano, bowling and that dress don't go together — then, raising her voice, she asks—. Please, did someone record this historical moment?! Someone needs to post it on Jen&Wa's funniest moments of the year.

— I did! —yells Mattia—. I know the girl; I know she gets clumsy when she drinks too much.

Mattia comes over and plays the video. Everyone is laughing again. It really is very funny. I ask Mattia to send it to me.

—Are you okay? —Mattia asks when the euphoria of the moment has passed.

—Yes!

Gabriella comes over.

—Darling, you're so funny. Honestly, you're not even trying.

—Thank you, honey, Mattia is funny too, I don't know if you've noticed — I say, trying to help them connect.

—Yes, it's true, I should spend more time with him just because of that — Gabriella says as if asking for approval.

—Yes, honey, of course!

Mattia gives me a slight smile with gratitude.

Gabriella invites me to go have a smoke, but my buttocks are throbbing from the blow, so I decline and decide to sit for a while.

I grab my phone to send the video to H so we can both laugh about it. He answers instantly.

*You fell like on Wii*

*Oh, that's true!! Like the Wii*

*characters*

*I remenber when I couldn't use the Wii on Saturdays because two intruders took over it.*

*Oh, yeah, and you didn't play with us.*

*They were two player games. And you were smaller. At those ages, the age gap is quite noticeable.*

*It's true.*
*That's why, Pucca.*

*¿Pucca?*
*You' re dressed like Pucca.*

*That's also true    hahahaha*

I take a look at the clothes I'm wearing, and, indeed, I'm a Pucca, out of place for the season with this autumn dress in the summer.

I quickly do an online search for Pucca and when I see Garu, I'm shocked by how much he looks like H.

*Hey, You're Garu, too.*

I send him a picture.

*Hahahahahaa*

Now I send him a picture of Garu when he was little, with a pacifier.

*Look, this is you when you were a baby*
*Haha, yeah, I can see the similarity. Now the question is, if you're a stalker like Pucca.*

*Well, I was a stalker when I was spending too much time at your house in Venezuela.*

*Let's see, stalker Pucca, tell me what your were doing.*

CHAPTER IV | Shadows of desire

*Well, one time you fell asleep on the sofa and I maybe took some pictures of you with my Blackberry Pearl, that I then spent hours looking at.*

*But do you want to hear the worst one? The most stalker thing I did when you were my platonic crush?*

I'm scared. But go ahead.

*You went to take a bath and Luismi and I stole your phone to check it and see what you had on it. You had a girlfriend at the time. Oriana, but I called her Choriana, because she had "choreado"[47] you from me. And then I opened the conversation with her. And you were arguing, I don't quite remember what it was about, but she was treating you badly, I remember I got so red with rage, I was thinking «I'm going to crack this bastards head open when I see her, how dare she treat my Hachito sweetie pie like that?». Luismi was telling me that you guys were fighting a lot, and I was just thinking «but who can be angry with*

...........................

[47] *Chorear* is a verb used in Venezuela, Argentina, Chile and Peru that means to steal. (Editor's Note)

*this boy? My God. I see his little face and I couldn't be angry, just seeing him would blow away any anger».*
*I was clearly a hormonal teenager, because right now I would get upset with you. Hahahahaha*

*That level of stalking is too much even for the real Pucca. Violation of privacy. Police, take her away.*

*Mr. policeman, put me away for having been a teenager with access to her platonic crush. Mr. policeman, life sentence.*

We both send each other laughing emojis.

# To the Netherlands and the Nether-worlds

It's Tuesday and H tells me he has to go shopping for vegetables. This is something he usually does on Sunday at the local market in his neighborhood, but he didn't get a chance to go because he is preparing for a marathon and went to a half marathon to practice with his friends, and he didn't get a chance to go yesterday, Monday, either because he left work late.

Thinking that he goes shopping for vegetables on Tuesdays, made me remember Maracaibo, our hometown. Over there, a supermarket had an advertisement in which they said that they had discounts on fruits and vegetables on Tuesdays. The advertisement was broadcast during the morning radio show that Luis Chataing hosted, and I am sure that all the millennials from Zulia listened to the program and the advertising while they were on their way to school.

«Country-side Tuesdays. Fifteen percent discount on fruits and vegetables». I say that in a voice note, impersonating a radio host.

*That's right, it's Country-side Tuesday.*

*Wow, brings back memories.*

*Anything else you should do today?*

*No. Nothing else. By the way, I'm going on a trip this weekend. I just bought the ticket.*

*Where are you going? Is it for work?*

*No, I'm going to a festival.*

He told me that he is going in party mode. It is the first weekend with good weather that is neither too hot nor too cold.

From the details he gave me, I get that he's going to a rave music festival, a place where H is known for using cigarettes that make you laugh, narcotics and other substances that are used in those nether worlds. The truth is that in my mind I give H a free pass at festivals, he can do and undo and I don't care, even if he disappears and reappears three days later, I wouldn't worry either, if I know where he is it's enough; besides, we're not boyfriend and girlfriend, and he should take advantage of the fact that we're like this now, long distance and in "friends" mode, because if we're together he'll never see another naked woman again in his life.

When we're husband and wife, I think I wouldn't mind if he wants to go to a festival here and there; of course, I wouldn't go because it's not my style, but if he wants to go to do drugs a few times a year, I wouldn't have a problem with that. I would let him come home drunk, I'll be waiting for him, warm in bed with a set of sexy lingerie so he can have the music, drugs and sex combo.

It's all a matter of balance. H and I are free souls. And H is extremely responsible, even I know that he needs his two minutes to let loose, after all he is still an Arian at almost thirty.

Now, today, if I found out that H was hanging out with a girl at his house, and she's part of his routine, I think I would be devastated, I would feel very betrayed.

> *Well, Hachito, enjoy your festival, do what you want, but be careful, I'm worried someone might spoil you for me. Use protection, because diseases are real. And if you get a woman pregnant who isn't me,*

> *I'll kill you. Simple as that. Your firstborn is mine. It's written in the Declaration of Independence, in the Bible, in the Akashic records, and in the hieroglyphs of Egypt.*

My conversations with H make me feel so comfortable that I can tell him absolutely everything that comes to mind, and I'm sure he won't skip a beat.

> *Wow! And where did all of that come from? Should I go to a bank and store my sperm and then get a vasectomy to be sure? On the other hand, in which declaration of independence?*
>
> > *Mijo, in the one of the independent state of Zulia.*
>
> *Hahaha*
>
> > *Are you going alone?*
>
> *Yes, I'm going alone, but there's nothing easier than making friends at a festival. And there are always like Facebook groups where people talk and comment and you can say that you are going alone and groups are made and that's it.*
>
> > *Is it a big festival?*
>
> *No, it's small. It's in a forest, and it has several settings. With different styles, so.*
>
> > *Hey, let's see if we can meet, okey? You should come over for my birthday next month or something, right?*

> *Yes, I'll be in touch, it depends on my schedule. This will be a crazy and quick getaway; I'm only going for the weekend.*
>
> *Well, yes, but for my birthday, okey?*
>
> *Yes, we'll figure something out.*

I don't know if it's because H doesn't like to make plans too far in advance or if he just doesn't want to see me. I decide to rush away any negative thoughts, I pretend it's nothing and wish him a good trip to the Netherlands.

# Gossip grenades

After making it clear to Fernanda that I could not make a hate club with her against H's ex, my friend spent several weeks without texting. I imagined that she was angry despite my «delicate touch», but I decided not to wind up the matter, «the absence of gossip isn't something to die for», I said to myself.

To my surprise, Fernanda sends me a message asking if she can make a video call with me, and I immediately say yes; regardless of her gossipy essence, I miss her.

—*Marica* [48], I've got to tell you something!

—What's the matter, girl?

—I just crossed paths with a friend who is the boyfriend or ex-boyfriend of the tramp.

—Which tramp?

I swear I thought Fernanda had already lived through her emotional hangover because of what I told her in our last conversation, and she was coming back with stories about the ex.

—The tramp who was in bed with H, the day of the party at Luis Miguel's house, when you were here in Madrid.

—And, how do you know about that?

—Do you remember that I was at the party at Luis Miguel's apartment?

---

[48] *Marica o marico*, in Venezuela, is a word that for a long time was used in a pejorative way towards homosexual people, but nowadays it is used as a form of nominal treatment: it replaces the name of the speaker or the word friend.

Well, that day you were talking to H all the time and you disappeared all of a sudden. In your absence, that tramp immediately jumped on him, it was so obvious that I said to myself «this girl just wants to fuck H», I saw her intentions, you know. But it was just a hypothesis, when Jennifer and I left the party there were still a lot of people. Well, I confirmed the hypotheses later, when I heard her talking about it on another occasion. She was all cocky saying that she was about to sleep with H and you walked in the room and *killed the vibe* [49].

—Aha! and why didn't you tell me you knew? —I interrupt her.

—Well, mija, you don't like gossip, you've already stressed it to me a million times.

—Okay. —And why are you telling me now?

—Because you told me that I could bring gossip about the «pro H» ones. And this is something that should interest you, girl, so don't interrupt me anymore. Well, the tramp was all cocky saying she was about to have sex with H and you walked into the room. Her exact words were: «I was about to have sex with H and that nosy bitch walked in and killed the vibe». Imagine that!

Hearing what she had called me made my blood boil. If I was showing restraint so far, and I had even limited Fernanda so that she wouldn't come with gossip, at that exact moment, my friend's comment dragged me towards hating that party tramp.

— Okay, if what you're telling me did happen, I can confirm that— if that's why you're calling me—but now, what about that disgusting bitch? — I ask vehemently.

—Mija, because I saw her ex at the gym, I saw him with his head hanging low and when I asked him what had happened, he told me

---

[49] *Killing the vibe* is an expression that in Venezuela means to ruin something pleasant suddenly. (Editor's Note)

that he and the tramp broke up and that the tramp went to meet with a fuckboy in the Netherlands. I immediately went to the tramp's Instagram account... And instead of telling you, I'm going to send you a screenshot of her stories in the Netherlands. There's a guy there, tell me if you recognize the guy.

My world stops. H told me he was going to the Netherlands. Fernanda doesn't have to tell me anything else. I know who he is. It's H. The gossip hit the mark. Right in my heart.

—Marica, I don't want to know anything else. I already know who you're talking about and I don't want to know anything else. —I hang up immediately.

The *arrechera* [50] not only makes my blood pressure rise, I also start having an anxiety attack. «Of all the women in the world that H Miguel can fuck at that festival, why did he arrange to meet her in the Netherlands? Why does he have that back and forth with me, but with that dirty tramp he just goes packs his bags and goes to see her?

---

[50] This expression, although it has other uses, is very often used to designate a state of extreme annoyance and indignation. It has a colloquial use, but it no longer registers as vulgarity. (Editor's Note)

# CHAPTER V
# At the edge of the twilight

«I shall keep on feeling less and less and remembering more and more, but what is memory if not the language of feeling, a dictionary of faces and days and smells which repeat themselves like the verbs and adjectives in a speech, sneaking in behind the thing itself, into the pure present, making us sad or teaching us vicariously until one's self becomes vicarious, the backward-looking face opens its eyes wide, the real face gradually becomes dim, like in old pictures».

—Julio Cortázar, *Hopscotch*

# The tower

The time that has passed since I found out what happened in the Netherlands and H's return to Paris, was not enough to lower my level of anger and disappointment. When H texts me to say that he has got home, I call him immediately. I don't ask him; I just do it.

—Hello —he answers. I go straight to the point.

—Quick question —I say, and I already have a lump in my throat. - Who were you with in the Netherlands?

—Alone —he says.

—Are you sure?

—What do you know?

—Why with her, H Miguel!?

—It's just sex, Maria Valentina. I'm not going to marry her, I'm not going to be her boyfriend, no nothing. It's just sex and that's it.

—How do you make it so easy to travel and go see her? — I ask crying—. But every time I ask you to see me, it's suddenly too hard for you.

—It's not the same!

—Why!? —I yell at him.

—Because with her it's just sex. With you it could never be just sex! And I'm not ready to give you what you deserve, Maria Valentina, I need you to wait for me.

—This waiting is hurting me!

—I hate reproaches. I don't ask you about who you're with, and I know that sometimes you go out there and do your own thing. And I know that for you it's just sex and that's it!

—Why are you so sure it's just sex and that's it? You just said that, didn't you? With me it couldn't be just that, don't you think that another man can feel the same as you? Do I only have value if I'm with you? Or am I your safe choice? Of course! I'm the stupid one, I'll wait for you while you mess around and when you're stuffed full of pussy then you'll come and look for me, and you and I can have something, right?

«Where does he get that I go out to "do my own thing"? That's probably because I called him from the club. On that occasion, I didn't tell him that I would go out, but when I talked to him, I told him that I didn't feel good when I kissed that guy. Maybe that's why, but with what I said, didn't he realize that I couldn't have sex with anyone unless there was an emotional bond?»

—Your worth is yours. You give that to yourself. And of course, any other man can see that worth in you, and if he doesn't, then he's an asshole. And what do you mean the safe option? Maria Valentina, you could never be someone's safe option. You are the riskiest option of them all. A man needs to have a clear and stable life to be with you. You have clear goals and directions in your life, and I am figuring out who I am on my own after being in a relationship with someone else for two years. Give me a chance, it's all I'm asking for, I can't right now.

If the love of my life had come to me after ending my relationship with Voldemort, I would have given him a chair to sit and wait for me while I picked up my pieces from the floor. That's what H is doing; giving me a chair. But this communication is killing me, every word, «every little star he draws on my scars» [51], as Taylor's song says, makes me fall in love with him more, and I can't deal with so much love anymore. It overflows me, I need to give it to him or put it on pause.

—I think we should stop talking. This is beyond me. I can't take it anymore. I love you, H, but I can't keep hurting myself like this — I say between sobs.

—I accept it. I'm not going to argue, or stop you. I'll respect your boundaries.

—It's final. I mean, I'm not waiting for you anymore, I'm moving on with my life.

When I end the call, I just throw myself on the floor crying. I remember Taylor all over again, «H is my Maserati on a dead-end street»[52]. I can feel all the horsepower when I make the engine roar, I feel the thrust, but I can't hit the gas, I can't make the most out of it. H unlocks more Taylor Swift songs for me than I can manage.

...............................

[51] Cardigan - Taylor Swift
[52] Red - Taylor Swift

# A menu of bitterness

It's been a week, and I'm still having a hard time sleeping. I feel him everywhere, his memory crosses me at every corner, on every street, in every car, in every number. I feel like a psycho. Spiritual and earthly psychosis, I really feel out of myself. I feel a horrible sadness inside me, an emptiness. I miss him, I miss telling him about my day. H made my days more bearable, he helped me with everything he could, even choosing my cereal. I once heard that when we are in the post-war, which in my case has been post-black plague, basic decisions become hard, like that one, like choosing a cereal. The truth is that I hadn't realized it until I saw myself in front of the supermarket aisle without H on the phone, either on a call or via chat to choose for me. How do I like my cereal? Chocolate or strawberry? None of them seems to be the right choice. H surely has the answer.

When I get back to my house, I realize that it's time to change the sheets and the truth is that I don't feel like it, perhaps the garbage can in the kitchen is also full. But it's just that I don't have the energy today, H sneaks back into my thoughts. H would call me when I had to do those two tasks, specifically, because they are the only ones I can't stand doing. H knew it and when I had to change the sheets or I had to take out the garbage can, he called me to keep me company and give me a push. I even told him once, «When we're together, these tasks will be officially yours, please, I just can't stand it». I remember that he said that he got up and changed the sheets immediately on Saturday, without fail. His weekend had to start with clean sheets.

Ugh! I wish I could stop spinning my daily thoughts around the routine I shared with H. I had never shared so much with someone, so much of my daily routine, so much of my day-to-day things, because in previous romantic relationships, I had kept that kind of things to myself and hadn't shared them with anyone, same with my fangirl part. Honestly, I wasn't going through life telling people that Justin Bieber had been my first love and that when I was in catechesis, we had read that verse from the Bible that says «Love is patient and kind, it is not envious, conceited or proud, it does not behave rudely, it is not selfish, it does not get angry easily, it does not hold grudges...» I had thought about how right that verse was, because that's how I felt my love for the blond Canadian was. Now, each word of that biblical text gains more strength, because my love for H feels like my love for Justin Bieber: pure and selfless.

I'm curled up in bed with the sheets that were changed over a phone call with the guy I love, who just doesn't feel like corresponding me.

I say a prayer and ask God to let me sleep and get up with energy to do my household chores.

A vibrating phone interrupts my hard-to-find sleep. The phone is on the wooden floor of the loft bed, so when it vibrates it makes a lot of noise. I grab it and I see that it is a +33. I know it's H. Although I deleted his number and our chat, no one else would call me from France.

The vibration of the phone scared me, but when I saw the number, I calmed down. I remember that I fell asleep crying for him. «It's H, it's just H, it's just him; the problem is when he's gone». I hesitate for a moment, whether I should answer or not, and I decide to take the call.

–Hello.

–MJ.

–Tell me –I answered, trying not to show my feelings.

—What were you doing?

—Well, I was asleep.

—Ah, but it's Saturday, didn't you go out somewhere?

—No, I stayed home. I'm not an alcoholic or a party girl. —I admit that my answer was somewhat tense, and H immediately got hooked.

—I'm not saying that you are.

—Better safe than sorry. —What were you doing? —I said, in a more relaxed tone, putting an end to what could end up in an argument.

—I was out and about, partying, because the truth is that I'm a bit of an alcoholic and a party boy. And because of that, you're not my friend anymore.

—Stuff happens...

—Well, yes.

—Is there anything you need? —I ask in a worried tone.

—Well, to talk to you.

—What do you want to talk about?

—I don't know, just talk.

«Trying to distract his mind from someone else? Or does he really want to talk to me?». I don't know. I wasn't going to ask him either, it would be too bitter, even in our current situation. So, I decide to make a game with the Aries energy that characterizes both of us.

—Well, imagine that you are in a restaurant. Okay?

—Okay.

H was already used to my games and puzzles, so I knew that he would tag along, no problem.

—You open the menu and have a list of meals.

—Okay, yeah.

—You have «Honest Chicken», «Forgotten Hamburger» and «Halfway potatoes». And you can have this menu with ice, with a pinch of salt or have it with a downpour.

—Okay, can I have a better description of the meals and drinks? Please.

- Honest Chicken comes with a verbal description of what I think about the last few days and what I think about you. Forgotten Hamburger comes with a we forget what happened and this phone call, and we move on with our lives. Half-way Potatoes means that I tell you half of what I think and we half forget this phone call and what happened. And you can have those dishes with ice, that is, as if it were nothing; with a pinch of salt, meaning, being a little skeptical of my words; and you can also take them with a downpour, meaning that you didn't even expect it.

—Please, miss, Honest Chicken. And I'll have it with rum and Coca Cola. That is, I'll take it the way I take things, calmly, trying to empathize with the other party. Thank you.

—Perfect, I'll take your order, sir. I'll bring it to you shortly.

I decided to get down from the loft bed and smoke a cigarette while I organize my thoughts about what I want to say to him. When I light the cigarette H cuts in.

—While the chicken is cooking, the restaurant lady has decided to light up a cigarette.

—Yeah, well, it's a good thing the smoke doesn't get over there. Right?

—Yes, it fades over the 1411 km.

I feel a jab to my heart.

While we remain silent, I look on my phone for the notes about the things I've written lately. I admit that this inspiration has come from watching poetry videos on Tik Tok, especially ones by Ricardo Bulle

—Okay. You picked Honest Chicken, right?

—Yes.

—Well, I've got some notes here— I say—. Shall I read you one?

—Yes.

I have notes on several things that I've written in the last few days, but the truth is that I hoped that H wouldn't get these notes, I wrote them in a moment of excitement, and I didn't read them anymore, I don't know for sure if they're embarrassing or not.

I randomly pick one, and start reciting.

—Home is an H word and H is the personification of the word. A home under construction. When I broke into the residence I placed my portraits, it was still summer. I decorated it to my liking, bought towels and sheets. I bought blankets, put them on the sofa in case we felt like snuggling there and placed my heart on the doorknob at the entrance. I'm sorry I didn't ask if you wanted it there or somewhere else. Now, I don't know where to put all this love; a feeling that I can't give to anyone else.

»At night, I come back to that home. I sneak in through the window. I sit on the sofa and wrap myself with the blanket. I see how my skin bristles in the autumn. I see how my mouth blows smoke. You're not there, but it's the only way to feel you. The only way to suffer you.

»You know? Perhaps time is to blame. He got it wrong. He put the wrong date on the calendar. With so many previous, parallel and future lives in which we coincided, he got confused along the way.

»Perhaps in a few days he'll come back to apologize to us. Because it's always been you and time knows it. Maybe he's forging windows and knitting blankets now, because he knows about the distant cold.

»Maybe I have to wait for Time to come and give me my keys to this home. When I come back, I'll dust off the portraits, and wash the sheets and towels. This time I'll place my heart in your hands and with my love I'll cement the ceramics.

»I will feel you. You will be there. I'll be there. We'll be in our home with the keys that belong to each of us.

—None of this would be happening if we lived in the same city or at least in the same country – replies H, almost immediately after I've finished reading.

—Time is to blame.

I had never believed when people talk about the right person at the wrong time, but H was my person, my home. It just wasn't the right time to be together. We had to let it go until time decided to put us together again.

—MJ…

—H, please. We have to let it go.

—I don't want to, not now, please, Maria Valentina.

—But tell me, what can we do? Are you coming? Shall I go?

—Let's just talk tonight —he answers in a low voice, too low.

I put out my cigarette, and return to sit on the couch.

—H Miguel, we could talk tonight, but everything would be the same tomorrow. You'll be there and I'll be here. I could move, but would you take that responsibility?

—No. I couldn't do that to you.

—Exactly. Then we have to stop hurting ourselves. Have a good night. I love you, always.

—I love you.

The moment I hang up the call, I start crying.

I love him. Intensely. He's the kindest thing that's ever happened to me. I feel like every vein in my heart is being ripped out raw. But it's the most logical thing to do. I feel guilty for hanging up on him, for not being there for him right now. But, to be honest, he has to live his loneliness out the same as me. Even worse, his loneliness is his own decision, he doesn't want me to go, mine is out of compliance.

# 432 Hz

I'm tossing and turning in bed looking for sleep, for the best position to find it, to fall into Morpheus' arms, but I can swear that the blankets have sandpaper. They make me hot, they bother me, they don't cradle me. H is the new hell in my head, thanks to him, I believe, the blankets burn me like fire.

«I must have my cortisol levels through the roof, I need to calm down», I tell myself.

I turn on YouTube, and I look for some frequency that helps me lower cortisol and sleep peacefully, I find an eight-hour video, 432 Hz; «to sleep in peace while the body heals», says the description.

I remember when I couldn't get through the night without healing frequencies or the holy rosary on; at midnight I would wake up sweating, with the bed totally soaked with sweat, drool and tears, I would tell myself «I'm healing»; I was like a post-war soldier with chills.

I understand that H isn't capable of hurting me that way, but when the nervous system comes from a war it doesn't know the difference between fireworks, a gunshot or the neighbor's television with an action movie playing; any noise is equally scary, and it can be the trigger to a nervous attack...

H let off fireworks that didn't end in lights and stars in the sky; it ended in an explosion. I sometimes wonder if it's a spoiled girl's whim, but I delete that thought, because when I think about it, I can feel all my love for him in my whole body. I refuse to believe that this firework isn't going to end with stars and bright lights in the sky.

But today, tonight, the pain I feel is unbearable; I must tear it out of my bowels so I can breathe, until God wants me to.

I've been crying my whole soul out anywhere no matter what. I cry in the street, when I'm on the subway, at work I go to the bathroom to dry the tears that escape, in the apartment I let go completely, with snot and weeping included. A full category cry-out session. Melancholy crying, tears that come out unintentionally; tears of sadness, every time I see an H, scandalous crying, in the bathroom when I try to wash my face from the previous crying. If I keep it up, Milan will be flooded. But I'm always crying alone, without company, and that makes it pure crying, without pollutants or diluents.

I have not wanted to go out, to not to be a black cloud that rains on dinner or lunch time. I know that the most rational thing would be to go to my Aunt Eugenia's, she would console me, but the twins are highly sensitive and seeing me like that would make them cry too, and making them feel bad makes me feel worse.

I feel lonely and miserable... When is it going to be my turn for things to go the way I want them to? I understand, on the other hand, that the plans God has for me are better than the ones I have, but right now it seems that Luci is the one planning my loving agenda. I shake off the thought quickly, and apologize to God for thinking that way.

I get down from the loft bed and I'm going to smoke a cigarette and take a melatonin pill to continue with my 432 Hz. I know it's been a lot of cigarettes for today and that makes me feel bad too, but I can't sleep.

When I have finished my dose of nicotine, I remember my psychologist telling me: «Valentina sometimes we don't have to let go, we have to let it be. That goes for feelings too. Because it's not like you let go of a helium filled balloon into the sky, sometimes the way to let it go is to let it be first».

I sit on the couch and I say to myself «you can let it be, my girl, cry as much as you have to».

The tears run fast down my cheeks, and the knot in my chest is too much. I lay down on the couch and let it be, to let it go. The music is still playing.

# Endless loops

After the crying session the other day, I have been feeling better; I think I emptied the pain until further notice. So, I've come to have a sleepover with the twins. My aunt and uncle have gone to dinner alone.

The twins are having fun with video games while I'm watching TikTok on my phone. I find a little strength and decide to go to the photo gallery; I must start deleting or putting in a folder where I can't see things from the last months that remind me of H.

Before doing it, I take a deep breath and tell myself: «"We are not going to cut ourselves, we will just organize the photo album so that it doesn't catch us by surprise at a time when we're not as strong».

I start to slide my finger over the gallery, I get screenshots of video calls from me and H, even one where he called me from his office, went to pee and put the phone in the sink, so I can see his back when facing the urinal. His jet-black hair is longer than usual dressed in a navy-blue shirt, a cream pullover, black dress pants and vans. You can't see his face, but even from the back and urinating, he seems to be the most attractive man in the world to me. I decided to place that image in «hidden».

I keep on cleaning and get to the pictures of Madrid, I find one of us in the bar, after our first kiss. In it, I have his glasses on because my eyes were red from the sun and he gave them to me. I still remember when Luismi took the picture and I stuck my tongue out. «Mmmm, don't tease», the great H said after that.

Then I found the picture of the book from when I bought the Libra bookmark for him. The book is called *Us on the moon* by Alice Kellen. I get out of the bed and go to iBook's, I look for it and buy it without reading what it's about. «Information comes to you at the right time, I tell myself, I'm sure there's something that this book wants to tell me»

I tell the twins it's time for bed, I help each of them to clean up. They both give me a kiss and fall asleep on the bunk bed. Before doing it, there was a little fight over who sleeps on the top or bottom bunk, but we managed to solve it. When the girls are fast asleep, I go to the couch to start reading.

The story is about Rhys and Ginger who meet by chance in... Paris. And then they start a long distance "friendship"...

The book was easy to read, so I was devouring it. When I get to the part when Rhys – after Ginger sent him a picture - touches the phone thinking about how beautiful Ginger looked, I lose it.

«Did H ever touch his phone or smile at the screen with any of my messages? With a picture? Did our conversations make him feel excited? Did they make him feel butterflies, or was it just noise in his loneliness, post wounded heart? Was I just a distraction or could this really be called love?».

When the tears' roll down my cheeks, I decide to go and get some human warmth. I lie down on the bottom bunk bed with Maria Celeste and she hugs me. By the merciful fortune of the Virgin of La Chinita, the girls are heavy sleepers, so if I sob a little, they won't wake up.

•—••⇾ ⇽••—•

When I open my eyes, I'm the only one in the bunk bed and I can hear the conversation my family is having outside while they're making breakfast.

- Mom, cuzzie spent all night crying.

-Yes, Mom, I had to get down and Celeste and I were hugging her, she was just crying - Maria Paz says.

—Is that right? —my aunt asks.

—Yes, Mom, cuzzie was asleep. She used to do that before, when she lived with Estefania — says Maria Celeste.

—Do you remember, Mom? —Maria Paz asks.

—Yes, I remember, love. We have to give a lot of kisses and hugs to your cuzzie, because life hasn't been very kind to her.

—That's right, girls, Valentina has been through a lot— my uncle chimes in—. Every time she comes over, we must give her a lot of love, so her heart can heal.

I find it inevitable to start crying. I remember these same conversations from my family during the black plague. It was me crying again without realizing it. Was it me, again, in the black plague? No. No. No. No. No. As much as this hurts me, I refuse to link H to the black plague. I'll call it the Hurricane, with an H for Heinrich.

# Not your ordinary day

I don't know when time passed by, but my birthday is just around the corner. The truth is that I just want to be with my family. I call my Aunt Eugenia and ask her if we can go to see Juliet again for my birthday; I have a pending conversation with the dramatic love heroine, but I don't tell her that part. My aunt agreed without hesitation, «of course, it's your birthday, baby girl» she said.

My birthday falls on a Thursday, so I have decided that I will go out to eat with my friends that day and the next day, that I asked for it off at work, I'll travel to spend that weekend with the twins, and, of course, with Juliet.

**Raindrops Are Near**

Like all pretty girls in the world, on our birthday we cried. Maybe a little too much because a birthday is a turn around the sun for the person «celebrating» their birthday. The crying maybe came from the fact that we expected things to be different, from the unfulfilled desires, for not having done more during that year that had passed, or maybe because we hoped that the important people in our life, by magic, had the need to make us feel special, and we cried knowing that that would not happen. Perhaps we were wishing for flowers and chocolates from our crush, a message from an absent parent, a balloon and a letter from a former best friend. We cried because that didn't happen in real life, because those we truly love rarely fight for us, even though we always fought for them. That's why, maybe, just maybe, we cute little girls cried on our birthdays.

The day of my birthday, as expected, the sun didn't come out extra bright or with cheerful butterflies telling the world the joy of having me being born into it. No, it was just another normal day for everyone, except that I was spending it swallowing up my tears. I got to the office wanting to concentrate and not cripple myself by thinking about H, or maybe, also, I came in hoping that some coworkers would say «happy birthday» to me and have something amazing happen.

It looks like in the last few months, I'm the baby on a tricycle from the movie The Incredibles, waiting for something incredible to happen. But the truth is that nothing incredible was going to happen.

My day at the office was just another work day; the work group congratulated me and Mattia didn't come because he felt bad.

When I'm on my way back to my house, the rain that never fails on any of my birthdays starts to fall and get me a little wet. I run to the subway and decide to add fuel to this sad fire inside me. In the end, it's my birthday, I have the right to feel as sad as I want. I play «Jueves»[53], and then I let myself be, I let time go as slow as it wants. And I let, just like the rain, the tears fall, and I don't mind crying in the subway. No matter the level of drama of that scene, I don't care if people see me. I'm a human being with the right to be sad.

When I get home, I take off my half-soaked clothes, and I go to take a warm bath before I catch a cold.

When I'm under the shower I stop crying. I decided to stop feeling miserable for today. I think about the song I was listening to from La Oreja de Van Gogh. It is a piece inspired by the diary of a girl found by the rescue teams after the terrorist attacks of March 11, 2004 in Madrid. A heartbreaking story. That girl had lost her life there and couldn't live out her love story. I am alive and I am going through a stage of it. I have the right to cry, I have the right to ask God why, but, above all that, I have the duty to live my life.

When exercising the right to live my life, I have accepted my friend's invitation to go to dinner, I have decided to lower the sadness switch and have a blast with the girls. While I'm on my way, I randomly hit play to the list of songs from the book of my life, and, in tune with my decision, «Feeling Good»[54] by Michael Buble starts playing.

---

The girls and I are having fun in the restaurant bar we chose, it's just the five of us. Due to the rain, we decided to stay here, after ten o'clock the karaoke starts and today's musical theme is iconic songs from movies.

The first group stands up and they sing "Singing in the Rain"[55]. Then other girls stand up and sing "Dancing Queen"[56] from *Mamma mia*. That's when Emiliana screams for us. We're going to sing the mashup of songs[57] from the end of the movie *Pitch Perfect*.

—Yes, but there are four girls singing, and there are five of us — I said, worried because I don't want to leave any of them out.

—I'll be the Asian girl with the fish gills!!! —says Margot.

We all crack up laughing.

—I'm the blonde, the leader of the Beauties. And you are Rebel Wilson —Corina says while pointing at Soffia —and, obviously, the birthday girl is Anna Kendrick.

—They're forgetting about half the cast! —Soffia says, almost having a heart attack—. There's the brunette who's kind of a lesbian, and the

---

[53] Jueves- La Oreja de Van Gogh
[54] Feeling Good - Michael Buble
[55] Singing in the Rain - Gene Kelly
[56] Dancing Queen - ABBA
[57] The Finals - Pitch Perfect (Mashup)

rowdy girl. And the redhead from the original Beauties.

—Oh, it's true!! —says Margot.

—Well, let's see, let's mash up the redhead with the blonde from the original Beauties. That's Corina. The fish girl with the rowdy one, that's Margot. Sofi, the brunette lesbian, and I'm Rebel Wilson, and, as Corina said and we all agreed, the birthday girl is Anna Kendrick. Okay? —Emiliana said.

—Yesss — we all replied.

And then it's our turn. Soffia asks the girl group that sang "Dancing Queen", to please record us with a phone.

We get on stage; we huddle around and I say:

—Don't forget, it's just for fun, so don't pay attention to tone or anything.

All right, let's get in position.

Luckily, this karaoke is not so karaoke because they play the YouTube video with the song and we sing on top of the voices. We have a screen in front of us and we can guide each other for the choreography.

The music starts.

«Price Tag» starts, and we're focused. Corina sings while we just «harmonize»

When it's the fish girl's turn, Margot makes it hilarious and we die laughing. We try to follow the choreography and Soffi enters. After her, it's Anna Kendrick's turn to sing the Breakfast Club song, and I remember the movie, the plot; I need all my focus to not start crying.

Between the hey, hey, hey, I imagine H in front of me, I imagine that H is Skylar Astin. I focus on that, and the fear disappears. I'm singing to him, and this is just a scene from the movie of my life.

*Don't you forget about me*
*As you walk on by*
*Will you call my name*

*As you walk on by*
*Will you call my name*
*As you walk on by*
*Will you call my name*

I'm waiting for the imaginary H to raise his hand, and for that to mean we choose each other. When it happens, I raise my hand as well in synchrony. We both choose each other.

Then comes the part where Margot is supposed to dance like a ballet dancer and then Sofi comes in singing «Pitbull».

Emiliana acting as Rebel is the funniest thing. It's so funny that no one can keep on harmonizing. We all simply die laughing. The crowd cheers, and we do a theatrical bow.

The girls from the previous group, the ones Soffia gave her phone to record us, give it back, and we decided to leave the bar to watch our video because we couldn't stand the laughter and curiosity.

When we're watching my part. Emiliana says:

—Wow, girl, you were in the zone. You did good.

—Yeah, well, maybe I imagined I had H in front of me.

—Mmm, what's up with that? Hasn't he texted you for your birthday? —Margot asks.

—No —I answer in a soft tone.

—Bah, fuck him — says Soffia angrily.

—Hey! Don't be like that! Let her be sad —comments Corina.

—Well, come on, let's take a shot of tequila —Emiliana orders and we go back to our table.

It's already midnight, so the girls have decided to sleep in my apartment to make sure that I'm not going to call H to confront him because he didn't text me, and to make sure I get up and take the train to Verona. Although my train leaves at noon and everyone has to work, they want to make sure I get up in a good mood to travel, they want to be sure that I won't be overcome by sadness due to the absence in communication from H, and that I will go to my aunts tomorrow.

We get to my house, like queens, a little tipsy, but not too much. We still decided to drink a liter and a half of water each to make sure we don't have a hangover in the morning. Soffia lights up a marijuana joint and smokes a little with Emiliana and Margot. Corina and I don't smoke weed, so we're just keeping our distance from it and play Uno.

Corina, Margot and I will sleep upstairs in the loft bed. Soffia and Emiliana will sleep on the pull-out couch. Emiliana tried to convince us that she could sleep on the floor on a yoga mat with a sheet. Everyone opposed, obviously, sometimes we had to remind her of her value. In part, self-esteem was the reason why it was so hard for her to leave her relationship with Giuliano.

The next morning, noise from the kitchen woke me up. I already felt when Margot and Corina got down from the loft bed, but I was too sleepy to pay attention to them, I was earthquake proof when I was asleep.

Suddenly the door separating the bedroom-living-dining room from the kitchen opens and I hear:

—*Tanti auguri a te Tanti auguri a te Tanti auguri Cara Tina Tanti auguri a te*.

I open my eyes; the girls are singing birthday to me. When I sit up, they're all downstairs with a cupcake and a candle.

Excited, I come down, as they scream:

—*Auguri* girlfriend!!

—Girl, make a wish —says Margot.

—I wish to be happy. —And I blow out the candle, everyone claps immediately.

This has been a long birthday, of sadness and absence, but also of happiness and company. A beautiful spring in the middle of winter.

# The wheel of Fortune

My uncles, the twins and I had dinner last night at L'evangelista Ristorante & Enoteca and ordered the winter tasting menu. I love this type of restaurant that has a fixed menu and you just taste things. Italian food is one of my favorites and the tasting menus have small portions, so if there's something I don't like, it's easy to give it to someone else. But in this case, everything on the menu was to my total liking.

The next day, Saturday morning, we decided to take a little walk to then have lunch and go to Juliet's.

With a full belly, we set off, and when we passed by the Basilica of San Zeno again, I asked my aunt to make a brief stop to go to the church.

In front of the church my aunt is talking to me about the architecture of the facade, she mentions something about the large rose window known as the «Wheel of Fortune», and the truth is I have a hard time paying attention to her because I have a tremendous desire to go inside, I don't know why.

When I get in, as if I'd done this thousands of times, and as if this would relieve the anxiety in me, I walk until I almost reach the altar, I kneel down on one of the chairs and begin to cry inconsolably.

«God, you know what I've been through. Please help me heal, help me to find peace in my heart. Please, God, I want to stop loving him so much. If I must live this feeling, at least help me not to burn, help me not to drown, help me to overcome it more nicely».

I am so involved in my crying and in my prayer that I don't feel when my aunt stands next to me.

I keep on sobbing and praying.

«If this love is to be, removes any external obstacle from our path: distance, people, traumas, fears... everything that needs to disappear. And if it's not for me, show me the way out».

So, I have an epiphany: the wheel of fortune! The tarot card, I've seen it. I make a mental note to check and see what it means.

When I have calmed down a bit, I have the twins on my left side hugging me and my aunt on the right.

—Maria Valentina, what's going on? Is everything all right? —my aunt asks, restless.

—I'm in love with someone— I answer, wiping away my tears.

—Oh...

—But love shouldn't hurt —says Maria Paz.

—Is your boyfriend a boy or an onion? —Maria Celeste adds.

—Know, cute things. I don't have a boyfriend. And love makes us emotional in all aspects, but I agree that it shouldn't hurt all the time. Right now, it does, it hurts like hell.

—What's his name? —Maria Paz asks.

—H.

—Just H?

—Well, Heinrich.

—And where is he from?

—Mija, from my hometown, where else — I answer with a Maracucho accent.

—And what's going on with H right now that hurts so much? —my aunt asks.

—Well, we decided to stop talking because of the distance between us. He lives in Paris.

—But Paris is an hour and thirty minutes from here. And if you get along, then you can move in together, right? —my aunt says.

—I'm the one who, in theory, has the least number of responsibilities and the one who could most easily move; because I am the one who has a stable legal status, he's still in the process. But he says he doesn't want to take that responsibility and I understand that.

—Well, it's all in the hands of God.

—Why do you think I'm kneeling in front of the Holy one? I'll leave it to him. I'll let go. God's plans are better than mine. I just have to trust him and his plans.

—Amen.

I'm not a religious fanatic, I'm a universalist. But with my aunt here, I'm a Catholic orthodox, who only believes in God. And the truth is that, in hard times, we all turn to God and to our mom. If things get tough, those two calls will always get an answer.

When I leave the church, I carefully check on Google the meaning of the Wheel of Fortune.

The website talks about the symbology of each of the elements in the chart, numerology. After karma, life cycles, destiny, which is in motion, changes.

Then it shows the specific meaning of each theme. I go to the section about love, and it has three parts, if you're single, if you're in a couple, or if you're in conflict with your couple. From my point of view, H and I have an important emotional bond, but we haven't declared ourselves as a couple, so how should I focus on this? I decided not to give it too much thought and just read the one about the conflict. It talks about renegotiation, above all, to show feelings, and put the cards on the table. Otherwise, there will be no moving forward.

Destiny. Karma. Renegotiation. Cards on the table

«What the fuck's going on, Juliet Chiquinquira?».

When I get to Juliet's statue, I stay back a little.

It makes my stomach churn again that people touch her private parts, or to be touched, in general.

«Hello, Juliet. I was just talking to God, and now it's your turn. The reality is that I would talk to the devil if I had to. I would strike a deal with death. But that's not the point. The point is this. I love him. Intensely. Deeply. He is the kindest thing that has ever happened to me and I would like to keep him».

I stop the diplomacy with the statue-woman, and I remind myself that I am also valid in my *arrecheras*. So, aha!

«*Verga*, you kind of like this mess, mija, honestly. I mean, let's see, jokes aside and all, but who the fuck came up with having my feelings caught with my teenage crush? Marica, it's fucking crazy. Who do I have to negotiate that with? Huh? Juliet Chiquinquira, I need help from Maria Bolivar. Because I don't understand shit.

# Parallelepiped

Finally, the girl's schedule and mine have lined up and we can finally see each other. Emiliana's situation, who is sometimes here on the weekends and sometimes isn't, it's been hard for us to organize ourselves and go out together. Emiliana and her guy have finally broken it off, but they still live together because they haven't managed to get an apartment. She travels to her mom's house in Perugia as much as she can and he goes to Faenza, his parents' village; that way they try to see each other as little as possible. Housing problems in big cities, a daily struggle.

Usually, when we go out as a group, the girls and I go to dinner first, and then we go to some bar to catch up with other friends.

I enter the Mexican restaurant called Mexicali where we made a reservation, the girl at the entrance takes me to the table and I am the first one seated, the restaurant is pretty simple, but it is authentic Mexican, the best tacos al pastor in the city.

Mmmm yum yummy, I drool just thinking about it. I think Latin American food is my favorite, a good Colombian ajiaco, a Peruvian chaufa, an Argentine asado, some tacos al pastor, a Cuban congri, a Venezuelan reina pepiada, yum! I love to eat, I love to feel hunger in my body, especially after Hurricane H, I think I feel too good today. I have a good energy and a good feeling. Today is a good day to be happy.

Now that I think about it, Emiliana broke up with her guy because he was unfaithful with his friend's girlfriend, which means that they also broke up, and I ended whatever I had with H, was Venus retrograde? Eclipses? What astrological event was happening in the sky that made love breakups so common?

I decide to find out, while I wait for my margarita to be brought and for the girls to arrive. The truth is I didn't find anything special, beyond the lunar cycles, not even Mercury retrograde. This is collective information, maybe something was happening on the person's astrological map, but I don't know how to read that myself.

Sometimes I think I'm in a state of alert for every astrological event, as if I want to control everything around me, predict it or even justify it. That's not to mention the state of hyper-vigilance of finding meaning and signs in everything. My therapist told me that this was the new spiritual delusion, it was okay to believe that there was something else, but I would get frantic even if I saw a feather outside my apartment. When I was with H, even car license plates made me frantic. Do you know how many car plates have HM? Or HG?, a lot, and it seemed that they were all chasing me, the numbers, 33 and 333, I found and saw everywhere. Today I've been able to relax a little, that's why, maybe, I have that feeling that it's a good day to be happy.

Once I was with the girls and our food was ready, we continued to catch up. We have decided, in an unspoken way, that Soffia will take center stage in the conversation at dinner today. Neither of us felt like talking about boys, not for any bad reason, but there just wasn't much to talk about beyond the fact that Emi and I were heartbroken and under construction. Therefore, Soffia was getting her head out of feminism and telling us the story of how she got her company to give her a promotion and make her creative director and raise her salary by thirty-five percent.

—Well girls, in the meeting with human resources and my manager, they told me that I would be assigned to training advertising and designer teams, and that they would give me a ten percent raise while doing that role. What's the matter? We have a new client, which is a new British English study center, and they're going to open branches here in Milan and in Rome. So, in other words, they wanted me to manage and direct the project and after the inauguration I would get back to being an advertising agent. What!? I told them «I've been here for two years; you can't do this to me. I want to be the creative director of the project, direct it from the beginning until the client wants, and then keep on being a director with up-coming projects». I warned them, informed them that otherwise that would be my last day at work, I said: «Give me what I deserve or I'm leaving».

—Wow! You go, girl! —says Margot while clapping excitedly.

—So, they had no choice but to give me what I asked for.

—That's it, damn it! —I say, joining in on the excitement—. It looks good when a woman gives herself her place, and the world has no choice but to lower their heads. A real fucking queen, my friend! I'm grateful to get to call you that, my friend.

---

We get the first snowfall of the year, and as the snowflakes fall, the five of us walk towards the bar. I feel like I am in an episode of Sex and the City. A beautiful happiness blooms inside me again and I'm grateful to have them with me, to laugh together, our broken hearts beating in tune. «More, please», I tell the universe in my mind, «more of this feeling of complete happiness with friends».

Before entering the bar, I tell the girls:

— Listen up, women of the twenty-first century, we will walk in that bar, we will drink, we will dance, we will party, but no one is leaving with a man. We will all go back to each other's house and share a taxi. Tonight, even though there are guys in the room, it's a girls' night, okay?

- OKAY! - they all scream and we make a pinky promise.

The bar we came to is one of those typical European places, where they play the soundtrack to Mamma Mia. So, we don't hesitate to scream and dance when «Dancing queen» is playing on the speakers.

*You are the dancing queen, young and sweet, only seventeen*
*Dancing queen, feel the beat from the tambourine*
*You can dance, you can jive, having the time of your life*
*See that girl, watch that scene, diggin' the dancing queen*

It's a big group, with our friends, and friends of our friends. Apparently, someone is celebrating their life anniversary and we're all kind of crashing their birthday party. I couldn't stop thinking that H was right, everything is more colorful here, but my color spectrum had only expanded when I met him. I no longer wanted Italy without his presence, because he was my home.

With his memory, the itch to start crying begins, and I say to myself quickly "Parallelepiped". That's my safe word to get me out of trains of thought that don't work for me at the moment, to bring me back to the present. According to my psychologist, that takes me out of the anxiety box, a box is a parallelepiped.

—Paralalalepide. —I'm trying to say that with some drinks in my system.

—What are you saying, girl? —Are you okay? —Soffi asks.

—Girl, paralalalepide —I try to say it again.

—Parallelepiped, is that what you're trying to say?

—Yes, that!

—Why do you want to say that?

—It's my anti-anxiety spell.

—Are you having an anxiety attack?

—I'm trying to avoid one.

—Soffi, who is also drunk already, climbs on the table and screams.

—Everybody, shout with me: PARALLELEPIPED!

Italians are not afraid of anything, and they do not know what shame is.

The crowd is screaming.

—Parallelepiped!

I'm laughing so hard my tummy hurts, Soffi gets off the table.

—Better?

—Much better!

—Giddy up! girl, come, I'll get you some water.

When we're walking to the bar to buy water, I try to find Margot, Corina and Emiliana at the bar because I don't know where they are, and I see them with the guy I made out with in the summer, Theo, that's his name, now that I remember. They're all sitting at a table with other guys who were also there that day, but I can't remember their names because I didn't make out with them, hehehe.

Water in hand, Sofi and I head over to the table where the girls and Theo are. It doesn't take long for him and I to get into a bubble where the main topic has been music.

The guy can't believe that American rap is my favorite music, and that, even though I love Taylor Swift, I love Kanye's music. The truth is that I don't usually separate the human from the artist, but Kanye is my guilty pleasure. My only exception. And sometimes, I'm a little embarrassed to admit it.

The Greek guys' favorite music, Theodore Angelopoulos (yes that's his full name) is Johnny Cash, and his guilty pleasure is Turkish music.

At this point we have made a playlist with a variety of music, very random, that we like, one of those playlists that you say, «I can't believe you're listening to this», even though it makes complete sense.

When it's time to go home, Theo says goodbye to me tenderly.

—When you're ready, let me know. I'm not asking you to marry me,

I'm just asking you on a date. Someday. Okay?

I nod shyly.

Although I am a Libra woman capable of having several connections and having a good time and having fun, like in the summer when I made out with Theo, the reality is that he scares me a little, he is very direct and to the point. Very different from H, who lacks the drive. That drive that Theo has, makes me doubt, it makes me feel like I'm talking to a Mr. Wickham. And that scares me.

I make a mental note to make an appointment with my psychologist and talk about this topic:

Dating after H.

There's no hurry, Christmas is coming and according to what Theo told me, he will go to Greece to spend those days with his family.

# Christmas

There are ways to have a white Christmas, really: my family and I have come to San Bernardino, Switzerland. I asked for a few days off at work. My friends left Italy: Emiliana is in Croatia, Corina is in southern France, Soffi went to the Canary Islands with her family and Margot is in Budapest seeing her grandmother.

Luckily, Estefania and Daniela Trunchbull went to Germany together.

So, we are all with whom we should be. And my place this Christmas is here with Maria Paz and Maria Celeste.

We've spent these days skiing, and I'm trying to go snowboarding. I'm a little bad at sports, except tennis and swimming, but I'm focused on improving, so the first step I have at hand is to put down the skis and switch to the board. I'm failing miserably. I have H's videos in the back of my mind, from that time we talked about sports, and obviously the kid is a fully blown Aries, he is excellent at sports, and of course snowboarding is no exception.

Every time I fall on the board, every bump against the snow is a reminder that I'm alone, that I have loved him, but perhaps, just as with snowboarding, I'm not up to the challenge and that's why he hasn't reciprocated me.

People spend too much time saying things like «after what I've been through, I deserve to be happy now»; I've never had a problem with deserving, I know exactly what I can create and what I can handle. But

H throws me off balance and brings out my most hidden insecurities.

I also understand that my mind throws too much information and too many memories, I admit that I have days when I feel my strength and drive, my strength and courage, and at other times I feel like a complete lunatic, and, other days – just like today – I don't feel worthy. I feel dirty, not enough for someone like H. I have a heavy suitcase in tow, full of abuse and traumas, maybe he needs someone more angelical and I still have five years to completely get rid of my last abusers DNA.

Maybe the tramp wasn't such a tramp, maybe Choriana lost her virginity to H, maybe her ex had an angelical and non-disruptive attitude. Perhaps they had been touched by fewer hands or perhaps the hands that had touched them were full of love. And I, well, the only love my body had ever experienced was that of H, with his two taps on the back of my hand.

I fall on the board again, and then I hear the voices of a couple of little girls.

—Cuzzieeee, we're coming to the rescue.

When they get there, they jump on top of me and fill me with kisses. Ugh! So sweet!

We've already had dinner and we're watching Frozen 2 because I hadn't seen it and the love I have for Olaf is not normal. While we're watching the movie, I have Maria Celeste on one side and Maria Paz on the other and both of them are already starting to close their eyes.

When the movie ends, the girls are asleep and my aunt and I get ready to wrap the presents for when they wake up.

I bought some unicorn headphones for each of them and a box of friendship bracelets.

My aunt bought two gifts, one from Santa and the other from her and my uncle Alessandro. Santa brought them some electric skateboards to go to school; and from their parents, the girls will get helmets and everything they need to protect themselves. Obviously, Paz's is pink and Celeste's is... light blue.

Seeing all that, makes me nervous.

—Hey, Aunty, but aren't the girls too young to go to school alone? And isn't that electric skateboard dangerous with all the rocks and stuff on the road? How fast can you go on them?

—I think the same, but what can I do? All the kids at school have one and they go to school with them. In fact, at school they opened a parking lot just for electric scooters; this thing is the new bicycle. I hate it, but you can't swim against the tide when it comes to two girls who are almost teenagers, and, moreover, encouraged by their surroundings.

And, it's true, I can't find any arguments to refute yours, my aunt is right. But I think that when I have my own kids, I'll take them by the hand even when they're in college. That makes me nervous.

The next morning, the girls wake up earlier than usual, for obvious reasons.

—Cuzzie, Santa came.

—Cuzzie, wake up!

I get out of bed and into the room where the AirBnB sponsored christmas is, and I lay eyes on our secret creation from last night.

My aunt and I are certain that the girls already know that Santa's gifts actually come from their parents, but that's part of the Christmas magic, so we sat around the tree, without breakfast, and we started to open the presents.

I want to stay forever in that special moment, listening to the wrapping paper getting ripped, seeing the happy faces and feeling the true affection that is in the air, but the girls can't contain their excitement and their screams when they see the skateboards, and, of course, they also hug me, happy and thankful for their bracelets and headphones.

If I had given them a chocolate, they would be showing their happiness; they are girls growing up in a happy home, without shortages, therefore, gifts are acts of love and not excuses to meet needs.

—Cuzzie, there's a gift from us —says Maria Paz.

—I hope you like it —adds Maria Celeste.

The girls pass me an envelope and I open it. It's a handmade letter by the girls that says: «God is with you at every step, and so are we. We love you. Don't fail to make all your dreams come true, we want to see you succeed». Tears are getting away from me.

—Thank you, my beautiful girls. I love you too!

—Cuzzie, take a good look at the envelope; there's also a gift from mom and dad.

I pull out a card and it says «GymRosa».

—It's a year-round subscription to a gym near your neighborhood —says my Aunt Eugenia—. They have different activities each day, Pilates, yoga, ballet, spinning, kick boxing. You could use some group activities to expand your circle of friends. There's nothing wrong with the ones you have, but meet new people, love, people who are on your same vibe too.

—Wow, auntie, thank you very much! Yes, this is amazing, just yesterday I was thinking that my resolution for the new year is to do more physical activities. So, it fits like a ring on my finger.

The other resolution is to focus on myself, and stop thinking so much about H. These activities will do me a lot of good. I should make a list of resolutions that are doable for this year

# Now, it's Luismi's turn

I'm getting back from walking by the lake here in Switzerland. The calm of this place makes me relaxed, makes me feel in communion with this splendid nature. Once home, I see that Luis Miguel has texted me, in a «drama king» mode, he's been arguing with Andres.

> *Mary Jane, I'm mad at Andres and I don't know what to do.*
> 
> *What happened? Tell me about it.*
> *It's nothing serious, it's not that we're breaking up, or anything like that, Santi, it's just that sometimes he puts me on edge, he put on a show at Christmas dinner and, well, we argued.*
> 
> *Okay, but tell me, what happened?*
> *I want to disappear for a few days. Besides, he's going to spend New Year's Eve with his family and I don't know what to do with my lonely body.*
> 
> *Visit me, my Luismi, come and spend these days with me*

Without thinking twice, I tell him to come over. It's true that I have to tighten up my pants to be as good a hostess as he was when I was in Madrid, but I love the idea of him spending a few days here, plus he's definitely my younger brother and I love him to bits. «Maybe if H sees that Luismi is with me, he'll decide to break zero contact».

Luis Miguel bought a ticket and we both arrived in Milan on the same day.

Once at home, I didn't want to fall behind on how he had treated me, so I made an asparagus risotto with goat cheese for him. Although I don't like to cook when I'm alone, I love making it for the people I love and I know I do it well, but Luismi is a picky eater and I don't know if he will like what I prepared for him. «Mmmm, did I pass this culinary test with Luismi?».

—What a delight —Luismi tells me, as he licks his lips—. What a great way to start Milan with a dish like this.

—I'm glad you liked it! I passed the test! I passed the test! —I scream super excited and Luis Miguel forces me to explain my reaction to him—. You know that I don't cook delicacies often, but I had to prepare something delicious for you as a welcome, and you are a magnificent cook, so this was a test for me. I'm very pleased that you liked it.

—Oh, Mary Jane, you're a nutcase. Don't worry, as long as I'm here I'll take care of the cooking, I love to do it.

I kiss him over and over. At times like this, I feel perfectly justified in loving him.

We spent three days touring Milan and eating delicious food. At one of the dinners he got me thinking: «Maybe Luismi's future is to be a famous chef» And my imagination flies: there's Luis Miguel receiving his third Michelin star with Hachito and me accompanying him. I shake it off, «Get him out of your head, he's not ready for you».

On New Year's Eve, once Luis Miguel and I get back from touring part of Via Montenapoleone (although we didn't buy anything I knew that Luis Miguel was going to love it), we're getting ready to go receive the new year at my aunt and uncle's house. While I'm putting on my lipstick, Luismi's phone rings with a video call.

—It's Graciela —he tells me.

He answers the call from his sister, next to me, and when the video comes on, I realize that Graciela is on the Vereda del Lago. I'm getting a little nervous because Luis Miguel told me that H went to Maracaibo to spend Christmas and New Year's Eve.

—Heeelloooo! —Graciela says.

—Heeelloooo! —Luismi and I say in unison.

—How are you doing? —she asks us.

—Fine, getting ready — says Luismi.

—Oh! Let me have a look at Santi!

I move closer to the phone, wave my hands and say:

—Here we are, getting ready to go to dinner. How are you? Who are you with? — I ask, because I know there is a possibility that she is with H.

—Just walking around, thinking about some things. —I can't help it, I ask her about H and she answers me with another question—: Santi, do you still have a platonic love with H?

—Oh! If only you knew — says Luismi. I shake my hands to shut him up, but it's too late.

—Tell me, because I want to know.

—No. Please. —I feel embarrassed— I say, ashamed.

—H and Santi had a summer love —Luismi reveals to her. It's not that he preferred to ignore my request in the face of his sister's, but he was desperate to tell the gossip. He never has a happier face than when he can give a scoop.

—No way! —Graciela says.

—Yes. It's the truth —Luismi continues.

I was mortified, I step aside, and then Graciela tells me:

—Santi, put your head in, I want to tell you something. —I reluctantly agreed and she continued—: Santi, listen to me. If there is anyone in this world whom I love, it's H, in fact, I always say it, when I grow up, I want to be like him. Yes, I want to be as disciplined and successful as my younger brother. And there's nothing wrong with loving him, wanting him, being in love with him. —My eyes are watering and she keeps talking—: If you are in love with him, as a woman I can tell you, honor your feelings. Now, tell me, where are you two standing right now?

—We don't talk to each other —I reply with a sad tone.

—Well, sometimes a man is not ready to have a wonderful woman like you in his life. And the truth is that I know H and I know you, and you deserve each other. Now, I'm going to have my heart full of excitement. Now I'll pray to God that it's you who will be with H. He deserves a woman like you, and you deserve a man like him.

The tears are already rolling down my cheeks, and when I turn to look at Luismi I realize that he's crying too.

—Thank you, Graciela. I've put everything in God's hands —I answered, and she burst into tears. The three of us are drenched in emotions, with longing that turns into crying. With my heart on the table, I continue—: I never imagined loving in this way. Honestly, despite everything that he and I have been through, things that are between me and him and that I am not in a position to tell, I can tell you that he has been my rock in super hard times, and the only thing that remains inside me, is a feeling of gratitude for him being in my life. I have always reproached him because he doesn't let people love him, he doesn't let me thank him for everything he has done for me. In this kind of situation, a woman has stronger feelings than a man, it's always the woman who gives more, but this is not the case. He has always given me more than I have been able to give him, and it's not that I don't want to, he doesn't allow me to.

—I know H, I know what you're talking about, I'll ask God to be the one to intercede and that my brother can give himself the opportunity to be loved the right way.

I still have tears in my eyes, but Luismi wants to get out of the emotional trance and screams:

—I want nephews! —Enough to make us all laugh with wet cheeks.

—Well —Graciela interrupts— I'll let you finish getting ready, God bless you both, and, Santi, you have my blessing. One last question, does my mom know this?

—Not that I'm aware of, no —I answer.

—Can I tell her? —Graciela asks.

—I don't know.

—Well, I'm not going to say anything then.

# Unapologetic

Luis Miguel and decided to walk to my Aunt Eugenia's house. It's a thirty-minute walk, but that way we have time to talk and we're not in a crowded subway. When we're leaving my building, Luis Miguel's phone rings again, he answers the video call and it's from his mom, Mrs. Marisela de Gil.

It makes me nervous to see her face. I haven't talked to her like that, one on one, for so long, but I remember her kindly. Of course, seeing and listening to her now is a different scenario for me. It's as if I was looking for H in her personality and expressions, of course, I do the same with Luis Miguel, who is like H's twin brother, and with Graciela, but mostly with his mom. I know that H is very attached to his mom. I even asked him once who he would take his broken heart to have it fixed, in case he needed it, and he said to his mom.

I know that they have a very special relationship, with such a connection, that he once told me that the only person he didn't need translations with, was her; his mom simply and naturally understands him. When H told me that, it felt sweet and soft, because I know that his mom and I have the same personal planets, that is, we have the same Venus-Mars energy that H has as well. Of course, they have their own language, they're an extension of one another. Seeing H and his mom is like seeing a couple of best friends. I guess, in a way, it's the same connection that Graciela and Luis Miguel have, they just understand each other.

I look at everything from this third-party perspective, feeling close to them, but also distant, not because of anything negative, but I know what my place is and I know the difference and how to respect boundaries. So, when it's my turn to say hello to Mrs. Marisela on the phone, I decide to do it based on the bond we have since I was thirteen years old.

—Mrs. Marisela, how are you? You look so beautiful! As always.

Mrs. Marisela is a Libra worthy of her Venus energy, she's got nice makeup on, and somehow, I can smell her perfume all the way over here.

—Santi, you too, my love, always beautiful and glowing. —That's right, we're two Libras who are giving each other compliments.

—Oh, Mrs. Marisela, you're making me blush. —We both laughed.

—How's the cold? —he asks.

—Well, what can I say, my pretty one. —Mrs. Marisela is a relaxed and carefree woman, so it's easy for me to talk to her as if she was a friend in her twenties—. My beautiful body is freezing.

—No, *mija*, take some *guarapo*[58] for that cold. Some *grappa*[59] —she says, with no inhibitions.

—Haha, when I get to my aunt and uncle's house.

—Oh, Santi, you look really beautiful. —I notice that she raises her voice as she settles in her chair, as if she wants someone else in the room to hear her. I wonder if H is around.

—Thank you, Mrs. Marisela, when are you planning to come over, so we can go out and party?

—Honey, I'll come when I can get my passport. I'm going to Madrid and Paris.

...........................................

[58] By guarapo they refer to fermented sugar cane juice.
[59] Grappa is an alcoholic beverage obtained by distilling wine residues.

Luis Miguel interrupts the conversation and says:

—Oh, we'll all see each other in Paris, and soon we'll all see each other again in marriage —he says mockingly, and proceeds to go away, leaving me with the phone in my hand.

I act stoic, but I decide *to act like I'm from Merida*[60] and continue with my conversation.

—Well, you could also spend a few days here in Italy, I'll be waiting for you with love —I say ignoring Luismi's uncomfortable comment.

Mrs. Marisela simply nods her head laughing. I think she didn't understand what Luismi said, and so I assume she doesn't know anything.

Impulsively, and without thinking too much about it, as if, out of nowhere, I suddenly had something stuck in my chest, I ask Mrs. Marisela if she is alone, and she says yes.

—Do you know why Luis Miguel made that comment? Just out of curiosity, Mrs. Marisela.

Mrs. Marisela softens her look. And then answers:

—I heard something, but I didn't ask. H is very private about his things and I don't want to intrude too much.

—Did he mention anything to you, or was it somebody else?

—He told me something once, and I've heard something from other sources.

I sense that Mrs. Marisela knows more than she claims to, but I also know that she is a woman like me, she respects other people's boundaries a lot. H is the same way.

—Mrs. Marisela, I love your son. I've always been in love with him, but now I have all the letters to make up the word love. —I tell her so fast that I'm out of breath. As if by telling her, face to face, that I love

---

[60] *Acting like from Merida* is an expression to say that some plays the misunderstood, pretends that what's going one doesn't have to do with them. (Editor's Note)

H, I was telling him.

- Well, my child, loving is a privilege for those who feel it. Sometimes we think that the one who wins is the loved one, and the truth is that loving is so beautiful that you are the lucky one, the one who feels it.

—Mrs. Marisela, I don't know where I'm standing with H right now. I don't know where we're coming from, where we are, or where we're going. But I want you to know that I love your son in a pure way. —I pause myself, the tears in my eyes are just as fast as my words.

—I just hope things turn out well, Heinrich is like his father, very taciturn.

I realized that Mrs. Marisela was somewhat surprised with my confidence, even though she knew something. I didn't need her approval, I just wanted her to know, but what I did was an outburst and I felt I needed to apologize.

—Mrs. Marisela, I'm sorry. I'm sorry that I threw all of this at you so drastically.

—There's nothing to apologize for. Women should not apologize for loving, much less so for loving with courage.

Perhaps Mrs. Marisela was protecting her son, perhaps she knew things about her previous daughters-in-law, perhaps she had already heard someone say that she loved her son and was then proven otherwise.

# Morning tales

Luis Miguel and I spent a wonderful New Year's Eve with my family here in Milan. He was happy, so was I, and he gets along super with the twins. For them, he is another «cuzzie», it even seems that Maria Celeste loves him more than me, her own flesh and blood. Luismi, besides not being shy at all, is as if he were part of the family, that's how we treated each other in Maracaibo and that's how we continue to treat each other here.

After we relived the hugs we give each other on New Year's Eve in my country during the celebration, we had dinner and decided to head back; we had several drinks in our system and it was better to have some sobriety to walk through the bustling city. Once home, we went to sleep, we were tired, the day was intense.

When I open my eyes, all I can hear is Luis Miguel's breathing, and I, who adore him, stroke his head.

—Oh, honey, it's so nice to sleep in your bed, it's so comfortable. And everything is so quiet, so calm. I'll get up in a minute, I want to stay in this peace and quiet.

—I'll wake you up when breakfast is ready —I say and give him a kiss on his forehead.

—No, love, no way. I'll make you breakfast, I'll get up right away then - he says, still sleepy.

—But I can cook and you can have a little more time.

—No, honey, I'm getting up now - he says frowning at me.

—Baby, I'll have some fruit and I'll wait for you.

—No, no, I'm getting up.

It's super clear that the love language of the Gil Montilla family is acts of service. I'm getting out of bed to go get cleaned up a little and at least put the coffee on. Once I'm done and the coffee is ready, I pour a cup for Luis Miguel and another for me.

Since he's my guest of honor I decide to give him the cup that my dad gave me when he came over that has an engraving in English with «*If nothing goes right go left, but always find a way*» [61].

When I enter the bedroom-living-dining room, Luismi tells me:

—Listen to this.

A voice note starts playing: «Send my greetings to Santi, I'm glad you are spending time together, may God bless her always».

—It's your dad – I say, stoically.

—Yeah, perhaps you're not talking to H, but think about it. My mom, dad and sister are all drooling over you.

Taking advantage of the fact that we're touching the topic, while I give him the cup of coffee, I say to him.

—You know I told your mom yesterday that I loved H, what do you think she'll think about that? I mean, now that I've got a cool head, I think I probably acted crazy.

—Oh, Mary Jane. Shut up —he tells me, and sips some coffee—. My mom is super chill. Besides, she adores you. She'll be happier than fuck, damn it, I can already imagine her going to La Chinita to ask her to join you in holy matrimony.

I laugh. And, then, I add:

—Can I ask you one thing that I shouldn't ask, but I'm curious about? —I ask, with a lump in my throat.

..............................................

[61] If nothing goes right, go left, but always look for a way

—Of course, Baby, ask away—Luismi replies, curious.

—What was H's ex's relationship like with all of you?

—Complicated, Santi, I'll be honest with you.

—Why?

—There was something that didn't quite add up for us. I don't know.

—Can I be honest with you?

—Yes, of course.

—I think H has been abused, emotionally, too many times. But she takes 1st place. I don't know how to explain it. I swear by my love of art that I'm not a woman who bad mouths another, I'm the first one that stands up for another woman, but I need to confess and I have no one to talk about it with.

—Do you think so? It doesn't sound illogical, honestly.

—That's why H and I haven't finally gotten things right. Because he's too hurt. But, on the other hand, it seems very indulgent to say that he's wounded, because I'm wounded, I'm a woman who is in post-war mode, and here I am, steady, with my heart in my hand ready to love him. Maybe, I'm just not the girl for H.

—Well, Baby, as far as I know H is going to therapy. So, we have to give him a chance, too. He's too closed up.

I didn't know H was going to therapy, but I'm not surprised. He's someone who commits to himself if he needs to, just like I have him on my affirmative wish list. I don't want to delve into the subject of therapy with Luismi because my concern is what H's mom might think, from my expression of love towards her son.

—But back to your mom. She just told me that she hoped everything would turn out fine and that H was very stubborn.

—Baby, stop spinning that idea in your head. You have to understand that my mom isn't used to a girl coming up being so straightforward and honest. You simply, *caught her off base* [62] —he says to me with a reassuring tone—. Now come here, let's eat. Everything will be OK. H and you have a red thread.

I let Luismi leave the bedroom-living-dining room and go up to the loft bed to make the bed.

«Luismi sees the red thread between us. Will fate find a way? It can't be that I love him this way and that God forbids me from living it, after everything I've been through, why don't things just end up going well? Why is my happiness always temporary? Was I perhaps too rude to H when I asked him to stop talking? Should I have been more patient and understanding.

---

[62] An expression that's used to say that it took someone by surprise, unprepared. (Editor's Note)

# CHAPTER VI
## Forming the unseen

«It's not good to dwell on dreams and forget about living».

–J.K. Rowling, *Harry Potter and the Philosopher's Stone*

# New year. New me.

The year has started with a bang. I have firm and strong convictions, one of them was to have a session with my therapist about the calls from the Gil Montilla family and about a possible first date with Theo.

My therapist advised me – and I agree with her – to take January to experiment and experience the things happening around me. Things that I could touch. Therefore, I have taken a week to go to all the gym classes, I have tried pilates, yoga, ballet... I even did a little swimming.

The girls are doing their own things, as always, and Theo has answered me a couple of stories on Instagram.

The last time I saw Theo was when I went out with my friends before Christmas; on that occasion, besides sharing musical tastes, we exchanged our phone numbers and social media. Sure, there were many naughty smiles and phrases with double intent, but it didn't move past that. I also didn't think, at that time, that I would give myself permission to date someone other than H, but it's a new year and I must, yes or yes, set myself expectations in the reality close to me.

After Theo's insistence, and after my session with Mariana, I have decided to go out with the Greek God for a first date and see how I feel. Whether it makes me feel comfortable, or not. The only times we have interacted has been in a group setting. So this would be the first time that the two of us would be alone, and my expectations are through the roof.

With my therapist I also came to the conclusion that, perhaps, the reason H has been in my life is to confirm that the guy on my list is possible; perfect men exist. Now, it might be the time to find him within a maximum radius of five kilometers. I've managed to change the narrative of H is my happily ever after, to if there is one H, there are others. I just have to get out there.

———•••⇥⇤•••———

This morning I got a call from Theo, his invitation was to a winery restaurant that offers a welcome package with a wine tasting. I had never been there and his idea convinced me completely; it seemed like an elegant and respectful invitation.

Maybe the idea of elegance behind a wine tasting was the one I had when I was fifteen, when I asked my mom to pay for a wine tasting course for me. I did it, but I had to spit out the wine, not because I was training as a professional taster, but because I was underage and shouldn't be drinking it. It was a whim, eleven years later I don't remember anything about smells, flavors or colors anymore, but I guess it's like when you don't remember a language, you get the hang of it after a while.

Theo's proposal seems to me worthy of a first date: distinguished and formal «Point for Theo. But that doesn't mean I'm going to sleep with him, he'll have to meet my standards first», I tell myself. I accept his invitation and remember H's advice; when I was about to ask him if he would send me a taxi or come and get me, he said first:

—Tina, can you send me your location to pick you up?

—Will you come get me or...? —I said, because it was what I had thought to ask him before he came forward.

—Of course, I'm going to pick you up. Do you think I'll let a princess like you walk around the city alone?

«Wow, I said to myself, this guy already has two points on my scale, he's respectful and kind». We set a time and I sent him my location via WhatsApp.

According to the schedule, Theo arrives on time, he smells to die for, he's wearing a navy-blue blazer and a half-open white shirt that shows his chest. For my part, I'm wearing a short black dress. I know it's provocative, but I didn't wear it with that intention, but because it's what is recommended for a wine tasting, because of possible stains. I'm wearing pantyhose and black heels. I know I'm dressed up. When Theo sees me, he breaks down with compliments, he makes me feel like a queen.

The wine tasting venue is beautiful, quite old and full of wood, they seat us at a high table and the tasting is random with five types of wine: two red, two white and one pink. After the tasting we could choose the bottle we would have liked and finish it with dinner; the dish would not be decided by us, but it would be from the wine we chose; all of that was told to us in a rather ceremonious explanation.

They bring us the first wine. It's a white wine without any other information. We will have the information in order, when we finish the five glasses of wine.

—Well, come to think of it, five glasses of wine sounds like too much for my big little body.

—Hahaha, take it easy, Tina. A glass has about a hundred and fifty milliliters of wine, here they'll only have fifty milliliters. Each sip should be more or less between ten and twenty milliliters, maybe about three sips per cup. If you take the whole glass, it would be about fifteen sips of wine, about two hundred and fifty milliliters for the whole tasting.

—Oh, well, that's true. The numbers don't sound that much. But don't call me Tina.

—That was the name you gave me.

—Right, but it's the name I use when I don't want to make a situation too personal. We're on a first date and we're sharing music. I think it's already personal enough for you to call me Valentina or Mava, whichever you prefer.

—Valentina. I'm flattered. Thank you.

I wink at him.

We started with the tasting and, as I figured, I started to remember my lessons.

—Mmm it has a floral aroma —I say after smelling it —with warm alcohol —after I taste it slowly.

—Wow, you know about this —Theo says, surprised.

—Actually, not much. I'm just remembering some lessons I had many years ago —and I'm telling him about the course paid for by my mom. I think that will be the most personal thing I will reveal to him about me tonight.

When we are being served the third glass of wine, I ask him if I can check his birth chart.

He has no idea what I'm talking about, so I give him my phone so he can put in his information on a website.

Once he gives my phone back, I hit continue and when I see the wheel with his astrological map, I take a brief look at it and I understand why there is this attraction that made me forget my mishap with H.

He asks me about what I'm doing and I confess my fondness for astrology.

—Explain more of that to me —he says —What do you see in my data?

—Well, you're a Taurus with Scorpio rising. You have Venus in Taurus and Mars in Virgo, and your Mars is in conjunction with Pluto, which means that your batteries are not running out.

—Okay, you're right. I know I have a lot of energy.

The only difficulty I see is that he has a Moon and Mercury in Cancer, and that could speak of a man who needs a lot of attention. But these are big words for this moment and I decided not to touch them.

But he, on the other hand, reveals himself to me completely. He tells me everything that he does. He works, reads, likes music and even has a band. I find it sweet that he wants me to get to know him, and he tries not to ask that much about me. I think he's afraid that if he corners me with questions, I will walk away, so we handle our conversation in a relaxed mode, trusting, but without intrusions.

When the time comes, we have to decide which wine to choose. I tell him that I liked the white one, perhaps because it was the first one we tried.

—I'll confess that it wasn't my favorite —he tells me —but I am here to please you.

I tell him that I like his honesty and that I'm flattered by his justification. Honestly, this guy makes me feel really good about myself. In my list, he already has three points.

The restaurant surprises us with smoked trout as the main course, accompanied with a fresh salad. Everything is delicious and definitely goes perfectly with wine.

When we're about to finish our dinner, Theo reminds me of what he said to me at the disco, the first time we met, and asks me how I'm feeling right now.

—I assure you, Valentina, that I've been thinking about you ever since that night. Do you remember that I told you that if you wanted we could just dance, that for cute girls like you there's always patience. I know you were going through some bad shit. Don't tell me if you don't want to, but tell me if you're over it.

—It's something I wouldn't like to talk about right now, agreeing to this date is part of the freedom I want to give myself, but I'm not ready for any commitment beyond this dinner just yet.

—I also like your honesty and I warn you —he smiles as he says it —I'll keep on insisting, and I'll tell you again, for a pretty girl like you, all of my patience.

The evening was fabulous. Theo took me back to my apartment and we said goodbye with a kiss that almost shook my decision not to have sex.

Once at home, I laugh when I remember what the funniest and friendliest nun at my school said when I was studying high school. Sister Ines, in a special class with just girls, told us that to avoid having sex we had to implement the pill method. «Pill?», «are there any pills to abstain from sex?» What's that?», we asked curiously. «Well, you put a pill between one leg and the other, knee height, and hold it there until the date is over. If you drop it, you're screwed». We were dying with laughter with her advice. Tonight, Sister Ines, was one of wine and stars, and I didn't drop the pill.

.

# Theo's pacience

After our first wine tasting date, Theo and I went out to the cinema. We were both «demure», we watched the movie, walked around the city a bit while we were talking about it and then he took me home. Nothing happened but two deep kisses, but, Oh boy! They sure shook me to the core. The boy knows how to kiss.

Since then, we've been chatting on the phone, and I have, in particular, been finding out more about his astral chart. I want to understand why I see him and all my resolutions of prudence get shaken. «What does this man and this Maria Valentina have in conjunction?».

It makes me laugh to think that these dates with Theo look like teenage dates with a first boyfriend, but I think that this strategy, that I self-imposed to not to go any further, is working out, today I've been thinking about him and his patient way of being. Apparently, Theo, with his patience, also has a purpose... thinking about that worries me a little because I don't know if I'm ready to have a serious relationship; the one I aspired to have with H. At this point, Theo seems to be a very special man, someone who would be an excellent prize in the contest of life, but he's not an Oscar and I don't know how I would feel if I had to cut his wings if this takes flight.

Theo lives with his best friend named Lucas, also Greek. Both are doing their master's degree in automotive engineering internships at Ferrari, and both are waiting for the company to offer them full-time work. During these days, his friend is out of Italy, on some training in London. Theo calls me, tells me about it, tells me he wants to make the most of the extra space and invites me to his apartment.

I find myself doubtful. I like the guy a lot, and over in his apartment, alone, it's going to be difficult for me to hold on to my decision of temporary chastity. But I'm willing to stay that way until the memory of H fades forever. It's just that for some reason I still feel like if I have sex with someone else, I'm failing him. I wonder if he feels the same as me. I remember that he couldn't do anything with the girl in Valencia, he felt that he owed me respect. Well, yes, but it must be over because he even traveled with that other tramp.

Theo seems to smell my doubts and my hesitation, so he texts me:

*Maria Valentina, we're not going to do anything you don't want, but I would like for you to simply know where I live and make a pizza together. I've already bought the ingredients, I just need to go get you, go on, say yes.*

*All right, come and pick me up, I'll be ready in half an hour.*

---

His apartment is nice, much more spacious and comfortable than mine. I tell him about that and we make a promise that one day he will visit me. Then, we start preparing the pizza, aprons included. I feel comfortable and happy, Theo does most of the work and I'm like his assistant. While cooking, we also drank some wine. It feels like a family Sunday. Many times, sparks fly between us, a repressed desire, but then comes my silence that Theo interprets perfectly.

I admit that the pizza was spectacular. We're eating and, maybe because it was delicious, a comment escape from me:

—You cook as deliciously as Luismi. —Big mistake on my end, not only because I have to clarify who Luismi is, but because of what comes attached to that memory.

—Anyone should I be worried about? —he asks me with a smile.

—No, no, he's a great friend of mine who lives in Madrid and has a partner, he's like my younger brother —I try to summarize, so that he doesn't ask me about it anymore. And he doesn't. He behaves like a gentleman.

Despite Theo's cordiality, with Luismi's memory, it becomes inevitable that H will get into my food. I feel a huge sadness because I realize that he raised the bar on my demands, he makes everyone else look childish and small.

Here I am in front of this Greek god who is magnificent, handsome, tender, respectful, who is determined to show himself as a man capable of making a home, and I think he is far away from the bar that H set up for my life. It's not fair to Theo. It's not fair to me.

Theo looks at me as if looking for words in my eyes, but he is not H, and I stay silent.

In the face of my silence, Theo realizes that something is up, but he doesn't interrupt me. He acts cautiously. He picks up the dishes, takes them to the kitchen and I decide to clear my head of H and go and wash them with him.

—Don't think you're going to do all the work alone — I tell him, and I get ready to continue being his assistant.

When we finish washing and drying the dishes, and picking up the mess we had left in the kitchen, Theo asks me what I would like to do next, and I propose that we go for a walk around the city.

—My apartment is not far away, you know that. You can walk with me if you want.

—Of course, Valentina. If that's what you want to do, that's what we'll do.

When I get there, I'm tempted to ask him to come up, I look at him and he seems so handsome that I want to send the idea of abstinence to hell, but I remember that I put up the blue towels I bought for H, and as long as H is still here, I won't do it. Today, Theo has raised his points in patience and his kisses are delicious. If this keeps up like this, I think I'll be able to fall in love.

# It's in the air

That horrible moment in life that comes for every woman is here, the least expected moment that always comes, and it's always frightening. I ran out of sunscreen and facial serums. Holy Virgin! That means spending a minimum wage in Latin America. Armed with courage, with a courage that all independent women have to find because, what else, girl! When it's time, it's time, so I put my little feet in gear and go to the mall.

When I get to the cosmetics store, I immediately head to the sunscreen section. I go to the dermatologist at least twice a year, and the last time I was there, the doctor told me that Australian sunscreens were *a shot to the floor* [63]. Therefore, after exhaustive research on YouTube, I have decided on the Bondi Sands SPF 50+ Face Fragrance Free, which is perfect for all weather conditions and will not disturb my acne-prone skin. I wonder if H has gotten sunscreen that doesn't leave his face like fried chicken... I shake the thought off immediately.

Sunscreen in hand, I go to the serums section. On my way, I stop in my tracks because of a smell that has reached my nose. I recognize it, and I start instinctively and frantically looking for the source of the aroma until I see it: a guy has just tried a perfume, the smell created an expansive wave towards me and when it hit, a tiny short circuit triggered my psyche. It's H's perfume, "Born in Roma", by Valentino.

Like a zombie, I walk up to the counter, grab the piece of paper they put to test and spray perfume on it. It smells delicious.

---

[63] A shot to the floor is an expression used to mean that doing something is easy, also, like in this case, it means that something is a safe bet. (Editor's Note)

It's amazing how H keeps sneaking into my life without me calling him. «Is this a heavenly conspiracy, Chinita, enlighten me, What should I do to get him out of my mind? Why don't they invent pills to forget?»

---

It's true that H is in the air, but so is Theo. Today I've managed to control my anxiety surrounding H, it's true that I haven't yet reached total indifference, but it no longer affects me and Theo is here with his gallantry, his beauty and his delicious kisses. I think it's time to take a step forward with him.

Today he invited me to dinner again. He has promised me that we will have a wonderful evening in a newly opened restaurant where he managed to make a reservation. And I, without hesitation, said yes. I feel too attracted to him. «Goodbye, Hachito, it's your loss».

Theo will be picking me up at eight, so I have to hurry because I'm going to dress up for him like a princess.

I've put on a short black skirt, with a turtleneck, high boots and my signature makeup when I want to elevate a look, that is, red lips. I know I'm to die for and that's what Theo tells me when he sees me. He has also dressed up elegantly and looks gorgeous, he deserves my compliments.

When we arrived at the restaurant, we didn't go unnoticed, eyes were chasing this handsome pair, we looked like two models walking down a catwalk. Of course, they didn't take long to serve us.

They bring us the hors d'oeuvres and we order a bottle of wine while we choose from the menu. We have a bite to eat, we have a drink, and I'm just melting for this guy. Following my instincts, I keep staring at him, I get close enough to make him uneasy.

When the waiter approaches, I raise my hand and make the sign that I want the bill.

—What's wrong? Don't you want to wait for dinner? — he asks nervously.
—No. We're going to skip dinner and go straight to dessert. Your place or mine? —I answer without hesitation, framing my face with my

eyebrows.

His eyes look at me without being able to believe what I just said, in reality, I don't believe my daring either. But I think that if Theo as much as blows on me right now, I'll have an orgasm. My scorpio venus is dripping for this man.

—Okay —Theo replies nervously.

The waiter brings the bill and Theo takes his card out.

Once the waiter comes back with the card, we get up, Theo has got his breath back, relaxed and took control of the situation; he leads the way with his hand resting on my back. Once outside, he hands over the ticket to the valet parking and they immediately bring his car.

When we enter his house, Theo closes the door behind me. And in less than one second, he is frantically kissing me, I accept his kiss with passion, and then he lifts me up. And he keeps on kissing my neck.

—Bedroom? Or can I have dessert on the kitchen counter?

—Kitchen is okay — I reply between gasps.

Theo, with agility, puts me on top of the kitchen counter and lays me down on it. When he pulls up my skirt and realizes I'm wearing garter belts, he breaths out heavily.

—Woman, you're going to kill me —he says.

He slides my thong to the side and without hesitation or embarrassment puts his head between my legs and licks my most sensitive part with frenzy. After a few seconds I have a loud and prolonged orgasm. Theo prolongs the assault of his mouth between my legs, even when I try to pull him away. When I finally succeed, I start to laugh. The Greek god quickly pulls me down from the counter and turns me over, exposing my buttocks, and spanks me hard. After such an orgasm, the spanking was the icing on the cake of this dessert.

Theo gets himself right behind me, gluing his body to mine. And he says in my ear:

—I hope you enjoyed the orgasm, because unfortunately mine isn't working today.

—I enjoyed it —I assure him, panting.

—Next time, I'll be more prepared.

He was intimidated. I was already familiar with the issue. I had experience with that..

# Intimate

I didn't wake up feeling good today, I stayed home, because I'm having a terrible time. I have a lot of stomach pain and my period isn't coming down. I haven't been able to eat right. When I start to feel my stomach pain rising, I'm aware that I am about to experience what I call «the belly fit». It's when the pain rises unexpectedly and becomes so unbearable that my body collapses to the point of losing consciousness, vomiting or my sphincters acting out. Thank God this has never happened to me in public, or in front of anyone. There is no painkiller that can help me, I just have to let it happen. It's an episode that lasts approximately ten minutes.

Aware of what is going to happen, I prepare myself a hot water compress that I place on my abdomen, while I wait for the tub to fill with hot water as well.

When the pain makes my legs shake, and I retch, I get into the tub, which isn't full yet, but it is warm, to help me get through the painful moment.

I'm in the tub basically praying, asking God not to let me faint or lose consciousness. When I choke on my own vomit, I quickly get out and throw up in the toilet bowl. I faint a little and fall on top of it, even though that seems disgusting and unhygienic.

Since I have a very regular period, I get it exactly every twenty-eight days, I take all the precautions I can. The day before I do some gentle exercises, I walk, eat well, and the day I'm going to have it, I take painkillers and disinfect the toilet because I know that despite all the forecasts, I cannot avoid extreme episodes. I have a real panic about my own period, I get nervous breakdowns a few days before.

When I manage to get my strength back, I get back in the tub. I wake up suddenly, choking with bathwater. The pain is still there, intense. I don't know if I fell asleep or if I passed out, but I know it's not safe to stay here like this. I decide to get up very carefully to not fall down, my legs are still shaking, I remove the plug from the bathtub, and turn on the shower.

I wash myself calmly, crying to see myself in this state. I get out of the shower, put on warm pajamas and go up to the loft bed; I have a bucket with me, in case I feel like throwing up; my laptop, because I'm supposed to be working; an analgesic gel, a protein bar and water.

I lay down in bed with the compress that keeps warm. I put the analgesic gel on my lower back and belly. I drink water and take a bite of my protein. Within a few minutes I fell asleep, exhausted from the pain.

The sound of a Teams notification wakes me up. It's my boss, she asks me to unlock an order, and I do it quickly. The process doesn't take more than two minutes, but I'm the only one with that access.

When I finish, I'm still sore. Although the pain is more manageable, I'm still exhausted. I'll try to get some more rest.

When I wake up, the pain is finally gone. I'm hungry and I'm feeling in a better mood; anyhow, I'll stay at home all day and maybe watch a movie or a series in the evening.

When I'm about to finish my work schedule, I get a message from Theo asking me out. At this point our communication is constant, but there is no good morning or good evening, or a detailed exchange of our day, as I used to do with another «Parallelepiped» person.

*Oh no    not today. Really. I got my period this morning and I almost died, really. I must rest and stay at home. I'll watch a serie.*

*Of course, Baby. Get some rest.*

I'm sitting on the couch watching a series when Theo calls me on the phone.

—Can I come over?

—What do you mean?
—If I could come over and hang out with you.
—But I have my period.
—We won't do anything; I just want to hang out with you.
—Okay. Yeah, I guess so.

Honestly, his company doesn't bother me, but the opposite is also true. At least at the moment.

There's a knock on the door, I know it's Theo. When I open it, I notice that he's carrying a paper bag.

—Hi, Baby. —He gives me a kiss on the lips.

He comes in and leaves the paper bag on the kitchen counter while I close the door.

He starts unpacking what he bought.

—I brought you chicken pho from the Vietnamese guy on the corner. Support your local business.

I'm shocked. Theo continues:

—I also brought you a Kinder surprise. It's chocolate with a small gift. And I brought popcorn for us to watch your series.

—Kinder surprises remind me of when I was in Venezuela and I took care of my little cousins, they always asked for one. And the answer was always No because they were too expensive and there were other priorities – I tell him.

—Kinder surprise eggs are expensive everywhere. They didn't buy them for me either. That's why I bought two. One for you and one for me.

Dear Theodore is so sweet and courteous.

—Thank you for all this, you are very kind.

—You're welcome, Baby. Now have some soup.

I help myself to some pho.

—It's delicious! —I say, and follow it up with—. I should start being more daring and try more things. I had never tried Pho, I had tried Vietnamese food. In fact, I used to eat with my cousin at a Vietnamese restaurant near our old apartment, but my order used to always be chicken bo bun. Definitely added to the list of foods that Maria

Valentina Santini Duque likes.

—Congratulations! —says Theo and smiles wide.

Finally, Theo has stayed with me for quite a long time. I'm sleepy and in a bit of pain so I take a painkiller and I offer to lie down in the loft bed.

Once upstairs, lying on the bed, Theo is quite warm, so I ask him to place his hands on my belly while the pain passes.

—I promise I'll get over it in a few minutes. Give me a chance.

—Take your time — and he gives me a kiss on my forehead.

After some time, with Theo's warm hands on my belly, I fall asleep.

We both slept until dawn. Theo is spooning me in a hug, and he puts his head behind my hair.

—I should get going. I have to work.

—Yes, me too— I reply still sleepy.

—Do you have to go too?

—No, I have to work too.

—Okay. Stay here, don't worry, I can find my way out. I'll leave you pho, when you get up, eat some, Baby. It will do you good, I hope you have a better day today.

I nod my head. And then he leaves.

It never ceases to amaze me how this relationship is going, we have no plans or expectations, we haven't created them, at least I haven't, we have simply gone with the flow. I like him, he likes me; he's sweet, and I love that, and we have reached this intimacy, the intimacy of sleeping together without doing anything else. It's the first time a guy has spent the night here, in my apartment, with me and for me, not just to have sex.

# Scary!

In the building where I live, each apartment has a doorbell number and a code. If somebody uses the doorbell number, the intercom sounds like a call, and if someone uses the code, the intercom rings with a beep. Theo has just left, and as soon as I hear the door closing, the intercom rings notifying that someone entered using my code.

I panic. The only person I can remember who has my code is Voldemort and since Theo just left, I'm overcome with paranoia. The morning after my first rape, Voldemort showed up at the old apartment and I immediately associate it to that. «Is it possible that this fucker is stalking me?».

I quickly get down from the loft bed, phone in hand, quickly get into the bathroom and open the window.

The bathroom window overlooks other apartments. I'm on the first floor, if I scream loudly, someone could help me, I could also get out of the window without hurting myself too much.

This is the only open window. The two large windows of the bedroom-living-dining room have a grille, so even if the glass is broken, no one can't get in, and the door is heavy, they can't break it down.

I'm thinking about all my possibilities.

I have the emergency number ready on my phone. And I stay silent waiting to see what happens.

They knock on the door in a hurry and loudly.

My heart is about to escape.

«God, help me. Don't let him in. Don't let me see him again. Don't let anyone hurt me».

A call comes in from my Aunt Eugenia. I ignore it.

Then a text.

> *My sweet sobri. Are you at home? I'm at the door*

My soul gets back in my body.

I get out of panic mode and out of the bathroom, and I'm going to open the door with my prayers on the top of my tongue.

—Auntie, you scared the shit out of me.

—Why? Who else has your code?

—My ex.

—Oh. That bastard —she starts jumping—. Let me go to the bathroom and pee. Pretty please.

When my aunt enters the bathroom, I run out to my room. I have to get rid of any trace of Theo! The cigarettes, what he brought for dinner…

I grab the cigarette pack from the counter and stuff it inside a jacket at the entrance. I take the remains of pho and throw them in the trash, I realize that they are visible at the bottom of the can, so I put it in the closet.

I hear my aunt flushing the toilet. A few seconds later she comes out of the bathroom.

— Sobri, I was in the area running an errand and I felt like taking a pee, and I said to myself, «I'm going to stop by to see if my beautiful sobri is home so we can have breakfast together». I know you don't work at the office on Fridays. I knew you'd be here.

—Of course, auntie. But I have to take a shower, will you wait for me?

—Yes, of course.

God! What a scare! Between thinking that Voldemort was coming to stalk me and then my aunt seeing the cigarettes… or worse… that she would have knocked on the door and I was in bed with Theo, OMG!

My aunt is not stupid. She surely knows that I smoke, and of course she knows that I'm not a virgin. But it's one thing for her to think or imagine something, and it's another thing for her to have evidence or get caught red-handed. My aunt is not the judging type, but I prefer to hold the line of respect.

---

The waiter brings our Italian cafes and pastries to the table, we have chosen the new and small cafe on the corner. Supporting local commerce. My aunt tells me.

—Mary, look, that man, your ex, can't hurt you. No more. You're in Italy, honey, there's laws here, and there's the police. He's not going to stalk you — My aunt was aware that he had been mean to me, that he had hurt me, but she really didn't know the whole story—. And if he does, remember Grandpa. All of a sudden, a kick in the balls and that's it. Your dad taught me how to defend myself. I'm sure he did the same with you, didn't he?

My dad is twelve years older than my Aunt Eugenia. There are four of them: two men and two women. My dad is the oldest, he is fifty-five years old right now; then, my aunt Fatima, with fifty-two; then my uncle Alberto, forty-seven; and the youngest, my aunt Eugenia, forty-three years old.

I was very fond of my aunt, and loved spending time with her. Although I sometimes went weeks without seeing her because I was lying in bed crying for H, or staying in bed doing other things, or hanging out with my friends. When I apologized to my aunt for not being so present, she only replied: «You are starting to live, between migrating, that bastard of your ex, and covid, it's as if you are really just now starting to live, you don't have to apologize for that».

—Yes, auntie, my dad taught me how to defend myself.

My dad has been a great dad, although I wouldn't have seen it that way in my teenage years, the reality is that my parents were very protective of me, and I thought they were clipping my wings. Now that I was out of their protection, I understood what they were protecting me from.

My aunt and I finished our breakfast and when it's time to leave, I promise to visit her soon because I know that the girls ask about me often.

# The unexpected

The encounters with Theo continue. I accepted his invitation to cook in his apartment again. He told me that he wants to follow a recipe for risotto, he wants to learn about local gastronomy and that he would love for me to be his «assistant».

He picks me up, we get to his apartment and do what we planned. Once the meal was over, we got ready to watch a movie in the living room. We decided on Mystery on board. A silly movie, but easy to digest.

We're on the couch laughing at the movie when, without preamble or hesitation, Theo pulls me towards him, puts me on his lap and starts assaulting my mouth. He gets carrying me and without stopping to kiss me, he takes me to his bedroom.

When I reach an orgasm, something happens. I don't laugh, instead I start crying and start to have a panic attack. Theo, not knowing what to do, quickly brings me water and then holds my face, blowing at me to give me some air.

—Baby, what's going on? —he says to me in a worried voice, still holding me in his hands.

Sobbing, I shake my head, with the movement I tell him that I don't know.

—Did I hurt you? Did I do something to you? Talk to me.

I'm still crying.

Theo takes me in his arms and wraps me with the duvet, while I keep on crying. He starts to rub my arm to comfort me, but the friction of the movement causes me to retch. I let go of his grip quickly, and then he looks at me bewildered.

—Tell me, what can I do for you? —he asks uneasily.

—Open the window, I need air — I reply panting.

Once the bedroom window is open, I shuffle over to it. The cold breeze touches my naked body and I start shivering from the cold. Theo pulls the duvet closer to me and covers me, but this time he's careful not to grope me too much.

I really don't know what happened to me. I came with full intentions of having a spectacular night and suddenly this happens to me, I don't know why this anxiety attack came. I feel like I should retire to think, forget, or what do I know, maybe live out my shame.

—Is it okay if I go home? —I say, ashamed.

—I'll take you, it's already late.

—It's just a few minutes walking.

—Baby, you just had an anxiety attack. Please, I know that you can go alone, that you are a strong girl. We'll walk if you want, but let me accompany you.

—OK —I reply without fighting him anymore.

We walked the blocks in silence, and by the time we got to my apartment I was feeling better and now I feel guilty for ruining Theo's night.

—Do you want to come up for some tea?

—Sure, I'd love to.

I am making two cups of tea with their own sachet, while Theo limits his conversation to commenting on the decorations in my apartment.

—Valentina, when you are ready to talk, I want to listen to you. Not to act like a Don Juan, but believe me, I've been with many women in my life and I know how to deduce certain things. I don't want you to feel like I'm putting pressure on you, just know that what happened tonight, is something that has happened to me with other girls before and I'm really sorry, Baby. I want you to know that I understand a No even without being told, it's an attitude thing or rather a guy thing.

Theo is a great human being; I've noticed that from the very beginning. He's a very genuine guy, there's nothing he would have done that triggered the anxiety attack, it had just happened. And he had behaved like a prince, and now with these words he was a prince becoming a king.

However, today I just don't feel like talking about ugly things that happened in the past. I guess talking about one thing will lead to another and I'll end up talking about H. And that's a subject I don't want to touch. This isn't a day to cut myself open.

I explain to Theo that I don't want to talk today, that maybe one day we will talk about this, he tells me that he understands and then I tell him that I want to go take a shower and go to bed.

—I don't want to leave you yet, is it okay if I stay here a while longer? You can take a shower and I'll wait for you.

The reality is that one of those alien things I have, is that I don't like guys with a golden retriever attitude, they tire and bore me. I am a black cat, a panther, and I'm attracted to black cat boys. H is, in short, a black cat, precise, he likes solitude, stillness and, although it's difficult for him to be sweet and friendly, he ends up being it when you earn his respect.

Parallelepiped I tell myself to stop the chain of thoughts that could end in another anxiety attack. I bring myself to the present. I'm at home, with Theo, a wonderful guy who is so comfortable with me that he wants to stay just like that for five more minutes.

—Okay. That's fine. I'm going to take a shower and, honestly, I'm going to take my time. I'll leave the apartment door open in case you want to leave.

—Valentina, take your time —he says to me gently, squeezing my shoulders.

When I get out of the shower, I see that Theo has picked up and folded the clothes that were drying on the clothesline next to the heating and has put them on the table in the bedroom-living-dining room.

—It was dry. I hope you don't mind. I didn't want to take it too far and put it away. Although I didn't lack for wants.

...............................................

[64] *Jalabolas* is an expression of Venezuelan origin. It's used in a pejorative way to say that someone is servile and sycophant. Its origin dates back to the beginning of the twentieth century, it was coined during the dictatorship of Juan Vicente Gómez. The prisoners were chained to a very heavy steel ball, and those who were detained, but had economic resources, paid the poorest prisoners to carry their ball. (Editor's Note)

«What are they giving these guys lately? So kind and considerate!», «*Jalabolas* [64], says another part of me.

I laugh at myself and my contradictions. «Be kind, Maria Valentina, don't be a bitch with this guy. He was all cute, he even folded your clothes. Ah, but if it was H, and you would have wet yourself. Deranged. Get it together».

I walk towards him and subtly kiss his cheek.

—Theodore, thank you for your kindness. I do a lot of laundry because I'm crazy, and if I wear something, I'll wash it. If you feel like it, you can come one day a week and help me — I say, batting my eyelashes.

—Valentina, I hope you know that I can also sweep, mop, wash dishes and I like to cook. Well, you already know that. Call me, Baby, for whatever, but call me.

—Noted — I give him another subtle kiss on the cheek and proceed to put on my pajamas.

When I finish putting on my pajamas, I sit down with him on the sofa, and the conversation moves on to family and the past. Theo tells me that his parents divorced when he was young, and that his dad wasn't around too much, that it was always just him, his mom, and his grandmother. That he was an excellent basketball player, even at the young age of seventeen, he was signed with the most important club in his country and they paid him a good amount of money, but that the situation went to his head to the point that his mom told him that he was unrecognizable. When his mom told him that, he quit and dedicated himself to studying and pursuing a quieter and more tangible career.

—There are two things I'm passionate about: cars and basketball. Right now, I'm focusing on cars, but I hope to be able to do some basketball in the future, and I'm not talking about playing. I'm talking about business decisions, like being a shareholder in a club and scouting for talent, and just being there. Giving athletes a proper club, so that what happened to me doesn't happen to them, with psychologists, and with a family atmosphere. The only positive and memorable memories with my dad are around basketball.

My heart is melting.

—It sounds like a super idea to me. You'll find a way to achieve all that. People are lost these days; it feels refreshing to talk to someone who knows exactly what they want.

—Valentina, thank you for your words, I hope to be like you one day.

—What are you talking about?

— Well, you're an independent woman, living in your own apartment, you crossed an entire ocean to be here, you know three languages, and speak all three elegantly. I still make mistakes when I speak English, and even more so with Italian.

— It's all a matter of practice, I've been speaking English since I was eleven and Italian since I was seventeen, and I've always been surrounded by Italian culture so it wasn't that difficult either.

—Valentina, you're exceptional. Believe me, I look at you and, wow! I admire you. Any man who approaches you is going to question whether he deserves you. Besides, you're successful in a career that you did not even study, you know, you're an audiovisual producer. And here you are, doing a career in finances and killing it. Just wow!

I was a very confident woman, I patted myself on the back. I really didn't need those words, but hey! They felt good. That's exactly what my therapist Mariana & I were talking about. I didn't need external validation, but I liked having it. I enjoyed it. It was like a confirmation that I was doing things right, in case I doubted myself.

—Well, thank you very much. I think you're exceptional, too. I mean, leaving basketball at the peak of your career because it went to your head, putting what your mom thinks about you in the first place, that's a wonderful thing. I don't know, nor am I sure it's the right thing to do, but it was something that worked for you personally.

Honestly, the boy has a Moon in Cancer, he needed validation from his mom, and he needs that from any important woman in his life. He's a man who's always drooling over women. Too much of a Mr. Bingley. Too sweet.

# My cortisol is on its own

The experience with Theo makes me set an appointment with Mariana. Because of H, I came to therapy and surfaced all the wounds left behind by Voldemort and the others. Now I have to do it, not because of Theo, but for me. What happened with Theo is just a symptom that something is not right, and if I want to be everything I am meant to be, I must heal any wound, even if that wound is spelled with an H. So here I am, in the office in front of Mariana.

—Let's see, Valentina. Tell me what you've been up to since we last met.

I tell Mariana everything that has happened in the last weeks, I explain to her that I managed to control my anxiety with H and that now it's just an anecdote, that what worries me was what happened with Theo, I tell her about my abstinence on the first dates and then the panic attack, because I don't know why or where it came from.

—Okay, let's see, then, the first time you had a sexual encounter, everything flowed nicely, but the second time, you had an anxiety attack. Is that right?

—Yes.

—Who had the initiative for the sexual encounter the first time?

—Well I did, at the restaurant, I told him we should leave.

—And the second time? Who initiated?

—Oh. I understand where this is going. He caught me off guard while I was laughing at the movie and put me on his lap.

—Do you see that?

- But I even went to his apartment with the intention of doing it.

—That's right, Valentina. And like you told me a few minutes ago, there was nothing he had done that had triggered your nervousness. Let's call that, shall we? Not anxiety, or panic. Nervousness.

It reminds me of Mrs. Bennet from Pride and Prejudice, who had «nervous issues».

—Okay —I replied.

Mariana continues.

—Let's say that when you have spent too much time in survival mode, and secreting so much cortisol, the brain could forget about what a sudden discharge of hormones like endorphin or dopamine, or in this case, oxytocin looks like, and especially if it was without warning as you mentioned in the second case. Let's say it was an unforeseen and huge discharge of oxytocin that made your brain go in shock and then, boom! Nervous breakdown to balance and a return to the chemical state you already know.

Now —Mariana continues—. What's our job? Well, to teach our nervous system that we no longer need that amount of cortisol, because we're safe. And if an event that puts our integrity at risk happens, we'll have the ability to act on our protection, because we're not the same person. On the other hand, my friend, you deserve to have an orgasm that makes the windows shake.

—Hahahaha —I'm laughing. Mariana is money well invested in myself.

Mariana gives me some tips on how to balance my nervous system, and among them she tells me:

—I know that showering is something therapeutic for you. So, since it's a calm space in your daily routine, I want every morning when you're showering to remind yourself that you are safe, that you have evolved, that whatever happens you'll have the ability to overcome it. I know that in the past you have used the shower as a calm zone in the middle of a storm. It's time to use this tool as prevention, not as a refuge.

I keep every word of this session in my brain imploring him to remind me of it and use this new *Mouseketool* [65].

---

[65] She's talking about to the tools offered to solve problems in the children's TV series called Mickey Mouse's house. (Editor's Note)

# From a breeze to a hurricane

Theo and I are walking in the park. I never get tired of comparing this relationship to a teenage courtship; although we've shared a lot about our tastes and future desires, we have barely had sex.

His admiration and tolerance for me sometimes feels sweet, and other times, causes rejection. He is definitely not a black cat, but his presence today relaxes me, makes me feel that if I do my part this can look like happiness.

We're holding hands, like two little sweethearts, watching the birds and listening to their song, and a gentle breeze wraps around us. I can't avoid the memory of a breeze on the street in Madrid and H looking at me, enchanted, but I push that away, here in Milan I have this Greek god and I can't keep getting my hopes up with the estranged H.

Suddenly, the breeze gets stronger and more furious, as if it wanted to interrupt «the Kodak moment», like my mom says. Apparently, that phrase was the advertising of the analog camera brand, and every time we lived a sweet and tender moment at home my mom came up with that «Kodak moment» phrase.

The fact is that the breeze has turned into a windstorm that makes us wobble, and I tell Theo that we should go to my house, that there we can order something at home for dinner. Theo gladly accepts, as always, because there's nothing I could say to him that he would disagree with; it's as if he's scared of saying no to me, and that's what I don't like about him, now it's a bit more clear to me, I don't like that he loses his personality because he's drooling over me, I don't like his lack of character.

Once home, while Theo is in the bathroom, I decide to check my phone for notifications, I answer my family group chat and I see that I have a Facebook message, when I enter the app, I'm struck speechless.

H has shared a memory that came up on Facebook, with me in it.

It's a picture of Luismi and him at a family party at his house, it was someone's birthday, but I don't know whose, and in the background, like a statue, I'm standing dazzled looking at H. I was a little girl, and the craziest thing is that I'm wearing a Spiderman t-shirt that belonged to Luismi.

H sent me a message along with the memory that says: «Pucca MJ stalking Garu since ancient times».

The world stops, with me in it.

Theo's touch brings me out of my trance.

—What's up, Baby? Is everything all right?

—H texted me —I say, without measuring my words.

—Who? —Theo grabs the phone out of my hands and then sees the message. Italian is similar to Spanish, but to understand what H wrote, he has to know our story—. Who are they, Valentina? Your cousins? —he asks.

—No. It's my best childhood friend and his brother.

—Okay, and why are you turning pale? You're even shaking, can you tell me what's going on?

I tell Theo everything.

He listened to me carefully, but since I started talking, he has become hard and cold as ice. It's like he's built a wall between us. He hasn't uttered a word and I don't stop talking, over-explaining things in detail. When I can't find what to say anymore, I just start sobbing.

—Valentina, listen. I'm not upset. These things happen, but everything you tell me leaves me completely out of place. Honestly, I'm not part of your life. Your friend was here just a couple of months ago and now this message… it's clear that this guy is the one who is in your life. He may not be present here at all, but he's the guy you expect to be here.

»Ever since I saw you, I had hopes of having something with you. Do you remember that first time at the disco? I assumed that you were going through a break up with someone and I decided to wait for you. An opportunity came along. When you decided to agree to go out with me for that wine tasting, I took it for granted that you were ready to start something with somebody else, and I felt happy that that «somebody» was me.

»I have been very patient —Theo continued with a bitter tone. From what I can see and from what you're telling me, your head and heart travel from Paris to Madrid to Maracaibo constantly. Between phone calls with his family, his brother, and now messages from him…

Theo pauses, he's sad, but he doesn't cry like I do, but carries on:

—I don't want to keep reproaching you. I have to thank you for the time we had; I enjoyed your company, and that's a gift from life, but at this point it's best that we end it here.

I start sobbing even harder, I don't want to lose him. I don't want to be alone. If I am alone there's a lot of silence, and if there's a lot of silence, I think a lot and if I think a lot, I inevitably think about H, and when H is in my head, I have no control over my emotions. Theo is my escape. Like for Taylor: «My Getaway car» .

—Permanently? —I ask, afraid of the answer.

—Yeah, Baby. Permanently.

—And if I fix my head? You said you'd wait.

—There's nothing to fix, you're not a car. We've already given each other a chance, I appreciate it, but it's time to go our separate ways.

He kisses me on the forehead, grabs his coat and scarf, and leaves.

When I can catch some air again, I take a ten-second breath and start describing the room; it's one of the strategies that Mariana has suggested to me to calm my «nerves».

There's a kitchen. The stove has four burners, next to it we have a refrigerator. It's white. If I open it, it has vegetables like tomato, onion, carrot. I go over and open it. I keep mentioning the things inside it. There's prosciutto cotto and crudo There's cheese, parmesan cheese and grana padano cheese. I close the fridge and continue with the descriptions. There's a sink, the only sink in the house. And there's a framed poster of *The kiss* by Gustav Klint, that painting is in a museum in Vienna.

When I finish describing the whole kitchen out loud, looking for logic to ground myself to, I pick up my phone again and look at the message. «What should I do?» I ask myself. Why did Theo have to wait until the last moment to show the character that I want in a man?

And then the Tarot reading sneaks into my thoughts. «This guy will come in and out of your life many times, each time he appears, he'll have the power to teach you something that will contribute to your personal growth. You're the queen of wands, and if the queen of wands wants it to rain, she will make it rain».

I look at the date on the calendar, and I see that H's birthday is only in a few days. We are in Aries season, I check the astrological map for today, and we have a beautiful Stellium in Aries. Impulsiveness is on fire: H didn't hesitate to contact me, Theo didn't hesitate to leave and I didn't hesitate to overshare. If I had kept quiet, I would still have Theo here, him and his smile. Now I can only hope that my beautiful getaway car reminded me, like a song, «in his wildest dreams» .

Or could it be that H smelled that I was being happy without him and had to come and ruin everything.

# CHAPTER VII
## The never ending Paris

«There is never any ending to Paris and the memory of each person who has lived in it differs from that of any other. We always returned to it no matter who we were or how it was changed or with what difficulties, or ease, it could be reached. Paris was always worth it».

—Ernest Hemingway, *A Moveable Feast*

# Blues in April

It's been a few days since Theo walked out the door of my house. He left through the front door, protecting himself and taking shelter from me. It wasn't about whether I deserved someone like him or not, or if we were both destined, the truth is, we both go with the flow. I deduced then, that perhaps in his past he had experienced something similar and that is why the sudden strong character put that final distance between us. Similar to H when I told him to stop talking: he didn't waver, he didn't stop, he just let the wall build between us.

What a blue April, and what a grey March. I cry, but not just because of Theo, but because of H too. I cry for losing Theo, and in anger with H, for being such an idiot and showing up at the worst moment, as if the psychosis of seeing him everywhere wasn't enough, of feeling him chasing me like a ghost, as if I didn't already think I was crazy. I don't know how many times I've thought about going to a mental institution, but on the other hand, I think that perhaps I'm just too spoiled, dramatic & stupid, so I cry some more.

I need this to stop, I want my mind to stop sabotaging me, I want to have clarity to know what is real and what isn't, either spiritually or down to earth.

I want to have the knowledge to discern, to make decisions based on the principle of «what's best for me» or at least on the principle of «what I want».

I open my wish notebook again, which I renamed «My life, my reality».

I reread my list of the perfect man, and the tears rolled down my cheeks even harder. He's all of this, he represents all of this. He's exactly what I asked for. Was I wrong in asking for this? Is there something inside of me that thinks I don't deserve it? Don't I deserve someone like him to love me? Did the same thing happen to me with Theo? Or am I not clear about what my needs are and what my approach should be?

I know I want to be H's girlfriend, at least I thought so when I just got back from Madrid. Now, honestly, what was I looking for in Theo? Why did I have so much energy with H, energy to create, to do, to even move, and even though Theo was so romantic, he didn't make me feel anything?

I remember that time I was on my search for a new therapist, post black plague, just before I found Mariana. I had a mini-session with a friend who is a psychologist and I had concerns about how to reconnect and bond with guys, romantically speaking, and she very aptly told me: «You will just know that you want to be with that person and you'll have to trust your instinct of wanting to love them, getting to know them will be like reading a new book which you cannot put aside, it just entertains you and fills you up».

Now, with everything that has happened, I agree with her. In social media, it's been popularized that after "healing" you meet a green flag and this flag, under the concept that your brain can't handle happiness, doesn't make you feel anything. It's partially true, at least in my reality. Theo made me feel comfortable, but I wasn't thrilled with the idea of falling in love with him. H, simply, made me feel excited, he made me feel nice, pure, unconditional, I finally understood what people mean when they say, «I fell in love with my best friend».

Ohhh, Heinrich Miguel, he has me melting with love, and without even lifting a finger, without even putting in the effort. How am I not going to give it another try? Another chance?

I close the «My life, my reality» and open the other one where I have written all the poems, songs and stories about H. That was my interactive personal diary, but this notebook is the diary of my interactive personal diary. I didn't give a name to this one, but it's like my little secret, I've even written down all the dreams I've had with him here: crazy dreams. I've also written down the tarot and astrology readings that I did about us, about him. I have what I wrote down a week before his birthday, his solar revolution, which was missing nothing.

I read out one of the dreams:

*I'm dressed as a bride looking at myself in the mirror, Romina, my childhood best friend says something to my Aunt Eugenia in her ear, my mom is finishing with fixing the purple orchid that I have in my hair, I turn to the left and look through the window, we're in a hotel room overlooking the beach, from the white sand and the crystal-clear water I know we are in Los Roques, I take a soft, long and short breath of air. With my hand on my heart, I made a small bow to the universe and mentally thanked it, I turn to see look at myself in the mirror and then I panic, I start breathing irregularly, everything starts to get confusing, my mom tells Romina to get me water, I'm going to pass out. When Romina is about to get going, I grab her by one arm and spit out:*

—Get the groom.

—Whaaaat!?

—GET ME THE GROOM NOW!

—The groom can't see you in your wedding dress, it's bad luck.

—Bad luck is not knowing who you're going to marry! WHO AM I GOING TO MARRY, ROMINA DEL CARMEN!?

*Romina gives me a look of understanding, she reads my thoughts, we were soulmates. She takes everyone out of the room and before closing the door she says to me: I'll bring you your sweetie pie.*

Her accent from Punto Fijo[68], her pink and purple Afro, and her small height gave me a breath of fresh air for a second, I thought, «She's here, we're friends», and then the door would close.

I look in the mirror again and the panic was still there, "WHO THE FUCK AM I GOING TO MARRY?!!

A few minutes pass, I'm rummaging around the room looking for a cigarette, when I hear a commotion outside. «Let him in», I hear Romina say.

---

[68] Referring to the name given to the inhabitants of Punto Fijo, city in the state of Falcon, in Venezuela

The door opens and he comes in.

I knew that jet black hair by heart, my fingertips tingled yearning to touch it, he had combed it back with a white liquiliqui [69]. With a gentle and calm voice, with a voice that I know, he tells me:

—Babe, what's up?

—Is that you? —I say and release the air that I had been holding in.

—Of course it's me, who else, then?

I run into his arms and fall apart when I have him close.

—It's you—I repeat—. It's just you.

—Yes, were you expecting someone else?

Tears were running fast down my eyes; he gave me my peace back. Gradually, my heartbeat was returning to a normal rhythm.

—It could only be you.

—I'm sure, Maria Valentina Santini, there are thousands of men begging to marry you, but really, do you think someone else is going to be at the altar? I mean, who else do you want there? Is there really anybody else.

I don't need anything else, information comes to you when it is useful to you, when you have the awareness to receive it. Although it had been a powerful dream, I had thousands, I had randomly chosen this one, and this one contained the information I needed to create a strategy for my next move with H.

I have to be stealthy; I have to be bold and plan it right. I can't drown him like maybe I have in the past, I have to take it easy. After all, if it's already written in my notebooks, in the declaration of independence, in the Bible, in the Akashic records, and in the hieroglyphs of Egypt that I am going to marry him, I don't have to hurry with anything. I must enjoy the moment, he belongs to me, he always has.

I close the notebook and say, «Universe, show me the message I should send to H to continue with our story».

I randomly open the notebook and come across the song I rewrote from «All too well»[70] by Taylor Swift.

---

[69] Typical costume used in the flatlands of Venezuela and Colombia, usually white colored. (Editor's Note)

[70] All Too Well - Taylor Swift (10 min version)

# All too well

*To HeinrichGil@emails.com*
*From MVSantiDuque@emails.com*
*Subject: All too well [71]. (Email version). (MJ version).*

*I walked through the door, you said "hi!"*
*It was warm, something in the air made me feel alive.*
*MJ left her Spiderman shirt in your brother's place,*
*And you still got it it in your drawer, even now.*

*Oh, your sweet disposition, my wide-eyed gaze,*
*We sang Taylor, got lost in the upstate haze.*
*Autumn leaves fell, like pieces into place,*
*I still picture it, after all this space.*

*And I know it's long gone, the magic's not here no more*
*I pretend I'm okey, but when I close my eyes, I disappear,*
*And I go to Madrid, where we are again.*
*In that little street, with the wind in my hair,*
*You almost got hit, but you were looking out for me,*
*Wind in my hair, I was there, and I remember it all too well.*

...............................................

[71] Taylor Swift's song «All Too Well». (Author's note)

*I slept in your room, blue sheets on the bed,*

*Your mother made tea, your father spoke French, I'm still misled.*

*You talked of the past, thinking the future was me,*

*You picked me up after every fall, like you were screaming from the stars:*

*"Fuck THE PATRIARCHY!"*

*You opened your ears when the world went deaf,*

*Solemnly swear that you were up to only good*

*You held me from a distance, arms stretching wide,*

*I felt safe in your hugs, nothing to hide.*

*You praised the art I created, just for you,*

*Every word, every image, a bond that felt true.*

*We talked and talked, until words lost their sound,*

*I thought at any moment, you'd say love had been found.*

*But you never said it, not even when I cried,*

*And after months of silence, I realized it died.*

*I called, full of rage, but all I felt was shame,*

*And you just held that dead body, like it was just a game.*

*The magic's gone, nothing left but the sound,*

*This queen of wands can't make it all turn around.*

*MJ only wants to forget, but she needs you still,*

*Then I remember us: kitchen at dawn, against our will.*

*The fridge hummed, the alarm went off, a secret kept tight,*

*You held me in silence, I held you in light.*

*You kept me a secret I kept you like an oath.*

*We promised we'd remember, and I'll keep that vow,*
*But maybe I asked for too much, maybe we lost our way somehow.*
*My sacred prayer, my knees in church.*
*We were a work of art, and you tore it apart,*
*You ran, and I stayed, remembering every part.*
*I called you out, but you just broke me down,*
*Like promises you break, when they don't fit your crown.*

*Everyone says this will pass, but here I stay,*
*I live in hell 'til you cross my mind today.*
*You said if we were closer, maybe we could have tried,*
*That thought alone makes me want to die.*

*The idea you have of me? Who is she?*
*A never-needy ever-lovely jewel*
*Whose shines reflects on you*
*I wipe my tears, but the bar's still cold,*
*Friends ask me what's wrong, and I just feel old.*

*H, that's the story I can't let go,*
*You captivated me, but now I'm left in the flow.*
*You chose my meal, the vodka for my Cosmo,*
*But all I wanted was a "Happy Birthday," a "Merry Christmas" to show.*

*They say time heals, but I'm frozen in place,*
*I can't find myself in this empty space.*
*After so many calls, you held me in the storm,*
*Now I walk back alone, wet, bruised, and torn.*

*But you kept my shirt, the one from Madrid,*
*You can't forget it, 'cause it's still where you hid.*
*You remember me, like I remember you,*
*We both know it's exceptional, it's something true.*

*The reality is that I hate the irony,*
*But every day I get closer to love, while you stay lost, unfree.*
*Your Eiffel Tower broke my bones, left me to stand,*
*But now I'm whole, with my weight and hair, just as planned.*

*So tell me, how's your love bruise now?*
*Have you cut again, in the same old vow?*
*In this city, I still remember my first cut,*
*And I know that blood, it's something we can't trust.*

# Peace treaty

I've sent H an email with my version of Taylor Swift's All Too Well. I'll let my sister, Taylor Allison, decide for us, to be the judge between the two. My excuse was his birthday, but the truth is that I made him wait, I waited and sent it a few days later. It's only right that he should also wait for my message, just as I waited for his... the one that never came.

Minutes later my thoughts are interrupted by an incoming call. France +33

—Hello — I say in a very low voice.

—Good morning, is this Maria Valentina Santini? —In a serious tone.

—Yes, this is her.

— I would like to propose a peace treaty between the parties.

—I'm all ears.

—To sign the contract, both parties must meet on neutral ground.

—I accept.

—How are you? — H asks.

—Everything is in order. Happy belated birthday. How was it?

—Thank you, my birthday gift arrived by email. I must say that it's the best text that anyone has written to me, even though it came from a heartbreak and your friend Taylor helped you out a little. I still liked it a lot.

—Bah, don't break my heart or I'll turn into a poet.

— It would never mean to do that, if I've done something, I apologize, it's really not on purpose.

—Yes, I know, I know your heart and I know that you wouldn't do something to hurt me directly.

—Well, I'm relieved you know that. Because it's very heavy. I mean, because of your past.

—Let's change the subject.

Although I always felt comfortable talking to H about my past, and even committed the sin of overexplaining, detailing and so on, I had decided when I sent him the email to try to change our dynamic, a little, in some aspects. This was part of it. I didn't want to talk too much about the past, I wanted us to talk about the present, to then have the basis to talk about the future.

H understands, so he decides to change the subject.

—For my birthday I went snowboarding with my friends, it was awesome.

—I changed skis for a board in December, I wasn't very successful.

—It's a matter of practice. A good instructor might be able to help you.

—Where would you recommend or choose that practice for me?

—Okay. We could go to Slovakia, I've heard that they have the best mountains and it's super cheap, so we can have a little luxury.

—I love the idea, and speaking of trips, how did it go in Venezuela?

—Amazingly, I went to Angel Falls.

—Wow! Really?

—Yes, I thought about you a lot while I was there.

—Why?

—Because I met someone. —H pauses and my blood pressure drops «he's got somebody, nooo», but I pull myself together and I don't interrupt him—. I met a British girl, with an audiovisual company like the one you want, I was asking her a lot of questions.

—Like what?

—Mostly about numbers, she was with her partner and they were both the owners of it. The company mostly does advertisements for small businesses. For example, a car dealership wants to advertise on social media, they offer their services. They work on projects. Your idea is more geared towards audiovisual art in general, right?

—Yes. My idea is more in tune with music videos, short films, theater plays. But let's be honest, as life goes by, we shape our dreams. Right now, that dream sounds very far away into the future. I have to focus on things that I can do.

—Do you have any ideas?

—Yes, for now, switching to a more creative job.

—Have you applied for jobs?

—Yes, for a couple.

I had applied to some job openings at Warner and the BBC, and in some audiovisual production companies, but I had received the No in less than twenty-four hours, and I was feeling discouraged. I had done it as a test before telling my boss Anna that I wanted to move forward with what we talked about back then, about Disney and her friend. I wanted to prove to myself that I could make my own opportunities.

—Any in Paris?

—You can't say that, and you know it.

—I'm just asking.

—Anything new going on? Did you find an apartment?

—Yes, I moved in when I got back from Venezuela. I found something livable, a little out of my budget, but I have my annual meeting soon so I can ask for a raise there.

—Congratulations.

—I also bought some plants.

—Ah, the lord of the plants.

—Yes. Any plans for the summer?

—No, it's still early, don't you think?

—Well, it's April, almost May. Does June sound good to you to sign the peace treaty?

—The truth is that the twins have their first communion in June and then at the beginning of July it's their birthday.

—Okay. Mid-July, what do you think?

—Yes. Where?

—We can meet in Madrid and then escape to Mallorca.

H and I have had a conversation for more than three hours on the phone. We didn't talk about the fight we had when he came back from the Netherlands. It feels as if time hasn't passed. Now I question everything, the pain I went through, was it really necessary? Was it justified? Or was I, perhaps, a little dramatic?

The truth is, it doesn't matter right now. What matters is that H and I have gotten back in touch. In a matter of hours, we made plans and we bought the ticket to meet in Madrid, and from there, perhaps, go to the beach for a few days. We bought a one-way ticket. This time, I'm taking my work laptop with me.

# Maslow

H and I have resumed our almost daily contact, although it's true that we don't talk to each other some days, or we talk very little, we are there, present, and the conversations continue to have the same tone as always: playful and philosophical.

On the other hand, the great advance on self-awareness that he has acquired in recent months is noticeable. His ideas are clearer, I think the distance between us has been beneficial, at least for him. I haven't told him details about the Greek, not because I want to keep it to myself, it's just that I haven't felt the need to do so for now. Just as I never felt the need to tell the Greek about H, until there was no escape.

I want to maintain the peace and dis-inhibition that we have in our current bond. Before, I would have felt anxious if he didn't answer his phone quickly. But I understand that was because of Voldemort and his abandonment, that made me feel insecure.

I also understand now that H's quick replies to offer emotional security are part of his habits; they are things he picked up with his ex-partners and hasn't detached from them; he does it unconsciously. But this time I want us to discover ourselves as two individual human beings willing to flow, and not as two people pulling traumatic weights from the past.

We've both been talking about Maslow's pyramid. We conclude on the importance that, individually, we are able to cover our needs; and that, in being with someone, that someone knows how to naturally cover their needs, not to take refuge in the other as a survival method.

We talked about the importance of eating, and eating right for our body.

Get the necessary hours of sleep.

To take care of our physical safety and our resources.

To have friends, real friends. Friendships are fundamental in the life of a human being.

To have a high self-esteem, to believe in our dreams and work towards fulfilling them.

We both have a perfect Maslow's pyramid, and we both have the ability and the habit of maintaining it. We are both two complete human beings, now, in a certain way, we want to give each other a chance, or that's what I feel with the signing of the peace treaty in neutral ground like Spain.

In that same dialogue about Maslow's pyramid, we talked about sexual needs and the need to be intimate. When we talked about it, H decided to talk about our disagreement. He admitted that the tramp invited him to the festival and he agreed. The last thing he imagined was that I would find out, and that if that happened, regardless of the reaction I had, we were just friends. And in that, he was right, basically I was in the friendzone.

A few days later we returned to the topic of intimacy. He confessed to me that he met with the girl from his summer in Valencia, the girl who was in the photo next to him. He told me that in both situations he just wanted to know how it felt, that he didn't think about it too much either.

We talked on one occasion about the fact that he has not made an effort to visit me, he admits that it's not that he doesn't want to see me, on the contrary: the more he talks to me, the more he is concerned about my well-being, and doubts if he can take care of me. He stresses that I am the riskiest option. At no point in his narrative is there any mention of him being ready to take a risk this time around. But if he needs a final push, I'll give it to him.

Also, now I understand that healing from a two-year relationship is not so simple. To understand that, I should have seen it from my own perspective: if my relationship with Voldemort was short and traumatic, and it took me so long to heal from it, how much can it take to forget a two-year relationship with life routines included?

In those cases, even if the panorama of why it is over is clear and even if there is a final resolution, routines hold on: «Do you hug an empty space in bed, H? Do you pour two coffees, even if you are alone? Do you hide the phone because you know there won't be a daily call anymore? How hard is it to break these habits, H?». I have never experienced a relationship like that, just imagining it causes me pain.

But I don't want to dwell on that, maybe it's time to simply see each other and re-experience our bond from a new perspectiv
.

# We have a wedding

Margot has had a long-distance boyfriend for quite a long time. Three years ago, she lived in Mexico and a year after being there she fell in love with a guy; since then, they're together, but they're not. The boy surprised her at Christmas in Budapest and asked her to go to Mexico for a while to try it out. The point is that they have suddenly decided to get married. I know, it's something exaggeratedly unexpected. It took them three years at a distance to decide to give themselves a chance.

Emi, Margot, Corina, Soffia and I are very different in our relationships, and we all have different experiences, but, for me, they're all valid. Understanding the authenticity of our emotional bonds is, from my perspective, fundamental. There is no book with rules on how relationships are managed; if they're all based on respect, love and admiration, they're more than valid, regardless of race, sex, distance or age. The books I've read have shown me the true beauty behind every love story and the validity of them all. I am very happy for Margot and her sudden engagement-marriage.

So, all of a sudden, we bought tickets to go to Hungary. The wedding will be at a place forty minutes from Budapest, in her grandmother's village called Szentendre. We will go on Thursday; the wedding is on Saturday and we will return on Monday. Margot has provided accommodations because we will be her bridesmaids. We'll all be accommodated on sofas and mattresses on the floor.

I would be lying if I didn't confess that this sudden wedding has been like fuel to the fire of my own illusions. No, it's not that I want to consider a similar relationship with H, I'll let ours flow, as we agreed, but this marriage shows me that distance is not, necessarily, separation.

If Margot and her long-distance boyfriend are about to get married, why couldn't the same thing happen between H and me? Why can't H and I be like Victoria and David Beckham or Sascha Fitness and Andy?

With that thought in my head I followed my impulses to invite H to be my "+1"; perhaps, as an echo of this story, he will be ready to take the plunge, and then I will be the one to arrange for my friends to stay in Los Roques.

I text him and tell him the necessary info to invite him to come with me.

*Hachitooo, What are you doing next weekend?.*

I immediately get an answer headed with a question mark emoji.

*Why?*

*You know, my friend Margot is getting married next weekend. I will be one of her bridesmaids. Would you like to come?*

*Phew, last minute invitation.*

*I just found out; it was a surprise for me too... What do you say?*

*MJ, I would love to, but it's impossible for me. This weekend I have training in Luxembourg for work, besides training it will also be an organizational meeting for new projects, and it was planned ahead for months. I can't miss it.*

*Ow, Okay.*

We'll stick to our peace treaty.

# Welcome to Budapest

The day has come, we are going to Budapest for a WEDDING, OMG. Emiliana, Corina, Soffia and I have agreed to travel together and we took the first hour flight, so we have a quick itinerary around the city. Margot came to pick us up at the airport and we started at once with our sightseeing, so we can take it easy tomorrow in Szentendre.

Our first stop is at the central market to have some *goulash*. Since it's not lunch time yet, there aren't that many people, and the market manages to show all its beauty.

I buy a couple of *matryoshkas* to take to my uncles. Margot says that the Hungarians claim that the dolls are Slavic in general, not just Russian. I associate that with the discussion around the Arepa, whether it's Venezuelan or Colombian, it is simply pre-Columbian and belongs to all of us because the borders of that time are not the same as they are now. And so are *matryoshkas*. I also bought a couple of Rubik's cubes for the girls, authentically Hungarian and without discussion, because their inventor was a Hungarian.

Our next stop is the Fisherman's Bastion. Margot tells us that she had a wedding photoshoot here a couple of days ago at five in the morning and that the whole place was empty.

—There was such a cold breeze that we were walking around with blankets, it's just that spring is colder here than in Italy — she points out, and my heart shrinks in sweetness.

We do a photo shoot ourselves. Margot with her film camera, me with my polaroid, Corina with her analog, Sofi obviously with her iPhone and Emi with a professional camera. It's funny to me, because we are exactly like that, we all like the same things, but each one in a different way.

We get off from the Bastion and make a technical stop at the Budapest Parliament. The whole aura of the city is very *dark* academia, very Harry Potter, and the parliament was Hogwarts.

When we finished, we headed to Deak Ferenc Ter to get on the wheel. And then we start to get hungry again. Margot tells us to have a *gyro* quickly and go to Szentendre, because her family is preparing traditional Hungarian food for us.

---

Last night we had a spectacular evening with Margot's family. We talked in English, Spanish, Italian and Hungarian. I already know how to introduce myself in Hungarian. «Valentina vagyok», «Venezolai vagyok», I also learned one or two bad words like «Kurva anyád».

This makes me think about sense within a language, I can say «Kurva anyád» without it generating any emotion, but the same doesn't happen with native speakers of the language who have the term loaded with an emotion of liberation, the same would happen if I taught them a bad word in our language, for them it would just be one more word, a word that would not move any feelings. That emotional charge in a language is also a point of rapport in the relationship with H, something that I can't have with anyone.

We went for a walk in Szentendre and it's quite a picturesque place.

Margot tells us that when she was a little girl and she came here, she went into a shop that was in front of the church. When she left mass she went straight to the store and there her grandmother would buy her a surprise gift that cost one euro. We came to see if the store still has surprise gifts for one euro.

When we got there, they still had them. With freshly bought lavender ice cream, each one grabs her surprise and, in the middle of the square under the colorful hanging umbrellas, we open our gifts.

Emiliana gets a mini emoji love plush; Soffia, a mini sculpture of a seagull; Margot, a fridge magnet with a cupid; Corina, a purse with traditional Hungarian fabric; and I got a heart-shaped keychain.

—When I was young, I also used to think that there was a message for me in these things, so let's figure out what they could mean —says Margot.

—Well, Corina, the universe wants you to save money, girlfriend— I say, and they all laugh. Margot, you obviously have a cupid because you're getting married, congratulations! —I shout, excited, and everyone applauds.

—Emi, I think this is talking to me about you falling in love with yourself again. It's time to discover yourself in freedom —says Margot, and adds—: Soffi, girl, your seagull tells you that it's time to fly.

For the first time since I've met her, Soffi starts crying.

—What's wrong? —Emiliana asks.

—Girls, I've just received an opportunity to go to Australia for a year and I'm afraid to take it.

—Nemo's seagulls in Sydney! —I say too fast and everyone is surprised by my reference.

—Girl, you are never afraid of anything. Why are you afraid of this? —Margot asks.

—I don't know. I don't know what's going on, I'm still figuring it out —she says between sobs—. Please, let's continue, and then we'll talk about this. Valentina, you got a heart keychain. Is it time to open the door to your heart?

—Maybe —I reply.

«It's for the keys to H's house, I thought, because in my poem I was given the keys. My path is guided by the divine. I commend myself to the angels of love and of course to H».

# Yes, I do.

As my dear friend says yes to her love, tears flow from my eyes. Of course, it's happening, how wouldn't it? I'm an emotional Barbie, of course I cry at weddings, and I don't care. I love seeing my friend happy, I love seeing the love of her family and of the boyfriend's family, I love seeing happy people, and, of course! I hope in my heart that I will get married one day, and I hope that person will be H.

My chicken heart is exploding, and I've done an unheard-of amount of spam to H with pictures from the wedding. Thinking that these two, that is, my friend and her husband, had a long-distance relationship for years, read again, YEARS, where they ended and got back together millions of times, where they saw each other every six months or once a year. And this guy in full zero contact mode surprised her at her family's house and asked her to marry him. In other words, the thing between me and H is possible, because the impossible can happen when you really love from your heart and you want it. It's true that sometimes it takes time, space, money, it's complicated… but you can be happy after all the difficulties. I couldn't stop thinking that maybe one day it would be my turn at the altar; and, of course, the song I would walk down the aisle with would be «Young and Beautiful» [72].

The ceremony took place on the bridge of a mini-castle, and the location for the party is close by.

We are approximately fifty people. Only a few of the groom's family came, because they'll have another wedding in Mexico, and of course I'm invited to that wedding, but it doesn't have a date yet.

---

[72] Young and Beautiful - Lana Del Rey

At this party they put on Latin, Italian and Hungarian music that the newlywed danced to without restraint. At midnight, my friend changed her dress and put on a red one as the Hungarian tradition dictates, and continued dancing. Of course, I danced too, but, as a good beginner astrologer, who has a few too many drinks on top, I have decided to give birth chart mini-readings to the guests.

Martin and Greta come up. Martin is Julio's brother; Julio is the groom. I offer them a synastry and composite letter reading. I clarify that I'm only doing this as a hobby and to please don't take anything personal, it's just for entertainment.

When I start doing the reading, I realize the beautiful connection they have, how they both look at each other, smile at each other, it seems super sweet to me. I finish my reading wishing them a lot of love and asking them to invite me to their wedding. They both laugh and thank me.

After giving brief readings to other guests, I excuse myself to smoke a cigarette and get some air because I'm a little drunk, I'm barely walking in a straight line anymore.

When I'm outside, I send a couple of messages to H. He's already asleep because he has a presentation the next day with his company. This time, he also sent me photos and has been more communicative than on his other trips. He is setting up a new project for a billionaire who wants to create an Alexa-style assistant with artificial intelligence for elderly patients in hospice care. Something like that was what he told me, the truth is that H's work is extremely interesting, but I understand little about it, robotic engineering is not my forte.

—Can I have a cigarette? —says a male voice. It's Martin. Without answering, I open the pack of cigarettes and hold one out to him, and then, with the same hand, I light it—. Where did you learn all that? —he asks.

—What? Astrology?

—Yes.

—Reading online, hahaha.

—Wow, apart from being beautiful, you're very smart. And when you talk, you have something very special, please tell me that you have a boyfriend that takes care of you right.

I hate the tone that he speaks in and his body language.

—Yes, I do, his name is Heinrich.

—And why didn't he come and take care of you here today? If I had the opportunity to be with a Venezuelan beauty like you, I would not leave her alone for a second.

—Heinrich is not an insecure man, and he respects my freedom as a woman.

—Tell me, what does he do?

— He is an engineer at a very important company, and apart from doing that, he makes me happy. From my perspective, he's the most attractive man in the world.

I'm trying to make sure that, with my answer, even if it's with a partially imaginary Heinrich, the idiot will take for granted my little interest in him, but airheads are abundant.

—Oh, so... He doesn't have his own company? He's just another employee. A salaried employee —he laughs. This Mr. Wickham, besides being an idiot, wallows in his stupidity.

—Well, anyone in their own country with the right opportunities can achieve that, having their own company, right? But try being an immigrant and start from scratch in a city like Paris. H is brilliant and successful at what he does. He is respected and doesn't need to go around talking bad about other people. Besides, what's all this about? Excuse me— I say, without losing my composure and I leave.

I run to the bathroom, and I start to feel an anxiety attack coming up. I call H and he answers after a few seconds.

—MJ, is everything okay?

—You can't imagine what just happened.

I told him that a guy with a girlfriend, a Mr. Wickham, had wanted to seduce me and then had tried to minimize him and that I had defended him.

—I'm sorry that guy tried to hit on you, on the one hand, but on the other, thanks for standing up for me.

—Thank you for being my imaginary boyfriend who stands up for me.

—Use me, remember that I am your toy, so I can also be your imaginary boyfriend and stand up for you when you need it.

—Do you think I should tell the girl, the guy's girlfriend, about what happened? I mean, warn her in a female sorority mode.

—If I'm being honest. No. A shit show could break out. The timing is off. I think that, if you want to tell her, wait until everyone is in their own country, let's respect your friend's space, and when there is no liquor and wedding involved you can tell her, if that's what you want.

—You're right, thanks, sorry to wake you up.

—You're never a bother. Whenever you want, call me.

—H... Can I tell you something? Can I make the most of the alcohol, vulnerability, wedding and the fact that I'm in another country, and in theory it's neutral ground and you're somewhere else too?

—Peace treaty?

—No. Love confessions.

—Oh, okay. Tell me.

—I'd like to be your friend, honestly. Without expecting anything else. I would like to know that we're going to see each other and that we will let things flow, but that isn't my reality. H, I'm in love with you. I want to be with you, have children with you, adopt children with you, rescue puppies and cats. Having a house, an apartment, a business with you. I want it all with you.

—Holy shit.

—I swear I tried to stay out of it, to take all this as a friendship. To leave the romantic initiatives on your end, things like the Netherlands didn't affect me. But since I saw you again, my world turns with you, everything I do is to get closer to you. Forgive me if I don't know how to be the best lover on the planet, but I swear to you, from the bottom of my heart, that what I feel is very deep and very beautiful and very pure. Please, I'm not asking for anything right now. I just want to turn to my readings and tell you that «if ever your heart heals and you find yourself in the position of loving again, please, I ask you: fall in love with me» [73]. You do not know the love that I can give you, you haven't experienced it. No one will love you the way and with the power of my love. No one is going to protect you more than I can do, I know that both of us, together, can achieve everything. When you're around I feel so capable, so complete, with so much energy, I refuse to believe that you can't feel the same as me, you just have to give yourself the opportunity.

—Maria Valentina, you're saying such beautiful things. I feel very flattered. Let's meet, talk and take things from there. What do you think?

—Yes, I agree.

«I take this magnetic force of a man to be my lover» [74]

---

[73] Tomado del libro de Colleen Hoover *Romper el círculo*. (Nota de la autora)
[74] Taken from the song «Lover» by Taylor Swift. (Author's note)

# Birthdays and empty spaces

In the last few weeks, communication with H has not been as intense as it used to be, I assume it's because the trip is a few days away and he'll be concentrating on getting everything ready at his job, so that when we are both in Madrid, we can dedicate ourselves to enjoying it.

On that line of thought, I decide to do exactly the same: I dedicate myself to my work. The truth is, I can't handle the excitement of seeing him again. The girls tell me not to have high hopes, but they didn't grow up reading fan fiction, it's obvious that I have all the expectations and illusions at the highest level, I'm in top gear.

I feel thousands of butterflies inside me, I dream about the moment, about being on the beach with him. I'm so excited that I already have the wardrobe for all the scenes inside my head, for the dates, going to the park, for going to the beach, to walk around… absolutely everything. So much so, that I have paid for a twenty-kilo suitcase plus the ten-kilo suitcase to make sure that I'll have everything with me. I've overdrawn my credit card for this trip. It's my way of telling the universe, «I'm ready to take this man as my lover forever."

I'm going ALL IN at this moment; I'm betting everything that the peace treaty in Madrid will become a colonization signature on my life and on H's. I'm betting everything that H's hands will be the kintsugi to the ceramic of my heart.

I put all my thoughts aside, and my half-packed suitcase in the living room, along with my illusions, to concentrate on the final checks before leaving for the twins' birthday.

My aunt has decided to make the girls' birthday in the small recreational area of her estate. My family lives on the border just between the outskirts of Milan and Milan itself in a family estate; a really adorable place. Anyone would say that these are the suburbs, and also for anyone it would be the perfect place to make life as a family, but my perspective, and that of H, is different.

I dream of a small apartment in the center of an elite city, making different productions every day, my office is the whole world, each day in a different place. Then, when I've already burned that stage and I want to be away from the chaos, I love the idea of having a house in Switzerland, and, if it's not too much, with a tennis court.

The crazy thing about all this is that when H and I had talked about our dream houses, he had described a house with a tennis court in Switzerland, and I had described a flat in an elite city. And the more we detailed the houses, the more we said, «Hey, that's my idea».

The only discussion we had at that time about houses, apartments and housing was that the little Aries boy intends to put a five-hundred-inch TV in each area. I had a small heart attack, «TVs all over the house?!!, negative procedure, there can be no televisions in my bedroom, and even less so in the sacred temple of my home - the library. You're not going to put a TV near my books! If you want, you can in the living room, or in the guest rooms». We got into a serious discussion, in which he basically made fun of me and said, «There's nothing you can do, we'll have five-hundred-inch TVs in every part of the house, plus it'll be a smart home with speakers even in the bathrooms." Shocked, I said no, until we reached an agreement that the TVs would not be visible. Secretly and intentionally, we returned to the topic of dream homes.

We completely agreed that our home would be eco-sustainable, with a gray water cleaning system to use for sewage, solar panels and other related things.

We also agreed to have a gym with all of the gadgets and the same for the kitchen. Very Taurus - Aries of us. H, Aries, rising in Taurus and I rising in Aries with a moon in Taurus.

When we talked about our dream home, I remembered the keychain that I got in Szentendre and I clung to every word spoken, to every consonant written or verbalized in our conversations. «God our hearts are in your hands, and may it be your hands that build the home that houses our hearts, including the five-hundred-inch televisions that H wants, Oh God, that man is going to kill me one day».

I'm remembering all this while I put Moana plates on the tables where we have the *pasapalos*[75]. In my Neptunian world, I dream that one day I will be doing the same with H and our children, but somewhere in Switzerland.

The girls are in the little playhouse and my aunt and I are sitting waiting for the guests to arrive.

There is a little neighbor, smaller than the girls, named Zoe, who has recently arrived in Italy, she's British. The three of them play without talking. The unspoken language. It's so nice to be young, without prejudices or fears.

—It won't be long before the children from the twins' school start arriving – my aunt comments.

—Yeah, well, let's wait a little.

—It won't be long before your uncle gets here, he went to get more things to drink because I didn't calculate right and there isn't enough juice for the children.

—Perfect, how many kids did you invite?

—I let each twin invite between four and five friends. They made their own cards and invited their classmates.

The sound of a call interrupts our conversation and my aunt gets up to answer. It's the mom of the twins' best friend. I know the girl's name is Stella. Minutes later the girl runs in the door and her mom says goodbye from the car.

The three girls run and hug each other. The gift that Stella has in her hand falls to the floor, the British girl picks it up and then joins in the hug and the four of them start jumping and saying things in

---

[75] In Venezuela, it refers to small portions of food that are served as companions to drinks. Elsewhere they are called snacks, tapas, aperitifs... (Editor's Note)

Spanish, Italian and English.

My aunt and I looked at each other, witnesses of that sweet moment.

- Awww, girlhood —I say, a little nostalgic, because I did not grow up being part of a community of girls, I was always the one who was left out, the one who was taken out of groups, the one who was not invited to the cinema or the shopping mall. I felt a lot of comfort knowing that the twins had that thing that I didn't have. I think I'm healing my feminine line through the femininity around me—. Let's sit down and keep waiting and talk about girl stuff.

My aunt and I have been waiting for an hour and no one else has arrived. I start to get nervous, «Is no one else coming?», I think to myself.

I tell my aunt about my concern and she gets up to ask the twins who are the children they invited to get in touch with their mothers. The girls gave her the names; they didn't have many guests.

My uncle, who's playing with the girls in the park, makes a concerned face when he hears the children's names.

—What's wrong? —my aunt asks.

My uncle makes a movement with his head to say let's talk in private.

We leave the girls in the park and the three of us step aside to talk.

Although the twins realize that we are stepping aside, they ignore it, because they understand when adults need the privacy of a conversation.

—You do know who those kids are, right? —my uncle asks.

—Schoolmates, right? —says my Aunt Eugenia.

—Yes, but do you know who they are? —my uncle insists.

—No. No idea, I've heard Celeste talk about liking Mateo, I guess that Mateo she named is the boy she likes, right? But I don't know about the rest.

—Okay, yeah. Mateo is the boy Celeste likes, but he's two grades older than her. He didn't even know Celeste existed before the invitation. We can rule that one out, a fifteen-year-old boy will not come to a park party of some girls that are turning thirteen - clarifies my uncle.

—What's wrong? —I ask to try and better understand.

—That the children they invited made different plans, they are like, very far ahead. And the twins, well, they're still girls. They won't come because they think the twins are silly and babies: they're thirteen and having a party in the park. Because of their age, these kids want to play video games. Paz has even told me that she's seen her classmates hiding to smoke vapers.

My aunt has a surprised and worried face. She paid attention to the twins' homework, their meals, and of everything being in order. Maternal energy comes from the Moon, and my aunt has a moon in Virgo. So, it was natural that her main focus with her daughters was having things in order. My uncle is a Libra, and his paternal instinct comes from his Sun, he is aware of all the gossip around his daughters. It's natural that my aunt had no idea about all this and my uncle did.

—So, they're not coming? —I'm trying to confirm the bad news.

—Don't even try to text their moms, it's better that way. I don't want my daughters around children like that – says my uncle to Aunt Eugenia.

—Then, you should change schools —I say—. I'm shocked by the idea of the twins interacting with children who are already smoking.

—It's a problem that's in every school, and the education there is good, we cannot put the girls in a bubble. This is the world, and the only thing we can do is teach and educate them – my uncle replies to my comment.

—It's true —my aunt adds.

—What should we do? What do we tell them? —I ask without restraint and my voice starts to break up —. I mean, no one's coming to their birthday party. Will they be lonely?

My aunt grabs my hand and says:

—Valentina, look at them, please. They're happy, playing. Let's not say anything, and if they ask, we'll tell them that we're probably very far away and gas is expensive. They live in their world as children, and they don't have an evil bone. What your uncle says is true, we can't protect them from everything, but if we can prolong the blow or soften it, we will.

Tears are running down my cheeks. Nobody likes my cousins. They're good girls. They deserve a birthday full of people. No one came to my birthdays either.

A lump starts to form in my throat and I step aside so that the girls don't see me crying. I go into the apartment and lie down on the girls' bunk bed, take Celeste's teddy bear and the Paz lion plush and lie down to cry a little.

I pick up my phone and call H. I know that talking to him will make me feel better, he'll validate what I'm feeling and turn it around, so, with his point of view, my tears will go away.

It rings, once, twice, three times, and he doesn't answer. I decided to cut the call and send him a picture with the stuffed animals and my red eyes. Since we are at a distance, video calls, photos, and voice memos are what we have at hand to give context to our experiences. Taking a photo of me crying is not something I would do in this scenario, so I sent him a voice note, sobbing and with my vocal cords showing my pain.

I tell him everything that's happening with the twins and the correlation with my own childhood. I act with him like when I was little and I would fall down and cry, and I would see Mom and cry harder, because she was my safe place to be vulnerable. The same thing happens to me with H. As I give him details about the birthday and the relationship I see with my memories as a child, the stream of pain grows bigger. I know that maybe it's silly, I know that maybe the reason for my crying is justified, even if the level is excessive, but they are my girls and, despite the fact that I sometimes feel there's a wall that distances me from my family, especially the twins, there are situations like these that hurt me badly.

When I've recovered my strength, I return to the garden with the girls and my uncles. I see that the parents of the British girl are also there.

We hang out talking while the girls play, laugh and do Tik Tok dances. There are a couple dances that I've and that I know, so I join them in some dances. Every now and then I distract myself by checking the phone to see if H has answered. But nothing.

«It's Saturday. His routine on Saturday is to go to the gym and then take a walk or go to a cafe. Weekends are when he takes the longest to answer because he takes those days to take a break from screens. However, it seems strange to me that he hasn't shown up for so many hours, especially given the kind of message I sent him», I think and I start to get a knot in my stomach. «What if something happened to him? What if he doesn't want to tell me so I don't worry?».

I have an incredible and inexhaustible source of uncontrollable concern for H, and he knows it. I have never been concerned about the well-being of a human being in this way. My brain starts playing with me, and it starts thinking about each catastrophic thing that could have happened to him... «he was hit by a car, fell down some stairs, injured his back at the gym, had a sugar crash and passed out. Paris is not a safe city, what if someone robbed him and he objected and got wounded with a sharp weapon?». Before I realize it, I'm on my knees on the floor gasping for air.

—Cuzziiiee —I hear one of the twins screaming.

A few seconds later the four girls come over.

—Cuzzie, are you okay? —Celeste asks.

—I'm fine, I just feel dizzy. —I lie, panting and faking a smile so i dont worry them.

—My mom also suffers from dizziness— Stella says—. It's called vertigo. The vertigo disease.

The girls are joined by my uncles and the neighbors.

—Hey, is everything okay? —my aunt asks.

—Yes, auntie, it's just... —she understands that I'm having a panic attack.

—Sobri, why don't you sit down? Can I get you some water? What can I do for you?

—Sitting's a good option. Come on — I reply, still panting.

My aunt walks next to me and everyone returns to the place where they were before the event. When there is enough distance between everyone, my aunt asks:

—Will the nervous breakdown, by any chance, have a first and last name?

I don't answer, I just nod my head and don't say a word. I'm too focused on getting oxygen into my lungs and I'm like, «Everything's fine. You have plane tickets, and you have plans. Have faith».

# Doubt-full Monday

It's Monday and I still haven't heard from H. This weekend is the trip and his silence makes me uneasy, fills me with doubts, «Did something happen to him? I can't deal with the anxiety and I send him several messages.

*Hi, H.*
*Is everything all right?*
*Please, answer me.*

There's a fantasy filled part of me that tells me he might be preparing a surprise for me. I hope it's for a good reason, and not that something happened to him.

At the end of the afternoon, the news arrives with a voice message:

«Hey, yes, I saw your message, but I didn't open it right away, I was doing other things. And then —hey, don't get scared or upset — I was out on a bike ride, a car ran a red light, it came in fast and hit me. I hurt my hand and they had to call an ambulance. I spent the night in the ER. They didn't know if I needed surgery, so I had to wait for a specialist to come and check on me. In the end, they just bandaged me up. I'm okay. But it was on my right hand, and I just wanted to rest. Like I said. Please don't be scared. I'm okay. I just need to rest».

When I finish listening to the message. I call him.

He's not answering.

Attached is a picture of his hand and hospital paperwork. Then, he sends me another voice message.

«This week I want to focus on getting some rest. See you in Madrid. You'll get there a few days before me, so as soon as I arrive, I'll let you know, okay?».

H is Moon in Pisces. What you can expect from them is that, if something happens, they seclude themselves. They need their time to process what's happening to them, especially emotionally. I think he's organizing his ideas, studying the possibilities, we're basically going to have a conversation that will be the conversation.

If the seclusion that H has decided to have until we see each other is a test, then I will be a queen and give him his space, I will not insist on calling him. On top of that, H knows that I'm a noisy person in an emotional sense, that I am shocked by any event that involves him, that I worry about him. Maybe he's not used to someone caring about him as loudly as I do.

I knew, from what Luis Miguel told me, that his ex-girlfriend had left him when he got covid, and apparently the virus hit him really hard. Apparently, he is used to solving things on his own, without help, and his words are just his way of saying I'll fix this and when I'm at one hundred percent we'll talk.

It made me a little sad to think about H with covid; going through that love breakup alone and sick. And now, imagining him alone in the hospital made my heart ache. «And if he got hungry? Did they have delivery service at the hospital? Did they give him food at the hospital? Did it hurt a lot?», I think, and I can't help but send him a message.

> Hi, I'm so sorry that happened to you. Thank God it wasn't anything serious, from what you tell me, and also from what the paperwork says. Of course, I'll give you your space to get better. Whatever you need, I'm still here, it makes me sad that I'm not around to help you or do something more useful than just texting you. I just wanted to ask; have you been eating right? Does it hurt?

Sometime later he answers me, with another voice message:

«I've been eating well, yes. And no. It doesn't hurt. I have a high pain threshold. But it does affect my mobility. I'm okay. Please, don't worry».

I am distressed by his repetitive «don't worry» when I'm more than worried. «My poor baby, I thought, my sweetie pie Hachito, my delicious Hachito, my wounded Hachito, all alone without me».

I can feel as if there is a wall between him and me right now, and I attribute it to the fact that he isn't used to someone's care; his habit is taking care of others. His attitude breaks my heart a little, and, as expected, I'm crying inconsolably again.

What a sea of tears I've become since H entered my life. When I decide to take a shower, I play the scene and imagine a car running over him, and then I feel nauseous. If something were to happen to him, I think I would die with him. The mere thought terrifies me uncontrollably. I have never loved so deeply, I think, perhaps, this is the first time I really love someone.

# Running away

In the last few months, I have been using, now and then, the year-round subscription that my aunt gave me. I'm really enjoying doing something different during the week, whether it's Pilates or kickboxing, something that isn't precisely gym and weights.

I have never been able to be a person who meditates and does yoga. My brain just can't turn off, it never shuts up, it doesn't stop working; these practices are about thinking about nothing, breathing and turning the brain off. Meditating or doing yoga doesn't work for me, if there's silence my brain collapses. Going to therapy I understood that meditating is also thinking about anything other than something deep or worrying. For example, in Pilates, you focus on making your movement perfect, not on whether your boss liked the Excel spreadsheet you did in the morning or on what H thinks about me.

The reason why the gym isn't working anymore is because I know my routine from head to toe, I know the exercises by heart. When I'm doing deadlifts, out of inertia, my posture is perfect, and then Excel spreadsheets or H fill up the blank. On the other hand, I like that I am meeting new people, like my aunt had told me, every day more girls join in to do different things.

My trip is just a few days away, I'm almost counting the hours, and the anxiety about seeing H is going to freak me out. I need to «turn off» my brain a little, and since I've finally been able to afford my half-point shoes along with my tutu, ballet is the plan for today.

Ballet class after about ten years. When I was a teenager, in the last years of school, I was in a dance academy where I mainly danced flamenco and ballet, I practiced only one hour each a week. At that time, I was throwing some bulerias worthy of the motherland, I really loved it! And although I never managed to handle things well with my hands, like the fan, castanets, or a mantle, or I never got to stand on end with ballet shoes, dancing for me is the true meaning of «turning off» my mind. It's the only activity where I really get to do that.

When the teacher enters the class, she introduces herself, and she's Russian. «Wow! I'll have an authentic experience». She says that she was a professional ballet dancer, but because of the Ukraine-Russia war, she had to emigrate, because her husband is Ukrainian. One of the girls who I assumed was Asian, says something to her in Russian, and the teacher looks to the floor and answers, and then gives her half a smile.

The truth is that I was obsessed with the news now and then, from time to time. A few months ago, I had been watching the news every day in Mexico about the missing girl, Debanhi Escobar, and they had finally found her. Dead. I remember getting up at dawn and saying, «Debahni, where are you?», while refreshing Twitter with her hashtag and then the news came that they had information about her whereabouts. I remember it, and I feel a twinge. As a woman, I saw myself, it could have been a friend of mine, it could have been me. The same way with Ukraine-Russia. It was news that felt close. That was felt in the heart, especially on the side of Ukraine because when they had protests in 2014, we were protesting too, and that year they were victorious, we were not as lucky, and now with what was going on, we seemed to be the «lucky ones».

All of us in this place were doing the exact same thing, running away. Escaping from reality, just for a few hours.

We were in a sacred place, where the only important thing was that the *grand pillé* and the *relevé* came out perfectly.

# CHAPTER VIII
## Kintsugi

«His dream must have seemed so close that he could hardly fail to grasp it».

—F. Scott Fitzgerald, *The great Gatsby*

# Wild and melancholic Madrid

I wake up from the landing and the pilot announces the arrival: «We have landed at the Adolfo Suárez Madrid-Barajas Airport. The local temperature is thirty-one degrees, please stay in your seats until the seatbelt sign turns off, thank you».

I have decided to give H his space, he has the pictures of my ticket so he knows I arrived and everything else. The truth is that the level of response to my messages has given me an enormous anxiety, but I remember the conversation with my psychologist and I feel better, calmer; I trust in what we have arranged to be here, on Madrid soil again.

H arrives the day after tomorrow. I decided to buy an earlier ticket because I also want to enjoy it with my friends without worrying, I don't want to abandon H to see them or share with others, I want H just for myself.

I'm waiting for the bags when I get a message from Jennifer.

*Girl, lunch is ready.*

*Let me know when you're in the taxi*

I decided to stay with Jennifer these days because she's temporarily sharing an apartment with Fernanda and Paola.

I knew that Fernanda and Paola lived together in a flat, but when their contract expired, the landlord raised their rent and they couldn't afford it, so Jennifer, taking advantage of the fact that her mom is away because she got a job outside Madrid, offered them to stay while they got a place to live.

I really don't know how many rooms the place has, or how it's set up, but I feel at peace, because H has the keys to Luis Miguel's apartment, and I, in case of any emergency, can call my friend Martina, the makeup artist, I know she would help me.

I had talked about the best and the worst scenarios with my psychologist, and how to react in different situations.

The best thing that can happen is to go to Luis Miguel's house with H, spend a couple of days together there, then go to a place by the sea and organize how we would be together, with the most likely scenario being that I would move to Paris.

And the worst thing that could happen is that H rejects me, or that we don't get along; in that case, I can spend a few days in Madrid with my friends, or go and visit some friends I have in Barcelona and go to the beach. Just thinking about that alternative makes me swallow thick.

Anyway, my therapist, my mom, my aunt Eugenia and I are betting that everything will turn out fine and this will end in marriage.

I ask God and the angels of love to open the way for me and let me be happy.

Once lunch is over, Jennifer proposes to go for a walk to El Retiro, to take Golfie out, the puppy of her current almost-something, who is traveling abroad for work.

Walking through the park, we're in a place I hadn't seen last time and it's the golden hour.

Jennifer is quite an Instagram model, and you could say that she is an influencer, she has very good taste when dressing and has impeccable aesthetics, Libra, with Venus in Virgo, of course.

I'm wearing something comfortable, with a simple orange dress that I bought in H&M sales and some chunky sandals that are fashionable and with no makeup. But she, on the other hand, has even got high heels on. It's funny to me to see how she walks perfectly even over grass and cobbles.

I'm admiring the scenery of the park when I hear Jennifer say:

—Girl, strike a pose, this light is amazing.

The warmth that the sun instills in my face and the thought of knowing that in a couple of days I will see H make me feel so happy that I decide to pose naturally and authentically, with a smile from ear to ear.

—Wow! Girl, you look so cute! What an aura! —says Jennifer and adds—: I mean, just look at that! You even have a rainbow on top of you. You're like an angel, radiating love.

She hands me the phone so that I see for myself what she's talking about, and sure enough, happiness is coming out of my pores.

We keep walking a little more, Golfie comes and goes and brings us things like sticks or rocks, he's the sweetest thing; he's a rottweiler, but he is super-gentle and well behaved.

We came to a place with climbing trees; at the top, there are three trees. When I see them, my skin bristles, and I feel a deep melancholy inside me all of a sudden.

—Jennifer, those trees are beautiful, but kind of sad, aren't they?

—Girl, you're so sensitive, those trees are a reminder of the terrorist attack that took place years ago here in Madrid, in the subway. Each tree represents a lost life.

—I can't believe it!

—Do you know that song «Jueves» by La Oreja de Van Gogh? Well, that song talks about that attack, it was really hard.

Yes, I know about that, but I don't tell her. I travel back in time, to my blue moments, to my birthday without H, I think again about the girl's diary and I think about Juliet. Tragic and frustrated love.

—Girl, do you really know why I came to Madrid? —I tell Jennifer, spitting it out.

—Well, on vacations, right? But go ahead.

—Do you remember Heinrich, Luis Miguel's brother?

—Of course, everyone's impossible love, all the girls were eternally in love with him.

—You too? —I ask, feeling a little discouraged to be just one more in the bunch.

—No, not me. But he and Paola had something, and at that time Paola was my best friend. More than once, I helped her escape from her house to see him. Why? Did you have something with him too?

—I have something with him. Present tense —I answer, looking at the floor in shame.

—Girl, then go all in. That boy is pure gold and he likes girls like you. Beautiful and smart. Strong and determined.

Her words comfort me and validate my feelings more than I can consciously admit. The reality is that I am a very confident woman, but I become vulnerable when H is in front of me. Although he makes me feel super strong and capable of facing this life, I become fragile in front of his eyes. When H is in front of me, it's me, with all my virtues and insecurities in superlatives.

—Well, I came here because he's coming. We've been talking and all that, in the last year.

The both of us, sitting on a bench in front of the trees that honor the lives of those victims, talked about our love misfortunes and our expectations.

I tell Jennifer everything in great detail, not only about Heinrich, but also about Voldemort and the other guys. The terrorist attack was a catastrophic and horrible event, and there is no way to compare anything that I have ever been through with what the victims lived and the pain their families felt, but, for some reason, I feel that every word I say about my past, every consonant and vowel pronounced, becomes a thread that connects me to them, especially to the girl from «Jueves» and her diary.

Jennifer, on the other hand, also opens up with me and tells me about her not so nice experiences, she tells me about the time one of her boyfriend's got into a traffic accident and it was so bad that she had to change his diapers when she was taking care of him, because the guy couldn't move, and everything she did was for nothing because once he recovered, he cheated and married another girl. She adds that he still writes to her from time to time and tells her that he would divorce his wife if she would only take him back. Such madness and insolence on behalf of that cockroach.

When we finished our confessions, whispered to the trees, I let myself believe that perhaps they—the trees and the victims—welcomed these intimacies, that they reminded them of what it meant to be alive. Maybe they wanted us to unburden our pain, silently assuring us that our feelings were valid. I like to think that nature itself acknowledges the weight of human suffering—that a terrorist attack, the horrors of human trafficking, a war, or decades of dictatorship are unspeakably tragic, each carrying an unfathomable depth of pain. Though some might argue there is no true comparison between different sorrows, pain remains pain; it carries the same weight. Perhaps, in their own quiet way, the trees and lost souls have whispered, «I'm sorry that happened to you» just as we, in turn, have offered them our own silent apologies.

There were atrocities a thousand times worse than the ones we had both experienced, we didn't know if it was too much, but for us it had been enough.

When we get up from the bench, I touch a tree with my right hand and mentally say: «I'm sorry, forgive me, thank you, I love you.». They are words that work like mantras in the ancient Hawaiian technique called "ho'oponopono", phrases that fill me with peace and help me shake off toxic memories.

Back at Jennifer's apartment with Golfie, we found the girls making a fuss: reggaeton playing on the speakers, phones charging, makeup everywhere, Jennifer's closet strewn all over the house, grinder, rollers and weed on the table.

—Saaantiii —Fernanda screams—. Sister, let's go out today! Take your clothes out of that suitcase and let's see what you've got. We've got a table at «Salvaje». From what I heard, there are some single footballers going, there is one that plays in second division that I want to introduce to you because the last time you were here, he asked very excitedly who you were when he saw you in a photo I posted on Instagram.

—And girl, he's cute. His teeth are a little crooked, but we can tell Luis Miguel to fix that, and you'll be a winner —says Paola.

—Well, all of us —says Fernanda while looking at Paola in complicity.

—First off, Hello. I'm okay, bitches —I jokingly tell them —thanks for asking. I am engaged to the love of my life and no footballer has a chance with me. Griezmann and Dybala can ask me out and I would say no to them. Now, we can go out to party. But I'll back to the house to sleep whenever I want to —I say in warning mode because I know that they all like to see the sunrise at intimate after parties.

—Heinrich Miguel Gil Montilla is the name of the lucky guy in case you're wondering —Jennifer says behind me as she takes off Golfie's leash, and I freeze.

My instinct is to look at Paola's face to analyze her reaction to the confession I didn't agree to, but that I have to face now.

—Girl, finally!! —Paola screams, and jumps around as if she had won a competition.

«Uh! Why finally? I don't understand».

—Valentina Santini and Heinrich Gil. Now this is truly big news! And of the good kind! —Paola continues.

I'm still quietly trying to figure out what's going on. Paola has always been somewhat toxic and violent. I was waiting for her to slap me for taking her ex-boyfriend, whom by the way I didn't even know was her ex-boyfriend. Anyway, I saw him first, H has been my crush since I was thirteen.

«Do I have a not yet deconstructed misogyny/patriarchy inside? What makes me believe that Paola could beat me up because of this?».

—Finally, a woman good enough for H, finally a woman who can compete with him, who is smart like him, beautiful too, not like his filthy ex. I bullied H so much when he just started with her, and let's not talk about the bullying I put him through when he was with that blonde the last time you came over. I thought that had ended there, that they had never talked again —Paola adds.

«Oh, somebody else is the one with misogyny/patriarchy. And she knows about that tramp, too. And what does she mean by bullying then and bullying afterwards? I mean, do they talk to each other? They have that much confidence? Is she another groupie?

—But why didn't you tell me?! —Fernanda screams in a victim tone that I don't like, as she goes ahead and slaps me on my arm.

Maybe she was hoping that my relationship with H would end forever after her gossip about the Netherlands thing, but I don't give her any explanations. I decided to ignore everything I just heard.

—Well, then, the outfit for today —I say, so that everyone understands that I will not continue with that conversation, then I turn around and go and get my suitcase to show them what I brought.

Paola, Fernanda and Jennifer walk behind me to the living room where I have my suitcase, I proceed to open it and I comfort myself for separating the clothes that I'll wear with H from the clothes to go out with my friends, that way I make sure that those clothes are not even close to the hands of these wild girls, like the place we're going to. Maybe that action had to do with my spiritual paranoia.

I understand that her world is not my world, her way of thinking is not mine, and as Luismi said some time ago, Jennifer is more my style, or maybe not, it's just that she accepts me as I am, with my peace of mind, and I know that these girls try to change me and make me more like them, it's like they want me to be part of their community, but I don't understand the reason behind it.

Our differences don't stop me from enjoying a night out at a disco with them and brainless footballers.

—But tell us everything about it, oh my God! What a mystery! —Fernanda resumes the conversation.

—What do you want me to tell you? —I say pretending that I don't understand what she's telling me and what she wants to know.

—Well, about H.

—Well, we're both just there, that's it.

—But are you boyfriend and girlfriend? —Paola insists.

—Mmmm.... —I say, looking at the ceiling.

—Ugh, you are just like him — says Paola —mysterious and quiet. Okay. But girl, it's a good thing that he's with you, because, I swear, I saw his ex and I was about to throw up. I'm sure she probably has hairy armpits.

—Disgusting —Fernanda says, and amplifies the word with her gesture—. I bet she smells bad and everything.

—Not to add fuel to the fire, but yes, honestly, that woman looks like she doesn't shower— says Jennifer.

That motherfucker doesn't even comb her hair, her hair is all tangled and burned — Paola continues.

—She seems pretty to me — I say to their comments.

I stand up for the girl. Although she isn't my best friend, she's a woman, and not just anyone, she's the woman who has been loved by the love of my life. Somehow, despite her Sun at Uranus, she had formed the man I had today, and that has to be respected and appreciated.

—Oh, but isn't that weird, Santi the public defendant —Fernanda brings out her sarcasm—. No one is going to give you an award for defending that hippie. Regardless of what it is, you are more beautiful, more of a woman, more feminine, more intelligent, more of everything than that tanned nobody. You deserve H more than her.

I stayed silent.

Far from feeling magnified by her words, I feel ashamed to make part of this conversation where a woman is treated like this. But I'm not on my own turf, I'm on someone else's turf, in someone else's house.

Once I was reading about Laveyan Satanism; a Church created in rejection of Catholic beliefs. Despite their name, they follow a sensible philosophy of life that they state some principles that seem right to me. One of them says that when we are in someone else's house, we should show respect for what that person says or does. That's why I didn't insist on stating the opposite.

I have shared this philosophy with H. In every space that has his name, I follow those principles to the letter. It's like an unspoken philosophical pact that we've both made to respect each other for the rest of our lives. Of all the contracts and treaties that H and I have agreed to, that's the second one. The first was to coincide and bond.

Another one of the principles of Laveyan Satanism points out that stupidity is a sin, and I consider that destroying a woman I do not know like this, is stupid. Therefore, I decide to ignore what they're talking about and not comment on the topic.

— Come on, leave Santi alone and let's focus on going out and having a time —says Jennifer, who has caught on to my discomfort.

—Yeah, but if she's married, we can't take her, if I invite her over to the table it's because someone is interested in her. You don't go to the disco to pray, much less to test loyalties – Fernanda said acidly.

—Well, I'll pay for her —Jennifer says, in disgust—. She'll be my date then. We're supposed to go all out and party, it's no problem if we're there, right?

—Yes, the truth is that there would be a problem. When Rodrigo invited us, he clearly said to take cute friends to hook up with —Paola explains— Not to be a bitch, but Fernanda is right, besides Rodrigo's friend is already in hunting mode with Santi.

—Girls, don't worry. I'm not going —I intervene. The reality is that you're going to party with your friends and to hook up. I just came to spend time with friends, so you guys go ahead. I'm staying here and watching a movie with Golfie.

— I'm staying with you – Jennifer says.

— Well, we'll finish getting ready —Fernanda says and pulls Paola out of the room by an arm.

# Tantrums and concerns

I feel a lick on my foot and I wake up scared. It's Golfie. I slept on a small mattress on the floor. Jennifer told me to stay in her room with her, but the truth is that I wanted some solitude, some silence after Paola and Fernanda's little show.

H is still «missing». According to his schedules and routines — which I know by heart — he writes to me when he starts working and before leaving, but this time he hasn't done it. I told him everything that happened yesterday, as my personal interactive diary, and I'm waiting for him to answer me, looking at my phone so that when he answers me, we can have a smooth conversation, like before... when answers came immediately.

I would be lying if I didn't say that I have reread our conversations almost from the beginning to the end looking for a reason, «I must have said something inappropriate for him to act like this», but since I don't find anything, I blame my anxious attachment and I scold myself for being so distrustful.

The truth is also that I have done three hundred tarot readings asking what he feels for me, what he thinks about me, what I can expect from this trip. And the tarot answers look normal, the only third party among us is his fear of being hurt again.

I've formed a friendship with Tatiana, my new tarot/astrologer, and she has very kindly been instructing me and wooing me with readings of all kinds.

From the first moment I gave her some context about H, she told me that it was a highly karmic relationship, which I already knew because he has a stellium in my 12th house. According to her, when we meet someone or see someone and there is an explosion of good and bad feelings, it has quite high karma.

According to Tatiana, all of the people who come and go in our life are karma, but there are different levels: mild, medium and high, and H and I were the highest karma she had seen in her career. Our karma seemed so high to her, that she called it a "birthright", which means that our bond, beyond being by destiny, is our right.

When my astrologer/tarot reader and I talked about karma, she made a list of key words that were covenants of our bond, she mentioned the pact of building companies and businesses together, the pact of being in each other's life for a lifetime, even if absent, the pact of protecting and respecting each other, the pact of me being the mother of his children. She told me that this was the reason why "peace treaties" exist between us, why in sacred places like Angel Falls, H would meet people who reminded him of me and who would make him think about my projects that were basically «ours», because I would dedicate myself to the creative part and he would do the same with the business part. «Everything is interconnected» were her exact words, even if H acts like he is from Merida and stands firm in his agnosticism.

It doesn't matter that he doesn't believe in our karma, I believe for the both of us.

I decided to get ready to go out to eat something and go for a walk with Golfie, I told Jennifer that I would take the dog out. I'll also take the opportunity to call Luismi when I'm at the park, because I told him I was coming, but I haven't called him to tell him that I'm already here. I'm keeping my distance at the moment because he was posting stories on Instagram with the tramp, and that really turns my stomach.

Once in the bathroom, I try to put some music on Spotify and I realize that it's not working. «Maybe the platform is down», is what I think and I don't think much about it: I decide to put YouTube instead. I find one of my old playlists, from when I was in school, and it's a mix of songs by Tecupae, Vos Veis, Reik and Camila, so I hit play in random mode.

By the time I'm rinsing the soap off my body, the smell takes me away; I wonder where I must have smelled this soap, I keep thinking and travel back in time to the moment when H was bathing in front of me after the anxiety attack. YouTube plays «De mí» , and the indigenous instrumental part begins along with an introduction:

«Imagine that you live without the fear of taking a risk and exploring life, you have nothing to lose, without fear of being alive in the world and without fear of dying. Imagine that you love yourself the way you are, that you love your body the way it is, and your feelings the way they are. To know that you're perfect, just the way you are»

I take the memory and the intro as a message, a confirmation that I am being guided by the divine.

As I get out of the shower, I notice that there is a commotion outside. I go out in nothing but a towel to see what's happening, because by the moans that I can hear, someone is crying.

Fernanda, Paola and Jennifer are all in the living room.

—He humiliated me, ignored me and rubbed that damn bitch in my face —I hear Fernanda say.

When I get to the living room, Fernanda is still dressed in yesterday's clothes. She complains, she cries, her mascara is all over the place, but I swear I can't pay attention to what she's saying; I'm impressed by how beautiful she looks even though she stayed up all night and her make up is all smeared.

Her short skirt —too short —in white color, leaves nothing to imagination. My friend doesn't have a bit of cellulite on her long athletic legs. She's lying on the floor, and I can still see her quadriceps. The matching crop top in white shows her perfect cleavage, because, of course, this woman has three hundred and eighty cubic centimeters in each breast! On her side, a tattoo that I had never seen before, of a butterfly. She has brown sugar colored skin, amber eyes and black hair down to her waist. Wherever you put her, wherever you look at, this woman is one hundred percent Venezuelan. When I open my vision and see the three of them, I realize how different I am from them, physically too.

The three of them are dolls from the Venezuelan factory, three hundred cubic centimeters in each implant, long hair or with extensions, perfectly chiseled abdomens, finely injected lips, rhinoplasty too, but they don't look plastic or too constructed; the surgeries on their bodies have been subtle, precise.

At some point I heard that they had all had surgery before entering college with the surgeon who did Misses; it was already customary in my country for plastic surgery, especially breast implants, to be a high school graduation gift from parents to their girls. I was sure the three of them could dance tambor and salsa baul.

On the other hand, I'm skinny, tall, maybe too tall, with bright red colored hair, I'm a natural redhead, but depending on the season, I make it darker or brighter. My hair isn't that long and I'm pale. Very pale, and when I go to the beach, I turn red like a shrimp. These girls with half an hour of sun already have a perfect tan. My breasts are small, and I would give the world about three hundred cubic centimeters in each one too. I remember when my mother offered me to get surgery as a gift and I refused, «Maria Valentina the hippie», I say to myself.

Jennifer scares away my thoughts by asking me to bring water for Fernanda and her crying.

I quickly go to the kitchen, fill a glass of water and when I come back, I ask what's going on.

—Marica, that Rodrigo invited a girl over, and we know she's into him and all that, and since she got there before us, she had already made room for herself with him and there was no way to separate them. Anyway, they left together —explains Paola—. So, Sergio, the friend that we supposedly had arranged for you, invited us to a private party, and we were there all right, having a good time, and when we saw Rodrigo arrived with the girl again and they were kissing and everything in front of us.

—And the fact is that the idiot and I had been talking and dating for a while. In fact, I even went to a football game with his mom and everything. I mean, he wanted to humiliate me, period —Fernanda says between sobs.

I stay silent, I don't know what to say, neither good, nor bad.

—Can you, please, stop judging me —Fernanda spits out with hatred while giving me a look like we're not friends.

—Don't be silly, no one is attacking you —Jennifer says with a reassuring tone.

—It's true. I'm not attacking you. That's just what my face looks like. And why would I judge you? you've done nothing wrong, wanting someone is not a crime, and what you went through is horse shit —I say, trying to appease the tense atmosphere that is unnecessarily being created.

—Of course! Since you're all smart, studied, who reads books, speaks several languages, with a body like a model, without implants, with a good position at a good company, all the guys want to marry you, apart from that you are the perfect daughter of the ladies from Las Lomas…

—Whaaaat!? — I said. Understanding absolutely nothing of what she says to me «That I, what? Where's she getting all of that from?»

—Fernanda, stop it! —Paola intervenes, clearly intoxicated from the alcohol.

—You think we don't know about all your ex-boyfriends and how they licked the floor for you and how they all wanted to marry you, and I'm sure H won't be the difference. The whole dental school knows that Carlos Daniel was dying for you, everyone knows how he talked about you, you don't know what it's like to be replaced. — Fernanda continued her assault—, and that all of the moms in Maracaibo from all of the schools had to do with you, and everybody was flattering you all the time.

«Wow! So that's what they say about me».

—Let's see, Fernanda —I say, already a little angry— You think that I've been locked up in paradise and from there I magically jumped over here. I know what it's like to have a broken heart. But you're right, in theory, I don't know what it's like to be replaced by someone else. — I continue—. But I will tell you that, indeed all the boyfriends you have met have been very open when it comes to communicating their desire to marry me, and the reality is that, before, the only way I would turn to see a guy was that, my friend, like you said, that he licked the floor I walk on.

»But know this about my «boyfriends»— I air-quote with my fingers —Carlos Daniel physically abused me, with the next one I had a slightly worrying age difference, I don't doubt that he loved me, but now, I question the validity of the love between us and of our relationship and even of his ethics, because he was seventeen years older than me, at that time I didn't even have my frontal lobe fully formed; and the next «boyfriend», And let's not even talk about the next one. But to sum it up, he was married with a child and I didn't know, and on top of that he raped and abused me in other ways, isolated me from the world, and came to control whether I had a job or not.

Jennifer is just looking at the floor, Paola is stoic and Fernanda has relaxed her body language. A couple of seconds pass with a mournful silence and now I'm the one lashing out:

—A relationship goes beyond the fact that someone wants to commit, it's more complex and deeper than that. And you don't have to have a «a model's body» — I'm air-quoting with my fingers again — or look a certain way for you to deserve to be loved.

I understood them, these girls modified their bodies to silence their insecurities when they just wanted a guy to turn and look at them. Their desires have changed, they want a home, and boys only do that: they turn to look at them. They are the sexy girls, to spend some time with, there's no commitment.

Fernanda's recrimination against me, towards the fact that I don't have three hundred cubic centimeters in each breast, reveals to me that she wants to change her body again to look less voluptuous, to not be the exotic girl just for a party; now she wants to have an appearance in which she looks more like the ladies someone would want to «marry».

They blame their bodies. But it's not their bodies that are the problem, it's the place and the how. And they still haven't discovered that they're not going to find the love of their life with a footballer in a nightclub in Madrid. The Messi's of the world looking for their Antonella's are not in the club and don't say «bring your friends».

Reflecting on and understanding Fernanda and her situation made me calm down.

—Hey, it's okay, you are really beautiful. I'm not attacking you. Come here – I hold out my hand and help her to her feet–. Let's get you showered and in bed to catch some sleep. We'll talk more when you're not intoxicated.

I helped Fernanda take a bath and Paola too, while Jennifer makes breakfast. It feels bad for the both of them, because, honestly, they're both beautiful and they're not mean girls, they're just looking for human warmth. I reflect on their relationships with their parents, and both of them have absent fathers. Your whole lives have been based on filling that void, but I'm not a therapist, so I can only recommend that you take care of that part of yourself. With all the subtlety I could, I sent them by WhatsApp the information for a group of medical psychologists in Venezuela who do online consultations.

I left the house with Golfie, who had already peed in the kitchen because he couldn't hold it in anymore.

On the way to the park, I call Luismi, after a few rings he picks up.

—You bastard, bitch. I already know you're here and I'm the last one you call.

«Drama king mode for today».

—My baby, no! You were the first one I told I was coming over. I'm calling you because yesterday and today were crazy. But obviously, I want to see you.

—Yeah, well. I can't today, I have to work until seven in the office because a patient called us and he had a broken implant. And, well, those overtime hours pay me super well.

—Oh! Well, baby, we're still talking and we'll see each other, okay? And... look, Baby, my usual question, what do you know?

I wanted to get some information out of him to see if there was anything about H that I didn't know. On our calls, conversations and visits, I had limited myself as much as I could with details so as not to say or talk more than I should, to keep our bond as private as possible.

—H?

—Obviously.

—Have you guys started talking to each other again?

—I'm the one asking the questions here —I answered. I take it for granted that Luismi still thinks that H and I haven't talked and I decide not to delve into that.

—Well, I don't know, about a month ago he told me that he was coming over, that he needed the apartment for a few days, and I told him that it was fine, but he didn't say anything else. And we haven't spoken anymore since then, you know, sometimes he interacts in the family group chat, but we haven't spoken privately.

Jumping to conclusions, H's family may not even know he was run over. The world is crumbling over me. «What if he's hurt? What if it was more serious than he had me believing? What if something worse happened to him and that's why he hasn't showed up?». As far as I can see, he hasn't even got in touch with his family. The only reassuring thing about all this, is that I now know it's not personal. It's not against me. There's something going on, but I don't know what.

—Okay. Okay —I'll drop the subject—. Thank you for telling me.

—Yeah, well, I know talking to you is talking about H too. It's inevitable. The red thread, I already told you. Neither you can escape from him, nor he can escape from you.

I laugh. It's one of those nervous but reassuring laughs. My surroundings are in tune with what my heart and my intuition are screaming at me. At some point, we'll get married.

# Ripples of friendship

H showed up shortly after talking to Luismi. He lectured me, telling me that I shouldn't bond with Jennifer, Paola or Fernanda. He stressed that we're very different and that, in that place, they don't value who I really am. Maybe he has a reason to say that, because he knows Paola. Fernanda, well, we all know who she is, but Jennifer seems honest to me, I think, just like any other girl, she is looking out for her own community, she wants friends and these are the friends that she has available today.

Migrating and making friends isn't easy, I was very lucky to meet Corina and Margot. We met by chance, we were training at a swimming pool and we had a connection. That same day, we went out and then Margot invited Emiliana, because they were neighbors. We met Soffi at a restaurant. I could say that she was my contribution to our community. We were eating and I saw Soffia was alone. I told my friends that she looked like a damsel in distress and that we should invite her over to our table, something like in a female sorority mode, they agreed and I was the daring one who invited her over. Soffia gladly accepted and we all loved her acid and straight-to-the-point personality. From then on, we were five for whatever happened.

But those are almost one-in-a-million situations, and it's not the circumstance of my Maracucho friends in Madrid, in their case, it's as if they were attached to each other until further notice or forever.

After H's lecture, I'm left wondering where to go. I'm not going to go to Luismi's for two reasons: first is because of his Instagram posts with the bitch from the Netherlands, an issue that bothers and angers me, I also have my «drama queen» moments, so; the second reason is that I don't want to be there when H arrives. This new encounter has to be spectacular and, no matter what, I'm going let this second «first time» fall into routine . Besides, it would be very hard to hide our intentions there, at his brother's house.

I got in touch with Martina, my YouTuber friend, right then and there – I met with her and her wife last summer - and I tell her that I'm in a bit of trouble. I explain the situation to her and that I no longer feel comfortable, I give her some details of what happened and I ask if I can go with her and her wife Andrea for a while, to spend the day with them. Her generosity has no limits, she immediately tells me that they are working at home and that I can leave with my luggage, and that I can stay with them.

Her very affectionate and supportive response makes me reflect again on friendship, on how these unexpected but powerful connections begin. I remember how my friendship with Martina and Andrea came about. I'm a follower of Martina's YouTube channel, in one of her videos she posted her marriage and I wrote a very long comment telling them how brave and beautiful they are and how much I loved to see them happy. That was enough to go from being her fan to being a very special friend. It may seem strange, but I believe that an extraordinary spiritual growth is needed to make us able to honestly say what we think and to listen with affection to authenticity. I think that happened with us.

I thank Martina for her offer. I'll take all my stuff, including my laptop, to get some work done myself.

I go back to the apartment. Fernanda and Paola are sleeping off their hangover and I take this opportunity to explain to Jennifer the reason for my untimely move. I omit certain details about H's generalization and I tell her that it's because of Fernanda and Paola. Jennifer understands me, she's even happy for me and tells me:

—Anyway, I'm going to keep calling just in case, girl.

We hug and I say goodbye because my taxi has arrived.

⋅—••→⇥⇤←••—⋅

I'm already at Martina and Andrea's apartment. We have ordered sushi for dinner while we watch Taylor Swift's Miss Americana documentary.

After dinner and the documentary, we're watching and listening to Taylor Swift songs. And I get on my phone to give them the list.

Popularly speaking, when a girl shows her «list» it's usually associated with the list of guys with whom she has been sexually or romantically involved with, but my list is the list of songs that H has chronologically unlocked for me. My list is split in two. One exclusively for Taylor Swift and the other for various artists. I decide that I will play one song at a time, and I warn them that, given the circumstances, I may get a little emotional. Martina, who is preparing a marijuana joint, offers me. For the first time in my life, I feel comfortable and confident enough to give it a try.

—Just give it a small puff, and then release it. Don't let the puff be too long or strong. It should be small, soft, and, let it out right away, don't hold it in because it hits harder. And I want us to go little by little and see how your body reacts. I want you to be comfortable —Martina says.

—Take it easy, we're here, we're listening to Taylor Swift, we just ate, if you get the *munchies* [77], there are more snacks, salty and sweet, if you feel sleepy, the bed we reserved for you is there, we have already taken your things to that room —says Andrea.

—Can it make you sleepy? I thought it just made you hungry —I asked.

—It can make you sleepy, hungry, thirsty, you can see the most vivid colors, feel more, all of your senses can get heightened—clarifies Martina.

The truth is, I think I would trust my life to these two girls, they are beautiful people at heart. I feel super comfortable with them.

—Okay, if I can get sleepy then I'll go put on my pajamas and do my skin care.

---

[77] Slang used by those who use marijuana to refer to an increased appetite that can be cause by its consumption

—Okey, we'll wait for you here - says Martina.

With pajamas on, and with my childhood teddy bear —which I take with me on my trips for moral support, and so that H can meet him this time —and Taylor Swift on the speakers, in an apartment in the city of Madrid, I take the first puff of marijuana in my life. After releasing the smoke, my throat closes and I start coughing non-stop.

Andrea offers me some water and Martina warns me that it's possible that it'll hit me quickly because of the cough. Indeed, within a few minutes, my teddy bear feels funny.

Andrea doesn't smoke and says that she very rarely accompanies Martina, and Martina likes it from time to time. I don't know why, but Andrea's serious face while she explains to me that she doesn't smoke makes me laugh, and I get into a laughter trance that I just can't stop.

—What a good trip. You're super high — says Martina with a smile from ear to ear.

—Girl, this is amazing! Why do I always take so long to do everything?

—What do you mean? —Andrea asks.

—Well, I gave my first kiss when I was sixteen, my first boyfriend when I was twenty, the first time I had sex was when I was like twenty-one, or around that, and the first time I'm smoking marijuana is today, at twenty-six.

—But that's not bad, you've taken your time, and you've done it when you've been comfortable —Andrea points out.

—Well, that's also true, I've done it when I've felt safe.

After savoring gummies, peanuts, potato chips, Coca Cola, and when I say savor, I mean savor, I've spent what seems like forever chewing on each of the goodies. I make signs to my friends that the list of songs begins and along with them, the explanation of why that song is for a specific moment.

—We inaugurate the emotional bond with "Enchanted" [78] —I say—.

---

[78] Enchanted - Taylor Swift

The second H opened the door for me and my eyes landed on his, so that after that my brain threw me the «this man has my life in his hands», that song started playing.

I told them how I forced myself to be involved in the conversations at the bar with people I knew, and conversations I knew by heart, and he was there, paying attention to me and to my needs. How everything seemed enchanted, straight out of a fairy tale. Then at about two o'clock in the morning, he came into Luismi's room to ask me if the distances were too long, as if he was asking me if I loved him, and I secretly replied that they were, with a bookmark passed under a table. And how my doubts and my decisions came and went, and how I had consciously asked about him all these years, and now that I had him, I unconsciously prayed that he wasn't in love with anyone else, or that no one was waiting for him, how I prayed that those moments would be the first pages on the book of the story of our lives, that that would be the beginning.

We move on to «Red», the song talks about the way we memorize our routines, the physical aspects, the tastes, and I explained to my friends how I did it too, including the way my dear H likes his bananas, or how he drinks his coffee.

—For me it's like listening to your old favorite song during any unplanned day, as it plays you remember it more and more, you know it, it's familiar, but at the same time it's like a discovery. That's how it feels to root my feelings to him and argue, just like the song says. It's like a crossword puzzle made by his father, Mr. Heinrich, only he knows the answer and you can't figure it out. It was his crossword puzzle, and to argue with him was to be validated by his thoughts, but never to be right. Later, during our breakup, my bluest and most melancholic moments, because I had never known a love like this. To love him honestly was red, vivid red, passion red. And when we were in zero contact, it was gray. It seemed like there was an absence of color, and I really tried to forget him, but it just didn't happen.

Next on my list is «Mr. Perfectly Fine» [79], even at the time of the breakup that song got stuck with me. And, of course! I have nothing to add, change or explain here. In this song my words are unnecessary, so I just keep silent and let the song play.

Then comes «You Belong With Me». This explains why every time I asked about him, and he had a girlfriend, I was the one in the stands while he was with a cheerleader. But I was taking action, because I remembered everything too well («All too well») and then I tell my friends how music and my story were consecutively linked together. After H sent me that picture to my Messenger and my «Getaway Car» left my life while I was waiting for him to remember me in his «Wildest Dreams», I had sent that email to H, with my version of «All too well».

And finally, «Lover» [80], the wedding song, and like Sister Taylor, I had saved a chair for him at that event. And how I would choose him, to be my lover. And like with each part of the anatomy of my broken heart, which he had repaired with his words and his care, he was a golden being doing kintsugi. And with my heart like that, fixed with gold, I chose him, my heart was now borrowed because it belonged to him, and his heart had been blue. And I swore that I would show myself like this, dramatic and honest in front of him. Honoring everything I felt for him. I didn't know if I had loved him since I saw him at the door, or if I had loved him for fourteen years. The fact is that I loved my magnetic man, my sweetie pie Hachito, my delicious Hachito, my beloved Hachito.

My friends have been paying attention to everything I said and have intervened here and there. Asking specific questions.

—Valentina Paris —Andrea says.

—Huh, why? Valentina's going to Paris? —Martina asks.

—No, love, please, look at her. Valentina is like Paris: romantic, melancholic, emotional, brave and charming. Obviously, H is melting over her, she is the epitome of the vibe of his home. Of both homes, Maracaibo and Paris.

«Ow, so cute. H is right, they didn't appreciate me where I was

---

[79] Mr. Perfectly Fine - Taylor Swift
[80] Lover - Taylor Swift

staying, here, where I am now, they really appreciate me, and just like H does, these two girls make me feel safe as a blanket. Unexpectedly, this moment roots a friendship».

I start crying. Honestly, it feels so nice.

—Thank you for being my friends —I tell them between sobs—. I have good friends, and you are part of them. Thank you for opening the doors of your home to me, my house is also your house. I love you, girls.

—Awww —they say in unison.

We shoved ourselves into a three-way hug.

—I want a beautiful relationship like the one you have —I add—. I briefly saw how you guys got engaged and your story on Martina's YouTube channel. Could you please tell me the things you couldn't say in the video?

—Hahahaha – they laugh

—Obviously —says Martina.

Andrea took care of telling everything herself, while Martina just added a comment here and there.

They studied together at the university, and on the first day of class, first thing in the morning, first class. Martina showed up late and interrupted the class when she walked in. Andrea said «I love her, I'm in love with her, she's the love of my life». Back then, Martina had a boyfriend and had never been with a girl, she declared that she was completely heterosexual.

So, Andrea, very chivalrous, took distance and decided to keep her love to herself. She says that she told the universe, «Show her the way towards me when we're both ready to be together», and did what people do when they are in love: she waited. Five years and two of Martina's boyfriends later, at the graduation party and after a couple of drinks, Martina stole a kiss from Andrea and said, «I think I like you». A year later, Martina came out of the closet in a YouTube video with an engagement ring on her finger.

The most romantic thing that has ever existed on the face of the earth, Andrea waited in silence, didn't force her, didn't manipulate her, didn't hurry or hinder a process that would take place naturally, because she knew in her heart that Martina belonged to her.

I'm a sea of tears with their story, and to think that all this friendship started because of the long comment I left on her video. All this makes me feel nice, I see my whole world again through rose colored glasses.

The effect of the marijuana has not gone down, and I decide to go to the bathroom with the excuse that I'm going to blow my nose, and wipe my tears a little. When I see myself in the mirror, I realize that I have tiny, very red eyes, and like this my iris looks even greener than usual. I decide to take a picture and send it to H. Along with the photo I text him:

> *I've sent you photos drunks, crying, happy, but never ever high, so, good night, Poliedro de Caracas.*

I get out of the bathroom and I have an epiphany. Taylor Swift is the Elizabeth Taylor of this generation. And just like the girls from Sex and the City and the whole generation of women of that time that referenced Elizabeth Taylor in their day-to-day life, this generation, mine, references Taylor Swift. Both Taylors, like all strong and successful women, have been judged and criticized by the media for living their freedom, for having «too many» men, for getting ahead despite the bumps in their lives... But we women understand, because only we in our femininity understand each other, the Taylors, the best friends of strong girls who have had to be born again multiple times from the ashes.

I share my epiphany with my friends, and they both agree with me. It's as if the universe had chosen the Taylors to live things first, so that we, somehow, through them, can intuit the endings to our stories. My heart is even more excited, «Oh, my God. I truly am in the «Lover» era after the «Reputation» era.

# Too much red, too much «Reputation»

Today is the day. H arrives in Madrid. My friends have to go on a trip tomorrow, but, given the circumstances, they have told me that they will leave me their key, no problem, that if I need to stay here longer, I can do it and that if I want to come here with H in case that Luis Miguel can't let us have his apartment, there wouldn't be a problem. I'm so grateful to have them, for their hospitality and for their trust in me, in lending me their home, even in their absence.

Jennifer called me early today to ask how I'm doing and told me that if I felt like going out to do something, to hang out while H was getting organized, to let her know. I thanked her and replied that I would call her if I decided to do something.

This encounter is truly being surrounded by a tribe of family and friends who are assembled with the purpose of carrying this out, the way my Libra heart likes things, that is, like a fairy tale.

I really wish I had the ability to act on something that doesn't have to do with H, but since I saw his plane land through the Flightradar24 app, my stomach has stopped working and my heart is just beating very fast.

I try to take it easy and stay all day at my friends' apartment. Each time my phone vibrates I hallucinate that it's H who's texting me. Every notification is like a heart attack. I sweat. I'm really nervous.

It's almost getting dark, H has been in Madrid for a couple of hours, Luismi hasn't published any unusual stories and H never posts anything on his Instagram. I'm watching Tarot readings videos on YouTube confirming that everything's fine, and trying to calm my anxious heart.

Martina knocks on the door, I pause the video, and I tell her she can come in. She peeks out and tells me:

—Vale, do you feel like doing your makeup? That way I can teach you how to do French makeup, so that when you have your date with H, you'll be glowing.

—Oh, that's so sweet. —Yes, I'd love to.

Martina finishes entering the guest room, this is actually her recording studio, here she has the bag with all her makeup. She proceeds to organize everything and turns on the lights in the studio and so on. And the both of us, with Lady Gaga playing, set out on the task.

I leave my phone charging and put it in «do not disturb» mode, so I won't get anxious about whether H texts me or not and I can concentrate on learning how to do a French makeup.

Half way through our makeup session, when we've finished with the skin and we're finishing with our eyes, I start to run out of breath, I deduce that I am having a nervous breakdown… «Calm down, Maria Valentina, I tell myself, everything will be fine, if he texted you, he can wait a while until you answer, he's not going to leave because it took you half a minute to answer, he's not going to stop loving you for making him wait». I breathe in deeply, hold it in for a few seconds and let go. I repeat the procedure. «Everything is fine, and if it doesn't go well, if it's a catastrophe, you've shown yourself that you can pull through, life doesn't start or end with a guy»… But this isn't any other guy. He's my person, he's the love of my life, he's the purest and greatest thing I have ever felt, he is… unconditional.

I couldn't stop thinking about all the Tarot readings. Both in reading my friend Tatiana did for me and the reading I did with help from YouTube, the seven of swords had appeared. Tatiana interpreted that card as my fear of getting hurt, and that this time, the damage would be permanent.

When I'm outlining my lips to put on some red lipstick, Martina tells me:

—Okay, Paris, *you're red. Very red*, red hair, red lips, red cheeks and that eyeliner looks amazing. For some perhaps it would be too much red, I say it just highlights your features.

I look at myself in the mirror and, wow! Yes, I look amazing, but it's also true that I have too many reddish tones on. I feel like my hair color is too bright and I don't like the way I have my nails anymore. They don't go with me or my moment, I declared that I'm in my «Lover» era, so I don't need such a strong copper orange in my hair, I need to soften it a little more to a brownish copper. Also, my hair has too many layers, like with too much movement, maybe I should cut it a little.

I get even more nervous, how am I going to show myself like this to H? My look is too «Reputation», I haven't changed my look since after the black plague. I need to close that cycle and thank my Mary Jane carrot orange hair for saving me.

Martina goes to get water and I run to check my phone to see if H has written to me, but still nothing. He has answered some things that I had asked him and sent me emojis, but there's still nothing. Still no real conversation.

Martina's back and we decide to take a couple of photos for an Instagram post, the truth is that I look very pretty.

I send Jennifer the photos and she, like the *Instagrammer* that she is, edits them, and encourages me to upload them to my Instagram so that H can see how gorgeous I look.

I decide to upload them to my stories so that there is no evidence of this makeup when we have our date; besides, the last Instagram posts I've uploaded have been approved by him first. I don't want to bother him right now with those types of questions and I don't want to upload it in a post without his approval, I don't want him to think that I'm ignoring him.

It's not like H controls what I post to my Instagram, it's more along the lines of when I was asking him what nail color to wear. It's just now part of our dynamic. I was an indecisive Libra on life's small decisions, like which photo to upload to Instagram.

The girls have gone to bed early because they have to leave at four in the morning. Knowing that H is already at Luismi's house, but that he hasn't yet given me the invitation I expect, makes me anxious. I decided to try to make the night bearable and put on episodes of Pucca & Garu to laugh for a while, with the resemblance between us both.

I die laughing and drown my loud laughter when I see the episode of Garu in the hospital, because, in short, that's how I would have been when he had the accident: I would have taken care of him, and he would be all grumpy with his «I can do it alone» attitude, I took a capture of Garu's buttocks in the episode, sent it to H and by added:

> *Pucca, dying even over Garu's buttocks*  .

I go to Instagram and I realize that he has seen all my stories and hasn't said a thing. «What is he doing? I wonder, does he not want to do this anymore? What's going on?». It's all very strange. Honestly, I can't take it anymore, I feel like a little girl waiting to be picked up at kindergarten and nobodies coming to pick her up. I start crying with fear, so I decided to just ask him.

> *Hey, Hachito, is everything okay?*
> *-Are you okay? What's up? Why do you barely answer me? Are you angry with me? Did I do something? Please talk to me. I feel very anxious. You're worrying me a lot, I'm scared. I don't know what's going on. I love you, always. If you see this message reply at once, I just want to know that you're OK.*

A few minutes pass and, the truth is, I can't take it anymore and text him again.

> *Hey, I'm going to call you in ten minutes, if you don't answer me. Sorry for being so intense. It's just that I need to know if everything is*

*okay*

I set a timer and after seven minutes he replies back.

*Hello. I'm okay. I'm at Luis Miguel's house. I had to solve a giant work problem when I landed and I was exhausted. I fell asleep. We'll arrange everything tomorrow. I'm not upset with anyone, and stop seeing yourself as intense. You're not intense and you never bother me.*

This is the first time since we started talking to each other that H labels a work problem as «giant». There were reasons for his silence. Relief fills every inch of my body. His message has been like putting an asthmatic patient on a ventilator. It was all in my head, I was scared.

# Like a Miss

I wake up, jumping from the phone's vibration. I know it's a call, of course I think it's from H, i am excited because I'm going to hear his voice invade me, but I don't give myself time to enjoy it, I jump on the phone and in milliseconds I grab to pick up the call.

—Hello.

—Baby, good morning, how did you sleep? Did H show up? —It's Jennifer.

—Hi, baby, all good. Yes, I slept well. —The truth is that I was able to sleep peacefully because H answered me—. Yeah, he showed up, told me we were arranging everything today.

—Well, look, near where you are there is a Venezuelan stylist who worked at the Miss Venezuela organization for many years. He's been doing my hair up and I'm on my way to an appointment I have with him right now because I want to pamper myself a little. Let me get to the place to see if they can do your hair too, if so, I'll send you a taxi and you can come over so that you can get pretty and be ready for when H invites you to dinner or something. What do you say?

—Yes, of course, but isn't that too expensive? I'm scared. I don't have a lot of money; the truth is that I still haven't got paid and I put a lot on the credit card buying clothes and paying for suitcases for the trip.

—One problem at a time, one thing at a time, first let me find out if they have an opening. I'm almost there, go take a bath. Bye.

—Oki, bye.

Jennifer has managed to get me an appointment, and I'm on my way to the hairdresser. When I get there, I ask the taxi how much I owed, and he tells me that Jennifer has already paid for it.

I get out of the car, I enter the salon and I see Jennifer sitting in one of the chairs, I greet the receptionist and I make a gesture to my friend that I'm coming over. When the stylist sees me, he shouts out saying:

—Explain to me right now how you're not Miss Venezuela! Explain to me why you're not in La Quinta! How old are you? To call Osmel this instant.

—I told you. She's of Miss Venezuela category —says Jennifer with a smile from ear to ear.

I laugh and blush.

—I'm twenty-six, I'm turning twenty-seven this year.

—No! That's so bad! You had a chance until this year. Well, at least I think, what if I call Osmel and ask him? —the stylist says.

—Thanks for the compliments, but I worked as a producer for Miss Venezuela, I had the opportunity, but the year I decided to do it was when the organization passed over to another manager, and there was that huge scandal and I decided to leave the country.

—A Miss Universe that we lost. With you, I would have had the seventh crown. What a shame! —he says with frustration.

—No, and on top of that she's super intelligent— says Jennifer. She would have beaten anyone in the questions.

A shower of compliments and unexpected stimuli have happened since I arrived in Madrid. In Milan it's super common for people to compliment me; Italians and the inhabitants of the city are characterized by their excessive need to passionately communicate what they think. So, something like this isn't strange to me. Lately I have set myself the task of giving back compliments, but I feel a little intimidated, because the compliments I get are usually like this; they leave me on the spot and I don't know what to say. I mean, what do I tell Mauricio the stylist?, «Hey, are you a Mr. Venezuela too?». I don't know. The only thing left is to be kind and receive compliments and stay humble.

Mauricio has asked me what I want to get done, he has the morning free for us. Jennifer explains that I'm about to go after a relationship with the guy I've liked since I was thirteen and that I must look like a doll.

I look at Jennifer like I had a heart attack, in my head that's as much money as the equivalent of five minimum wages in some Latin American country. Mauricio excuses himself to go and do something and when we're alone I tell Jennifer my concerns about the payment again.

—Girl, calm down. I've got it under control. I get discounts for posting stories, and clients always come thanks to me. If they do the both us, they'll give us a discount, but, if you don't want to post anything, you don't have to. Anyway, you have, what? Five thousand followers? — I nod, still scared—. We should put your account to work, but we'll talk about that later. On the other hand, the girls helped me with the rent and I have that extra cash. And besides, I have Gregorio's card, my boyfriend. So don't worry. I'll pay. You can get everything you want, please, the whole package: hair, nails, everything, please don't think about it. Join in the thought of abundance, look at it as an investment in yourself and your future. Think that in a few months you'll be in Paris in an apartment with the love of your life. And in one year, with a ring and in two with a big pregnant belly. Your life begins today. Don't worry about it. Right now, it's done!

I don't like Jennifer's idea about fixing myself up and seeing it as an «investment», it's as if I was considering that H is the economic solution to my life, and it's not like that. I love him and my idea is that the two of us together can build a promising future. I know she doesn't mean it that way, so I put aside my questions and focus on the words that give me an energy boost. What she told me about today being the beginning of my life is true, so I'm getting on that boat. I get on the boat of happiness; I choose to be happy.

When Mauricio comes back, without stuttering, I tell him what I want and how I want it.

Four hours later and after a lunch eaten in parts, Mauricio turns the chair and then I can see myself in the mirror.

I really do. Somebody should call Osmel. I look so beautiful. I feel incredible. I was right, I needed to take down some layers, the copper brown color suits me better in this new era, I look more like a princess from Las Lomas. The nail color with a perfect French manicure. Now I look and feel like Heinrich Miguel Gil Montilla's girlfriend. «Go get it, Maria Valentina —I do an imaginary toast— in a couple of years you'll be in Los Roques saying the Yes, I Do, and in another two, putting your first-born child's little feet into the sea».

When I leave the salon, I know exactly where I want to go.

—Come with me.

—Where to? —asks Jennifer.

—To church, to thank God —I answer, resolutely.

—Of course, let's go to church. We can walk; it's close by.

Once in the church, I kneel down immediately. Jennifer sits down next to me and I close my eyes.

«Dear God, I've come all this way to thank you for all the kindness you've shown me these past few days. You know what's in my heart, you know about what I want and the things I miss. But anyway, I'll still tell you about them. I am a woman who has been through a lot, I know that even in my darkest moments you hug me and have been with me, I know that you put this man in my path so that we can both learn from each other. I know that this last year, in which you gave me the opportunity to get to know his heart and know his fears, was to strengthen our love, this was our test, and I want to let you know that I'm ready to be happy now. I would love to be able to be happy with him. I thank you for the tribe of people that you have put at my disposal to help me with this, the friends, my relatives, the prayers that have been sent by my mom, my aunt and even by H's relatives, as Graciela told me that time. I want to start a family with him. I ask you, again, in case it's necessary, to remove any third parties, and above all, remove the fear, from both of us. Lord, listen to me with every part of my broken heart repaired with kintsugi, I take this man and choose this man to accompany me in this life, and, if you allow it, when I get to heaven, let me continue being with him».

When I open my tear-stained eyes I take Jennifer's hand and kiss it.

—May God multiply everything you're doing for me and for others —I tell her.

—I love you. Please be happy. It's about damn time! —she says to me, and places our hands on her chest, as a prayer.

—It's about time for you too— I reply.

Her little eyes are watering up too.

When I set foot outside the church, I get a notification from H.

> *Hello. Dinner reservation at ten p.m. We'll have a drink at the restaurant bar first, so we can by there by nine o'clock.*

I show Jennifer the message and we both scream and jump. The cars that pass by honk their horns and people shout and clap, joining in on our frenzy. Jennifer yells at someone passing by:

—My friend is going to marry a guy she's been in love with for fourteen years!!!!

She looked like Charlotte in *Sex and the City* when Carrie told her she was marrying Big.

# Handbags on the run

We ran fast to choose the outfit. Despite Jennifer's pleas to go to her apartment to get ready there, we came to Martina and Andrea's house, I have my suitcases here with the outfit I decided for this occasion. Of course, I called them first, I needed to ask their permission to go with Jennifer; for me, arriving with my friend without notifying them would be abusive. They told me that there was no problem, and not only that, Martina also suggested that I could go into her closet and have a look if I needed anything.

Jennifer is shocked that I'm not going to wear high heels, but H is slightly shorter than me, if I wear heels the height difference increases, and I like the idea that we're on the same level.

I have put on a long off-white silk skirt with some ballerinas that look like ballet flats, light pink; a basic white shirt, slightly oversize, which we have tucked inside the skirt. I've done the makeup that Martina showed me yesterday, and with what I'm wearing, the color tones work perfectly. I make sure to put highlighter on the corner of my eye to make me look innocent, and with that, like I did with my hair, I lower my Aries rising and raise my Sun in Libra.

I call Martina to ask her if I can borrow her heart shaped earrings, and she stresses, almost shouting, that she already told me, to take whatever I want, that there's no problem. When I'm ready, I put on some perfume and then Jennifer and I panic: I don't have a handbag that works with what I'm wearing. My friend claims that she has a perfect white one in her house. While we panic, I give five hundred puffs to the vape I bought so I wouldn't be smoking out of anxiety. The idea of lighting up a cigarette and then kissing my Prince Charming doesn't please me, besides, I remember that I once told God that when I found the man who was going to be the father of my children, I would stop smoking, so I have to start quitting.

It's seven forty-five, we need to act fast.

I get a WhatsApp from H that says:
> *Let me know when you're ready and the address to send a taxi to pick you up.*
>
> *I'm ready. But I'm missing one thing that my married friends' house doesn't haves.*

I tell him that so he knows I'm at Martina and Andrea's.
> *So, I'm looking for a way to fix it. I think the best thing is for me to go and look for it, and then I'll send you another address when I'm ready for you to call me a taxi to.*
>
> *What don't you have? What do you need?*
>
> *A handbag that works with my outfit.*
>
> *Valentina. Come as you are.*

He wrote to me in an imposing tone, and once again the fear was back, «But what's up with him?, I know my cattle[81], at any other time he would have made a joke about it».

> *I want my bag, H Miguel.*

I show him the spoiled version of Maria Valentina.
> *Okay. I'm going to call the taxi to take you from where you are to where you need to go. Tell the taxi driver to wait for you, get the handbag and when you're ready let me know and I'll put the other address in the app. And tell the taxi driver I'll give him a tip, for waiting for you, when he drops you off.*

---

[81] It's an expression used in Venezuela to say that you know the other person you are talking to very well. (Editor's Note)

*Thank you, you're a sunshine,*
*Hachito sweetie pie.*

I answer lovingly; I've gotten away with it.

I do as he tells me, when I get to Jennifer's house, I stay in the car waiting for her to bring it down. When she arrives, we swap handbags in less than two seconds. Then, Jennifer gives me a pill, still in its wrapper and a bottle of water. I keep looking at her, curiously, without understanding.

—It's a Xanax. Take it. Breath before answering any questions he asks. Keep your mind focused. Visualize yourself. And, above all, enjoy. Today your dream life begins, think about all the things you will build with him, including your audiovisual company.

I nod. I take the pill and say goodbye.

On the way over I text my mom and my aunt Eugenia that I'm on my way. That the next thing they'll hear from me is the date of our wedding.

# Seven of swords

When I get to the destination, I text H, but he doesn't answer. I call him and it sounds like the phone is disconnected. I ask the taxi driver if everything is paid for and he says yes, so I open my wallet and give him a ten-euro bill as a tip. Perhaps it's too much, but the man is from Venezuela. When I get out, he says:

—Good luck, doll, that boy is very lucky.

I give him a smile and walk to the restaurant. I feel calm, the Xanax started to work.

The employee asks me if I have a reservation, I tell her that I will meet someone at the bar and the girl shows me the way.

When I get there, I see him from behind. His jet-black hair is more mine than his; it's at a point that I like so much, when the tips of his hair almost curl up. It's been three hundred and eighty-four days since I last saw him, and I feel like I'm going to marry him, like he's waiting for me at the altar. My imagination is running wild.

I have my Sun and Mercury in Libra, in the Versailles gardens in a pink dress, running and singing «Can I Have this Dance» [82] from High School Musical. My Moon in Taurus is in a princess bed watching Pride and Prejudice while a downpour is falling outside. My Venus in Scorpio brings a glass of red wine stained with red lipstick while she looks in the mirror and puts on a pearl necklace, behind her is her jet-haired lover kissing her back, telling her how much he loves her and how horrible the world would be without her. My Mars in Scorpio takes a *pre-workout* [83], dressed all in black Nike clothes, with her lover's

---

[82] Can I Have this Dance - Troy & Gabriela, High School Musical
[83] Also called pre-train. Any nutritious drink used before physical activity to enhance performance.

cap on ready to run freely at midnight in NYC. And my dear and chaotic Aries rising, I carry that part with me, in my chest, pumping my blood and keeping me alive to face this moment with full freedom.

Aaaah, the great H is wearing a white linen shirt, black pants and loafers. I fantasize that his Sun in Aries is here, keeping him alive, along with his Mercury in Aries, both ready to go. His Moon in Pisces, I hope that it's on a quiet beach like Los Roques, just watching the waves come gently to his feet. His Venus in Pisces, excited and idealizing, taking note of all the needs of his princess to satisfy them, to then be rewarded with a tender kiss on the cheek and a «you're the best thing that has happened to me»; his Mars in Pisces, I imagine it as a smart octopus camouflaging himself from predators, but today, he camouflages himself with the color of the sea to disappear for a minute, because his Taurus rising needs that peace, to make the calm and down to earth decisions he needs.

I walk towards him, perhaps too quickly. I touch his shoulder, and, without hesitating, he turns around. He has already ordered a drink. He has a wrist brace on his left hand.

— Hello — I say to him, whispering because when his eyes landed on mine, I ran out of breath. I feel nostalgic inside and I think I want to hug him so hard.

— Hello — he answers, in a dry tone. He gets up to give me two quick kisses on my cheeks.

He beckons me to sit next to him and when I do, I instinctively sit down so that our knees are touching, and I put my hand on his leg.

—Is everything all right? —I ask, with anguish.

—Yes, everything's fine, and you? How was the ride over here?

—Well, my chaperon didn't come to open the door. I had to do it by myself. Can you believe that? I'm a damsel in distress — I answer in a dramatic tone, to break the ice.

—Oooh, I forgot. I'm sorry. I've been all over the place lately.

—Nooo! Really? —I say, adding even more drama to my tone, —I hadn't noticed. Except that I've died about thirty-three times in the last month. Including the stroke I got when you told me about this — I point to his wrist.

—I'm fine— he answers dryly, and proceeds to get up a little from the chair and move away from me.

—Hey, I don't bite —I say—. Only when I have to— I joke with him.

—It's just that the air conditioning hits me directly here.

The bartender takes my order for a Cosmo, without help from any vodka experts.

I realize that H is not mentally here. He's not looking at me and now I think he moved his chair to put some distance between us. I decide to ignore my intrusive thoughts and when I get my Cosmo, I take a long sip.

Another Cosmo later, H has barely looked me in the face, he hasn't held his gaze with me. When he talks, he looks around but he doesn't look at me. He doesn't make any comments about my hair. He doesn't see that I learned how to do this makeup last night, that I bought this outfit to show it off to him, that I paid extra for luggage, that I've paid Tarot readings, astrology and so on with money that I don't have just because I hope that this is the night when our forever after begins.

In front of me I have the purest and most beautiful thing that has happened to me in my life, and he doesn't seem to realize the magic of the moment. I start to get hot with rage, with fear, with stress... I don't know if the vodka has cut the effect of Xanax, but I feel disillusioned, disappointed, abandoned, I can feel like H, with his attitude, deliberately takes the fantasy out of my fairy tale. He is more than aware of what I'm doing sitting here, and what my intentions are. I confessed my wishes to him and he proposed this meeting to me. I take the drive from the rage I'm feeling, and decide to put him between a rock and a hard place.

—You either tell me right now what's going on or I'm leaving.

H takes a long swig at his rum, and, without looking me in the face, spits it out at me:

—When the accident happened, they called my emergency contact. My medical emergency contact was my ex. Since then, we've met to talk and I thought she just wanted to iron out any rough edges. But no.

She wants us to get back together and is waiting for an answer. I told her I would give her one after this trip.

A shot in the leg hurts less than this. Being thrown against a kitchen counter hurts less than this. Getting raped twice hurts less than this. Being forced to have an abortion hurts less than this. I can't speak for other women. I'm speaking for myself. And I swear by my love of art that everything I just mentioned hurts less.

I start laughing. But it's not a mocking laugh, it's a nervous laughter, full of pain and surprise.

—Okay —I answered—. Thank you for telling me — I control myself and dust off the Maria Valentina who put up with the shouting when she worked in production, the insults of that despot Jackson, Daniela's bad intentions. Basically, in the language of a fan of The Vampire Diaries, I turn off my humanity.

I finish my Cosmo in one gulp.

— I'm not going to convince you to choose me. I'm a fucking Yes every day. Not a maybe. And I've already been to hell and back enough times to grab my things right now and leave — I tell him with the calm of a serial killer recounting his crimes. Emotionless, stoic—. Be happy.

When I've left the restaurant, I realize that H didn't come after me. I feel how my emotions quickly invade me, and I begin to tremble with anxiety. Everything is cloudy in my head. I struggle to open my wallet, take out a cigarette and light it. After a few drags, H comes out.

Without saying a word and with the calm that characterizes him, he stands next to me without saying a single word. I get my strength back and I keep looking at the street, copying what H is doing, or maybe he is the one copying me. When I finish the cigarette, I look for where to throw it, I see an ashtray at the doors of the restaurant and then H takes the cigarette bud from my hands and proceeds to throw it away. When he comes back, he doesn't say a word, he just looks at the floor.

—Should I call you a taxi? —asks the former love of my life.

—Yes —I answer, with my heart broken into pieces.

H raises his hand and a taxi pulls up on the opposite side of the street. H walks towards it and I just follow him. He doesn't even turn around, to make sure if I'm walking behind him. When I get to the taxi, he hesitates whether to open the door for me or not. Each one of his actions breaks my heart even more. After his internal struggle about whether to open the door for me or not, he opens it for me and I get in. He gets in on the other side.

Through the window, I watch as someone gets mugged. When the thief is about to leave, he turns to his victim to give him one last look.

—Seven of Swords —I whisper.

The car is already moving. I turn to look at H, and he says to me:

—Let's go to Luis Miguel's place.

I don't say a thing. When we have arrived the taxi driver passes the dataphone to H for him to pay, and then I see his impatience, his desperation. As if he wanted to get rid of something already, at that instant.

I get out of the car without waiting for him to open the door for me. I don't want to see his doubts again, or feel the disappointment. We go upstairs to the apartment.

When we walk in, the heat suffocates me because the air conditioning is turned off. H proceeds to turn it on.

By the time he returns, I have taken off all my accessories and put them inside the handbag. He offers me a drink and I accept.

Both of us, in unison, took the drink as if it were a shot. As we put the glasses on the table, H pounces on me and starts kissing me furiously. But he's not there, it's not him. His kiss doesn't taste like him, his touch isn't his, his smell isn't his, when I touch his hair, it doesn't even have the texture that my fingers can remember. I'm starting to feel nauseous, like the first time I made out with Theo. I pull myself from his embrace, and I can feel the tingle of the rapturous assault my mouth has had. And no. This is not my H. I wipe my mouth with the back of my hand, disgusted even from the smell of his saliva.

He knows me, I know him. This being that is standing in front of me is a stranger.

—Stay. I'll sleep on the couch.

I say No with my head. I don't stay with strangers.

—Call a taxi for me, please, if you'd be so kind.

H nods. While ordering a car on his phone, I analyze the situation. «Did he bring me here to have sex with me, so he could make up his mind?». I felt more nauseous, «Did he put something in my drink?».

—Did you put something in my drink?

He looks into my eyes. For the first time he really looks into my eyes.

—No, Maria Valentina —he replies gently.

I look at him as he answers me, and now it's him, the H I know. I want to get down on my knees and implore that that H to stay with me. But he takes his gaze to his phone and the stranger returns.

We spent no more than five minutes in silence, until he tells me:

—The taxi is almost here.

—I'm heading downstairs, then.

—Okay —he answers.

Without hesitating, without saying goodbye and in silence, I leave the apartment with my legs shaking. I walk slowly to see if he is coming after me. I call the elevator and head down the stairs; if he regrets this and decides to follow me, he'll have the elevator there. Five floors down, with my legs almost not obeying me anymore, I leave the building; the taxi is already in front. I get in and the taxi driver says:

—Heinrich?

—Yes —I answer.

I take a last look at the building, I feel tempted to tell the taxi driver to wait a few minutes, but the reality is that, even if we wait all night, it seems that he's not coming.

The end

# About the author

**María José Pahmer** (San Cristobal, Venezuela, 1995) is a journalist, actress and writer who has dedicated her life to creative expression in various forms. She studied Journalism with a major in Audiovisual Studies and is currently pursuing a master's degree in Audiovisual Screenwriting.

In the professional field, after graduating, she worked as an audiovisual producer, a profession she had to leave behind when she had to emigrate from her country. Like any emigrant, she has worked in different jobs - and in different countries - far from her interest in the artistic world. She currently lives in Budapest, Hungary, and in her spare time she's dedicated herself to getting closer to the field she's passionate about: Art.

Since she was a child, Maria Jose decided that she would live a life of telling stories, whether on the boards of a theater, under the lights of a studio, or through writing. At the age of fifteen, she attempted to write her first work and has filled countless notebooks with her dreams and stories. Her passion for writing has been a constant throughout her life, and it finally culminated in her first novel.

Inspired by her own story, with just the right dose of fiction, 384 Days offers an intimate and courageous story in which Maria Jose dares to say: "I have lived this, and this is what I am today". Through her work, she touches on themes such as love, abuse, emigration and the post-Covid era, with a deep sensitivity that reflects both her personal experience and her professional training.

384 Days is her first published work and marks the beginning of a promising career in the world of literature.

# Playlist

i     Long Story Short - Taylor Swift
ii     Irresistible - Wisin y Yandel
iii     Tras de mí - RBD
iv     Dakiti - Bad Bunny
v     Ay, te dejo Madrid - Shakira
vi     Cúrame - Rauw Alejandro
vii     Sal y Perrea - Sech
viii     Hello, Amiguis, Hello - Somos tú y yo
ix     When I Look at You - Miley Cyrus
x     You Belong With Me (Taylor's Version) - Taylor Swift
xi     Sarah Smiles - Panic! At the Disco
xii     Me! - Taylor Swift (feat. Brendon Urie from Panic! At The Disco)
xiii     Cardigan - Taylor Swift
xiv     Red (Taylor's Version) - Taylor Swift
xv     Jueves - La Oreja de Van Gogh
xvi     Feeling Good - Michael Buble
xvii     Singing in the Rain - Gene Kelly
xviii     Dancing Queen - ABBA
xix     The Finals - Pitch Perfect (Mashup)
xx     Getaway Car - Taylor Swift
xxi     Wildest Dreams (Taylor's Version) - Taylor Swift
xxii     All too Well (Taylor's version) - Taylor Swift (10 Minute Version)
xxiii     Young and Beautiful - Lana Del Rey
xxiv     De mí - Camila
xxv     Enchanted (Taylor's version) - Taylor Swift
xxvi     Mr. Perfectly Fine (Taylor's version) - Taylor Swift
xxvii     Lover - Taylor Swift
xxviii     Can i Have this Dance - Troy y Gabriela, High School Musical

*Life is a challenging journey with no manuals or certainties.*

*If you or someone close to you is going through difficult times, remember that you are not alone. There are outstretched hands, willing hearts, and open doors for those who seek support. The first step to healing is to ask for help, because it is never too late to find comfort and strength. On the following pages, you will find resources for those who are facing violence, the weight of loneliness, or the echoes of dislocation. We all deserve a safe space, no matter who we are or where we come from. For those who are no longer with us, we continue to fight. Together we are stronger, more human. There is always a path to the light, even when the darkness seems endless.*

# Support Resources

## Psychological Resources

1. **Latin America**
    **Mexico:**
    - **Lational Hotline for Family and Sexual Violence:** 800 108 4053 (24/7 support).
    - **Origen Foundation Shelter:** Emotional support and guidance for women victims of violence. Phone: 800 015 1617
    - **National Network of Shelters:** Provides protection, shelter, and psychological support. rednacionalderefugios.org.mx
    
    **Argentina:**
    - **Line 144:** Free and confidential assistance for women experiencing violence. Phone: 144.
    - **Casa del Encuentro:** Shelter, legal support, and psychological assistance. lacasadelencuentro.org
    
    **Colombia:**
    - **Purple Line:** 01 8000 112 137 (psychological support for women victims of violence).
    - **Casa de la Mujer:** Shelter and support services. casadelamujer.org
    
    **Venezuela:**
    - **AVESA** (Venezuelan Association for Alternative Sexual Education): Provides support and guidance in cases of gender violence.
    - **CEPAZ** (Center for Justice and Peace): Psychological support and legal advice. cepaz.org2.

2. **Europe**
    **Spain:**
    - **Línea 016:** Assistance for victims of gender violence (24/7, free and confidential). Phone: 016..
    - **Ana Bella Foundation:** Support network for survivors, offering shelter and counseling. fundacionanabella.org
    - **Women's Health Association:** Therapy and psychological support. mujeresparalasalud.or
    - **Network of Emergency Centers and Shelters:** Immediate refuge across all autonomous communities

**Italy:**
- **Telefono Rosa:** National helpline. Phone: 1522 (24/7, multilingual support)
- **D.i.Re (Women's Network Against Violence):** Anti-violence centers and shelters. direcontrolaviolenza.it
- **Differenza Donna Association:** Shelter and psychological support. differenzadonna.org
- **Casa delle Donne:** Shelter and support center.

**France:**
- **Violences Femmes Info:** Domestic violence helpline. Phone: 3919 (free and confidential).
- **La Maison des Femmes:** Comprehensive support center. lamaisonparis.fr
- **FNSF (Fédération Nationale Solidarité Femmes):** Network of shelters and support centers. solidaritefemmes.org
- **En Avant Toutes:** Confidential chat line for young people experiencing gender-based violence. commentonsaime.fr

**Hungary:**
- **NANE Women's Rights Association:** Helpline for domestic violence. Phone: (+36) 80 505 101.
- **Patent Association:** Legal and psychological support. patent.org.hu
- **OKIT:** Crisis hotline. Phone: (+36) 80 630 101.
- **Békés Otthon:** Shelter and support for women and children. bekesotthon.hu

## 3. Global Aditional Resources
- **UN Women:** Support for women affected by violence. unwomen.org
- **Refugee Women Connect:** Assistance for refugee women. refugeewomenconnect.org.uk

## Safe Abortion Resources

1. **Latin America**
   México:
   - Safe Abortion Hotline CDMX: +52 55 3341 3121
   - GIRE: Information on reproductive rights. gire.org.mx
   
   Argentina:
   - Abortion Information Hotline: 0800-222-3444
   - Socorristas en Red: Guidance for safe abortion. socorristasenred.org
   
   Colombia:
   - Orientame: Legal abortion services. orientame.org.co
   - La Mesa por la Vida: Legal advice and support. despenalizaciondelaborto.org.co
   
   Venezuela:
   - Faldas-R: Information on abortion in restrictive contexts. Instagram: @faldas_r

2. **Europe**
   Spain:
   - Clínicas ACAI: Network of accredited clinics. acai.es
   - Abortion Information Hotline (FPFE): Phone: +34 915 412 900
   - Dator Clínica: Abortion clinic in Madrid. clinicadator.com
   
   Italy:
   - Voluntary Termination of Pregnancy (IVG) Hotline: Available in each region through public hospitals.
   - Laiga (Libera Associazione Italiana Ginecologi per l'Applicazione della Legge 194): Information on Italy's abortion law.
   - Non Una di Meno: Feminist movement supporting abortion access. nonunadimeno.wordpress.com
   
   France:
   - IVG Info: SAbortion information service. Phone: 0800 08 11 11.
   - Planning Familial: Abortion services. planning-familial.org
   - Fil Santé Jeunes: Youth support line. Phone: 0800 235 236
   
   Hungary:
   - Patent Association: Legal and reproductive health counseling. patent.org.hu
   - Magyar Női Érdekérvényesítő Szövetség: Feminist reproductive health resources
   - Kék Vonal: Youth helpline. Phone: (+36) 116 111.

3. Global Safe Abortion Resources
- **Women on Web:** Abortion pill delivery for restricted regions. womenonweb.org
- **Safe2Choose:** PGlobal abortion counseling. safe2choose.org
- **Aid Access:** Abortion medication access. aidaccess.org

## Support for Immigrants and Refugees

1. For Venezuelans
- **ACNUR:** Legal protection and humanitarian aid. acnur.org
- **CAVID:** Legal aid and integration support
- **Venezuelans in the World (VEM):** Health, legal, and education resources. venmundo.com
- **Venezuelan American Alliance:** Legal, medical, and community support in the U.S. venezuelanamericanalliance.org

2. For Ukranians
- **Help Ukraine Center:** Humanitarian aid. helpukraine.center
- **United Help Ukraine:** Medical aid and refugee support. unitedhelpukraine.org

## Mental Health Support

**Spain:**
 Teléfono de la Esperanza: 717 003 717
**Venezuela:**
 Psicólogos Sin Fronteras Venezuela: (+58) 0414-3380835
**Hungary:**
 Kék Vonal: Available in English) +36 116 111.: (+36) 116 111
**Global:**
 Lifeline International: Suicide prevention. befrienders.org
 Crisis Text Line: Text "HELLO" to 741741 (24/7 confidential support)

Made in United States
Troutdale, OR
05/01/2025